da
Novak

The Talk of Coyote Canyon

mira

mira™

Recycling programs
for this product may
not exist in your area.

ISBN-13: 978-0-7783-3428-6

The Talk of Coyote Canyon

Mira
22 Adelaide St. West, 41st Floor
Toronto, Ontario M5H 4E3, Canada
www.Harlequin.com

Printed in U.S.A.

Praise for the novels of Brenda Novak

"*Summer on the Island* is a big, tantalizing read!"
—Susan Elizabeth Phillips,
New York Times bestselling author

"*Summer on the Island* will resonate with many readers who, in the midst of a global pandemic, may be rethinking what is truly important in life." —*Booklist*

"*The Bookstore on the Beach* is a page-turner with a deep heart."
—Nancy Thayer, *New York Times* bestselling author
of *Girls of Summer*

"The prose is fast-paced and exciting, making this a breathless page-turner." —*New York Journal of Books*
on *The Bookstore on the Beach*

"An abundance of heart and humor. *The Bookstore on the Beach* is an escapist treat with emotional heft."
—*Apple Books*, Best Book of the Month selection

"This heartwarming story of sisters who bond as adults is sure to please the many fans of Novak as well as those who enjoy books by Susan Mallery and Debbie Macomber."
—*Library Journal* on *One Perfect Summer*

"I adore everything Brenda Novak writes. Her books are compelling, emotional, tender stories about people I would love to know in real life."
—RaeAnne Thayne, *New York Times* bestselling author

"Brenda Novak is always a joy to read."
—Debbie Macomber, #1 *New York Times* bestselling author

"Brenda Novak doesn't just write fabulous stories, she writes keepers."
—Susan Mallery, #1 *New York Times* bestselling author

Also by Brenda Novak

For a full list of Brenda's books,
visit www.brendanovak.com.

Look for Brenda Novak's next novel
THE MESSY LIFE OF JANE TANNER
available soon from MIRA.

As we were just coming out of COVID, my mother was diagnosed with dementia. A scammer had drained her bank account (stole over $50,000), and she could no longer care for herself, so I had to take over as guardian even though she was hostile, living in a different state and absolutely insistent that she didn't want or need my help—which meant a lawyer had to be involved. As I battled to make sure she got the care she needed, she kept trying to send the scammer more money, thinking she'd won some kind of sweepstakes he was going to bring her if only I wasn't standing in the way, and the land she owned was going through an adjudication, which was something she was unaware of and I was completely unfamiliar with. By the time I was legally able to jump in to try to save her water rights, it was almost too late. Then the neighbor (a preacher, no less) locked me out of the well, which forced me to spend a great deal of money to drill a new one because there wasn't time to go to court to enforce our easement. I had to miss my anniversary trip to Hawaii (which was already paid for, so my family went without me) and spend an entire month in a motel room in another state, trying to fix an almost impossible problem while struggling to keep up with my already pressing deadlines. And then, before I could write "the end" on this story, my stepfather passed away and my mother soon followed (on the heels of my father-in-law's passing, so I lost three parents within the same year).

A period like that definitely shows you the best and worst of human nature. The people I dealt with were total strangers. They had no reason to be sympathetic, and most weren't. But there were a few rare, exceptional individuals who showed me some kindness and compassion when it mattered most. They are the ones who pulled me through. And this book is for them.

One

Hendrix Durrant eyed his longtime neighbor, speaking with a hard-edged frustration he didn't bother to conceal. "You're hiring Ellen? Really, Jay? You've been talking to me about getting this well dug for the past eight months. You've had me meet you out here two or three times for details on where to drill, how deep to go, what size pump you'll need to get enough water, what we'll do if we encounter sand, and on and on. And now you're going with my competitor?"

Jay Haslem, a forty-something mechanic who was finally getting the chance to build a nicer home outside the small town of Coyote Canyon, Montana, where Hendrix had lived since he was eleven and Jay had lived his whole life, shoved his hands in the pockets of his grease-stained overalls and stared down at the dirt. "Well, she's not *really* your competitor, is she?"

Hendrix rested his hands on his hips. "She does the same thing I do, but her business is completely separate from mine. Wouldn't you call that competition?"

"Yeah, but…she's Stuart's daughter. And he's married to your aunt Lynn. I know you're not related, but you're sort of…connected, right?" He offered Hendrix a weak grin, which Hendrix immediately wiped from his face with a heated retort.

"Not only are we not related, I barely know her and hate that she moved to town two and a half years ago, because ever since then, she's made a concerted effort to become a major pain in my ass."

"It's just that…her dad's married to your aunt," Jay said again.

Lynn had raised Hendrix from the first year she married Stuart, after his mother died of breast cancer. Everyone knew he'd been taken in out of the goodness of her heart, that he would've gone into the foster care system otherwise. It wasn't as if he had a father, like most other kids. His mother, Angie, who'd lived and worked as a venture capital analyst in San Francisco, where attitudes were more liberal in general, had been so determined to have a child on her own terms she'd used a sperm bank, never imagining what might happen to him if she wasn't around. That meant, once she was gone, he'd been lucky to have extended family who would give him a home. "I don't care. That doesn't change anything."

Jay winced as he pulled on his beard. "My wife likes her, Hendrix. Thea's the one who promised her the job. Not me. Ellen's a tough little thing, a go-getter. We… I don't know, we admire that kind of gumption, I guess. After all, there aren't many women in your field."

Jay's, either. Not too many female mechanics around… But Hendrix was too focused on other things to point that out. "You admire her gumption," he echoed, chuckling humorlessly. "You're giving her the job because she's—" he used air quotes "—a tough little thing."

Once again, Jay shifted uncomfortably. "That and… she's saving us a few bucks, of course."

"Of course," Hendrix echoed flatly. Ellen had been undercutting him and Stuart since she moved to town. "How much is a few bucks?"

"She said—" He stopped and cleared his throat before finishing in a mumble, "She said she'd do it for a thousand less than whatever you bid."

"Excuse me?" Hendrix had heard him fine, but he wanted to make his neighbor state, clearly, the reason he'd chosen Ellen. This wasn't about supporting a female-owned company in a largely male-dominated field, as Jay had tried to claim a few minutes ago. This was nothing more than pure self-interest. Ellen had been working day and night since she moved to Coyote Canyon, just to best him and Stuart, her father. Hendrix knew that was true because, in some cases, she was—*had* to be—drilling wells and replacing and repairing pumps for next to no profit, other than the pleasure of taking jobs that would otherwise have gone to them.

"She said she didn't have the time to come out and bid, but she'd do it for a thousand less than what you said you'd do it for," Jay repeated. "All we had to do was give her the paperwork you left with us."

"You handed over my bid? Now she can order the supplies and get you on her schedule without spending any of the time I've invested in assessing your needs."

Jay hung his head. "I'm sorry. You know I don't have a lot of money. Thea and I have held on to this property for several years, hoping to save enough to start improving it, or...or I would've gone with you no matter what."

Drawing a deep breath, which he immediately blew out, Hendrix stared over Jay's shoulder at the rugged Montana terrain that constituted his neighbor's five-acre dream parcel. Ever since Ellen Truesdale came to town, he'd made a point of avoiding her. If he ran into her by accident—in a population of only three thousand it was impossible not to encounter each other every once in a while—he nodded politely, so she wouldn't know how much it bothered him to have her around. But she never responded. She just gave him that unflinching, steely-eyed gaze of hers that let him know she was gunning for him.

Despite that, he'd remained determined not to let her get to him. But as time wore on, and she stole more business from him and Stuart, she was harder and harder to ignore.

Why couldn't she have sold the place her grandparents had given her here in town and remained in Anaconda, where she'd been born and raised? Anaconda was twice the size of Coyote Canyon; there had to be more people in that part of the state who were looking to drill a water well. Actually, he knew that to be true because he and Stuart occasionally drilled a well or helped with a pump out that way—Fetterman Well Services ranged over the whole state and even went into Utah and Nevada. And if Ellen had stayed in Anaconda, which was almost two hours from Coyote Canyon, their paths would most likely never have crossed.

But Hendrix knew her decision had very little to do with where she could make the most money—or even where she might be happiest. She had a vendetta against her father, who'd left her mother when Ellen was only ten to marry Hendrix's aunt, and she was determined to make him pay for walking out on them. Hendrix and his cousin, Leo, whom he considered as close as a brother, were just the visible representation of all she resented.

"No problem," he told his neighbor as he started back to his truck. "Here's hoping she does a decent job for you."

"Are you saying she might not?" Jay called after him, sounding alarmed.

Hendrix didn't acknowledge the question, let alone answer it. Undermining Jay's trust in Ellen was a cheap shot—beneath him, really. Ellen knew what she was doing. In many ways, she ran her business better than Stuart ran the one Hendrix had helped him build since he was brought from San Francisco. She didn't have the resources or the experience they did, but she was a quick study. From what he'd heard, she was also detail-oriented—stayed right on top of everything—and since Fetterman had two crews consisting of three employees each, and covered a much bigger area, he had no doubt she was operating with far less overhead, so she could be nimble.

Although Stuart insisted they didn't have anything to worry about when it came to Ellen—that she'd give up trying to get back at him and eventually move on—Hendrix was beginning to realize that wasn't true. Stuart was just avoiding the problem because he felt guilty about the past. And the more he avoided it, the worse it got.

When Ellen Truesdale heard a vehicle pull up, she assumed it was Ben Anderson, her only employee. She'd finally sent him out to grab some lunch. Since breakfast early this morning, they'd been too busy to eat, and she was starving. He had to be, too; it was almost three. At twenty-one, he seemed to consume twice his body weight in food each day. But when she finished welding the steel casing they were putting down the well and flipped up her helmet, she saw that it wasn't Ben. Hendrix Durrant had just parked next to her older and much less expensive pickup.

Since Hendrix hadn't actually spoken to her since she came to town, she was more than a little surprised he'd driven out to her jobsite. That meant he was here with a very specific intention.

Setting her torch aside, she removed her helmet entirely and shoved up the long sleeves of her shirt. She had no idea what he wanted, but whatever it was…she couldn't imagine she was going to like it.

Instead of approaching her right away, he slipped his hands into the pockets of his well-worn jeans and studied her GEFCO rotary drilling rig. Maybe he'd assumed she couldn't afford a top-head drive, which enabled her to advance the casing that blocked off the sand and gravel as she drilled, and was shocked to see it. She could understand why that might be true. A rig like hers cost almost a million dollars, and *she'd* never had the luxury of being able to ride on her father's coattails. If she hadn't been able to take out a loan against the house and property her paternal grandparents had passed on to her, she wouldn't have had the down payment necessary to purchase it. And if she'd had to settle for an older rig, it would've made her job much more difficult.

As it was, her payments were almost ten thousand a month, and that didn't include the water truck she'd also had to buy. Fortunately, it wasn't nearly as expensive as the rig. She'd managed to find a used one in Moab, Utah, for only fifty thousand. But it all added up. She had a lot on the line, which was why she worked so damn hard.

"Is there something I can do for you?" she asked, tensing in spite of all the self-talk that insisted there was no reason to be nervous. She didn't care if she had a confrontation with her father and those connected to him. She'd been spoiling for a fight with them almost as far back as she could remember. Except for Leo, of course. Leo was harmless. Everyone knew that.

Hendrix turned to face her. She hadn't moved toward him, hadn't closed one inch of the gap between them. If he wanted to speak to her, he was going to have to cross that distance himself—which he did, reluctantly from what she could tell.

"You've been in town for two and a half years now," he said.

She wiped the sweat from her face before giving him a smirk. "I didn't realize you'd been counting."

His eyebrows slid up. "I've only been counting because you've been doing everything you possibly can to make me notice you—and now I have."

She barked a laugh. "Am I supposed to be excited about that?" She had to admit most women would be. With sandy-blond hair, smooth golden skin and wide, sky blue eyes, he reminded her of Brad Pitt in *Troy*— mostly because of the structure of his face but also his build. She couldn't claim he was hard to look at.

"I was hoping to convince you to come over and talk to your father," he said. "Scream and yell, say whatever you want, but quit trying to punish him by ruining our business."

She removed her leather gloves and slapped them against her thigh, which made him take a step back to avoid breathing in the resulting cloud of dust. "I have nothing to say to my father."

"Obviously you do, or you wouldn't be living here."

"In case you're not aware of it, my grandparents gave me their house, and it happens to be here. I guess you didn't quite manage to replace me in *their* affections."

"I didn't try to replace you at all. I'm sorry if you feel

I did. But just so you know, your grandpa and grandma Fetterman have been good to me, too."

She shrugged off his words. "Only because they're nice to everyone."

"Maybe so, but just because you got their house doesn't mean you have to live in it. You could sell if you wanted to…"

"That's the thing." It took effort, but she brightened her smile for his benefit. "I like it here."

"Come on," he said. "Be honest. You're only staying because you think it bugs your father."

"That's not all," she said with a taunting grin. "I'm staying because it bugs you, too."

"And that makes you happy?"

"Happ*ier*," she clarified.

He shook his head. "There's something wrong with you. What're you trying to do? Prove you can build the same business we've built on your own?"

"And do it even better," she said with apparent satisfaction. That had been her goal for a long time, ever since she'd finished college at Montana State with a degree in business and returned to Anaconda to help her mother make ends meet. After seeing her father become successful drilling water wells, she'd decided to do the same thing. She knew she didn't want to get stuck waiting tables forever, and Anaconda didn't offer a great deal of opportunity.

But it hadn't been easy to get started. If she hadn't managed to convince Ross Moore, a successful driller in Anaconda, to hire her, she wouldn't have had the chance. But she'd needed only two years of experience, drilling fifteen wells under a licensed contractor, in order to get her own license. So Ross had eventually agreed—just to be a nice guy, she thought—and wound up being so happy with her work he'd kept her as his business expanded until her grandparents gave her their house in Coyote Canyon two and a half years ago, and she decided to go out on her own.

Hendrix's eyes narrowed. "I've been pleasant so far, haven't lifted a finger to stop you. I don't want to—" he spread out his hands "—do anything that would harm you, even financially."

"If there was anything you could do to me *financially*, you would've done it already," she pointed out, which only seemed to enrage him further.

"Our company's bigger than yours," he said with a hard set to his jaw.

Our company. She was Stuart's daughter. Hendrix was only his second wife's nephew. He stood to take over the business when Stuart died, since Leo wasn't capable, but he wasn't even considered a true partner at this point. As she understood it, he was only on salary. And yet, when Hendrix lost his mother to breast cancer, her father had not only allowed Lynn to take him into their home, he'd chosen Hendrix over her in every regard. No doubt Stuart assumed Hendrix was stronger and more capable than she was, but she was bound and determined to prove he'd significantly underestimated her abilities. "That's obvious." She gave him the once-over. "But bigger isn't always better."

He stepped closer, too close for comfort, which was probably his intent, and glared down his nose at her. "It is in this case. *Don't* make me put you out of business."

He turned on his heel to stalk back to his truck, but she called after him. "You couldn't put me out of business if you tried!"

He stopped before opening his door. "We have deeper pockets than you do, Ellen. We can play the price game, too. What if I were to go around to all your jobs and offer to drill cheaper? You're saying I couldn't steal your next six months of work from you?"

"You'll be taking a heavy loss if you do!"

He studied her for several seconds. "I'm beginning to think it would be worth it."

The size of her monthly bills—the payment she had to make on her rig alone—sent a tremor of foreboding through her. She couldn't withstand a full-on battle with her father and Hendrix. Not one that went on for very long, at least. She needed to back off. But she couldn't. "You don't scare me!" she yelled. "I'll take you on. I'll take on both you sons of bitches!"

His tires spun dirt and gravel as he backed up and nearly hit Ben, who was just coming back in his Jeep.

Ben slammed on his brakes in the nick of time and waited for Hendrix to swerve around him. Then he got out, wide-eyed and slack-jawed, and walked over to where Ellen stood at the rig. "That was Hendrix Durrant, wasn't it?" he said. "I told you he wouldn't like what we've been doing. He confronted you about it, didn't he? What'd he say?"

"Nothing," she retorted. She couldn't bring herself to admit that the resentment driving her might have caused her to sign the death warrant on her fledgling business—the only thing that was currently keeping a roof over *both* their heads.

Damn her! What's wrong with her? Hendrix fumed as he drove, probably a little too recklessly, to Lynn and Stuart's. At thirty-one, he no longer lived with them, but his house wasn't far away, and he was at their place a lot to see his cousin, Leo, who had Down Syndrome. The office for the drilling business was in one section of the barn, too, and most of their drilling equipment was parked on the property.

Leo was in the wide front yard wearing a snowsuit—even though it was the end of March and edging toward spring and there were only little patches of white in the shadows—playing with his dog, Zeus. He lit up like a Christmas tree the second he saw Hendrix turn in, and came running to the truck.

"Hi, Hendrix!" he said, waving enthusiastically as Hendrix got out. "I been waitin' for ya. I knew you'd come!"

Because Hendrix came almost every day. He typically brought Leo a donut or other treat, and he would've again today, except Lynn had told him he had to stop. Leo was gaining too much weight. It was hard for Hendrix to disappoint him, but he had no other choice. "I know you're probably hoping I've got a donut for you, bud, but I couldn't get over there in time to buy one. I'm sorry."

Leo's shoulders slumped, and the corners of his mouth turned down, which made Hendrix feel terrible. But in typical Leo style, he perked up right away. "That's okay, Hendrix," he said as they started to walk, with Zeus, toward the office. "You'll bring me one tomorrow, right? I like the chocolate with sprinkles. It's my favorite. I bet that's the one you'll buy me. You'll bring me the chocolate one tomorrow, won't you, Hendrix?"

Hendrix eyed his thickening middle and offered to take him on a walk instead, but Leo was having none of it.

"After I eat my donut?" he asked.

"Yeah, after you eat your donut," Hendrix said, finally relenting. He couldn't refuse, despite Leo's weight.

He'd just have to take Leo somewhere else to eat it so Lynn wouldn't catch them. He hated to contribute to the problem when she'd asked him not to, but he couldn't deny his cousin the few simple pleasures he enjoyed so much. Maybe the walk after would zero it out.

"Thank you, Hendrix. I can't wait!" He rubbed his hands in anticipation as they reached the office. "What are you doing today?" he asked before Hendrix could open the door. "Are you drilling another well? Can I get my steel-toed boots and my hard hat and go with you?"

It was Friday, Hendrix's day for picking up parts, fixing broken equipment, giving estimates and helping catch up on any paperwork Lynn was holding back because of questions she had. She helped in the office while they did the drilling, but she must be in the house or getting her hair done or something else today, because Hendrix didn't see her when he swung open the door. "For the next little while, I'm mostly hanging out here with Stuart, okay, bud?" he said. "But if I have to run an errand or two, you can come along."

Leo smiled widely—something he did almost all the time. "Maybe we could buy a candy bar while we're out!"

"No treats, Leo," he said. "They aren't good for you, remember?"

Leo's shoulders rounded again, until he thought of the donut. "But you'll bring me a donut tomorrow?"

Hendrix barely refrained from groaning. He'd never known anyone with such a sweet tooth. Leo was at him for candy, soda and other junk food all the time. "Yes," Hendrix told him. "I said I would."

"I love you, Hendrix," he said. "You're the best!"

It was hard to remain angry about anything in the face of his childlike exuberance. "I love you, too," Hendrix said with a chuckle.

But when he walked into the office and Stuart glanced up, he remembered why he'd come skidding into the driveway of their house in the first place.

"You need to do something about Ellen," he said bluntly.

"Ellen *Truesdale*?" Leo piped up before Stuart, who was sitting at his desk, could respond.

Hendrix wasn't surprised Leo knew who Ellen was. With her bleached blond hair, cut in a short, jagged style, nose ring and ear piercings, together with the tattoo sleeve that covered one arm, she stood out in the ultraconservative community in which he'd been raised. Not only had she been a hot topic around town, she'd come up in plenty of conversations between Stuart and Lynn.

Hendrix *was* surprised, however, that Leo remembered her last name. It wasn't as if they knew any other Truesdales. As soon as she'd turned eighteen, Ellen had legally changed her last name to her mother's maiden name—another of her many attempts to get back at Stuart. Leo's father had been an alcoholic who'd raised and sold hunting dogs—before he shot himself when Lynn left him. Stuart adopted Leo when he and Lynn married three years later, so Leo went by Fetterman. And since Hendrix's father was found in a tube of sperm cells in a lab somewhere, he'd retained his mother's last name and went by Durrant.

"Yes, Ellen Truesdale," Hendrix told him.

Stuart sighed as he rocked back in his chair. "What's she done this time?"

"Took the Haslem job from us."

His father looked startled. "I thought we had that one in the bag. Isn't Jay your neighbor?"

About four years ago, Hendrix had bought a small, two-bedroom, two-bath, log-cabin-style home on a couple of acres about five minutes away. Jay lived in the mobile home next door—until he could move to his other property, anyway. "Yeah, well, I guess loyalty doesn't count for much when money's involved."

"She undercut us again?"

"Word's getting around that she'll beat any price we give. At least, that's what I'm guessing. All Jay told me was that he was hiring her because it would save him some money."

The beard growth on Stuart's chin rasped as he rubbed it. "Drillin's hard work. I can't believe she'd do it that cheaply—and that she's actually doing a decent job. She's only about five foot four, maybe a hundred pounds soaking wet."

"You know she has Ben Anderson to help her, right? She hired him right out of high school when she first got here."

"I know she's got Ben, but it has to be difficult for her even with a hired hand."

Hearing the grudging admiration in his voice made Hendrix's hackles rise again. "She's trying to damage our business. You realize that."

"She's not going to damage it for long," Stuart said dismissively. "I've been drillin' wells and servicing pumps for forty years. We'll reach a new equilibrium sooner or later."

"I'm not so sure," Hendrix argued. "Can't you meet with her? Have a discussion? Folks talk, especially in a small town like this. If word has it that she's the cheapest around, and she's a good driller…" He shook his head. "It's been two and a half years since she moved here. She's only getting a firmer foothold as the days go by."

"What do you want me to say to her?" his uncle asked. "She's not doing anything wrong."

"Purposely targeting our business isn't doing anything wrong?"

"It's a free market," he said with a shrug. "There's nothin' to say another driller can't move in here and compete with us. Whether it's her or someone else…"

"*I'll* talk to Ellen!" Leo volunteered. "She's *so* pretty. And such a little thing. I bet I could pick her up."

"Don't ever try that," Hendrix told him. "I don't think she'd like it."

"Oh, I'd never hurt her," Leo hurried to reassure him.

Hendrix knew he'd never hurt her intentionally. Leo would never hurt anyone intentionally. But he was a big man, and he didn't know his own strength. Sometimes he reminded Hendrix of Lennie in *Of Mice and Men*, not least because he himself identified with George Milton in the role of Leo's protector. During his teens, he'd been in more fights than he could remember trying to defend Leo from the bullies who'd tease and make fun of him. "I know you wouldn't, bud. You just have to remember not to touch her, okay? *Ever.*"

"Okay," Leo said dutifully.

"So will you talk to her?" Hendrix asked, turning back to Stuart.

Stuart blanched. "I don't know what to say to her," he admitted. "I mean…what *can* I say? I didn't do right by her, and there's no changing that now."

"Then apologize," Hendrix said, "before she makes me lose my mind."

Stuart stared at the paperwork on his desk for several seconds before finally—and grudgingly—relenting. "If I get the opportunity, I'll see what I can do."

"Let me give you the opportunity," he said. "She's drilling the Slemboskis a well right now. Should be there another day, at least. Maybe longer."

His uncle's jaw had dropped as soon as he heard the name. "The Slemboskis went with her, too? Slim Slemboski's on my bowling team!"

Hendrix threw up his hands. "See what I mean?"

Stuart winced as he went back to rubbing his jaw. "O-kay," he said on a downbeat, as if agreeing to talk to Ellen was tantamount to walking the plank. "I'll go over there tomorrow, see what I can do."

Two

"You did...*what*?" Talulah Elway cried.

Ellen cast her friend a sheepish glance. She hadn't known Talulah her whole life, like most of Talulah's other friends in Coyote Canyon—Talulah had grown up here—but they'd become close in the year since they'd met. The property Ellen had received when her grandparents moved to Phoenix was set away from town, adjacent to the old farmhouse and acreage Talulah had purchased from her great-aunt Phoebe's estate when she came home to handle the funeral. Talulah had planned on going back to her dessert diner in Seattle, which she'd started with a partner, but while she was in town, she fell in love with Brant Elway—a rancher Ellen had dated for a short time herself when she was new to the area. After Talulah married him, she sold her interest in the diner and had recently opened a new one downtown.

"I couldn't help myself," Ellen grumbled, sinking deeper—thanks to dejection and exhaustion—into the porch swing where they were sitting and rocking while gazing out at the gathering twilight. The rig had blown a hydraulic hose just before she and Ben were about to quit for the day, so he was the only one who'd left. She'd had to work late to get it fixed. Otherwise, they wouldn't be able to continue drilling in the morning. She hadn't even had a chance to shower yet. When she drove past Talulah's on her way home, she'd noticed the lights were on but Brant's truck was gone, meaning her friend was probably home alone and she wouldn't be interrupting anything they were doing together if she stopped by. So she was still in her jeans, work boots and the long-sleeved T-shirt she wore to protect her arms from sparks when she had to cut and weld—which she did with the casing almost every hour while she was drilling.

"I think you might've gone too far," Talulah said. "Your father's business is well established. Hendrix is right when he says they have deeper pockets than you do."

"They also have bigger overhead." She'd been telling herself that ever since Hendrix had stormed off, but her father's office was on the same property as his home, and for all she knew, he'd paid off his trucks and equipment over the years. He had to cover Hendrix's salary, of course, and she had no doubt Hendrix was earning way more than she was paying Ben, who was much younger. He also had to pay his other employees, and he had quite a few more than she did. But *she* was paying for her equipment and she had spare parts and supplies, like the pumps she needed to keep on hand, each of which cost a couple of thousand dollars, charged to her credit cards.

Using credit wasn't the safest way to build a business. But at least she didn't have a house payment beyond what she'd borrowed for the rig.

Talulah bit her lip. "Maybe I could go talk to him, tell him you didn't mean what you said today and try to work out some sort of truce."

"No!" Ellen sat up straight. "I'll be fine. I know what I'm doing."

"I admire your grit," Talulah said. "No one could fault your courage. But…you don't want this to turn into all-out war, do you?"

She manufactured a shrug. "There's nothing they can do to me."

The sullen note in her voice had given her away. Clearly, Talulah wasn't convinced Ellen meant what she'd just said. "I know you might not want to hear this, but I don't believe Hendrix is a bad guy. He drilled a well for Brant out at the ranch several years ago and is friends with Brant's younger brothers. Brant really likes him."

Everyone said Hendrix was a stand-up guy and admired him for the way he looked out for his cousin, who was a year older. But Ellen didn't want to hear it. Her father had already chosen him over her, sharing his longtime business and treating him more like a son than he ever treated her like a daughter. The praise Hendrix received only made her feel worse. "I thought you were supposed to be cheering me up."

"I'm just saying that maybe you should let the past go—for your own good."

That was easier said than done. Didn't Talulah believe she'd tried? "I don't have a problem with the past," she said, even though they both knew it wasn't true. "I'd better go," she added and stopped the swing. "I need a shower." She needed some sleep, too. Six o'clock came awfully early when she got home so late.

"Ellen!" Talulah called as she stepped off the porch.

Ellen no longer wanted to talk. She regretted stopping in the first place. But she turned.

"You're a wonderful person. It's your father who

missed out. Don't let the decisions he made when you were young rob you of the chance to be happy now."

"I *am* happy," she insisted.

But once she got home and walked into the empty house that had belonged to her grandparents all the time she was growing up, she was overwhelmed by the memories of coming to visit them. Memories of seeing the pictures of her father hanging on the walls and gracing the side tables—and knowing he was in the area but couldn't be bothered to see her, other than meeting them to get an ice cream cone at his parents' urging. His defection still cut so deeply, even now, that she flinched.

She had to banish those memories. Her father was an asshole. All she'd ever wanted was a few crumbs of his attention. But it was Hendrix who'd gotten everything. Hendrix, who wasn't his son, wasn't any kind of relation—except the boy Stuart had always wanted.

Hendrix sucked the foam off the top of his beer while waiting for Kurt Elway to take his turn at billiards. Coyote Canyon offered plenty of things to do—camping, fishing, four-wheeling, hiking, hunting and more, most of which he loved, but those things took place during the day. There was far less to do at night. Dinner and whatever movie was playing at the drive-in theater was a possibility. But even then, the drive-in was only open during the summer and typically featured older flicks the owners could bring in on a budget. That left hanging out with his buddies and having a drink at Hank's Bar & Grill while listening to music—a live band on weekends—and playing darts and billiards, which Hendrix did probably once a week.

"Damn. Missed," Kurt said as he stood and lifted his cue.

Kurt would probably beat him despite flubbing his turn. They were fairly equal when it came to pool, but tonight Hendrix couldn't concentrate—couldn't quit thinking about Ellen, who'd been getting under his skin for a long time. He simply couldn't ignore what she was doing anymore. The confrontation he'd had with her earlier played in a loop in his mind. She'd been so defensive when he approached her. He wasn't sure he'd ever met a woman with a bigger chip on her shoulder. Her stormy green eyes, the stubborn set of her jaw and the tenseness of her body telegraphed her animosity toward him.

Despite his preoccupation, he managed to sink two balls and even up the game. He felt pretty good about that, until Kurt went up by one immediately after.

It was March Madness, so basketball played on the plethora of TVs in the bar. Whenever he was waiting to take his turn, Hendrix watched New Mexico State battle it out with Vermont, so he didn't see Ben Anderson come in. By the time he noticed Ben was there, he'd lost at pool, Kurt had gone to the bathroom and he was on his way to get another drink.

Ellen's employee was sitting at the bar, eating a burger. Hendrix knew he had a girlfriend. He'd seen them together around town. But she wasn't with him tonight.

He looked up as Hendrix drew close, then immediately yanked his gaze away. Hendrix almost let it go at that. Maybe Ben worked for Ellen, but he wasn't responsible for how she ran her business. Hendrix told himself to ignore the kid and carry on with his night, but the look in Ben's eyes suggested he felt uncomfortable and understood that they were on opposing teams.

Seeing Hendrix approach, the bartender came close enough to be heard. "You want another beer?"

"Sure. This time I'll take a Corona," Hendrix said, and as the bartender turned away, he decided to sit down and have a little talk with Ben.

His close proximity seemed to startle the kid, who glanced over at him twice before continuing to eat.

"Hey." Hendrix had to speak loudly to be heard above the cover band.

Ben stuffed a French fry in his mouth. "Hey."

"You work for Ellen Truesdale, don't you?"

Ben swallowed before answering. "Yeah. That was me you almost crashed into today when you were leaving our jobsite. I was coming back with lunch."

"Sorry about that. Didn't see ya."

"No problem. You seemed to be in a hurry."

He *had* been in a hurry—to get away from Ellen.

The bartender returned with Hendrix's beer, then went to make someone else a drink while Hendrix squeezed the accompanying wedge of lime into the bottle. "How do you like working with Ellen?" he asked Ben.

The kid seemed taken aback by the question. "I like it fine. I'm glad I have a job."

"You don't plan to go to college?"

"Nah." He dipped some fries in ketchup. "I hate school."

"But she treats you right…"

"We get along."

"Somehow I didn't expect you to say that."

He lifted his own beer and took a long swig. "Why not?"

"She seems like a difficult person, if you ask me."

Ben bit into his burger, then had to talk while he chewed. "She probably wouldn't like me telling *you* this, but she's not as badass as she wants everyone to believe."

"Really…"

"Really. She'd be the first person to wade out into a flood and risk drowning while trying to rescue some flea-bitten feral cat, you know?"

Ben chuckled but Hendrix didn't. An idea had popped into his head, a way to show Ellen that there were consequences to picking a fight with him. A way to show her without having to go so far as to lose money drilling for even less than she was. "Don't you get tired of doing all the heavy lifting while she takes home the majority of the pay?"

Ben didn't seem to know how to answer that question. After several seconds, he took another swallow of beer, then said, "She owns the business. I figure she *should* take home the majority of the pay. She certainly works hard enough—harder than most men, if you want the truth."

The respect in his voice irritated Hendrix. Because of her attitude and the way Ellen bleached her hair—or turned it pink or purple, depending on her mood—and the piercings and tattoos, most people in Coyote Canyon steered clear of her. She made her own way and didn't apologize for it, and they didn't like that she dared to be different.

But he was talking to someone who'd spent a great deal of time with her in the past two and a half years, and Ben clearly admired her. "She pulls her own weight, huh?" he said, still digging to see if there was an opportunity here.

"And then some." Ben drained his glass. "What she lacks in physical strength she makes up for with determination. If we need to get something done, she figures it out. I've never known anybody like her."

"Still. You gotta look out for yourself," Hendrix said,

pointing at him with his bottle of beer. "Do what's best for *you*."

"What do you mean by that?"

"I have a job opening. One of my drillers is moving at the end of the month, which means I'm going to have to replace him."

Uncertainty descended on Ben's face, but what Hendrix had said was true. Randy Bettencourt was relocating to Billings so he and his wife could be closer to her family when they had their first child, due in three months. Hendrix was going to have to hire someone to replace him and suddenly saw this as a way to solve both problems.

"And…" Ben prompted.

"I'm thinking the job might be of interest to you. You've had a couple years of experience now, and I'm assuming she's trained you right."

"I'm a good driller," he said. "What's the pay like?"

"It'd be a lot more than you're making now. Probably twenty or thirty percent more."

Ben put down his burger. "You'd pay me that much?"

"You'd be earning it. Heading up a drill crew comes with a lot of responsibility."

Again, the kid didn't seem to know what to say. After a few beats, and a long exhalation, he finally admitted, "That's a good offer."

"It is." Hendrix got up and gave his shoulder a squeeze. "Why don't you consider it and come talk to me sometime next week."

Ben's forehead wrinkled in consternation. "I don't think I could do that to Ellen…"

"She's your boss, not your wife, Ben," he said with a laugh. "For one reason or another, business owners lose employees all the time. It's just part of free enterprise."

Ben scratched his neck. "This is a little different."

"How? If she's as great as you say, I can't imagine she'd begrudge you a better offer. I mean, you deserve to succeed, too. Can't you use the raise?"

"Of course I could use the raise..."

"And you'd be a driller, not a driller's helper. There's something to be said for that, too. It's always nice to come up in the world—make your parents proud." He saw that Kurt was out of the bathroom and looking for him, so he and Ben exchanged numbers and he grabbed his beer. "I'll be waiting for a call from you," he said and waved to get his friend's attention.

"What were you doing over there with Ben Anderson?" Kurt asked when Hendrix got close enough to hear him.

Hendrix wasn't surprised Kurt knew Ben. The town was small enough that most folks were connected in one way or another. "After two and a half years, I'm finally hitting back."

"What?" Kurt said, looking confused.

Hendrix glanced at the bar to see that Ben was still watching him. "Don't worry about it."

Ellen's muscles were sometimes so sore she could hardly get out of bed. But at least she had jobs lined up for the next several months and would be able to pay her bills.

With a yawn, she groaned as she pushed herself out of bed. A shower and a cup of coffee would make all the difference, she told herself. It was worth getting an early start. If she and Ben could finish the Slemboski well today, maybe she could get paid. Although she collected half the cost up front, that only covered a portion of her expenses. The back half covered the rest and went to overhead and profit. As always, she was eager for her final check and to be free to move on to her next project. The faster she worked, the more she'd earn and the closer she'd be to buying a pump pulling unit, a piece of equipment that would make it much easier to fix or replace pumps in existing wells. She guessed her father made half or more of his income from "out of water" calls.

She put on some coffee before checking her phone to see if Ben could meet her at seven. She'd texted him last night to tell him she'd fixed the hose that'd gone out, so they were good to continue drilling today, but since she hadn't yet received a response, she sent him another message.

Hey, you up? Let's knock this out and have the rest of the day to relax. Then we'll have tomorrow off and hit it hard again on Monday.

Unless she was under a tight deadline, she generally took Sundays off. Sometimes she was tempted to work seven days a week. But she knew her body probably couldn't take the abuse. She pushed herself hard and needed to rest now and then.

Besides, she'd promised to help at the dessert diner so Talulah and Brant could spend the day together in Bozeman. With its wonderful smells, bright, cheerful colors and so many beautiful and tasty confections, Ellen didn't mind serving customers and working the register for a few hours. It was nice to get cleaned up and do something different, have somewhere to go. Talulah always paid her. It wasn't much—not nearly as much as she could make drilling—but enough to give her a change of pace and a small amount of cash.

By the time she stepped out of the shower, the coffee was ready. She poured herself a cup and drank it mixed with a little almond milk while scrambling two eggs. She knew better than to leave the house without breakfast. Since she rarely took time to pack a lunch and often got caught up in what she was doing, it could be quite a while before she ate again—just like yesterday.

A ding signaled a text while she was buttering her toast. Assuming Ben was finally answering her, she grabbed her phone.

But it wasn't Ben. It was her mother.

Call me when you can.

Jan typically wasn't up this early. So what was going on now?

Ellen was almost afraid to find out. Her mother went from one hard-luck story to another, which was part of the reason Ellen resented her father so much. After he'd left, nothing was the same. Her mother writhed in the bitterness she felt toward Lynn for "stealing" her husband and couldn't get over the loss of her marriage, couldn't make it on her own, let alone support a child, even in an emotional sense. And since, more often than not, she'd had to fight Stuart for the child support he owed her, they rarely had the money they needed. There were times Jan couldn't even make herself get off the couch. Ellen felt she'd done more to take care of her mother over the years than her mother had ever done to take care of her.

Because that was still the case, she didn't want to hear the latest. She'd moved away from Jan on purpose—had to get a break from the constant neediness, and her grandparents had made that possible. But unlike her father, she felt a responsibility to help. So she returned Jan's call as soon as she sat down at the table to eat.

"There you are," her mother said, sounding frantic.

"What's going on?" Ellen kept one eye on the clock as she shoveled eggs into her mouth. "What are you doing up this early?"

"My landlord was just here, banging on my door."

"*Banging?* Why would he be banging?"

"He's mad because I can't cover my rent this month."

Ellen paused with her fork halfway to her mouth. *Of course.* "Why can't you cover your rent?"

Jan lived in a tiny, cheap duplex. And that was about the only payment she had, besides utilities, gas and groceries. She'd ruined her credit long ago, didn't have any charge cards. And since Ellen already had a truck, she'd given Jan the reliable car her grandparents had left when they passed on the Coyote Canyon property.

"I'm not getting enough shifts at the pancake house," she complained. "Oliver hired someone else last month, and he's been giving her most of my shifts. The way he talks to her and touches her at every opportunity, I think he's hoping she'll work after hours, if you know what I mean."

Jan had dated her manager for a while, too. Sadly, it hadn't worked out. Or maybe Ellen should be grateful. Oliver sounded like he was a hot mess, too. "How much do you need?" she asked.

"Five hundred."

The amount took Ellen by surprise. "I loaned you three hundred last month."

"I know. And I'll pay you back as soon as I get on my feet. I promise."

Ellen stifled a sigh. Problem was…she never seemed to get on her feet. "So what are you going to do to change things up for next month? Are you looking for another job?"

"I've put out a few feelers. One of the cooks at the pancake house told me he heard they need a clerk over at the dollar store. His wife works there. She's going to talk to her boss about me."

That was nice of the cook, but if Jan's reputation preceded her, she wouldn't get the job. She'd been fired more times than Ellen could count—was always late or calling in sick or having to leave early for a doctor's appointment—usually fictional.

"I have bills to pay myself, Mom. But I'll see what I can do."

Ellen would come up with the money somehow. She couldn't leave her mother in the lurch. But she also didn't want Jan to make a habit of coming to her for help. Jan didn't seem completely committed to taking care of herself. She leaned on anyone who'd allow it— and that was mainly Ellen.

"Or maybe you can talk to that father of yours and get the back child support he owes me," Jan grumbled.

Ellen had heard her mother complain about Stuart for years. If Jan had been more functional, she probably could've sued Stuart to force him to pay his child support. But she didn't have her life together enough to see anything through. "I'm not speaking to him," Ellen said. "You know that."

"Then why don't you come back to Anaconda? What are you still doing in Coyote Canyon?"

"I'm building a business here, Mom." She only needed to drill one well a month to stay afloat, and lately she'd been averaging one and a half. Even if she couldn't get a new well, she could squeeze by repairing old ones or repairing or replacing pumps. Considering the start-up costs of getting into her line of work, the difficulty of finding new clients and the physical demands of drilling, she was proud of what she'd accomplished. Not just anyone could do it. She couldn't tell her mother that, though. If Jan thought for a second that she had extra money coming in, the requests for help would never stop.

Besides, Ellen didn't *want* to go back to Anaconda. Then Jan would ask to live with her, and the next thing Ellen knew she'd be supporting her mother entirely. Jan had to stand on her own two feet for as long as possible. And Coyote Canyon was probably the only place that would allow Ellen to keep a safe distance. Since Stuart lived here with the dreaded "other woman" Jan had hated for the past twenty years, unless she was enraged about something she wouldn't even come close.

"You could build a business here just as easily, especially if you sell the house you have there. Then you'd have plenty of cash to buy another place."

No way would Ellen fall into the trap her mother had just set for her with that statement. "It's the equity in the house that enabled me to afford my drilling rig. Besides, I wouldn't want to have to train a new assistant. Ben's working out great. And then there are my friends..."

"You don't talk about your friends much."

"I've mentioned Talulah."

"Why isn't there a man in your life?" her mother asked.

Because, with one rare exception when she briefly dated Brant, she couldn't seem to pick a good one. She hadn't been in a serious relationship since leaving Anaconda. Even then, there was no one she stayed in contact with. "I don't get out much. Been too busy working."

"Seems to me all you do is work."

Ellen almost said, "That's not an entirely bad thing.

At least I can pay my bills." But she swallowed those words and tried to get off the phone instead. "Today's packed, Mom. I'd better run. But I'll look at what money I've got coming in and get back to you tonight or to-morrow, okay?"

"You can't let me know now? I need to have some-thing to tell my landlord."

"Tell him I think I can do it and send me his Venmo information."

"Thanks, honey." She sounded relieved, but it wasn't as if the anxiety this had caused her would teach her a lesson. She'd forget about it the next time she had to choose between picking up an extra shift at the pancake house or sleeping in.

"I have to run. I've got a well to finish today."

"You sound just like your father," her mother com-plained.

Except that she hadn't abandoned Jan. Stung, Ellen shoved her half-finished plate of eggs away. "If I fin-ish, I might get a check, which will help both of us."

"Okay. Let me know about the money as soon as you can."

Ellen promised she would and, relieved to have the conversation behind her, disconnected. While she'd been talking, another text had come in. This one was from Ben, but it wasn't about meeting her this morning.

We've been working six days a week for the past two and a half years, ever since you hired me.

She didn't know how to respond. Was he asking for the day off? Are you saying you'd rather not work today?

I'm wondering if you think I've been doing a good job.

Why would he be asking her this right now? Couldn't they talk about it while they were drilling? They'd have plenty of time for conversation. Yes, I do. I've told you that before. I'm grateful for your help.

I'm happy to hear it, because Hendrix Durrant just made me an offer I might not be able to refuse.

Ellen's blood ran cold. Hendrix had approached Ben? "Please say it isn't true," she whispered. She'd thought he might go after her future drilling jobs, but she'd never dreamed he'd try to steal her only employee. When?

Last night.

What'd you tell him?

I haven't told him anything yet.

Which meant he might be open to staying. But it would cost her.

The chair scraped the floor with a squeal as she stood. "Shit!" she yelled. There went any hope of being able to save up for her pump puller.

Three

As soon as they finished drilling and set the pump, Ellen let Ben go home, which meant she couldn't install the pressure tank today. If she were stronger, she might be able to maneuver it into place in the Slemboskis' garage, but it was heavy and awkward and there was no way she could do it by herself. She'd have Ben help her on Monday. Then she could wire up the control box. She'd wanted to push through; it'd been hard for her to quit when they were so close. But it was already four o'clock, and she knew Ben wouldn't react kindly to being asked to stay late. He'd been too eager to go celebrate their new deal.

She'd needed a break from him after negotiating with him, anyway. She fully believed there'd be months when he'd be making more than she was—at least until she could pay off her equipment or increase the number of wells she was drilling, neither of which was guaranteed. She was disappointed he'd driven such a hard bargain. She'd told him she didn't think she'd have enough money to keep the business afloat if she had to give him such a big raise. She definitely wouldn't if her mother kept bugging her for money. But he had a better offer in hand, and that had given her very little bargaining power. He wanted to make as much as possible. Anyone would. It was Hendrix who was to blame for what'd happened.

At least she'd ultimately talked Ben into staying on. She should probably hire someone else and train him or her as soon as possible. But if she brought in another employee, it would be all too easy for Ben to guess she was planning to replace him now that he was demanding so much. He'd leave at that point, anyway.

There wasn't a good answer. For the next month, she'd just have to limp by and see how things went. She had too many wells scheduled now that spring was almost here. Too bad it was impossible to drill alone. She wished she could, but it required at least two people.

Moving the rig would also have to wait until Monday, but she handled the derrick to get it ready and was hooking the trailer containing the rest of the casing up to her truck when she saw an expensive Ford pickup with a double-cab and dual tires come trundling down the drive. She would've assumed it was a visitor for the Slemboskis. After all, she was at their house. But even though the sun was glinting off the front windshield and she couldn't see the driver, she recognized the truck.

Straightening, she watched warily as her father parked, got out and came toward her.

They'd always avoided each other—looked the other way if their eyes ever met at town events like the Christmas-tree lighting ceremony or the Fourth of July fireworks, circumvented each other if they happened to pass in the street, left a restaurant, grocery store or gas station if they arrived to find the other one there. This was the first time he'd ever purposely approached her since she'd moved to town, and it caused a flood of unexpected emotions. All the hurt, anger and betrayal she'd felt as a kid came welling up, along with fresh anger over what Hendrix had done in trying to steal Ben from her last night.

"What do *you* want?" she asked as soon as he got close.

"I think… Maybe it's time we talked," he replied.

She removed her leather gloves. "About your attempt to steal my driller?"

His eyebrows shot up. "Excuse me?"

"Hendrix offered my driller way more than I'm paying him to come work for you. What's going on? After being here all these years, you can't get your own employees?"

He opened his mouth, closed it again and cleared his throat.

Stepping closer, she poured all the malevolence she was feeling into her voice, mostly to mask emotions she hadn't been able to stamp out even after all the years she'd told herself she hated this man. "So is that what you came here to talk about?"

With a sigh, he stared down at the dirt. Then he kicked a small pebble a few feet. "No, never mind," he said. "I'll leave you alone."

Ellen watched him go, both angry at herself for not giving him a chance to say what he'd come to say, and proud of herself for managing to conceal the terrible longing he evoked whenever she thought of him or encountered him. Her life could've been so different, so much easier. *He* was the one who'd had the power to make it that way. He could've loved her and protected her like other fathers loved and protected their daughters.

Instead, he'd let her down so terribly she knew she'd bear the scars of his neglect for the rest of her life. Because of his rejection, she wasn't sure she could ever truly believe she was worthy of the love she craved and, of course, that interfered when it came to other men. The only guy she'd ever gotten serious with, in Anaconda, had anger issues himself and had gotten in trouble with the law over and over again, and yet, when she finally broke up with him, he told her *she* was too combative. "You're always trying to measure up against the boy your father chose over you—that nephew of his wife's— and it keeps you too guarded. I can't break down your walls, can't get close to you," he'd said. "You won't allow it."

She supposed he was right. She was so jealous of Hendrix she couldn't help hating him just for being alive. And she was angry almost all the time, which made her prickly.

"He wasn't going to say anything that would make a difference," she mumbled, watching the plume of dust kicked up by his tires as he drove off. But she broke into tears as soon as she climbed into her truck and had the privacy to let the emotion that was tearing her up come out.

"Did you do it?" Hendrix asked when his uncle returned to the office.

Stuart didn't even look at him. "Do what?"

Lynn came into the room, with Leo and Zeus trailing behind, before Hendrix could clarify.

"I told you Hendrix was here," Leo said, pointing to him the second he came through the door as if he'd solved a great riddle.

Hendrix's truck was in the drive. It must've been obvious to Lynn that he was there. Leo was just expressing his excitement. Hendrix had taken him out earlier for a donut and a walk, but almost every time Leo encountered him, he acted as though they hadn't seen each other in a long while.

"Hey, Aunt Lynn." Hendrix hoped Leo wouldn't mention the donut. He'd told him not to tell, but that didn't always make a difference. Leo could decide that he should thank Hendrix *again* for the delicious chocolate donut *with the sprinkles* without even realizing that the people who weren't supposed to know were in the room.

But no sooner had Hendrix thought about the donut than he noticed his aunt's remonstrative look, which indicated he no longer needed to worry about her finding out. She already knew.

"Really, Hendrix?" she said, clearly displeased. "You *had* to take Leo to the donut shop when I've asked you— over and over again—not to feed him sweets?"

Leo clapped a beefy hand over his mouth but spoke through his thick fingers. "How'd she know?" he whispered like a shocked child. "*I* didn't tell her, Hendrix! I told her we *didn't* get a donut."

"Yes. You volunteered that little nugget, but it might've been more believable if you hadn't done it with chocolate frosting on your lips," Lynn said.

Hendrix gave his aunt a sheepish look. "I'm sorry. I took him and Zeus for a walk afterward, if that helps."

"It doesn't. Not enough," she said sulkily. "You're not helping him by undermining me, you know."

Hendrix bent to scratch Zeus behind the ears, partly to avoid his aunt's eyes. He'd agreed to help keep Leo on his diet, and yet he hadn't come through for her. "It's just so hard to tell him no. I mean…come on. If I can make his whole day just by giving him a donut…"

"The doctor says he needs to lose some weight," she said. "You don't do that by eating donuts."

Hendrix patted Zeus before standing up. "Fine. I'll try harder."

Her expression softened. "I know you love him. But it's because I love him, too, that I'm asking you to do this."

Hendrix nodded. She should be able to rely on him to support her efforts. "Okay." He had a candy bar in his pocket right now. It was a habit to pick up one for Leo whenever he got gas, but he promised himself he'd save it for when his cousin had lost some weight and it was okay with Lynn.

"Have you been to our PO box recently?" she asked, continuing to her desk, which was in the back corner. "I need to make a deposit when I go to town in an hour or so, and there should be some checks waiting for us."

"I haven't been by today. I'll go in a few minutes."

"Sooner would be better than later." She gestured at the desk next to hers, which they'd given Leo. "Have a seat, Leo. That coloring book I bought you is in the top drawer, remember? Maybe you can color me a picture."

He hung his head as he shuffled to his desk. "Are you mad at me?" he asked her, clearly heartbroken at the mere thought.

"No, of course not," she replied to reassure him.

He lifted his head. "Are you mad at Hendrix? Because I don't want you to be mad at Hendrix, either."

"Hendrix broke the rules," she said, attempting to be a bit harder on her nephew.

"I just wanted a donut," Leo mumbled, sounding dejected, and she immediately relented.

"Don't get upset," she said. "Everything's fine. Isn't it, Hendrix?"

"It is now," Hendrix joked, giving her a victorious smile and stood up to go get the mail—but then he noticed that Stuart hadn't said a word throughout the exchange and wouldn't really catch his eye. "Uncle Stu?" he said, remembering what he'd been asking about before. "Are you going to tell me what happened with Ellen?"

Stuart went over and poured himself a cup of coffee. "Nothing happened."

Lynn looked up. "What are you talking about?"

"He finally went to confront Ellen about stealing our business." Hendrix didn't mind telling her that. After all, she'd been complaining about it, too, and asking Stuart to do something. "I'm just wondering how it went."

"I don't want to talk about it," he said.

Hendrix exchanged a glance with Lynn. "You're not even going to tell us what she had to say?"

He put down his coffee cup. "She said you tried to recruit her driller by offering him more pay. Is that true?"

What had felt like a brilliant idea last night suddenly seemed too provocative. He'd had a few beers when he'd made that decision, or he probably wouldn't have done it. He could only imagine how Ellen felt about him now. "Ben already told her about that?"

"Must've. Essentially, you kicked the wasp's nest before sending me over to check on the wasps. So…how'd you expect it to go?"

"She started it," he grumbled, but still felt like an ass. She'd had to pull herself up by her bootstraps, with so much less to work with than *he'd* been given. It felt like he was playing dirty, but he didn't know what to do. He didn't want to fight her by going after her jobs, and yet they couldn't simply let her destroy their business. He just wanted her to move away, go somewhere else and leave them alone.

"I don't care," Stuart said. "Don't *ever* do anything that might harm her or her business again. Is that understood?"

Stuart didn't get on him very often. He was generally a pretty mellow dude. But Hendrix could tell this was one of those times when he meant every word. "Yeah, it was a dumb move," he admitted. "I'm sorry."

His aunt said nothing. Hendrix knew she understood that Ellen hadn't had an easy life. He'd long heard her and Stuart muttering about his ex and how difficult she was—and he knew Stuart felt terrible that he hadn't stepped in to do more for Ellen when she was a child. That was why he'd never tried to stop her from damaging their business before now, and this probably wasn't the turning point Hendrix had hoped it was.

Hendrix was just pulling into his driveway at six fifteen when he received a call from Ben. He saw the name on his screen and couldn't make up his mind whether to answer. What if Ben had decided to come work for him? What would he say?

He couldn't hire Ellen's driller, not without feeling even worse about what he'd done. He doubted Stuart would go along with it, anyway. He shouldn't have made such an offer in the first place. But what was he supposed to do about Ellen? Continue to let her undercut them?

He wouldn't have any compunction about fighting back if he was dealing with another man—some guy who'd moved to town and was trying to put them out of business. But Ellen was different. Everything to do with her was complicated.

"Shit," he muttered as he sat in his truck and stared down at his phone. He was tired of work, tired of the constant problems they encountered. Drilling wasn't an easy business. There was always a new challenge to overcome. And he'd probably just made things a lot harder for her.

Even if he had, she deserved it, didn't she? Why couldn't she just go live somewhere else? She obviously had no love for her father. And he couldn't blame her. He didn't know everything that'd gone on when she was a kid, but he did know that Stuart hadn't been part of her life after he left her mother for Lynn. Hendrix had the impression he'd been so relieved to be out of his first marriage, that he'd simply moved on and tried to forget the mistake he'd made by getting involved with Jan in the first place.

Sadly, that meant leaving Ellen behind, too. Maybe things would've been different if Lynn had been more supportive toward Ellen. But she'd never done anything to change the situation where Stuart's child was concerned. It was easier to pretend he'd never been married before. She had her own son to raise, a boy with Down Syndrome. And then she'd taken responsibility for Hendrix after his mother's death. Maybe she'd felt her son and her nephew wouldn't be able to compete for Stuart's affections if Ellen was around. Hendrix couldn't say for sure.

His phone buzzed again, and because he *had* made Ben the offer, he answered. He had to be accountable at some point, couldn't put off dealing with this forever. With any luck, Ben was calling to turn him down. That would take care of everything. "'Lo?"

"Hendrix?"

"Yes?"

"This is Ben Anderson."

"What's up?"

"I just wanted to tell you that I won't be able to come work for you after all. But I really appreciate the offer."

Breathing a sigh of relief, Hendrix said, "No problem. You're staying with Ellen, then? You like her that much?"

"She's a decent boss. That's not why I'm staying, though. Like you told me at Hank's, this is business. My girlfriend and I might want to get married down the road, and it'd be smart to start making more and saving more. Thanks to you, she gave me a fat raise today."

Hendrix bit back a groan. "How fat?"

"Thirty percent."

Dropping his head in his hand, he rubbed his forehead. "That's a lot."

"I demanded it. When I told her that was how much you were going to pay me, she couldn't believe it. Tried saying she wasn't sure she could continue to run the business if she had to give me that much. But I know she needs me. We've got a lot of wells lined up in the coming weeks. So I wouldn't relent, and she ultimately agreed."

Ben wasn't calling to accept his offer. But it was because of him that Ellen would have to pay her employee a great deal more. And she was already working on slim margins. "I'm excited for you," he said, trying to sound as if it were true.

"I owe it all to you, really, so… I'd love to take you out for dinner when you're free."

No way was Hendrix going to accept anything for what he'd done. But he couldn't say that without revealing his regret. "Sounds good. I'll give you a call when I have the chance."

"Great. Thanks again."

Hendrix cursed as he hit the Disconnect button. He should be happy, he told himself. He'd landed a solid blow to his only competitor, who hadn't been playing fair to begin with. That was what he'd intended to do, wasn't it?

It was. But somehow it didn't feel like much of a victory. She'd probably been telling the truth about being unable to afford such a raise. If anyone knew how difficult it was to run a drilling crew, it was him. There'd been plenty of years when he and Stuart had struggled, and Stuart had a lot more ties to the community since he'd grown up in town. Not only did he have an established reputation, he didn't have any tattoos or a nose ring that might make the people of Coyote Canyon look askance at him.

But the damage was done. Hendrix couldn't see any way to fix it now.

With any luck this would finally make Ellen leave. Moving would be expensive and difficult, especially since she had several jobs lined up. But most of those jobs should've been theirs to begin with.

He got out of his truck and went inside to shower and eat. But, somehow, he couldn't stop thinking about Ellen. She was the David in this scenario, and he was the Goliath. He couldn't allow himself to take advantage of having more power. It made him feel like a bully after spending years fighting bullies for the sake of his cousin.

He ate and cleaned up. Then he watched a college basketball game and had to tell himself to relax all through it. He just…couldn't.

Finally, he got up and grabbed his keys. He hated to do it, but he was going to have to go talk to her.

* * *

Ellen was asleep in her grandfather's old recliner—
her grandparents had been downsizing when they moved
to warmer climes, so they'd left her with most of their
furniture—when she heard a knock. At first, she thought
it was the TV, which was droning on. But when she
heard it again, she assumed it was Talulah, who came
over two or three times a week to have a glass of wine
or chat when Brant was off doing something at his family's ranch.

She answered the door without even checking the
peephole. Then she froze. Hendrix was standing on the
stoop. After living there for nearly three years during
which he'd avoided her like the plague, she couldn't
believe he'd shown up at her jobsite yesterday, her father had appeared at her jobsite today and now Hendrix was at her house. What was it with all the sudden
contact? "Has something changed that I don't know
about?" she asked.

He seemed confused. "I'm not sure…what you mean."

"You've ignored me for two and a half years. Acted
as if I didn't exist. Which I prefer, by the way. And now
you're popping up everywhere. I don't get it."

He shifted uncomfortably. "Look, I know things have
been…awkward between us. I won't pretend that I'm
happy to be here. But I just couldn't… I wanted to…"

She tightened the belt on the fluffy robe she'd pulled
on after her shower. She wasn't wearing anything underneath except a pair of panties, so she felt awkward
and exposed, even though she was adequately covered.
"To…" she prompted when his words fell off.

His gaze dipped to where her robe came together; she
could tell he was a bit rattled by her attire. "To apologize

for what I did at Hank's last night. I should never have offered Ben a job. I'm sorry," he said and walked off.

Ellen was so surprised she didn't react. Hendrix had just *apologized*? Why would he care enough to even bother?

But then she understood. He knew he had it better than she did, that he was in a more favorable position. "Don't you feel sorry for me!" she yelled after him. "Don't you *ever* feel sorry for me!"

He didn't respond. He just got in his truck and drove away, and she was left feeling rather strange—angry but sort of breathless at the same time as she remembered the flash of interest on his face and how decidedly he'd jerked his gaze up after it'd fallen to the opening of her robe.

Four

Hendrix believed he'd done the right thing by going to Ellen's. So why did he feel worse instead of better?

On second thought, he couldn't say he felt *worse*. It was more that he felt...unsettled. His mind kept presenting him with the image of her standing in the doorway looking as cute as any woman he'd ever seen, with her short hair spiking in every direction, her big, expressive eyes studying him as if he were the Big Bad Wolf, her body swallowed up in that furry robe and her bare feet peeking out underneath. Her toenails had been painted bright red, a detail that was so incongruous with the heavy work boots she wore during the day he couldn't help but notice.

Actually, he hadn't just noticed; in spite of all her efforts to appear tough—to make him believe no one could ever hurt her—he'd found her dainty feet incredibly sexy.

Rolling his eyes at his own reaction, he gave his truck more gas as he sped away from her house. If he was thinking about *Ellen* that way, it'd been far too long since he'd been with a woman. In the past few days alone, she'd made him feel furious, guilt-ridden, frustrated and...*attracted*?

No. No way. He wouldn't allow it.

Pulling out his phone, he called Veronica Salvo, who worked for a small local branch of a commercial insurance agency. She flirted with him whenever they interacted—had given him her cell number two months ago when Stuart sent him in to renew their policy—but he'd never asked her out. He wasn't all that interested, and he didn't want to start something that could end badly only to face her again whenever he had an insurance issue.

But tonight, he was willing to take her out for a drink. Anything to get his mind off Ellen. He would've called Jennifer Pullman, the woman he'd been seeing for the past several years, but she'd moved away. Although they still spoke on the phone once in a while, mostly because he missed Loki, the Alaskan Husky he'd given her, he knew she'd lost patience with him. Since their relationship had never developed into the marriage proposal she'd been hoping for, she'd cut him off six months ago and relocated to Flagstaff, Arizona, where she was dating other men.

Jennifer must've meant more to him than he'd thought. Or living without a woman wasn't as easy as it'd seemed so far. That had to be the reason he'd had such a strange reaction to Ellen a few minutes ago…

He didn't have anything to worry about, he reassured himself. He liked his women soft and curvy, and Ellen did not fit that description. He guessed she had nice breasts—at least they looked nice under her clothes. And he'd seen her in a pair of shorts, so he knew she had great legs. But she was lean and sinewy, not voluptuous and soft like Jennifer, who'd probably been the most feminine woman he'd ever met, with her long hair, pink lip gloss, thick eyelashes and fake fingernails—something Ellen would never be able to wear doing the work she did.

Ellen seemed far more quick-witted, which appealed

to him, but she was also a sharp-tongued, belligerent little pixie. Because of their unique situation, she was off-limits to him, anyway.

"Hello?"

Veronica had answered.

"Hey, it's Hendrix."

Veronica's voice grew softer, huskier. "I'm glad you called."

He shifted his hands on the wheel, wondering if he wouldn't be better off heading home to watch a movie. But then he thought of Ellen again in that damn robe and forged ahead. "I was wondering if you'd like to grab a drink."

"Tonight?"

"If you're available."

"I'd love to, but I'm babysitting for my brother and sister-in-law. They're out for the evening."

"No problem," he said, more relieved than disappointed. "We'll try another time."

"What are you doing tomorrow?" she asked before he could end the call.

Tomorrow was Sunday. He wasn't sure it would be convincing if he claimed he was working. "I have a few projects around the house."

"Do you think you'd have time to visit Talulah's Dessert Diner with me? I've heard great things about it, but I haven't had a chance to check it out. We could meet there and have a slice of cake and a cup of coffee..."

He'd tried some of Talulah's baked goods and found them to be the best he'd ever tasted, so his level of interest went up significantly. "Sure. What time?"

"Would afternoon be okay? That'd give you the morning to get a good start on whatever you're hoping to accomplish. I'm thinking...two?"

"Sounds good. I'll see you there."

When he hung up, he didn't regret calling. He could continue to be lonely and miss the companionship he'd had with Jennifer, or he could attempt to move on and find another relationship to fill the void she'd left. After all, there was more to life than work. This particular relationship might not turn out to be the best fit, but he'd be giving it a chance. Finding a woman he enjoyed spending time with required effort and risk.

Stuart called as he pulled into his own driveway.

He hit the Talk button. "Hey, Stu."

"Lynn and I were thinking about driving over to Billings to visit her friend Pamela tomorrow, but Leo doesn't like riding in the car for that long. We were hoping we could leave him with you. Would you mind?"

Hendrix had just agreed to meet Veronica. But having Leo along would make the date even more casual, which could translate into making it more comfortable, as well. "It's a possibility. I need to check with a friend I'm having coffee with. But even if it's okay with her to bring Leo, there'd be more treats in his future. We're going to Talulah's Dessert Diner. Lynn won't be happy about that, but if I take him there, I won't try to tell him he can't have cake."

"I don't blame you. He wouldn't be happy about that. Just a sec." Hendrix heard Stuart say something to Lynn before coming back on the phone. "She said it's nice of you to be willing to help out, and he can start his diet again on Monday."

"No problem. Tell him we're going to get some of Talulah's chocolate cake tomorrow. It'll make his day."

"It's okay to tell him? You haven't checked with whoever you're meeting..."

"If she's not cool with it, I'll reschedule with her and take Leo, anyway."

"You must not be overly excited to see her," his uncle joked.

That he was merely trying to distract himself from whatever weirdness had come over him at Ellen's door was nothing he planned to confide in anyone, least of all her father. "I doubt she'll mind. It's Veronica, who works at Master's Insurance, so she's met Leo before. He was with me when I renewed our policy. Besides, it's the first time we've ever gotten together socially. It's nothing serious."

"Well, you're not getting any younger…"

"What's that supposed to mean?" he asked.

"You need to quit being so damn picky."

With the way he was feeling about Ellen he needed to be pickier than ever. "Considering the situation, I doubt you truly mean that."

"What?" Stuart said.

"Nothing," Hendrix replied and disconnected.

Rocko Schneider, who owned the burger joint next door, stared into the display case at the variety of fancy cakes and pies Talulah had made before she left early this morning. Ellen couldn't believe he really wanted to order anything. If he did, he was sure taking his time about it. Because he generally parked out back like she did, he had to have seen her truck. He almost always showed up when she was working at the diner.

She guessed he was trying to summon the nerve to ask her out—and wished he wouldn't. She'd just have to turn him down. For one, she had zero interest. For another, he was almost as old as her father. And his ex-wife still lived in Coyote Canyon and would make her life a living hell. Two months ago, Debbie Schneider had purposely crashed her minivan into the Toyota of the last woman Rocko had tried to date. Ellen knew because it'd been front-page news in the local paper.

Fortunately, no one was seriously injured. Debbie had to pay for the repairs, but other than that, she got off with a slap on the wrist—a traffic ticket and some community service, according to the gossip—which didn't give Ellen a great deal of confidence that something similar wouldn't happen to the next woman he dated.

"The coconut almond cake is good," she suggested, hoping to get Rocko to order and leave.

He smoothed down what little hair he had left, which he'd recently dyed jet-black. He'd also lost some of the bulk around his middle and purchased a motorcycle she'd seen him riding around town in a new leather jacket he wore almost everywhere. "I'm not big on coconut."

"The chocolate is our most popular dessert. Maybe you'd like a piece of that."

"I might," he said, still looking stumped.

Ellen slid her gaze over to the clock on the wall. She had another three hours before she could close at five. She was growing more and more certain that she was finally going to have to tell Rocko she wouldn't go out with him. She hated being put in that position, but just when he turned to her and opened his mouth, the bell rang over the door. She doubted he'd suggest they go anywhere together if other people were around to overhear, so she would've breathed a sigh of relief—except when she looked up, she saw Hendrix and Leo walk in with some woman she'd never met.

The expression on Hendrix's face made it plain that he hadn't expected to encounter her, either, but Leo acted as if he couldn't be more delighted. "Look!" He spoke loudly while pointing at her. "There's Ellen!"

She couldn't say how he knew her. They hadn't had

any contact for years. Even then they'd only been together a few times. But she'd seen him around town and
could only guess that her name had been bandied about
the household—probably the business, too. After what
he must've heard about her, she couldn't believe he'd
be friendly, but based on what people had told her, Leo
was like that. Talulah had said she didn't think he was
capable of having a bad thought about anyone.

When Hendrix didn't react, Leo tapped him on the
shoulder. "Do you see Ellen?"

"I see her, bud," Hendrix replied, keeping his voice
much lower than his cousin's.

"Hi, Ellen!" Leo waved frantically. "It's Leo!"

No matter what she thought of her father and Hendrix, Ellen held nothing against Leo. She also knew his
excitement over seeing her had to be driving Hendrix
crazy, so she decided to play into it.

"Hi, Leo!" She beamed at him just as he was beam-
ing at her. "Have you been in before?"

"I have. I love it here!"

"Wonderful! I have something new you might like.
It has strawberries in it. Do you like strawberries?"

His eyes went wide. "I *love* strawberries, Ellen. But…"
he looked seriously torn "…can I have strawberry *and*
chocolate? Because chocolate's my favorite."

"Pick only one, Leo," Hendrix said. "One's enough
for anybody."

"I could save it," he said sulkily.

Ellen winked at Leo. "Maybe I can slice off a small
taste of the strawberry one, so you can at least try it."

"She's going to give me a taste, Hendrix," he said.
"A taste is okay, isn't it? Can I have a taste?"

Hendrix's eyes immediately caught and held Ellen's—
and there was a warning in them. He was sizing her up,

trying to decide if she was poking fun at Leo and letting her know she'd better not cross that line. His protectiveness actually made her respect him. She'd heard the stories around town, knew how fiercely he'd always stood up for his cousin.

But she shot him a dirty look, anyway—to let him know she took exception to the thought that she might mistreat someone like Leo—and saw him visibly relax. They were more comfortable being enemies than allies. "Did you decide what you'd like?" she asked, turning back to Rocko.

Rocko frowned. "I'll have a piece of coconut cream pie."

She blinked in surprise. "I thought you didn't like coconut."

"Oh, um, it's not for me."

She didn't care who he was giving it to. At least he was making a purchase. She knew Talulah had a lot riding on the diner and was always thinking of ways to make it a bigger success. "Got it. So this is to go?"

He shot a disgruntled glance at Hendrix's party. "I guess so."

She sliced his pie, put it in a container and rang him up. She wasn't exactly thrilled to see Hendrix, but his sudden appearance had stopped an awkward situation from developing. She had to be grateful for that. As it was, Rocko left her a ten-dollar tip, which was way too much and added to her conviction that he'd been after more than dessert; she knew the interruption wouldn't be a long-term deterrent. "Thanks for coming in," she said as he took his bag and left.

Hendrix ordered a piece of red velvet cake with a cup of black coffee, and the woman he was with chose a slice of caramel apple spice cake with a latte. Leo wanted a glass of water and remained loyal to his favorite—the chocolate cake—but he reminded her, twice, of her promise to add a little of the strawberries and cream cake.

As Leo and Hendrix's date, or whoever she was, left the counter to get a table, and Hendrix paid the bill, he lowered his voice. "What are you doing here?"

"Just helping out," Ellen muttered.

"Do me a favor and don't poison me, okay?"

"Don't tempt me," she responded and set about getting their order.

She could hear some of the conversation between Hendrix and the woman, could tell they were just getting to know each other. Apparently, she had the pleasure of being present for their first date. She had to smile at that. Hendrix had to hate the mere thought.

When Ellen carried their orders over, Leo was so excited, he jumped to his feet. "Look, Hendrix! She gave me a *big* of piece of strawberry. It's not little. It's big," he exclaimed.

Ellen could feel Hendrix's gaze as she put the plates and cups down but refused to look at him. Then she went back behind the counter and set about cleaning what she could while attempting to ignore the only patrons in the restaurant, which didn't prove easy to do—not with Leo in the café.

"Do you want a bite?" he asked his cousin.

"No, I've got enough here," Hendrix responded.

"Veronica, do *you* want a bite?" Leo held out the fork he'd been using to the woman's mouth, but she politely declined.

"It's good, Ellen," Leo shouted to her. "You were right. Strawberry's good."

"I'm glad you like it," Ellen called back.

As soon as he finished stuffing the rest of it in his

mouth, he came over to her. "I'm big," he said, tapping his own chest. "See how big I am?"

"You're certainly tall." He had an inch or more on his cousin and probably fifty pounds.

"I could pick you up, but I won't," he added quickly. "Hendrix said I can't."

They'd actually had this conversation? Ellen got the impression they had, even though it made no sense.

Hendrix's chair scraped the floor as he turned it so that he could watch his cousin without leaving the table. "Leo, could you come sit down with us?"

"Why?" Leo asked, genuinely perplexed. "I'm done."

"*We're* not done," Hendrix pointed out. "You have to remember your manners."

When Leo's face fell, Ellen decided to rescue the poor guy. "Actually, if your cousin doesn't mind, I could use your help with something," she told Leo.

"Did you hear that, Hendrix?" Leo called out. "Ellen needs my help."

"Doing what?" Hendrix asked skeptically.

"I have a giant bag of flour I was hoping you'd move for me—since you're so big and strong."

"Oh, I bet I can do that. Can I help Ellen?" he asked, turning back to his cousin.

Hendrix's gaze slid over to Ellen. He didn't fully trust her, but he was in an awkward situation, trying to make everything nice for his date. "Fine. But come back as soon as you're done."

"I will," he promised, and Ellen let him behind the counter.

"This is what it looks like in here?" he said, sounding awestruck when she led him into the back.

"This is where Talulah makes all her cakes and other treats. It's called a commercial kitchen." Ellen showed him the large refrigerator that stored the extra desserts, the giant ovens, the commercial mixers and the sprayer that washed the dishes. As she'd assumed, he was delighted with it all, particularly the sprayer, so she let him play in the deep sink with some soapy bubbles, washing pans and dishes she knew she'd just have to wash again afterward. She wasn't sure why she was being kind enough to let Hendrix have time alone with his lady friend, but it got her out of the room with them. And she liked Leo. She told herself she was doing it for his sake.

She was just mopping up the water he'd accidentally gotten on the floor when Hendrix poked his head into the kitchen. "Hey, what happened to coming right back, bud?" he said, chastising his cousin.

"Sorry, Hendrix. I've been washing dishes. Ellen needed my help."

Ellen grinned at his innocence as she finished mopping but didn't correct him.

"Did you get the sack of flour moved?" Hendrix asked.

"It's okay," Ellen told him. "I can get that. Are you finished with your date?"

"It's not a…" He looked behind him. "Never mind. Yeah, we're done."

Ellen handed Leo a towel. "Looks like it's time to go, Leo. You'll have to dry off and come back to help me another time when I'm standing in for Talulah, okay?"

Leo looked disappointed. "Do I have to go? Hendrix could come back and get me. Couldn't you, Hendrix?"

"Maybe another time," Hendrix said.

Sensing his cousin's resolve, Leo heaved a sigh of disappointment. "O-kay," he said with a heavy emphasis on the second syllable.

Hendrix held the door for his cousin to come back into the front, and Ellen assumed that would be that, but after Leo went out, Hendrix turned to her. "Thanks for…thanks for watching him," he said tersely and left.

"Ellen's so nice. Don't you think she's nice, Hendrix?" Leo asked after they'd said goodbye to Veronica and were pulling away from the curb in front of the dessert diner.

Hendrix barely refrained from rolling his eyes. Ellen hadn't been nice to Leo out of kindness, he decided. Making his cousin her biggest fan was just another way to torture him. How did she know he'd never hear the end of how she'd let him lick the frosting from one of the bowls and turn on the big mixer? Or about the sprayer?

God, the sprayer. Leo's shirt was soaked, but he'd had such a grand time Hendrix couldn't even be mad at her for what she'd done.

"Do you think she'll let me come back tomorrow?" he asked.

"I don't think she'll be working there tomorrow," Hendrix replied and was irked enough to add, "She'll be back at her regular job, where she'll continue to steal more and more of our business."

"She's stealing our business?" Leo looked horrified, but before Hendrix could calm him down with some benign explanation that would take it all back, a confused expression replaced the shock. "What's our business?"

"Never mind."

"I could talk to her, Hendrix," he offered. "I could tell her she's hurting your feelings."

"She *not* hurting my feelings," he clarified immediately. No way did he want Leo to get that in his head. If he did, Hendrix had no doubt he'd tell Ellen at the first opportunity.

"Whatever she's doing, I bet she would stop. If I asked her to. She's *really* nice, Hendrix. Ellen is my friend."

Hendrix nearly groaned aloud. "Oh, my God! How clever can you be?"

Leo seemed uncertain. "Me, Hendrix? What'd I do?"

Hendrix had been referring to Ellen, of course. "You didn't do anything, bud. Just…forget it. Everything's okay."

Leo continued to watch him carefully. He knew he was missing something but couldn't quite figure out what. "Should we go back? I bet Ellen would say sorry to you for…for why you're mad."

Hendrix knew it would be a cold day in hell when Ellen apologized to him for anything, especially after he'd tried to hire away her driller. Last night *he'd* had to apologize to *her*. "I'm not mad."

"You seem mad."

"Well, I'm not. So…what'd you think of Veronica?" he asked, trying to change the subject.

"I don't know."

Leo didn't sound too enthusiastic about Veronica. He didn't dislike anyone, but Hendrix could tell that Veronica hadn't made much of an impression—certainly nothing like the impression Ellen had made. "You didn't say much to her," he said.

"She doesn't have any pretty pictures on her arm, Hendrix. Ellen has a dragon right here." He indicated his left arm. "And a guitar up here. She has the solar system somewhere, too. She told me."

Hendrix couldn't help wondering where that was, couldn't help conjuring up an image of what she might look like naked. "You know what the solar system is?"

"She said it was where we belonged in the universe."

"And the universe is…"

"I asked her that, too. She said it was everything around us."

Both good answers. Hendrix gripped the steering wheel that much harder. "I'll tell you what."

"What?" Leo said eagerly.

"If you don't mention Ellen to me again for the rest of the day, I'll take you to get a chocolate donut next week."

He covered his mouth as if Hendrix had just said something naughty. "What about Mom? She told me no more chocolate donuts."

"As long as I don't have to hear Ellen's name again, it'll be worth it."

"Okay," he said.

But it was only fifteen minutes later that he forgot their bargain. "Ellen let me use the sprayer," he piped up as Hendrix turned into his own driveway. "And she said I could come back. Can you take me back?"

"Someday," Hendrix said.

"Tomorrow?"

They'd already been over this. Hendrix didn't answer. He called Stuart instead. "What time did you say you'd be back?" he asked.

"Not until later tonight," Stuart replied. "Why? Is everything okay?"

Hendrix swallowed a sigh as he glanced over at Leo. "Yeah. Everything's fine," he insisted but as soon as they walked into the house, he put on a Disney movie for Leo, hoping that would be enough to finally make him forget about Ellen.

Aladdin seemed to work. Leo was so caught up in the genie's antics that he didn't mention her again. Hendrix would've been relieved, except he couldn't get her off his mind even without Leo constantly reminding him. And that gave him even more reason to be annoyed.

Five

Talulah knocked on Ellen's door holding a box of French macarons she'd purchased in Bozeman. She and Brant had just returned from their day trip. While he relaxed and caught up on sports news at home, she was eager to check with her friend to see how everything had gone at the diner and to thank her for filling in.

But when Ellen opened the door, Talulah was so surprised she forgot to hand over the cookies. Ellen was wearing a dusty pink dress that fell to just below the knee and had a high neck and no sleeves. This was nothing like what her friend normally wore. Ellen typically wore work boots, tank tops, flannel shirts, denim cutoffs and ball caps. And that wasn't a bad thing. She was good at mixing opposites—masculine with feminine, lace with camouflage, work boots with cutoffs and that sort of thing. She put them together in a way that was unexpectedly stylish. But Talulah had never seen her hit the bull's-eye for "feminine." Not like this. Where was the contrast that revealed so much about her personality? "Where'd you get *that*?" she asked, gesturing.

Ellen's cheeks bloomed red as she stepped back to give Talulah enough space to walk in—and her reaction came as another surprise. Ellen didn't blush often. She was good at hiding embarrassment along with all her other emotions, except perhaps anger. But Talulah, who knew her better than most people, believed her tattoos and piercings—even what she did to her hair—was mostly an attempt to look tough. She wanted to put the world on notice, to essentially say, "You can't hurt me," even though it wasn't true, of course. She'd been hurt badly over the years, by her father *and* her mother. The bravado she exhibited was just an attempt to protect her soft heart.

"In town," she replied.

"Is someone you know getting married?"

"No. I just…saw it in the window of the store down the street when I went to grab some Chinese takeout and I bought it on impulse. I shouldn't have. I don't really have anywhere to wear it. Not in this town. And with my mom needing help again…it was a mistake to spend the money."

And yet she'd wanted it badly enough to buy it, anyway. What had triggered such an uncharacteristic purchase? "Did you get it at Linda's? Or Cammie's?" Both shops were down the street from the diner, along with a few others that were less likely to have this type of clothing.

"Linda's. She was already closed for the day. But when she saw me standing on the sidewalk, gazing at the mannequin while she was cleaning up inside, she walked out to say hello—and eventually convinced me to come in and try it on." She smoothed the delicate chiffon-like fabric over her hips before checking the tags, which were still attached under one arm. "I could take it back, I suppose…"

"No, don't. It looks amazing on you." Finally remembering the cookies, Talulah handed them over. "I thought you might like these. They literally melt in your mouth."

"Thanks." After untying the ribbon and removing

the lid, Ellen selected an espresso-flavored macaron from the stack of eight different flavors before offering one to Talulah.

Talulah shook her head. "I've had enough."

When Ellen took her first bite, she moaned as she chewed. "Oh, wow. You're so right. These are delicious."

"Not just anyone can make a good French macaron," Talulah said. "Maybe *I* should try making them."

"You should. I bet they'd go over big at the diner."

Talulah frowned as she considered the idea. "I would if they didn't get stale so fast. Until I reach the point where I'm selling almost everything I make before the end of the day, I think I'll hold off. They'd be too much work to waste all the ones that were left." She sat on the worn leather couch Ellen had purchased from a second-hand store and mixed with the furniture her grandparents had left behind. She had the same talent with decorating she had with clothes. She could make anything look cool—had even helped Talulah furnish her and Brant's house after they got married, which had saved them a lot of money. "Anyway, how'd it go at the diner today?"

Perching on the round, contemporary chair across from her—which she'd bought at a garage sale for only fifty bucks and was another example of her ability to bring very different looks together in a great way—Ellen helped herself to a second cookie. "It was a little slow at first, but it got busier as the day wore on. I walked over to the bank after I bought this dress and deposited the day's receipts in the night drop like you asked me to."

"I appreciate it." Talulah shifted so she could remove a throw pillow she'd sat on. "Anything interesting happen while you were there?"

"Not really. Why?"

Talulah peered at her more closely. "Brant and I ran into Rocko when we stopped for gas a little while ago."

Ellen rolled her eyes. "What'd the Burger Meister have to say?"

"He asked me why I don't have you help out more often," she replied with a laugh.

"Dude makes me uncomfortable."

"He's definitely got a thing for you."

"Don't tell his ex," Ellen joked. "I don't want Debbie coming after me."

Talulah sobered. "That wasn't the only thing he said."

"What do you mean?"

"He told me that Hendrix and Leo came in while you were there."

"Can you believe it? They were with a woman I'd never met."

What Talulah couldn't believe was that Ellen hadn't volunteered this information the second she opened the door, that she'd served her nemesis today and hadn't found it remarkable enough to mention. "What was her name?"

"I have no idea."

"How long were they there?"

"Forty, fifty minutes."

"That's a long time for you and Hendrix to be in the same room," Talulah said. "Why weren't you going to tell me?"

"What's to tell?"

Ellen *always* complained about Hendrix. As jealous as she was—and hurt by her father's neglect—she noticed everything about him. "Hendrix is the bane of your existence, remember?"

"True," she said wryly. "But Leo was there, too."

It was less clear how Ellen felt about Leo. He, too, had replaced her in her father's affections, which had to hurt, but she seemed to hold only Hendrix responsible. Probably because Leo was too harmless to be blamed for anything. "Leo is the sweetest," Talulah allowed. "But in the past, you've been careful to steer clear of him, too."

"I don't have any reason to get close to either one of them."

Leaning forward so she could reach the macarons Ellen had put on the coffee table, she broke down and had another one in spite of what she'd said earlier. "So how'd it go? Did you get the impression the woman Hendrix brought in was a friend or a relative or..."

"I'm pretty sure she was a date. He insisted on paying for the food, anyway. And the two of them spent the whole time talking and getting to know each other."

"You heard their conversation?"

"Only the first part. There was no way I could miss it—until I took Leo in the back so he could see the kitchen and play with the sprayer over the sink."

"You took Leo in the back?"

Ellen spread out her hands. "Yeah. Go figure. He wanted to be with me more than he wanted to be with them. And he *loved* the kitchen. You would've thought I'd taken him to Disneyland."

"There's always plenty of frosting in the fridge."

"Exactly. I let him lick one of the bowls before I washed it."

Talulah was having trouble imagining how this had gone down. Ellen and Hendrix, as well as the Fettermans, had fallen into a routine of avoiding each other over the years. But maybe Hendrix didn't feel as though he could just walk out once he saw her behind the counter.

That made sense, given that he was on a date. Walking out probably would've seemed weird. "Hendrix didn't mind you disappearing with Leo? He's usually very protective of him—and with the way you two feel about each other…"

"What could he say? He had that woman to worry about. I got the impression he was just glad I kept Leo happy and out of the way—and that *I* was no longer in the room."

"I guess I can see why that might be the case. It was probably awkward for him. *You* must've hated having them there."

"It wasn't a big deal," Ellen said. "Leo was worth it."

Talulah rocked back. *"You liked him?"*

She nodded. "How could anyone *not* like him? He wants to come back next time I work."

"And you wouldn't mind having him do that…"

Although Ellen took a moment to consider the question, she ultimately shook her head. "There's something about him."

"He's easy to love," Talulah suggested.

"That's it," she said with a fond smile.

Then Talulah understood. Ellen had been isolated for so long—first when she'd been left on her own to care for her mother all the years she was growing up, and then, while devoting herself to building a business that was particularly unfriendly to women. She needed love, could only deny herself for so long. And in spite of who his family was, Leo was completely safe.

Hendrix heard the car as it pulled into the driveway, so he stepped outside before his uncle and aunt could reach the landing and knock. "Hey," he said as they came toward him. "You two have a good time?"

His aunt was the first to start up the four steps to

his door. "It was great to get away. Thanks for watching Leo."

"No problem. As a matter of fact, you might want to leave him here until morning. He's already asleep. There's no reason to wake him."

Stuart checked his watch. "What's he doing sleeping at eight thirty?"

"After dinner, I took him over to the high school to run around the track."

"He was willing to *run*?" Lynn exclaimed. They all knew how much Leo hated exercise. "I've all but given up trying to take him walking with me every morning. He usually tells me he'd rather watch cartoons, and he's so big I can't make him move if he doesn't want to."

"He went over to the track with me but wouldn't do much running. He mostly walked and waved at anyone who came close enough while I ran."

"If he's already asleep, even that much exercise must've tuckered him out," Stuart said.

"Must have. I need to take him there more often so he can get in better shape. Then maybe we won't have to worry so much about what he eats."

"Too bad we don't have a gym nearby," Lynn said. "I think he'd like going to a Zumba class—something involving music and friends."

"Leo thinks everyone's a friend, even the people who used to be mean to him," Hendrix said.

"He's not capable of holding a grudge," Lynn agreed.

Stuart leaned against the railing. "How'd your date go? I hope Leo didn't screw it up just by being there."

"Not at all. It wasn't really a date, anyway," Hendrix said. "I was just meeting someone for coffee."

"Someone?" Lynn said.

"Veronica from our insurance place."

"Oh, I've met her," she said. "She's a pretty girl."

And yet he hadn't felt any attraction. "She's nice, too," he agreed blandly.

"So...do you like her?" Stuart asked.

"More or less."

Lynn frowned. "That sounds pretty neutral."

"It is," he confirmed.

Stuart shoved his hands in his pockets. "Then you won't be asking her out again."

"Probably not. But Leo fell in love while we were out."

"With Veronica?" Lynn asked.

"With Ellen," he clarified.

Lynn frowned. "Not... Ellen Ellen."

Hendrix folded his arms as he leaned against the railing, too. "Yep. That Ellen."

"How?" she cried. *"Why?"*

Stuart remained conspicuously silent.

"She was working at the dessert diner today—and for some reason, Leo took an immediate liking to her."

"He was probably drawn to her tattoos," Lynn said with a grimace. "He loves them and has been begging to get one. How'd she react?"

"She was surprisingly...sweet."

"Sweet?" Stuart echoed. "That isn't an adjective I've heard used in connection with my daughter very often."

Hendrix recalled the smile she'd given Leo and was still impressed by how genuine it had seemed. He'd gotten a tiny glimpse of how Ellen behaved when she actually liked someone. "Apparently she doesn't feel as though Leo deserves her hatred as much as the rest of us."

"At least she's not cruel enough to mistreat someone like him," Lynn said.

"I doubt she's cruel at all," Stuart said. "She's angry. And she's got a right to be."

Lynn scowled at her husband for sticking up for Ellen. Hendrix knew his aunt felt threatened by Stuart's daughter—and probably guilty, as well, for walling her out when she should've been more inclusive. He knew Lynn to be kind and loving. She'd been a second mother to him. But he could see where she could've done more for Ellen, who was a year younger than he was and had been only ten when Stuart left Jan.

"She got a bum deal," he admitted for probably the first time.

Lynn didn't like him supporting Ellen any more than she liked Stuart doing it and broke off the conversation right there. "I guess we'll leave Leo here with you, then. You can just bring him when you come to work in the morning."

"I will," Hendrix told her. "I have to stop by the office, anyway."

"Thanks for watching him." Stuart started to follow his wife back to the car but then turned. "Did Ellen say anything to you about your attempt to steal her driller?"

"No." Thank God. Hendrix had been afraid she might start an argument in front of Veronica, even though he'd apologized. Ellen had to resent what he'd done, and an apology did little to fix it.

"She was nice to Leo?"

He'd already acknowledged that but nodded to confirm it again. He couldn't fault Ellen for the way she'd behaved—and not just with Leo. As a matter of fact, he'd found it quite generous, considering she could easily have made a snide comment or two, if only to embarrass him in front of his date.

Stuart said, "Sounds like you got off easy."

That was true. But not as easy as he could've gotten off. Why'd she have to be there in the first place?

he wondered. Why'd his cousin have to take such a big interest in her? And why was he suddenly finding it so hard to dislike and dismiss her?

Don't you feel sorry for me! Don't you ever feel sorry for me!

He remembered her yelling that at him, essentially throwing his apology back in his face. That should've made him mad.

But if he was being honest, he couldn't help but respect her.

It rained the next day. By the time Ellen got home, she was wet, cold and muddy. "What a glamorous life I lead," she mumbled as she peeled off her clothes, tossed everything except her boots and her coat in the washer and headed for the shower. After she got warm and clean, she planned to heat up a can of soup and watch whatever looked interesting on TV until she fell asleep. She was exhausted. Today had been rough in more ways than just the weather. Ben had come to work and helped her set the pressure tank in the Slemboskis' garage before they moved the rig to their next drill site. But winning the salary battle they'd had on Saturday had imbued him with too much of a sense of his own power. It was one thing to have to pay him more; it was another to have to put up with him acting as though he was suddenly in control of the whole business.

Damn Hendrix Durrant. If something didn't change, she'd have to let Ben go. She was already thinking of how she could spread out her jobs to make time to interview and train someone else. It would mean she'd have to move more slowly in the months ahead, which would impact her bottom line. But it could arguably be the cheaper route...

She'd just stepped out of the shower, pulled on some

sweats, shoved her feet into a pair of fluffy slippers and traipsed into the kitchen, where she started going through the cupboards looking for some vegetable soup, when she heard her phone ring. The Slemboskis had paid her today, so she'd already let her mother know she'd be able to send the money for rent as soon as the check cleared. She was hoping this wasn't about that again, but she had a sinking feeling it was more of the same. Jan tended to be obsessive.

Ellen followed the sound until she located her phone. She'd left it while undressing in the laundry room. But it wasn't her mother. Although the call was coming from a number she didn't recognize, she answered. It had a local area code, which meant it could be someone trying to reach her about a well. "Hello?"

"Ellen?"

Immediately recognizing Rocko's voice, she kicked herself for being so eager to answer. "Yes?"

"It's Rocko. From the burger joint."

"I know," she said. "But… I'm curious. How'd you get my number?"

"I found your business card on the bulletin board at the Chamber of Commerce."

She'd posted it there to draw in more business, and to keep things simple and save money, she used her cell for everything. "Oh, right." Of course she'd get this kind of call and not the opportunity that sort of advertising was intended to create.

"How are you?" he asked.

She was hungry and tired, but she said, "Fine. You?"

"I'm great. I was just calling to see if you'd like to go out with me tonight to grab a bite to eat."

The meal part of his offer was actually tempting. She was tired of soup, which she ate more nights than not.

But there was no way she was going to allow something to get started with Rocko. "I'm afraid not. I just got out of the shower and I'm planning to stay in for the night. But thanks for the offer."

"What about tomorrow night—or another night this week?" he asked.

She knew it had to be hard to ask someone out and was sensitive to how it would feel to be rejected. So she said, "I'm sorry, but I… I'm seeing someone."

"You have a boyfriend?"

"Sort of," she said.

"Who?" he asked in surprise.

Most of the town assumed she was unattached, since she was never seen with anyone—other than Brant a few times early on—who might qualify as a partner. But several months ago, during a low moment and at Talulah's urging, she'd created a profile on an online dating site that had put her in touch with a few guys. She still corresponded with two of them, and last week she'd given her number to one who was a dentist. Dr. Jordan Forbes hadn't called yet, so it was a stretch to say they were *in a relationship*. But it was an easier, kinder way to let Rocko down. And for all she knew, the situation with Jordan could grow serious at some point—not that she was particularly planning on it. "A guy I met online."

"Does he live around here?"

"No. But he's not far," she added. "He lives in Libby." She probably shouldn't have volunteered that detail. It was unnecessary. But she was trying to make her story believable enough that he wouldn't suspect how she truly felt.

"That's a long drive."

"Only about five hours."

"I didn't realize you were with someone."

"It's…new," she said. So new even Jordan didn't know about it…

"So…what about me?"

"I'm sorry…what about you?"

"I thought you liked me. Have you just been…leading me on?"

He sounded dumbstruck. *She* was dumbstruck, too. How could he have interpreted anything she'd said or done in such a manner? "Of course not! I've never acted as though I'm interested in you… I mean…"

"What about that big tip I gave you? Do you think I'd hand over ten dollars on a piece of cake to just anyone?"

"I'm happy to give that back to you," she said. "I felt bad taking it in the first place, because I could tell… I just didn't know what else to do. It seemed kinder to keep it than chase you down to say I'm not interested when you hadn't even tried to ask me out yet."

"Wow. Apparently, you're as big a bitch as my ex-wife," he said and disconnected before she could respond.

Ellen was a little shaken by his reaction. He had to be as unstable as Debbie, she decided. As far as she was concerned, they deserved each other.

Trying to shrug off the pall Rocko had cast over her mood, she took a deep breath and tossed her phone on the couch as if she could shake off the emotional residue of that call just as easily. She was looking forward to having the rest of the night to herself. With some solitude, maybe she'd be able to find her center again.

But after she'd eaten and settled in to watch TV, she heard a knock at the door.

The last time she'd assumed it would be Talulah on her doorstep, it'd been Hendrix, so she twisted around and lifted the blinds on the window facing her front yard to check.

She couldn't see *anyone* at the door. Maybe her visitor was standing slightly out of range, but she noticed a flash of red taillights as someone in a car or truck rocketed down the road away from her place. What was going on?

Curious, she went to the door, opened it a crack and peered out.

Sure enough, no one was there. Why would someone knock and then run? She remembered doing that sort of thing in the neighborhood where she lived as a child, but there weren't any kids around. She wasn't even part of a neighborhood anymore. She was out in the country on five acres, and her closest neighbor was Talulah, who also had some land.

She waited several seconds to see what might happen as she stared down the road where she'd briefly glimpsed those taillights. But whoever it was didn't come back. It wasn't until she started to close the door that she saw a rock on her doormat.

"Someone brought me a rock?" she said but as soon as she bent to retrieve it, she could see it wasn't just any rock. It was a geode that'd been cut open and polished—and it was filled with hundreds of amethyst crystals.

She'd seen this sort of thing in gift shops and always admired them. But…was this a present? If so, she couldn't imagine who'd given it to her.

It had to be Talulah, she decided. But even that didn't make sense. Her best friend wouldn't leave it on her doorstep and drive away. She'd stay to see how Ellen liked it. She lived in the other direction from where that vehicle had turned, anyway.

Ellen looked beneath the mat and searched the front

porch for a card or note but found nothing. She waited a few seconds after that, too, in case whoever it was returned to see if it was gone. But the night remained quiet and still. All she could hear was a chorus of frogs coming from the stream that ran alongside her property.

Finally, she took the geode inside and set it on her coffee table.

Could Ben have given this to her as an apology for being such a douchebag?

No... He wasn't self-aware enough to even realize how he was behaving. And he wouldn't spend so much. A quick search on the internet convinced her that what she'd been given could cost as much as three hundred dollars.

While attempting to puzzle out the mystery, she texted her mother.

Did you have someone bring me a geode?

Is that a typo? What's a geode? Jan responded.

Ellen chuckled. She'd known her mother would be unlikely to have thought of something this unique. She didn't have the money to buy anything right now, anyway. And who did Jan know in Coyote Canyon she could ask to deliver a gift?

Never mind, she wrote.

What's going on? her mother asked.

That was the thing. Ellen didn't know. Nothing. Forget I asked, she wrote back. But finding such a beautiful item on her front porch after a hard day was certainly a pleasant surprise.

Her eyes returned to it again and again while she watched TV. She even carried it into the bedroom with her when she went to bed.

Six

Jordan called on Thursday. After they talked and laughed for an hour, he said he could drive down for a couple of days, and Ellen had agreed. She wasn't sure why, except that having a visitor would help get her mind off her father and Hendrix, who seemed to be more of a focal point lately. For some strange reason, she couldn't quit reliving the moment Hendrix had arrived at her door to apologize for trying to steal Ben. She couldn't figure out why he would humble himself enough to do that.

It seemed too soon to meet Jordan in person—and yet she knew he'd suspect her of stalling if she put him off. She'd been called "emotionally inaccessible" by enough men that she didn't want it to happen again.

At least he was planning to get a motel room. That would help. But he didn't know anyone else in town. She'd feel a great deal of pressure to entertain him, regardless.

What had she been thinking, putting herself out there on an online dating platform? Doing that was what had started the whole thing.

The answer, however, was obvious. She was lonely. Since moving to town, she'd put everything she had into her work and was beginning to wonder if there wasn't more to life. Besides, she'd watched Talulah and Brant over the past year, seen how happy they were together. She craved something similar.

But she'd always craved more love than she could find, so she knew better than to allow that need—that vulnerability—to get the best of her. True intimacy seemed to be reserved for other people. If her own father couldn't love her enough to stay, or even make her a part of his life after he left, there had to be something inherently wrong with her. Although her mother insisted it was *his* problem and not hers, by all accounts he had a good relationship with Leo and Hendrix. That made her feel like it *had* to be her, that things would've gone differently if she wasn't so impossible to love.

As she sat in her truck eating the salad she'd picked up for lunch, she grumbled, "I don't need anyone." Sometimes she had to remind herself of that. But Ben, who was striding purposefully toward her even though she'd already taken his food to the rig, proved an immediate contradiction. She had to have a helper at work, or she couldn't drill. And despite the raise, he didn't seem any more committed to what they had to get done in the next few months, which came as a letdown. She felt she deserved more resolve on his part—more of a willingness to help push the business farther and faster.

Instead, as soon as he'd arrived this morning, he'd told her he needed to take Friday, Saturday and Sunday off next week so he could attend a wedding with his girlfriend in Salt Lake City.

Surely, whoever was getting married had sent out the invitations long before now. Why hadn't he given her more notice so she could've planned ahead?

Now she had to call clients and put them off, which never went over very well...

As he drew closer, she rolled down the window. "Something wrong?"

"Did you get extra dressing?"

She'd already given him two of the four packets that'd come with their food, but she wasn't willing to hear him complain about not being able to finish his salad, so she handed him *her* extra packet just to buy a few more minutes of peace before she had to return to the rig herself.

"Thanks," he said and went back to finish his salad.

"Hallelujah," she muttered as she watched him go. That she wasn't feeling all that great toward him made the long hours they spent together far less enjoyable. Having him disrupt next week's schedule so cavalierly certainly didn't help.

But at least Ben's trip to Salt Lake would coincide with Jordan's visit, so she wouldn't have to juggle having a visitor with trying to work each day. Jordan planned to arrive Friday night, the same day Ben would get up early and drive to Utah, so she could spend a few hours getting caught up on paperwork and still have plenty of time to clean her place and grab groceries in case she decided to have Jordan over or cook. Then she'd have Saturday and most of Sunday with him—until he drove home to Libby—and she could get back to drilling on Monday.

A text came in from her mother: Thanks for helping with my rent, honey.

Ellen took another bite of her salad, then frowned at the words. She seemed to be growing more disgruntled with everyone in her life. Everyone except Talulah. Talulah hadn't done anything wrong.

No problem, she wrote back. Her mother would

only press her if she didn't respond and, again, she just wanted a few more minutes of peace.

She'd just finished her salad and was stuffing the container back into the sack when another text came in, this one from Talulah. Did you ever figure out who gave you that geode?

She hadn't. She'd put it back on her coffee table, where she was reminded of the mystery every time she saw it. But she'd asked everyone she knew, and no one seemed to have any clue where it'd come from or why it'd been left on *her* doorstep.

"That's a weird gift," Ben had said when she'd mentioned it to him.

She supposed he was right. It probably wasn't something most people thought to look for. But she liked it. For her, it was symbolic of the beauty that could be found inside a rather plain or unattractive exterior. Contrasts like that had always appealed to her. "I guess I'm a weird girl," she'd told him with a shrug.

"You think?" Ben had said, giving her the once-over.

Apparently, he wasn't impressed with "weird," and he was feeling more and more comfortable letting her know it. He liked women looking as much like Barbie dolls as possible, and she definitely didn't fit that mold.

But she refused to live her life to please him or anyone else. If she couldn't even please her own father, she figured that was an impossible task. So she did the exact opposite—and made sure she lived large and didn't seek approval.

When Kurt sent a text message on Friday of the following week to see if Hendrix would like to meet him at Hank's to play pool again—this time with two of his brothers, Ranson and Miles—Hendrix almost refused. He wasn't in the mood to be sociable. It'd been almost two weeks since he'd taken Leo to the dessert diner, and yet Leo had just called to see if he could find out if Ellen was working there again this weekend. He wanted to go back and wouldn't take no for an answer. He insisted she'd need his help, but Hendrix suspected there was more at play. Leo believed he'd made a new friend, and a new friend, especially one who treated him as kindly as Ellen had, was so magical that he couldn't get her out of his mind.

She was the real draw. And Hendrix didn't know what to do about it. Was she planning some kind of revenge for what he'd done with Ben? Was it possible, even after he'd apologized, that she was still angry enough to strike back at him by hurting the one person he cared about most?

He hated to suspect her of being that callous, but it was plausible. After all, what he'd done was costing her a significant amount of money.

Kurt texted again. Hendrix had taken too long to respond. His other option was to stay in by himself. Would that make things any better?

He didn't think so. Besides, if they had four players, they could form teams.

Yeah. I'll head over in fifteen.

Cool. We'll be waiting for you.

He'd just hit Send when Lynn called.

"Leo's in his room crying because you told him he couldn't go back to the dessert diner. He's convinced Ellen will be there, waiting for him this weekend and he needs to show up," she said.

"She treated him well when he saw her there and she made it fun," he responded.

"She must have. The question is why? Is she trying to divide us as a family?"

Hendrix couldn't answer that question with certainty.

"I don't think so," he said. "It seems different than that. She doesn't hate him like she does us, so she treated him the way she'd treat anyone in his situation."

He didn't add that he'd been impressed by how she'd interacted with Leo, how intuitive she'd been when it came to communicating with him and making him happy. He guessed she'd also be good with kids. But instead of continuing the conversation with his aunt, he told her Kurt was expecting him soon.

He took a quick shower and didn't see Lynn's text message until he was gathering his keys.

Stu won't do anything when it comes to her, so you'll have to. Can you tell her to stay away from Leo? Please?

Lynn had always been able to count on him to look out for her son. But how could he tell Ellen to stay away from Leo when she wasn't the one who'd approached him? He and Leo had gone into the dessert diner where she happened to be working. That wasn't *her* fault. The only thing she'd done to create this problem was to be friendly, which was hardly something he could complain about.

I'm afraid that will only make matters worse. Leo will forget about her eventually.

I'm not so sure about that. He's convinced she really likes him.

Hendrix got the impression she did. He just didn't know if he could trust that impression—or her.

Ellen had never met Jordan in person. She had no idea how well he'd match the pictures he'd posted on the dating app. So she was relieved to find she recognized him as soon as he got out of his Audi sedan and started across the parking lot toward her. Because he'd had a patient with a dental emergency this morning, he was getting in later than he'd originally planned—and he'd indicated he was hungry—which was why she'd told him to meet her at Hank's Bar & Grill. There was probably more fun to be found at Hank's than anywhere else in Coyote Canyon. They could have dinner, listen to live music, dance a little—*if* he danced—and play a few games of darts or billiards. Also, since she didn't know Jordan very well, she thought it would be smarter to meet him at a public place rather than invite him to her house. Talulah had insisted she'd be foolish to trust him too soon.

"I know you think you're bulletproof and are used to hanging with the guys but being too confident could get you into a difficult situation," her friend had advised.

"He's a dentist, for God's sake," Ellen had responded. "Dentists are the most steady, reliable people on the planet. Other than accountants, of course."

Talulah had rolled her eyes. "Those are stereotypes. You have to be careful. He could just as easily be an axe-murderer."

"From what I know of him so far, I highly doubt he's dangerous. Besides, you don't have to worry about me. You know I can't let my guard down even when I should."

"There's a difference between protecting your heart and your person," Talulah had said. "We've all heard

terrible stories about meeting someone online. So…
just be careful."

After that, Ellen hadn't argued. Talulah was right.
She'd be stupid not to approach anyone she didn't know
with caution.

Besides, she was grateful she had an excuse for *not*
inviting him to her house. While he seemed perfectly
safe from the standpoint Talulah was taking, having
Jordan stay at a motel gave her just enough space that
she might actually enjoy his visit.

Her phone buzzed before he could reach her. Talulah
had sent her a text. Is he there yet?

He was. And he looked about as benign as a guy
could look. But she didn't have time to write Talulah
back. Jordan was too close.

"Happy to finally meet you," he said.

Ellen smiled. She'd made sure her pictures were ac-
curate representations, too, so he'd known who she was
without confirming. But, to play it safe, she'd dressed
more conventionally than usual in a brown off-the-
shoulder sweater and faded jeans with boots. Although
she would never admit it to Talulah, she really hoped
this worked out. It would be nice to have someone she
could care about who also cared about her. "Same here,
except…you look even more conservative in person."

About six feet tall, he had a slender build with short
dark hair, brown eyes and round, wire-rimmed glasses.
He had no tats or piercings she could see. Dressed in a
blue button-down shirt and a pair of chinos, he came
across as a soft-spoken, educated professional. The only
thing missing was a tie. Since most men she knew wore
jeans, boots, T-shirts and denim jackets, she had to
admit he didn't fit in. But he'd relocated to Libby from

Portland only last year. That was probably why. He was a city boy who'd recently moved to the country.

"Are you sure I'm what you were expecting?" she asked uncertainly. She'd hate it if he suddenly had regrets, but his eyes crinkled at the edges as he laughed.

"The pics you posted made it pretty clear what to expect."

"And you still wanted to meet me?" she said disbelievingly.

"I did. There was something about what you wrote in your profile that appealed to me. You were so real, so transparent, saying you could be a little standoffish, you didn't trust easily, you weren't willing to put up with much bullshit and you didn't want to hear from anyone who was insincere. It wasn't a fluffy sales pitch, unlike so many of the others who talked about loving travel and the outdoors."

She hadn't wanted to sound like everyone else because she wasn't like everyone else and felt she needed to be honest about that.

"I admire a woman who is obviously her own person," he added and surprised her by offering to take her hand.

She thought it was a confident move, as well as a nice gesture, so she slipped her fingers through his as they started toward the entrance.

A dentist, she thought, gazing down at his loafers. She'd never dated anyone like Jordan. White-collar dudes didn't typically show much interest in her. First of all, there weren't a lot of professionals in the two small Montana towns where she'd lived. There were many more farmers, ranchers, welders and that sort of thing. Chase, the guy she'd dated on and off for years—from high school through college and beyond—had been a cement contractor. It wasn't until he'd spent three years in prison for drug trafficking and pulling a knife on a man in a bar, and started to get more and more controlling of *her*, that she'd cut him off for good.

But the next guy she'd dated wasn't a whole lot different. For some reason, she tended to be attracted to reckless, devil-may-care, adrenaline-fueled losers, and those antisocial types didn't make good marriage material. According to Talulah, she didn't have her expectations set highly enough, and maybe that was true.

But moving to Coyote Canyon and not dating anyone for the last couple of years had allowed her to clean the slate and regroup. Now that she was older and had a stronger sense of who she was and what she wanted her life to be, she was determined to raise her standards and go for a guy who had his act together—like Jordan.

"Is the food good here?" he asked as he let go of her to be able to open the door.

"It's not bad," she replied. "I like the veggie burger."

He cast her a sidelong glance. "Don't tell me you're a vegetarian…"

She would've gotten a similar response from any of the blue-collar guys she'd dated in the past, so she supposed Jordan wasn't *entirely* unlike them. "Would that be a problem?"

"Not really. I knew you and I were going to be different from the beginning." He winked at her. "And that's okay. Different makes life more interesting."

The band was so loud as they walked in that Ellen didn't bother screaming above the music just to tell him she wasn't a strict vegetarian.

The place was crowded; they had to wait for a table. Fortunately, it didn't take long. After about ten minutes, the hostess sat them and handed them each a menu.

They were close to the bar, which wasn't ideal since there were so many people trying to get a drink, but she figured they were lucky to get in at all tonight.

"You any good at billiards?" Ellen asked, once Jordan put aside his menu. She'd been hoping they could play after dinner.

"Not really," he said. "I don't have much experience. You?"

Chase had taught her how to play on an old table his stepfather kept in the back of his sandwich shop. They'd hung out there so often in high school she'd gotten good enough to be able to make money in college hustling guys who assumed they could beat her. But she didn't want to overstate her talents. "I'm decent. What about darts?"

"Not my game, either."

"What do you like to play?" she asked.

He studied her for several seconds. "I can play a mean game of chess."

Fortunately, she liked chess, too. "Then tomorrow morning, I'll take you on at chess," she said. "We can meet at the dessert diner down the street for a breakfast bun. My friend owns the place, and her breakfast buns are legendary and a highly sought-after item on Saturday mornings. If it's warm enough outside, we can play on one of the tables on the sidewalk. Talulah puts out some chess sets, and you'll occasionally see some older guys hanging out there and playing on weekends. But it's still chilly in the mornings so it shouldn't be crowded quite yet."

"I'm already looking forward to it. But...do I need to worry about getting beat?" he asked jokingly.

She sized him up. "I'll be honest. I'm not as good at chess as I am at pool. So...if I had to bet, I'd probably bet on you."

"Note to self," he said. "I'm going to get beat at pool but might have a chance at chess."

The waitress approached to take their order, and Jordan indicated he'd get the veggie burger. When Ellen looked up in surprise, he said, "Why not? It's what you recommended, isn't it?"

He was flexible. She liked that about him—flexible *and* nice. She could use a little nice in her life. She was just thinking she was glad she'd agreed to have him come see her when she heard a voice that jerked her back into the world she'd been living in most recently: *Hendrix*. He was standing at the bar only a couple of feet away with Kurt, Brant's brother, talking and laughing about a hard-won billiards match while ordering another beer.

Ellen was fairly confident he didn't know she was sitting right behind him and hoped he'd get his drink and move away without noticing. She didn't want to become as self-conscious and overly aware of him as he usually made her feel, not when she finally had the chance to concentrate on a man who might make a good love interest. It'd been forever since she'd had a man in her bed. She was sort of hoping this relationship would drift in that direction—not this trip but maybe a future one—and wanted to be able to get to know Jordan without any distractions.

But then Hendrix turned, and their eyes met.

Hendrix would've glanced away and walked right back to the billiards tables as though he hadn't seen Ellen. But Kurt noticed her at the same time and pointed the top of his beer bottle in her direction. "Hey, Ellen. How are you?" he said, taking the only step required to reach her table.

Hendrix could see a measure of wariness enter her eyes.

She always grew leery when he was around. But she managed a pleasant smile for Kurt's sake. He had no doubt she would've smiled at Brant's other brothers, too, if they hadn't already left with a couple of women from the next town. She seemed to be making friends with almost everyone in Coyote Canyon—except him and the Fettermans.

On second thought, now that she was friends with Leo, she was making inroads even there.

"I'm good." She kept her gaze attached to Kurt as though Hendrix wasn't standing right beside him. "You?"

"Can't complain." Kurt took a pull from his beer. "Did you ever find a plumber to fix that leak under your sink?"

Hendrix had no idea when the two of them had discussed a leak, probably at an event hosted by Talulah and Brant. Kurt didn't typically talk about Ellen, not to him. Almost everyone in town understood they were mortal enemies and they simply accepted the situation for what it was and carried on.

"Not yet," she replied. "I replaced the connections but that didn't help."

"Must be a corroded pipe."

"It's possible. I haven't had time to mess with it further. But it's in the guest bath, so I just turned off the water to that sink for now."

"Bet I could fix it," he said. "I'm not a plumber, but I've had to do a lot of that kind of work at the ranch over the years. Want me to come over and take a look?"

Eager to escape, Hendrix leaned closer to Kurt and mumbled, "I'll meet you at the pool tables," but Kurt was just drunk enough to grab hold of his arm.

"Whoa! Hang on. We'll go over in a sec."

"No need to worry about the leak," Ellen told him as if Hendrix hadn't interrupted. "I'll take care of it myself. You have enough to worry about. You don't need to be saddled with my stuff, too."

There was that fierce independence again. Hendrix was starting to see a lot of positive traits in her—and that bugged him more than anything else. *Keep your mind on what she's done to Fetterman Well Services,* he reminded himself.

"I wouldn't mind," Kurt insisted. "I'll stop by the next time I'm at Talulah and Brant's."

Hendrix felt his muscles tense. Why was Kurt being so solicitous of Ellen? Could it be that he found her attractive? Since Kurt never mentioned her, Hendrix hadn't seen *that* coming. When she first arrived in town, Kurt had laughed at her tattoos and piercings and the way she dressed right along with Hendrix. But they'd stopped doing that quite a while ago. She had a way of making whatever she did look cool, so what had seemed too odd or unusual at first had slowly become appealing.

"If you happen to think of it," she said.

Assuming that would be the end of the conversation, Hendrix almost stepped away. He hated standing awkwardly by as Ellen spoke to one of his best friends. But Kurt didn't move. He looked at the man Ellen was with—someone Hendrix had never seen before.

Noticing the shift in Kurt's attention, Ellen cleared her throat. "Sorry. Jordan, this is…this is my best friend's husband's younger brother Kurt and…" She hesitated as though she preferred not to introduce Hendrix, but it would've been too blatantly rude to ignore him. "And this is Hendrix Durrant, another driller in the area."

"And your best friend is named Talulah," Jordan said. "Isn't that right? I think you've mentioned her before."

The more they talked, the more Hendrix began to

believe that Ellen and this dude didn't know each other very well. So...what was the connection between them?

"One of them," Ellen clarified.

She had others? Hendrix had never seen her hang out with anyone besides Talulah. Or, occasionally, he spotted her in town with Ben, getting parts, gassing up or grabbing lunch.

"Talulah lives next to her," Kurt volunteered. "You know that Victorian farmhouse on the property just beyond Ellen's? That belongs to Brant and Talulah."

"Jordan's never been to my house," Ellen explained. "He's...he's from Libby."

"Libby, huh?" Kurt said. "What do you do up there?"

"I'm a dentist."

Kurt's eyebrows slid up. "Really. I have a cousin who lives there. You don't know a Don Taylor, do you?"

"I'm afraid not," Jordan replied. "I haven't lived there long. I was born and raised in Portland, only decided to move to Libby a year ago when I heard that the father of a friend I went to dental school with was retiring and selling his practice."

The waitress arrived with their food. Hendrix stepped back and pulled Kurt out of the way so she could put down their plates. It was the perfect opportunity to disengage. But he'd become so intrigued by Jordan's connection to Ellen, he had to ask the dentist a question himself. "So...is this your first time in Coyote Canyon?"

Jordan unwrapped his silverware so he could put his napkin in his lap. "It is."

"Then you must've lived in Anaconda for a while," Kurt said. "Otherwise, how'd you meet Ellen?"

"I've never lived in Anaconda." Jordan picked up his burger. "We met online a few weeks ago."

"Online?" Kurt repeated. "You mean like…on a dating app?"

That struck Hendrix as odd, too. Not the online dating part. A lot of people used the internet to meet someone. It was that Ellen was looking for a man in the first place. She was so waspish she was practically unapproachable, which was probably why he couldn't remember her being associated with any of the guys in Coyote Canyon—not since she'd gone out with Brant for a few months after she first moved to town.

"Yeah." Irritation had flared up and showed in Jordan's expression. "Is there something wrong with that?"

Kurt lifted his hands. "Of course not. I just…"

When his words dwindled away, Hendrix took charge. He couldn't imagine Ellen putting up a profile any more than Kurt could, but all the pieces were beginning to fit together. This was a date. The dentist was all cleaned up, freshly shaved and wearing cologne—and he and Ellen were just getting to know each other. "Sorry," he said. "In case you can't tell, Kurt's had a little too much to drink. We'll let the two of you enjoy your dinner."

Ellen and Jordan mumbled something polite in return and nodded as Hendrix dragged Kurt away.

"Did you hear that?" Kurt asked as they weaved through the crowded bar to reach the gaming section in back.

"Hear what?" Hendrix asked.

"Ellen's been using a dating site. Why, for God's sake? I mean…there are plenty of guys around here who'd be happy to go out with her. What's wrong with one of us?"

Hendrix looked over his shoulder, but Ellen's eyes were still following them, so he immediately glanced away. "Don't tell me *you* want to date her," he said, even though Kurt had already made that fairly clear.

His friend jerked out of Hendrix's grasp. "Hell, yeah,

I'd like to date her. Who wouldn't—besides you? She's hot, man. And I bet she'd be a wildcat in bed."

Hendrix got the same feeling. He knew she was a passionate person—and he was becoming converted to her sex appeal. He just couldn't bring himself to acknowledge it. "She doesn't seem like your type."

"I didn't think so at first, either," Kurt admitted. "But thanks to Brant and Talulah, I've had the chance to get to know her. I understand why *you* hate her, but *I* think she's cool."

Hendrix didn't respond. He and Stuart had lost a lot of business to Ellen. He didn't want to lose his friends to her, too. He couldn't argue the point, anyway. There was no question she had plenty of charisma. It was just that it didn't hit you at first. It built gradually, sort of snuck up on a person. That night when he'd gone to her place to apologize and she'd come to the door in her robe, he'd felt something different than ever before—a sudden upwelling of desire, which concerned him more than anything had in a long time.

It would be the greatest irony in the world if he ended up wanting Ellen. He could only imagine how she'd relish the power that would give her.

He had to stamp out the attraction. He just wasn't sure how.

"Don't you think she's pretty?" Kurt asked, still clearly upset that some stranger from out of town had swooped in to take what he'd been hoping to get himself.

"Not at all," Hendrix replied, but that was such a blatant lie he was afraid Kurt would be able to see right through it.

Seven

For the next couple of hours, Hendrix couldn't stop surreptitiously watching Ellen and her date. And he wasn't the only one. Kurt commented on every move they made. "Look at that," he said with disgust. "Look how close they're dancing."

Hendrix had seen Jordan lead Ellen onto the dance floor. Ellen had smiled up into her date's face and let him hold her tight, which—even though Hendrix would've denied it with his last breath—bothered him almost as much as it did Kurt. What was going on with her? He'd never seen her so open and accommodating.

"'Tonight's the Night'? Are you kidding me?" Kurt continued, complaining about what the band was playing. "This song's so ancient it was old when my mother was a kid. Why are they playing Rod Stewart?"

"No clue," Hendrix mumbled, but the lyrics conjured images of Ellen and Jordan he'd rather not see. Trying to ignore the song, he rounded the pool table, looking for his next shot. "Maybe it's the only slow song they know."

"If that's all they know, they need to learn some new stuff."

"Maybe they got a request."

"If so, it was probably from Jordan. I have no doubt he's hoping to get lucky tonight." Kurt cast another disgruntled glance toward Ellen and her new friend. "How much do you think a dentist makes, anyway?"

"I have no idea," Hendrix said. "I guess it would depend on the size of the practice."

"A dentist in Libby couldn't make *that* much."

Hendrix had finally decided on the angle he wanted, but instead of taking the shot, he straightened. "What makes you say that?"

"Have you ever been to Libby?"

"Not that I can remember."

"Thanks to that whole asbestos nightmare, it hasn't exactly been thriving over the past several decades."

Hendrix knew what Kurt was referring to. Most people had heard about the asbestos problem in that part of the state. Home to one of the worst man-made environmental disasters in the country, the town had lost hundreds of residents to asbestos-related illnesses due to contaminated vermiculite mines in the area, which had stayed open and operated for years even though the company that owned them had been told they posed serious health risks. The EPA had finally come in to clean everything up, but that was back when Stuart was just marrying his aunt. And the work had taken forever. It was only a few years ago that the town had been deemed safe. "Maybe it's bouncing back now that the EPA has done its job."

"Maybe," Kurt allowed. "I haven't been there recently. Been meaning to go up and see my cousin, but with Brant getting married, I've had to do a lot more at the ranch than I ever did before. It's been tough to get away."

Brant, Kurt's oldest brother, still worked at the ranch

the four Elway boys had inherited when their parents retired. He just wasn't there 24/7 anymore. Since he'd married Talulah and moved into her house, his younger brothers had had to grow up and take on more responsibility. "Has your cousin said if he likes living in Libby?"

"Hasn't said he doesn't," Kurt responded.

"Maybe Ellen will marry this guy and move up there..."

Kurt gave him a wry look. "I bet that's what *you're* hoping. If she sells her place and heads north, all your problems will be solved."

"Exactly. Let her drill in that part of the state. Or sell her equipment, have a couple of kids and live the bougie life of a dentist's wife."

A skeptical expression came over Kurt's face. "I can't see Ellen ever becoming a stay-at-home mom, can you?"

The answer to that question was *no*. Hendrix couldn't see it, either. But why would he care what she did in Libby—or anywhere else, for that matter—as long as she left Coyote Canyon? For the sake of Fetterman Well Services, he'd wanted her to move away since the day she arrived. But now that her strange appeal was beginning to act on him, too, the stakes were higher than ever.

"What's wrong?" Jordan asked.

"Nothing." Ellen upped the wattage of her smile for his benefit, but she could feel Kurt and Hendrix watching her at every opportunity, and it made her uncomfortable. A first date was awkward enough. Why couldn't they just focus on their game?

Because they weren't used to seeing her with anyone, she supposed. It didn't help that Jordan was an outsider. Several of the other locals cast them curious glances, too.

"Are you getting bored? Would you like to leave?"

she asked Jordan as they walked off the dance floor. She didn't dare take him back to her house. She didn't want him to expect to stay the night. But it'd probably been a long day for him, what with that dental emergency he'd had to handle early this morning. Maybe he was tired and ready to go to the motel.

"I'm not bored at all," he said. "But I'd be happy to go somewhere else, if you'd rather do that than stay here."

He didn't sound as though he was ready to call it a night. So…what else could they do? It was too late to drive to the lookout to watch the sunset. The sun had gone down before he'd even arrived. And nothing else would be open. "I'm fine. I just…didn't want to keep you out too late if you're tired."

He checked his watch as they reached their table. "It's only ten fifteen. Let's get another drink and hang out for an hour or so."

That would mean an additional sixty minutes of feeling like she was swimming in a fish tank. But she nodded. She was trying to be congenial so she wouldn't kill this relationship before it could even get started. Jordan seemed like a solid citizen. He worked hard and earned a decent living, and he treated her kindly and showed plenty of interest.

He certainly wasn't someone to be passed over too quickly. They didn't seem to have a lot in common, but… there were worse things to overcome in a relationship.

She was determined to make more of an effort— give Jordan an honest chance. Forget Hendrix. He could stare all he wanted to. If she was going to build a better future, she couldn't let anyone get in her way. If she didn't turn her attention to developing other areas of her life, her job would continue to be all she had. "Yeah.

Another drink sounds good. But I need to visit the ladies' room first."

Once Jordan acknowledged her response, she slipped down the hallway that led to the restrooms.

When she returned, she found that he'd already ordered a fresh cosmopolitan for her and a beer for himself. The drinks were at the table, but he wasn't.

Assuming he must've gone to the restroom, too, she was about to sit down to wait for him when she heard him call her name and looked up to see him halfway between her and the pool tables, beckoning her forward. "Your friends have challenged us to a game of pool," he shouted above the music once she reached him. "Want to play?"

Her friends? *Shit.* She shifted her gaze ever so slightly and saw Hendrix and Kurt waiting for them, cue sticks in hand. "Not a chance," she muttered under her breath. But because she'd introduced Hendrix and Kurt to Jordan, he had no way of knowing she wouldn't be pleased that he'd accepted their invitation, especially since she'd also shown an interest in playing pool.

"What'd you say?" he asked, taking a step toward her.

She drew a deep breath. "I said it...sounds like fun."

He seemed slightly baffled, as though he could tell he was missing something. "Are you sure?"

She could only answer *yes*—unless she was ready to do a lot of explaining. And this was a first date. The last thing she wanted to do was delve into her personal history.

Besides, she liked Brant's brothers. Kurt made the prospect of playing pool with Hendrix a bit more palatable.

She managed to convince Jordan that she was happy he'd gotten them a game, before they walked over and waited for Kurt to rack the balls.

She thought maybe Hendrix was the one who'd asked

Jordan if they wanted to play—to irritate her by putting her in the same position he'd been in when he brought that woman to the dessert diner. But it soon became apparent that he wasn't any happier to be spending his evening with her than she was with him. He remained quiet and stood off to one side whenever possible, stepping up only to take his turn.

She and Jordan lost the first game—so badly it was embarrassing. Her dentist date had been telling the truth when he said he wasn't any good. But she played better than she ever had in her life in game two and managed to pull off the upset.

"Nice job!" Kurt exclaimed when she sank four balls in a row to finish them off.

If Hendrix was impressed, he did nothing to indicate it. It wasn't until Kurt had drawn Jordan to the other side of the table to coach him on how to take a basic shot, that he leaned over and murmured, "This dude could never make you happy. I hope you realize that."

Blinking in surprise, she turned to gape at him. "Because he can't play pool?"

"Because putting the two of you together would be like pairing a mustang with a...a packhorse."

"You're saying I'm too wild for him."

"I'm saying he's too domesticated for you. You're complete opposites."

"How do *you* know?" she asked.

His gaze swept over Jordan all the way down to his loafers. "It's obvious. It has to be obvious to you, too. You just don't want to accept it—for whatever reason."

Because the men who were more interesting to her— the ones she was truly attracted to—would only break her heart. She was changing things up, being smart about her love life. "You don't know anything about me," she said.

He put his cue stick away. "I know more than you think," he replied and excused himself, saying he couldn't play another game, after all, because he'd just remembered something he had to do.

Kurt clearly wasn't pleased that Hendrix was leaving before they could start the rubber match, but Ellen said she was getting tired, too, so he wouldn't try to recruit a stand-in.

After they'd all said goodbye, she watched Hendrix navigate his way to the door while she and Jordan returned to their table. She would've bet her life that he didn't really have to leave. He'd just had enough of being anywhere near her.

Unfortunately, she also knew that he was probably right about Jordan. As hard as she'd been trying to ignore reality by focusing on her date's many virtues, she felt no attraction to him and would be doing them both a disservice to pretend otherwise.

She scowled after Hendrix as he flung open the door and stepped outside. *You bastard*, she thought. His opinion had ruined the illusion she'd been trying to create and forced her to see the truth.

But she couldn't really blame him for being right.

Why'd he have to say something to Ellen? Hendrix wondered. He'd just agreed with Kurt that he'd be much better off—his business would be better off, too—if Ellen married Dr. Jordan Whoever and moved to Libby. And yet he'd taken the first opportunity to warn her that she was making a big mistake.

"That was stupid," he mumbled as he climbed into his truck. For one thing, he didn't know for certain that she'd be unhappy with Jordan. *He* couldn't see them to-gether, but sometimes opposites worked just fine. He'd been speaking more from jealousy than anything else and hoped to God she didn't realize that.

Bottom line, he needed to stay out of her life. He typically managed to do that; he wasn't sure why he was letting circumstances get the better of him lately. Maybe it was because they'd been thrown together more often than usual.

Or…maybe it wasn't that at all. If he was being hon-est, it'd been a bumpy ride from the beginning, and there were certain times she got to him more than others.

When Ellen first came to town, Stuart wouldn't say much, but Lynn had gone on and on, mostly to Stuart, about every sighting of her, what she was doing, say-ing, had tattooed on her body—and every new well-drilling application she filed. *Why'd she have to come here of all places?*

There was nothing Lynn could do, nothing any of them could do. He figured she was venting, and he could understand why she'd feel the need. He resented Ellen's intrusion into their lives almost as much as she did. There were just a lot of other emotions mixed up with the resentment. The more he'd watched Ellen, the more he'd come to respect and admire her indepen-dence, resilience and determination.

He'd tried to adopt a "live and let live" approach—and ignore what she was doing the way Stuart did. But after a while, even neutral tolerance had given way to something else, and it was that something else that frightened him.

He should never have started to sympathize with her. That was partly what had whittled away his defenses. But most people had family to support them. She hadn't had anyone, from the age of ten, except a mother who was more of a liability. Even with all the things she had going against her, she'd managed to pull through what had to be a difficult adolescence to graduate from high school, earn a college degree and start her own business in a challenging field. *Their* field. And he was keenly aware that his aunt was part of the reason she'd been left to do it on her own. Shouldn't someone have done more to stand by her and make sure she received the love and attention she deserved?

Yes. Her father should've done more. And Lynn should've supported him in it. If they had, maybe Ellen wouldn't be so angry and determined to put them out of business.

It wasn't Hendrix who'd let her down. He shouldn't feel partly responsible for the damage that'd been done—and yet he did. So how did he resolve that?

He could try to establish a friendship with Ellen. But if all he felt was friendship, it wouldn't have bothered him to learn that Kurt was interested in her, because Kurt was a good guy. It wouldn't have bothered him to see her dancing so close to that dentist, either. As much as he hated to admit it, he was attracted to Ellen, which just made the whole situation weirder and more difficult.

He knew what he had to do. He would acknowledge that Lynn and Stuart were wrong to do what they'd done and offer her his friendship.

If he knew the boundaries going in, he could certainly respect them—couldn't he? he thought and turned his truck around.

Tightly gripping the steering wheel of her truck, Ellen glanced into the rearview mirror. She was fairly certain the headlights she saw behind her belonged to the Audi Jordan Forbes had driven to Coyote Canyon. Was he following her? If so, why? What did he hope to achieve? After they left Hank's and were standing in the parking lot she'd told him that she didn't want to pursue a relationship with him. He should be heading to his motel to get some sleep before driving back to Libby in the morning.

The last of the streetlights faded behind her as she drove out of town, and another glance in the rearview mirror—and then another—showed the same pair of headlights. If it was Jordan, she was leading him right to her house. But what else could she do? Pull over and confront him on the side of the road? Call Talulah and have her wake up Brant? Go to the police?

Those seemed to be her only options. But she didn't want to be standing in the dark on the side of the road arguing with a man who was little more than a stranger to her. She hated to disturb Talulah and Brant, especially so late, for something that probably wouldn't amount to more than a few final remarks. And going to the police seemed extreme. What could they do? Jordan hadn't threatened her, and she didn't feel she was in serious danger. She just wanted to be rid of him.

How ironic, she thought as she passed Talulah and Brant's house. She'd thought Jordan Forbes would be different—*better*—than most of the men she'd dated in the past, only to find that he wasn't. He seemed to think—just because she had tattoos and a few piercings—that he was superior and she owed him more than she'd given him so far.

"You had me drive all the way to this piece-of-shit town just to get a few drinks at a local bar?" he'd said when she'd first suggested they call off the rest of the weekend.

Self-conscious, she'd glanced around, hoping there was no one in the parking lot to overhear them. "You're the one who offered to come."

"Because I wanted to meet you—badly enough that I rearranged my whole schedule. I could've worked today!"

"I told you it would be fine to come tomorrow, but you insisted on driving down tonight," she'd argued.

"Because I thought we were going to spend the whole weekend together!"

She'd tried to explain that she already knew they weren't compatible. But he wouldn't take no for an answer.

"You don't even know me!" he'd cried. "How can you say we won't be any good together when we've spent only a few hours eating and playing pool?"

"I can just...tell," she'd insisted. She could've said she felt no attraction to him, but she wasn't out to hurt him.

"Wait, wait, wait." He'd put up his hands. "You're pulling the plug too soon. Why don't we just calm down and go to the motel—or your place—where we can talk?"

She knew there was no point. She'd realized as soon as Hendrix had spoken that she'd been forcing the relationship, pushing herself to accept something she didn't really want. She'd tried to tell Jordan that if he needed to discuss anything they could talk on the phone another time—but putting him off only made him angrier.

"Who do you think you are? You're damn lucky a man like me would take an interest in you."

"A man like you?" she'd echoed.

"Yeah. What do *you* have to offer? You're just a... physical laborer with no prospects in some out-of-the-way place. I can't believe you're already blowing things up between us. You've caused me to drive five fucking hours—ten if you count the return—and ruined my weekend."

"I didn't offer you any guarantees when you decided to visit Coyote Canyon!" she'd said. "With dating, sometimes there's attraction and sometimes there's not. I was hoping things would go better, so I'm disappointed, too."

"In *me*? You're not attracted to me?"

The genuine shock on his face astonished her. "That… that it's not going to work out," she'd clarified, still trying to be as pleasant as she possibly could.

"But…how did you come to that conclusion so fast?" he'd asked, raising his voice. "You're judging me based on…what? The fact that I'm no good at pool? I'm not one of the losers who live around here and spend all my time at the pool hall, okay? I have degrees, a practice. Do you know how many other women have messaged me on the dating app? I could've spent the weekend with any one of them. I chose you because I thought you'd be a hell of a lot more fun, so *I'm* the one who's disappointed."

"You entitled son of a bitch!" she'd snapped. "If you want the truth, I think I'm just as special as you are. *And* I'm good at pool."

He hadn't been happy that she'd fought back instead of apologizing and changing her mind. His attitude suggested he was used to getting his way. "Being with a guy like me could change your life."

There'd been people streaming out of the bar. Ellen had held her temper as best she could, but she'd told him that she was done and didn't want to hear from him ever again. Then she'd turned to get in her truck.

He'd reached out to stop her but let go when Kurt came out and yelled good-night. The fact that she could sim-

ply call out to her friend if she wanted to had prompted
Jordan to back off enough that she could get inside her
truck, start the engine and leave.

She'd thought that would be the end of her adven-
ture with Dr. Jordan Forbes and was eager to get home
where she could begin to forget her latest dating deba-
cle when she'd noticed the car behind her was making
all the same turns.

She dug through her purse to find her phone, scrolled
to Talulah's number and kept her finger hovering over
the Call button as she drove the last two miles to her
house, parked in her driveway and got out.

Sure enough, it was Jordan behind her. He pulled in
almost to the bumper of her truck before shutting off
the engine of his Audi and opening the door.

"What are you doing here?" she demanded.

He stepped out of the car. "I just want to talk to you,
okay? Things got out of hand in the parking lot at Hank's,
and I'm sorry for that. I don't want you to have a bad
impression of me. I don't want our weekend to end like
this, either. We can work things out. Let's just go inside."

This guy was nothing like he'd seemed. Ellen couldn't
believe the change even a small amount of resistance
had brought about. He'd expected her to be a pushover,
someone who was glad to have him in her life and probably in her bed. And he couldn't tolerate rejection. She'd
already told him she didn't want him to come over; there
was no way she was going to let him in her house. "I
told you at Hank's that I don't want to talk, Jordan. You
need to go back to the motel, get some sleep and return
to Libby."

An angry scowl cut deep crevices in his forehead.
"You can't make me leave Coyote Canyon. You don't
own this town."

"It was a mistake for me to have you come. It was too soon. We didn't know each other well enough."

"This is how you get to know someone!"

"I've seen all I want to see, okay? God, I'm sorry I agreed to meet you. Look at how you're behaving. Just make things simple and…and leave me alone."

His hand whipped out, knocking her phone to the ground so fast it shocked her. "What the hell!" She bent to pick it up, but he caught her by the wrist and dragged her up against him.

In that split second she knew she should've called Talulah and Brant while she had the chance. This guy was an arrogant asshole. He might even be dangerous. "You bastard!" She tried to knee him in the nuts so she could free herself, but he anticipated her move and shifted just in time.

"Call me what you will, but I won't let a stupid blue-collar bitch like you play games with me."

"I'm not playing—" she started to say when his wet mouth landed on hers.

Other than Brant, Ellen hadn't dated men with impeccable reputations. She'd be the first to admit that. But she'd never been *assaulted*. She'd worked around the opposite sex her entire adult life, believed she'd be able to fight her way out of any attempt at dominance. But she couldn't escape. Jordan had too tight a hold on her, and the more she struggled, the angrier he became.

"Stop it!" he yelled, sliding his hands up her arms to her shoulders and giving her a good shake. "You're the one who asked for this. You invited me to come, and here I am. We could be having a great time—we could even be making love right now—if you weren't acting this way. Instead, you're trying to end things for no reason whatsoever."

She could feel the rage welling up inside him, was prepared for a fight—one she was pretty sure she'd lose. She knew she had to act quickly. Screaming as loudly as she could, she raked her nails down his face at the same time.

She fully expected him to hit her but that didn't happen. A man came charging out of nowhere, roaring something unintelligible—like a battle cry—and the next thing she knew, she was pulled away from Jordan and she stumbled.

The jolt when she hit the ground knocked the wind out of her. Only after she could haul in a big, stabilizing breath was she able to rise up on her elbows. Then she saw who had interceded. It was Hendrix! She had no idea where he'd come from or why he would be anywhere near her house tonight, but he'd stopped Jordan and was now making him pay.

Determined to reach her phone, which had skidded to the edge of the grass, she staggered to her feet.

Fortunately, despite a cracked screen, it still worked. She dialed 9-1-1 amidst the grunts and groans of Hendrix and Jordan going at each other. But the fight was over before the call could even go through. She watched Hendrix shove Jordan, who was bleeding from his nose and mouth, back behind the wheel of his Audi and heard him tell the dentist to get the hell out of Coyote Canyon and never come back.

"K-keep him here. I'm c-calling the police," Ellen told Hendrix, stuttering and shaking from the adrenaline surging through her.

Hendrix's chest rose and fell quickly as he labored to catch his breath. "Don't bother."

A voice came on the phone. "9-1-1. What's your emergency?"

She didn't know how to respond. "Why not?" she asked Hendrix in surprise.

"They won't be able to do anything."

"I guess... I guess we have it under control," she told the operator and disconnected before asking Hendrix, "Why don't we have the police come? He attacked me!"

"He forced you to kiss him. He won't go to jail for that—at least not for any length of time."

Something else might've happened. Would probably have happened. But Hendrix had jumped in before it could.

"Call them back," Jordan shouted, pointing at Hendrix. "So I can tell them how this bastard attacked me!"

Hendrix didn't seem concerned about the accusation. "I didn't attack you," he said. "I beat your ass because you got out of line. There's a difference. And I'll do it again if I ever see you around here. Do you understand? You'd better go now, and you'd better forget about Ellen. Don't ever contact her again."

Ellen was so astonished she didn't know what to say. She'd always had to fight her own battles; there'd never been anyone to stand up for her. And even if that hadn't been the case, Hendrix would be the last person she'd ever expect to come to her defense.

"You got it all wrong," Jordan said. "We were just... kissing good-night."

"Sure you were, buddy," Hendrix said. "I saw what was going on."

How? How had he seen? Ellen planned to ask as soon as they got rid of Jordan. But she was rattled enough that she just stood there while her dentist "match" started his car and peeled out of the drive.

"I can't believe that happened," she said in the sudden silence.

Hendrix winced in pain as he shook out his right hand. "Dude deserved a lot more than I gave him."

Ellen gaped at her unexpected rescuer. "I—I appreciate the help. I don't know how far it would've gone without you. The situation was certainly escalating. And I never saw it coming, never dreamed *that* guy, of all guys, would cross the line."

"I can see why you wouldn't." He examined his damaged knuckles. "You wouldn't expect it from such a dink. Shocked the hell out of me, too."

"Aren't dentists supposed to be nice?" she said. "I mean…it takes a lot of self-discipline to get through all those years of school. A certain amount of intelligence, too. That's got to mean something. It *should* mean something." She'd been relying on it, had almost entirely dropped her guard.

"I guess it just goes to show anyone can be an asshole."

The past ten minutes could've taken a much darker turn. But Hendrix had protected her against the worst—*Hendrix Durrant!* She still couldn't believe he'd come out of nowhere right when she needed him most. How was it that he was so close? "What were you doing here?" she asked.

He kept his attention on his hand, which he seemed to be testing by opening and closing it again. "Just happened to be in the area."

"How? And why'd you bother to stop and help?"

He looked at her with a shocked expression. "You think I'd stand by and let a woman—any woman—be hurt?"

"We're not talking about any woman," she said. He hated her, wanted her gone. Plenty of people around town had told her that. And she could understand why. Her father was the only one of the two of them who'd really wronged her. She just hated Hendrix because he'd taken a lot of what she otherwise would've had.

"God, Ellen," he said with a scowl. "How bad do you think I am? I've never been out to get you personally."

She thought of Ben and how much more she was having to pay him since Hendrix had tried to hire him away. That pissed her off. But she'd done her fair share of damage to Fetterman Well Services, too; she figured she'd deserved some kind of retaliation. Part of her was even grateful Hendrix had finally done something to hurt her. After so many months of being ignored, it gave her something concrete to hold against him, made her feel that much more justified in disliking him.

"I—I don't think you're...*bad*," she said but she didn't sound convinced, even to her own ears, which was probably why he shot her a dirty look.

"Thanks a lot."

She shook her head. She had so many questions. She still didn't understand how he'd been able to step in at such a critical moment—and she knew she owed him her gratitude for that, at least. She would've assumed he'd been visiting Brant and Talulah and just happened to notice the scuffle as he was driving away. But she'd never seen him at their place before. And Talulah's had been dark when she passed it.

She opened her mouth to ask again, but his knuckles were busted up, his shirt was torn and stained with blood, and it was a lot cooler than it'd been earlier in the day. The wind felt like it was slicing right through her; he had to be cold, too. She figured they could talk inside. "C-come on in where it's warm, and...and you can get cleaned up."

Eight

Hendrix had never expected to find himself inside Ellen's house. Actually, he'd been in the house before, many times, when Stuart's parents owned it. But it was different now. Ellen had been in Coyote Canyon long enough to put her own stamp on the place. She'd brought a hippie vibe to what had been a straight-up ranch-style rambler by adding a lot of houseplants, contemporary art and eclectic furniture, most of which came off as quirky as she was.

He liked her style. At least she had one. That was more than he could say about any other driller he'd known, including him. As far as household items went, he owned a leather couch and a recliner, a couple of large-screen TVs, a king-size bed, some bookshelves and a basic dining set. Practical. Period. He hadn't even bothered to furnish his extra bedroom, which was why Leo slept on the couch whenever he stayed over. Hendrix hadn't hung many pictures, either—only the framed photograph he'd taken of a bear he'd encountered a few years back, while he was fishing.

"I like what you've done," he said.

She looked startled by the comment. "With the house?"

"Yeah."

"Thank you," she said, but without much conviction, as if she didn't trust the compliment in the first place.

She led him past the guest bath to the primary bedroom, explaining that the guest bath had a leak under the sink.

He remembered Kurt mentioning that at Hank's and was glad it was currently unusable. Otherwise, he wouldn't have been ushered into Ellen's bedroom, and he was curious enough about her that he was eager to see the whole house, especially the parts guests typically never saw. It helped him understand who she was and what she was really like—showed him the human side of Ellen, which broke down the prejudice his aunt had fostered in him from the time he'd moved in with her.

Hard as it was to admit, he was beginning to realize that the loyalty he'd given Lynn had led him to help her shut Ellen out. But the older he got, the more unfair he realized that was. Lynn's own insecurities and unwillingness to share Stuart had convinced him that Ellen posed some kind of existential threat to their happiness and well-being.

Stuart's daughter *did* pose a threat to Fetterman Well Services, of course, which was what had kept him so defensive as an adult. But that factor—her competitiveness on the business front—had developed much later and probably as a result of their actions toward her.

Her room was decorated in beige and white, and the carpet he remembered, along with a lot of gold plastic wall decorations, had been removed. The original hardwood floors had plenty of scratches and some wear but looked much better. "Wow. Great job in here. That old blue carpet was the worst."

"I need to tear out the carpet in the rest of the house,

too, but I'm so tired when I get home at night that it's the last thing I want to do."

She was drilling wells they would've drilled if she hadn't come to town, but he was trying to look beyond that, for once. "You did the work yourself?"

"Yep. You can learn anything on YouTube—except how to fix the leak under my other sink, apparently. I've tried everything short of replacing the pipes. Kurt must be right that they're corroded."

"I can take a look at it while I'm here, if you want."

"That's okay," she said warily. "I've got it."

She didn't trust him. That was obvious. But since he'd saved her from whatever Jordan was going to do, it was difficult for her to rebuff him. Kindness was proving to be the best way to disarm her. He wasn't sure why he hadn't tried that before.

She had all white linens on her bed—even the duvet was a crisp white—with a beige sweater-knit throw across the bottom. She hadn't bothered to make the bed this morning, but other than that her house was clean and tidy. He knew Lynn would rather believe she was some kind of slob, but she clearly wasn't. He especially liked the way her house smelled. The diffuser in the bathroom gave off a lemony, earthy aroma he found very appealing. "I need to get one of these," he said, picking it up.

She blinked several times before politely—and with evident uncertainty—saying, "I ordered it online. I can send you the link, if you want."

That was a courtesy she'd provide to anyone. Lots of people shared such information. But this type of conversation was brand-new territory for them.

"That'd be great." He doubted she'd meant she'd do it right away, but he tugged her phone from her pocket, turned it so that her face recognition software unlocked it and proceeded to enter his number. Then he called himself, so he'd have her number, too, and handed it back with a smile. "Now you can send it to me whenever you're ready."

He'd expected her to protest or grab her phone away from him before he could finish. Instead, her eyebrows knitted together as she accepted her phone and slid it back into her pocket. "You still haven't told me what you were doing so close to my house that you could see what was going on with Jordan," she said.

"I was waiting for you to get home."

She pressed a hand to her chest. "*Me?* Why?"

"Because I wanted to talk to you."

"About what?"

"About calling a truce."

Her eyes narrowed in suspicion. "And how, exactly, would that work?"

"Let me get washed up. Then we can discuss it."

He got the impression she was tempted to insist he tell her right away, but one glance at his bloody shirt and she nodded. "Fine. Here's a towel and a washcloth you can use," she said, pulling both from a basket near the tub.

He stretched out the fingers of the hand he'd used to punch Jordan. They still throbbed but, thankfully, he didn't believe he'd broken anything. He knew what that felt like; he'd fractured several bones in the opposite hand when he rolled his ATV a few years back.

"Looks to me like it's beginning to swell," she said as she put the towel and washcloth on the counter. "Maybe you should go see a doctor."

He grimaced. "Nah. It'll be fine by tomorrow."

"I hope you're right."

"I'm always right," he said jokingly.

Her eyes met his in the mirror. "I have to admit it's very uncomfortable being on the same side as you."

He chuckled. "It's definitely a switch. But maybe I'm not the bad guy you want to believe I am."

"And maybe you're setting me up." She held out her hand. "Give me your shirt. I'll throw it in the laundry and grab some bandages."

"What a cynic!" He pulled his shirt over his head and noticed how quickly she averted her eyes once it came off.

"I'll be right back," she mumbled and blindly took it from him.

While she was gone, he washed his hands, face, neck and chest. He even took the opportunity to snoop around in her medicine cabinet and bathroom drawers. While he knew that wasn't polite, he was becoming so curious about her that the temptation proved too great.

He found the usual. Makeup. Blow-dryer. Tampax. No birth control, but maybe she kept it elsewhere.

Or she wasn't sexually active.

That was interesting—more interesting than he wanted it to be.

Then he noticed a theme. Ellen used products that were as eco-friendly as possible. She had a bamboo toothbrush, pure-castile soap in the shower and one of those organic shampoo bars that were popular among hipsters. She cared more about the environment than most people in Coyote Canyon, hardly any of whom even bothered to recycle. The "hard-nosed bitch" who'd come to town seemed far more concerned about the people and things around her than he would've expected.

He closed the cabinets when he heard her tread in

the hallway and was just finishing drying off when she returned with a giant backpack.

This time she set her shoulders and didn't look away from him. She moved her finger in a circular motion to indicate she needed him to turn around. "What?" he said when he'd shown her his back.

"No other injuries?" she responded.

He felt guilty for going through her bathroom while she was gone. She already had trust issues, especially when it came to *him*, since he was fairly certain she believed he "stole" her father away from her. "You expected more?"

"You had so much blood on your shirt…"

"All of which belonged to Jordan. Noses tend to bleed a lot."

She caught her bottom lip between her teeth. "What if you broke his nose? Aren't you worried that he might file charges against you?"

"He attacked you first. I don't think a dentist—someone who has a reputation to protect—will want to risk having this go any further, do you?"

"That's why you let him off so easy?"

"Although at the time I wanted to do more, a lot more, now I think he was probably adequately punished." He shrugged. "If we let it go, he and I can both walk away. Why? Do you think he deserves a greater punishment?"

"I don't know how far he would've gone if you hadn't interceded, so that's tough to say." She set the giant backpack on the counter and dug through it until she came up with some antiseptic, which she dabbed on his scraped and bruised knuckles before wrapping them in gauze.

"That's an extensive first aid kit," he commented as she secured the gauze with surgical tape. "I doubt very many people have something like that in the house. Were you considering becoming a paramedic before you decided to start your own drilling business?" He dropped his voice meaningfully. "Or have you only ever been after my job?"

He was teasing—something he'd never done with her, which was probably why she didn't seem to know how to react. "It's come in handy on more than one occasion," she said, ignoring the last part of his statement.

"For you or for someone else?"

"Both. Drilling can be dangerous, as you know. I keep it in my truck."

That she could handle such a tough job and do it well enough to compete with him was beginning to turn him on now that he was stepping away from his own emotional involvement enough to look at it objectively. He'd never known another woman like her. She was taking business away from Fetterman Well Services, and yet he was impressed with her drive and determination.

He'd never felt so conflicted about anyone, which was why he typically stayed away from her. It was easier to ignore her, or so he'd thought until he couldn't ignore her any longer. "That's a good idea. I know drillers who've lost an eye or a finger—even a hand. Have you ever been hurt?"

She pushed up the sleeve of her brown off-the-shoulder sweater to reveal a long scar on her forearm. "Got this when a cable broke. Required twenty stitches."

Without her pointing it out, he wouldn't have noticed it even if she'd been sleeveless. It was covered that well by her tattoos.

Turning, she lifted her sweater so he could see a round, puncture-like scar on her back, which she'd made into the sun and the center of her solar system tattoo. So now he knew right where it was—and for no good reason he could think of, he sort of liked having that knowledge. "Got this when a water hose blew with so much pressure it threw me against the drill." She rolled up her faded jeans. "And a piece of slag cut right through my pants and embedded itself in my leg. A surgeon had to remove it." She put her pant leg back down. "Those are just the injuries that've left scars. You?"

"The worst injury I ever received didn't leave a scar. I was hooking a cable to a drilling tool when the heating device backfired and blasted me in the face with gasoline. Spent five days in the hospital for that one."

"Sounds bad."

"It was. In our line of work, almost anything can go wrong." He showed her a small scar where he'd put his teeth through his upper lip. "This wasn't exactly on the job, but I fell asleep while moving a rig to Wyoming. It was like…three in the morning. I simply couldn't keep my eyes open—and crashed into the back of our own water truck as we were all coming to a stop."

She laughed. "Really?"

"Really. I was barely seventeen. Probably shouldn't have been helping. I was missing a few days of school to do it. Fortunately, my lip only required three stitches, no one else was hurt and there was minimal damage to the equipment. But, man, did Stuart get mad. It's not like I could just go to school and get involved in sports like other boys my age. He wanted me with him every extra moment—" He'd been about to tell her how Stuart demanded so much of his time and involvement in the business. But he let his words fade away because the smile had slid from her face, making him realize he'd inadvertently brought up a very touchy subject. "Sorry," he said. "I didn't mean to—"

"To what?" she broke in, her voice slightly defensive if not outright belligerent.

She was pretending that what he'd said didn't bother her, but it obviously did. He hadn't meant to rub her nose in something so painful, but he couldn't explain that to her because she had too much pride to even admit Stuart's neglect still hurt.

"Nothing," he said.

"I'm really tired and would like to get to bed," she said. "But I've got a T-shirt that should fit you. You could wear it home. You could even keep it. I have no use for it. I'll bring your shirt over tomorrow, once I've had a chance to finish washing it, if that's okay."

He'd told her he wanted to talk, to call a truce, and she'd seemed somewhat open to having that conversation. At least, she'd been curious about what he had to say. Now that was off the table. She'd shut down completely.

He wished he could take back his blunder, but it was too late. And thanks to Jordan the Dentist, it'd already been an emotional night. Maybe it would be smarter to back off, for now. "Okay," he said. "If that's what you want."

Turning away, she went out and started digging through her drawers while he leaned against the doorjamb of her bathroom and watched her.

When she found what she was looking for, she brought it over and he pulled it on. It was a little too snug across the shoulders and in the sleeves, but it was fine for the trip home.

Being polite again—*overly* polite, in his opinion—she thanked him for helping her as if he was a kind stranger and walked him to the front door. Those few seconds of feeling as though he was connecting with her—for the first time—were gone. He was trying to figure out what he could say to make everything right again but couldn't decide how to go about that. He was afraid she wouldn't give him the chance even if he could come up with a way to take back that thoughtless mention of Stuart.

"I'll drop your shirt by tomorrow," she reiterated as he stepped outside.

He turned to face her. "I hope you didn't think I *intentionally* brought up a sore subject." He'd merely been trying to share his experience. Couldn't she tell? Or did it not matter? Was it because he was who he was and she wouldn't forgive him for that, no matter how well he behaved?

"Of course not," she said.

Discouraged by her brittle smile and stubborn courtesy, he drew a deep breath. "Okay, I'm leaving," he said and walked away.

When he didn't hear the door shut behind him, he knew she was watching him. He hoped she'd call him back so they could talk, after all. But she was probably waiting to see where he'd parked. No doubt she wanted to know why she hadn't realized he was there before Jordan grabbed her.

Once he reached his truck, which he'd left down the road well beyond her place so that if she brought Jordan home he could get away without her ever knowing he was there, he looked back. She'd had to come all the way out onto the porch steps to see where he was going. But as soon as she realized he was looking at her, she hurried inside and the porch light went off.

Ellen climbed into bed and pulled the duvet up under her chin. The weight of the down feathers inside it felt reassuring at a time when her childhood seemed far too close. She hated the emotions any thought of the past evoked and tried to avoid the more difficult memories, but they snuck up on her every now and then.

In a last-ditch effort to distract herself tonight, she wondered if Jordan had gone back to the motel or left town. In his place, she would've been so humiliated she would've driven home immediately, despite the late hour. But as long as he left her alone, she didn't really care one way or the other.

Which brought her back to Hendrix. *He* was the real issue. Having him in her house. Seeing him without his shirt while they were both in such a confined space. Feeling that strange sensation in the pit of her stomach when he smiled at her. What the heck was going on?

The answer to that question was obvious, but there was no way she could allow herself to be attracted to him. That would give him the upper hand, which was something she could *never* do. She'd been so terribly hurt by her father. And Hendrix had always been party to that. She'd be a fool to trust him, even as a friend.

She had to admit she'd been lucky he was around when she got home, though. What had happened with Jordan wasn't good. She had no idea where it would've ended without some sort of intervention. While it was possible the dentist would've stopped on his own, the opposite was also true.

But…what was Hendrix doing at her house in the first place? He must've walked closer after he'd parked down the street, where she'd seen him go when he was leaving, or he wouldn't have heard her scream. And he'd done that because he wanted a few minutes with her to possibly call a truce?

That was what he'd said, but she didn't want to get involved in any type of agreement with him. She hadn't done anything to her father, his wife *or* Hendrix—

nothing like what they'd done to her, anyway. She was merely competing in a free market, and she was going to continue.

Maybe he'd been planning to threaten to go after her business again if she didn't back off…

She dismissed that possibility as soon as it crossed her mind. He hadn't been acting hostile. He'd been different…*friendly.* Why the sudden change?

"Don't worry about him," she muttered into the darkness. "Even if he was friendly, it won't last." It couldn't. His aunt would never tolerate any type of a relationship between them. Ellen had no idea why Lynn had hated her so much right from the start, but she could still remember meeting her father's wife for the first time and feeling her resentment and animosity.

Jan blamed Lynn's reaction on jealousy. She said Lynn didn't want to run the risk of Stuart loving another female as much or more than he did her. Lynn also didn't want any competition for his care and attention when it came to her family—her son and her nephew. But Ellen had been only ten years old at the time. She hadn't been capable of defending her own heart. How could a grown woman be so petty?

Forget about Stuart, Lynn, Hendrix—even Leo. She had to ignore them, couldn't give them the power to hurt her, or they would.

But in the dark quiet of her room, the memories she tried so hard to contain began to bombard her again.

After Stuart had moved from Anaconda to Coyote Canyon, where he and Lynn had grown up, Grandma and Grandpa Fetterman had tried to include Ellen—and get their son to include her, as well. Ellen remembered staying with them for a week or two each summer, during which she'd hear Grandma Lilly on the phone in the other room, talking in a low voice while beseeching Stuart to show up for dinner, meet them for a picnic or even stop by to say hello. All too often, she'd come out of the room with red, swollen eyes, and then she'd try to smile and continue to entertain Ellen on her own, as though nothing had happened.

Ellen loved her grandma for the kindness she'd shown. Jan's father, a truck driver, had died in a big rig accident before Jan got married, and her mother had lived with her sister clear across the country, in Virginia, ever since. Other than a birthday card, a Christmas gift or a call here and there, neither of them had been too involved in Ellen's life. But at least she'd had one set of grandparents who loved her. A lot of kids who went through a rocky divorce didn't have that much.

Ellen was barely sixteen when Lilly was diagnosed with Alzheimer's. Although Lilly's decline had been slower than most people's, Grandpa Pete's attention had shifted away from the farm and everything else at that point, so he could take care of the woman he'd loved for nearly fifty years. That was why, once Lilly couldn't remember even those who were closest to her, he'd given Ellen the farm and taken his wife to an assisted living facility in Phoenix, which was where their daughter, who was a nurse, lived.

Fortunately, Ellen had been pretty self-sufficient by the time Lilly was no longer fully functional. That was the only thing that'd saved her.

Still, she missed the long, hot summer days she'd spent in Coyote Canyon, helping Grandpa Pete in the garden or learning to cook or can in the kitchen with Grandma Lilly. They were some of the happiest moments of her life. But those brief interludes never lasted long enough. All too soon, she'd have to go home to a mother who was emotionally unstable, who wouldn't bother to cook or clean, let alone help with homework or attend a school function, and who couldn't keep a job, which meant they'd had to move from one cheap duplex or mobile home to another. The only way to survive was to take over as the responsible person in the household, and that was exactly what Ellen had done.

Why'd it have to go that way? That was the question that had haunted Ellen for years. Why would her father let his new wife dictate how he treated his daughter? He'd been a good dad until he'd divorced Jan to move back to Coyote Canyon to be with Lynn. And, at ten, Ellen had had no idea her future happiness would depend on pleasing the cold, sharp-tongued interloper who'd caused the complete destruction of her world. The less welcoming her stepmother was, the angrier and more resentful she became, creating a vicious cycle that ended after only ten months, when Lynn refused to have her over at all.

Ellen remembered the first and only time, after she'd been banned from her father's house, that Grandma Lilly was able to prevail upon Stuart to drop off "the boys." Lilly had wanted to build a bridge between Stuart's daughter and his wife's son and nephew, hoping the situation might get better.

But Stuart only dropped off Hendrix—Leo was somewhere with his mother—and Hendrix had no interest in getting to know her. He'd spent his time avoiding or ignoring her, and the initial excitement she'd felt at possibly having someone in the Fetterman household who might finally accept her had quickly faded into a long day that turned out to be one of the loneliest she could remember. She was embarrassed, now, by how hard she'd tried to please him. She'd even given him the ten dollars her grandparents had put in a card for her birthday—which was all the money she had—and he'd taken it and shrugged it off as if it was nothing.

With a grimace at her eagerness and stupidity, she rubbed her stomach, which was beginning to ache from the angst she was feeling. She had to stop stewing about the past, or she'd give herself an ulcer.

Forget, she told herself. She was an adult now, in charge of her own destiny. She no longer needed her father, Hendrix, her mother or anyone else.

Her phone lit up in the dark room. Who would be texting her at one in the morning? "It'd better not be Jordan," she grumbled as she rolled over to check.

It was Hendrix.

I'm sorry I upset you.

Shit. Now that he had her number he could text her whenever he wanted.

She almost wrote back that he had it all wrong. Nothing he did or said could ever upset her. She didn't want him to believe he had that kind of power. She didn't trust him not to abuse it. But the saying *Methinks thou dost protest too much* popped into her mind in time to stop her.

After putting her phone back on the charger without responding, she eventually fell into the welcome respite of sleep.

Nine

Talulah could tell Ellen was agitated this morning. Her friend also had dark circles under her eyes. She didn't seem to be getting enough sleep. They often talked about how hard she was working—too hard in Talulah's opinion. But running your own business wasn't easy; Talulah knew that from experience. And today she was worried about something else. "I think you should go to the police and file a report on Jordan Forbes. Who knows how far things would've gone last night if Hendrix hadn't stepped in."

Talulah had heard a knock on the back door of the dessert diner before dawn and opened it to find Ellen, who'd insisted on helping her get ready for business. Ellen did that occasionally when she had the time, especially if she needed to talk. So while they'd finished baking Talulah's popular breakfast buns and opened the doors for the customers who lined up on the sidewalk each Saturday, Ellen had shared what'd happened with her date.

"I tried to call the police, but Hendrix stopped me," she responded. "And now, after how it went... I mean, Jordan got his ass handed to him. I don't want him to react by going after Hendrix for assault."

Talulah arched her eyebrows. "You're worried about what might happen to *Hendrix*?"

They'd survived the morning rush. After putting a sign on the door to indicate they were sold out of breakfast buns and closed for a short break, they were sitting at one of the small tables Brant had helped Talulah arrange out front, enjoying the warm spring weather, a cup of coffee and a croissant. Business slowed about this time every Saturday, and the bulk of the work at the diner was done for the day, but Ellen didn't seem very relaxed. "I'm not *worried*, exactly," she said. "I just don't want to turn it into a big deal when he was only trying to help. I'd feel the same about anyone who stepped in."

Cammie Cartwright, who owned the clothing shop down the street, walked by and gave Talulah a finger wave. Talulah nodded in return before continuing her conversation with Ellen. "I'd hate to see anything bad happen to Hendrix, too. And considering all the animosity of the past and present, I can see why you might not want his aunt and your father to know he was ever at your house. I'm just afraid if we don't do something about Dr. Forbes, he might try something similar on another woman."

"I'm going to report him on the dating site we've been using. He'll probably be kicked off. Or they'll put a warning label on his profile, letting potential matches know he's under review. That should make him leave the site on his own. Other than that, there's nothing more I can do. He didn't cross the line far enough to create any real legal troubles."

"He kissed you against your will," Talulah pointed out.

"True. But let's be honest. Even if I filed a complaint and Hendrix backed me up as a witness—which he might not be willing to do because that would attach his name to mine—I doubt Jordan would be arrested. The police might contact him and ask a few questions, but unless there've been other reports filed documenting something worse, like rape or molestation, they have too many bigger crimes to investigate. You can't punish people for every little thing they do, even if it's wrong. It's not practical."

"Sometimes you're too realistic. You know that?"

"You mean jaded?" Ellen said with a laugh.

Talulah took a sip of her coffee. "That, too."

"So much for online dating." Ellen tore off a piece of her croissant. "I knew it would be a mistake."

Talulah wasn't excited to hear Ellen say that. It wasn't easy meeting someone in such a small town, especially when you were a little too progressive for the area. She'd been hoping online dating would be the answer. Talulah wanted to see Ellen find someone who could love and appreciate her as much as she deserved. "One bad experience doesn't ruin everything," she argued.

"It does for me," Ellen responded with a grimace. "I was leery of going online to begin with."

"Does that mean you're getting off Together Forever?"

"I think so."

Talulah frowned. "Ellen, don't. It's a decent way to meet people if you're careful. Besides, it took us too long to create your profile to give up after the first guy." She was only half joking about the profile. She and Brant had taken the pictures Ellen had used, which had been a real chore since Ellen had been so critical of every one. Talulah had only persevered because she knew the pictures weren't the real problem. Ellen was afraid of failure. What'd happened with her father had convinced her that she didn't deserve love, so she refused to open herself up to the quick and easy rejection that came with online dating.

"You can say that after last night?"

"Hang in there. You'll meet the right guy eventually."

"That's not a given. Why risk another Jordan, especially when I'm fine with being alone?"

She was the most guarded person Talulah had ever met, and she had reason to be. Her past, not only with her family but with her previous boyfriends, had made her determined to get through life without ever being vulnerable again. But love required vulnerability. And Ellen needed love. Everyone did.

"What was Hendrix doing at your place so late at night, anyway?" Talulah asked, changing the subject. "That's what I don't understand."

"I told you. He said he came over to talk about a truce."

She'd mentioned that, but then they'd gotten busy and Talulah hadn't been able to ask for more details. "You never explained what the truce would entail."

Ellen set down her cup. "Because we never actually talked about it."

"Why not?"

"I had him leave. I don't want to call a truce. I don't want anything to do with him."

Talulah eyed her closely. Ellen often pretended she didn't want what she really wanted. It was a defense mechanism, in case she was disappointed. She'd been dying for her father's love and attention ever since he'd left her mother, and yet she insisted she hated him and wouldn't speak to him even if he tried to have a relationship with her. Talulah suspected the same might hold true for Hendrix—that deep down what she really wanted was to be accepted by him. "You couldn't have listened to him long enough to find out what he had to say?"

"There was no point. It wouldn't change anything."

"It would've satisfied my curiosity," Talulah pointed out with a grin. "Aren't *you* curious?"

Ellen finished the last of her croissant and dusted off her fingers. "Not at all."

Talulah couldn't fully believe that, either. But Averil Gerhart was coming down the sidewalk, and it was always awkward to run into her. They'd been friends since Talulah could remember, but in recent years their relationship had been difficult for several reasons, and it hadn't grown any easier after Talulah moved back to town and married the man Averil had hoped to get.

"Hey," Averil said. Normally she had Mitch, her six-year-old son, with her but today she was alone.

"Hey." Talulah smiled as brightly as possible. "What's up?"

Her eyes shifted to Ellen, which made Talulah even more uncomfortable. She didn't want this to turn into a confrontation. Several weeks ago, Ellen had overheard Averil and her mother talking about Talulah while grocery shopping, and it'd made Ellen mad enough that she'd approached them and told them off. Ellen was like that—fiercely defensive of those she loved.

Talulah hadn't seen Averil much since that incident, but what she had seen of her indicated she was going to pretend that it never happened, and Talulah was fine with that. She knew the Gerharts thought poorly of her, that her relationship with Averil would never be the way it was before. In ways, she couldn't blame them. She *had* hurt Averil's brother, Charlie, and she'd hurt Averil, too, when she fell in love with Brant.

But Ellen didn't like Averil, and after that incident in the grocery store, Talulah had no doubt the feeling was mutual.

"Hi, Ellen," Averil said.

Ellen narrowed her eyes but lifted her hand. It was a half-hearted wave at best. But Talulah was grateful she'd offered Averil that much. With any luck, it'd be enough to get them through the next few minutes without having an argument break out on the street. She knew Ellen certainly wouldn't back down from that sort of thing. She cared more about being honest than about what other people might think of her.

"Where's Mitch?" Talulah asked, partly to draw Averil's attention away from Ellen.

"He's with his father," Averil said.

Talulah had expected her to say Mitch was with his grandparents. Averil had been living with them ever since her divorce a few years back. Her parents helped her out a lot. "Cash is stepping up, at last?" Besides being neglectful and difficult to deal with, Averil's ex lived in California, so he wasn't close and didn't see his son very often.

"Not really. But his family is having a reunion and his mother begged me to let Mitch attend."

"I'm sorry things haven't gotten any better." That was a rather formal way to respond, and Talulah knew it. She sincerely wished the situation with Cash would improve, but she didn't know how to connect with Averil anymore. She almost wished they no longer lived in the same town. She would've stayed in Seattle and had Brant move there, but his family's cattle ranch kept him in Coyote Canyon.

Averil's eyes moved to the sign Talulah had posted on the door. "You're out of breakfast buns? That's too bad. I thought I'd stop in, say hello and grab one."

Talulah got up. "I'm afraid we sold out really fast today. But let me get you a croissant or something else. You can join Ellen and me and have a cup of coffee."

Once again Averil's gaze shot over to Ellen before landing on Talulah. "That's okay. I don't have much time. I just…thought I'd take my chances. With the bun, I mean."

"If you give me some notice that you're coming by, I'll save you one next week." Talulah only made them on Saturdays. Since she typically created and sold after-dinner desserts and not donuts, breakfast foods and the like, she didn't open the diner until much later on Sunday and weekdays.

"I'll do that." Averil slid a giant leather bag off her shoulder. "Oh, I almost forgot. I ran across some old photographs I thought you might like to have."

"Of…"

"Prom our senior year," she said as she pulled out a large manila envelope. "My mother took so many pictures—of all of us, remember?"

Her mother had done that because Charlie, Averil's older brother, had been Talulah's date. Charlie had been her boyfriend for years; she'd almost married him. It was jilting him at the altar that had initially ruined her friendship with Averil. Talulah took responsibility for that. But she'd been such a pleaser and so uncertain whether she'd be making a mistake giving up a guy who loved her so deeply she simply hadn't known how to get out of it any sooner—and then panicked at the last minute. "That's nice of you," she said but wondered at the same time if Averil was being passive-aggressive. Talulah already had her own pictures from prom that year. The previous year, too.

Was Averil trying to tell her that these photographs no longer mattered to Charlie or his family? That they preferred to be rid of them? Was that the message here?

"Thank you. I appreciate it," she said, trying to assume the best. "Are you sure I can't get you a croissant before you go?"

"No." Averil ran her hands over her hips. "I couldn't have refused a breakfast bun, so I'm sort of glad you're out of them. I'm trying to lose a few pounds."

Talulah wanted to ask if Averil was dating anyone. That was something she would've asked if things were still the way they used to be. But since she'd gotten involved with Brant, she knew how negatively that question would be interpreted. "You look great," she said instead, and Averil waved before walking away.

Ellen picked up the envelope Talulah put on the table when she sat back down, took the pictures out and looked them over. "Really?" she said flatly. "Why would you want these?"

"I have no idea," Talulah admitted. "I guess she's just trying to remind me what a terrible person I am to break her brother's heart by refusing to marry him and then stealing the man *she* wanted."

"It's her way of reminding you that you wronged her way more than she wronged you by talking bad about you in the grocery store. She wanted to let you know *you* committed the greater sin."

"I have no doubt you're right."

Ellen tossed the pictures aside. "She has to know Brant wouldn't want to see these, either."

What Ellen said was true. Charlie used to be his best friend, so when Brant got involved with Talulah, even though it'd been years since she and Charlie had nearly married, it had changed their relationship a great deal, too. "One of the downsides of living in a small town," she muttered with a sigh.

Ellen narrowed her eyes as she leaned around Talulah to watch Averil disappear down the street. "You'd better watch your back. You can't trust her."

Talulah didn't trust her. She just wouldn't admit it. She was trying to maintain her loyalty to a friendship that'd once meant a great deal to her. But she knew Ellen was right.

Hendrix had taken Leo with him to the hardware store. He could've waited until Monday, when he was working, but Leo had called, hoping he had somewhere to go, and Hendrix had decided to pick him up and grab a few things in town. His cousin loved running errands. He'd roll down the passenger window of Hendrix's pickup and wave enthusiastically at everyone they passed, calling most people by name, and since there were a lot of folks out on a Saturday morning, especially now that the weather was growing warmer, Hendrix knew it would be particularly fun for him.

"Why are we going so slow, Hendrix?" As happy as Leo was to be out, he was growing impatient. He wasn't as enthusiastic about this part of town, where the businesses were more spread out. He wanted to roll through the main intersection so he could see who was visiting the shops and eateries.

Hendrix slowed even more as they passed the Coyote Lodge, one of only two motels in town. "I'm looking for something."

"For what?"

"A car," Hendrix told him.

"What kind of car?"

"An Audi." He wanted to make sure Dr. Forbes had left town and wasn't hanging around to cause more trouble.

"What's an Audi?" Leo knew truck brands; he didn't know many car brands.

"A high performance car."

He looked confused. "What for? Are you going to buy it?"

"No." Hendrix relaxed when he didn't see Jordan's car. He hadn't found it when they drove past the Welcome Inn on the other side of town, either. Chances were Jordan had checked out and left like he was supposed to.

Leo probably would've followed up with another question. His curiosity knew no bounds. But they were approaching the Western wear shop at the edge of the central district—and then the bank—signaling that they were close to where he wanted to be.

"Hi, Chelsea!" he called out as the woman who cut their hair crossed the street in front of them while they waited at one of only two stoplights in town.

Chelsea looked up and waved.

"I'm out for a ride with my cousin," Leo told her, yelling louder since she was moving away from them. "We're looking for an Audi."

"Have fun!" she called back.

Probably because she couldn't really hear him, she hadn't asked *why* they were looking for an Audi, and Hendrix was glad. The fact that he'd been checking to see if Dr. Forbes was gone wasn't a national secret or anything, but he wasn't eager to explain that he'd beaten up some guy who'd gotten too forceful with Ellen. The details of where and when it happened would be weird, given that everyone believed them to be sworn enemies.

And they were enemies. Of course. They always would be, except…he wasn't feeling nearly as antagonistic toward her as he'd felt before. Truth be told, she was entering his thoughts far too often—and not in a negative way.

The light turned green while he weighed the cost-benefit ratio of telling Leo not to mention the Audi again and decided against it. That would only give his cousin more reason to remember it. Then he might make it part of every conversation he had today.

They passed two people Hendrix didn't recognize. Apparently, Leo didn't know who they were, either, but that didn't stop him from yelling out to them. "Hello! My name is Leo."

Startled, they looked over as if he'd thrown something at them, but Leo didn't seem to notice that they found his greeting a little too exuberant. He was grinning and hanging as far out the window as his seat belt would allow when they came to Talulah's Dessert Diner.

In his peripheral vision, Hendrix saw two people sitting out front, but there were always people at Talulah's on a Saturday morning. He was paying more attention to the traffic than what was happening elsewhere on the street. He was prepared for Leo to beg him to stop and get a treat and knew he had to say no; he wasn't prepared for Leo to yell, "Stop! That's Ellen! She's right there. See, Hendrix? That's her!"

Sure enough, it was Ellen. She looked over to see what all the fuss was about, and Hendrix saw her eyes widen when she realized it was them. She was wearing a tiered dress with a bulky sweater, big hoop earrings and work boots, and she looked so feminine, despite the boots, which weren't the type most women would pair with a dress, that Hendrix felt slightly out of sync. What was going on with him? He was starting to think she was pretty—*really* pretty. It was also becoming more and more appealing that she was bold and uncompromising and did things her own way even when it came to fashion.

Unfortunately, the car in front of them had to stop for someone at a crosswalk, bringing them to a standstill right in front of her and Talulah, who was sitting at the table with her. And as if Leo wasn't drawing too much attention already, he began to bang on the outside of his door. "Hi, Ellen! It's me, Leo! I can help you at the diner today. I'm here. Want me to help?" He tried to take off his seat belt as if he'd jump out and join her right then and there, but Hendrix stopped him.

"No, buddy. You have to leave that on while I'm driving. You know that."

Leo didn't get a chance to respond before Ellen yelled back, every bit as loudly, "Hi!" She didn't seem to care if she turned every head on the street. She even got up and hurried to his side of the vehicle to give him a quick hug while they were stopped. "I'm not working today," she told him. "But you can come tomorrow, okay? We'll give Talulah a break and take over the diner for a few hours."

"You want me to come tomorrow?" Leo looked immediately at Hendrix. "Can I? Will you drive me over, Hendrix? Will you? Please?"

Hendrix shifted his gaze away from his cousin's pleading eyes and met Ellen's instead. He expected to see the old hostility in them. But he didn't get the impression she was feeling hostile at all. What he saw was confusion. Things were changing between them, and she could feel it, too.

The car in front of them drove off, so Hendrix was free to go. But he kept his foot on the brake for another moment. Stuart and Lynn wouldn't like him fostering a relationship between Ellen and Leo, but the two seemed genuinely drawn to each other. "Sure," he said. "What time?"

"Did you just tell Leo that you'd let him help you here at the diner tomorrow?" Talulah asked when Ellen walked back to their table.

Ellen was almost as surprised as Talulah was. The invitation had tumbled out of her mouth before she could think of all the implications—or even ask her friend for permission. "He loved being in the kitchen so much last time that… I don't know. Sunday afternoons are usually a little slow. It won't hurt to let him come, will it? If you don't want to take the time off and leave the diner to us, maybe he and I could join you for an hour or so, and I'll chaperone while he does a few things to help."

Talulah started to laugh.

"What?" Ellen said.

"You are the biggest softie I've ever met. And yet I've never seen anyone try harder to hide it."

Ellen rolled her eyes. "Stop. I'm not soft. I just… couldn't disappoint him. I'm not going to hold what I feel for my derelict father and my *Hansel and Gretel–*like stepmother against Leo. He's completely innocent."

"And he *loves* you."

Ellen wouldn't go that far. They barely knew each other. But that was the beauty of Leo. He opened his heart to everyone. He seemed to accept her and everyone else exactly as they were—no qualifying necessary. "He loves everyone," she pointed out.

Talulah began to gather up their dishes. "You seem to be a new favorite. But that doesn't surprise me. You're way easier to love than you think."

"It's okay, then?"

"Of course it's okay. Brant will be thrilled to hear I have another day off. I've been putting so much into my business that we haven't been able to finish a few of the projects we've been working on around the house—like getting our storage organized in the basement."

"You should ask me to run the diner more often. I can spell you."

"You work hard enough as it is. It's so nice of you to do this for me and for Leo. But I have to admit, I'm surprised Hendrix would agree to bring him here tomorrow so he can be with you."

That had taken Ellen aback, too. He'd been hesitant to agree—she'd read that in his expression after she'd made the offer—but not quite opposed to the idea. Otherwise, he would've said no. That he'd agreed signaled a monumental shift. "Leo only needs a ride. Not a big deal."

"It *is* a big deal. Hendrix has to cross the Wicked Witch of the North in order to give his cousin that ride, which is saying something."

Ellen hadn't considered that he'd been making a choice between her and his aunt. Or maybe it was between Leo and his aunt, and that was why he'd done it. "Then why do you think he agreed?" she asked.

Talulah smiled. "I think Leo's not the only one who's starting to like you."

It was Ellen's turn to laugh. "It'll be a cold day in hell when Hendrix likes me. It wasn't that long ago he tried to steal my driller. The increase in Ben's wages is killing me, and I have Hendrix to thank for that."

Talulah started toward the door. "You have to get Ben to be reasonable again."

That was easier said than done, or Ellen would've made it happen already. But after struggling through the past week, she'd come to the same conclusion. She couldn't continue to employ him, not at the wage he was demanding. "I know. I have to tell him that I'm going to hire and train someone else, and he can go work for Hendrix."

Concern filled Talulah's face as she turned. "Will you be able to manage until you can get up to full speed again?"

"I'll have to. What's happening now isn't sustainable."

"Then he either accepts what you can pay, or he moves on."

"He won't have any other choice—because I don't have any other choice." Ellen held the door so Talulah could carry in the dishes, then took down their "break" sign. "He's attending an out-of-town wedding, and I don't want to ruin it for him, so I'll wait until Monday to talk to him, when he's back."

A fork fell and clattered on the floor as Talulah whisked around the counter. "It'll be interesting to see if Hendrix will really hire him," she said as Ellen picked it up for her. "Especially at the salary he offered."

"Maybe I've actually raised the price for him. That would be poetic justice, wouldn't it?"

"Indeed."

Ellen followed her friend into the kitchen to get her purse and keys. The morning rush was over. She was going to leave Talulah at the diner and head to the hardware store so she could try, once again, to fix the sink in her guest bathroom. "Yeah. I give up. If Hendrix wants Ben, he can have him."

Talulah deposited the dishes in the sink. "What if Hendrix wasn't making him a sincere offer?"

"What do you mean?"

"It could be that he was only trying to get under your skin and show you some of the things he *could* do if he ever really decided to come after you."

Ellen hadn't even considered that. "We'll find out soon enough," she said. "Because if that's the case, I'm about to call his bluff."

Ten

Hendrix didn't go out that night. He was too busy thinking about Ellen. He couldn't stop seeing her in that dress with her sweater falling casually off one shoulder and work boots on her feet—and somehow liking the unusual combination. Her appearance had been growing on him. But her unique beauty, especially her doe-like eyes, was making more of an impact all the time.

What was he going to do about Ellen? What *could* he do? Between his aunt and what she'd demanded of her husband—which was a full and unequivocal commitment to her, her son and her nephew at the sacrifice of his daughter—and how much Ellen resented all of them for cutting her out of the family, there didn't seem to be anything he could do to improve the situation.

For his own sake, he should draw a hard line and continue to ignore her presence in town. Because if he let his heart soften and started to care about her, he'd only be handing her a weapon she could use to exact revenge.

But it was already too late. The disappointment he'd felt last night when she wouldn't even hear him out was proof that he'd already started to care. So...how could he regain his distance, especially if he was also battling

Leo's growing fascination with her? Did he try to put a stop to that, too?

No way. Leo would never allow it.

Lynn would die if she knew her son and her nephew were so taken with Ellen. He was willing to bet she would never forgive him for that...

He'd just taken a seat in front of the TV when he saw a flash of light at the window. A car was turning into his drive. Kurt had mentioned stopping by to watch an NBA game and generally smacked the door once to announce his presence before letting himself in, especially if Hendrix was already expecting him. But there was no knock. It wasn't until he saw the same lights through the window that he realized whoever had pulled into his yard was already leaving.

He got up and opened the door. There was a bag on his front mat, and inside was his freshly laundered shirt. After the way Forbes had grabbed it and ripped it during their fight, the neck would never be quite the same, but Ellen had found a way to get it clean and had folded it carefully before putting it in the sack.

He held the cotton fabric to his nose. It smelled good—like her house.

She could've brought it to the diner and given it to him tomorrow, and yet she'd made a special trip. Could that signify anything? A possible softening?

No, he decided. She probably hadn't wanted anyone to see her return something like that to him. It might invite speculation.

She could've knocked on the door and handed it to him in person, though. His truck was parked in the drive. She had to have known he was home.

Instead, she'd quietly dropped it off and left.

He pulled his phone from his pocket as he went back inside. You could've said hello.

No response.

We don't have to be enemies, you know, he wrote, trying again.

Finally, he saw the three dots that indicated she was typing something.

I appreciate your help last night.

No comment on his offer of friendship. That's all you have to say?

That and I'm going to fire Ben on Monday. He's all yours.

"Shit," he muttered and sank onto the couch as he tossed his phone on the side table.

Talulah had called first thing to say she'd open the diner and would leave when Ellen arrived. Since her parents and sister lived elsewhere, it was rare that Talulah had someone to stand in for her, so Ellen could see why she might want to take advantage of every opportunity.

She hadn't set a specific time with Hendrix and Leo, but she took over for Talulah at one and didn't have long to wait. Hendrix showed up with Leo at ten to two—about the same time they'd come before.

"Hi, Ellen!" Leo called, blasting through the door with the power of a gale force wind. "I'm here! I came to help you like I said I would."

"And I'm all ready for you," Ellen told him.

Hendrix entered several seconds after Leo, moving far more casually.

"Are we going to wash dishes again?" Leo asked.

"We can do that later if you like. I thought you might want to help me serve customers for a while first."

Leo's eyes went wide. "Did you hear that, Hendrix? I get to serve customers!"

Hendrix removed his sunglasses. Sadly, he looked stronger and more handsome than ever in a Fetterman Well Services T-shirt and a pair of loose-fitting jeans that fell low on his hips. It was slightly enraging that he'd turned out to be such a perfect male specimen. As far as Ellen was concerned, he'd had plenty of luck in other areas—did he deserve this, too? For years, she'd tried to identify some fatal flaw in him, some character trait or shortcoming that would enable her to feel slightly superior in at least one or two areas.

But if he had a flaw, it certainly wasn't in the looks department.

"I heard, buddy," he said. "I know you'll do a great job."

Ellen tried not to catch Hendrix's eye. She could tell he had something to say to her. He probably wanted to tell her to take good care of Leo. But she would do that regardless of any input from him. She didn't need him to say it. The less interaction they had, the better.

She got the apron she'd brought from home—the one Grandpa Pete always wore when he took over the canning after Grandma Lilly started to decline—and helped Leo get it on over his head. It wasn't branded. He was so big Talulah had nothing with the diner logo that would fit him. But she was guessing he wouldn't know the difference. "Turn around and I'll tie it for you," she told him.

He smoothed the canvas fabric again and again, obviously excited to feel so official, as he allowed her to tie the strings. Then he yelled out to his cousin. "Do you see this, Hendrix? I have my own apron and everything!"

Hendrix remained just inside the door. Maybe he could feel her resistance to having him stay because he didn't come any closer. "I can see that," he said. "You look very sharp."

As soon as Ellen finished tying the apron, Leo loped over to the windows. "When do you think we'll get a customer?"

"I hope soon," Ellen said. "We want a big sales day for Talulah, don't we?"

"Yes!" he answered as if it was his most fervent wish.

Hendrix slipped his sunglasses into the pocket of his T-shirt. "Has it been busy so far?"

Ellen began to rearrange the cash register area, even though everything was already where it should be. "Talulah opened. She said the first hour was busy—people coming to pick up dessert for dinner before certain pies and cakes could sell out. After the first little bit, Sundays can be slow, although we typically get another flurry right before we close."

"You know a lot about the diner."

"Talulah's my best friend and my neighbor. She's talked about it since before she opened it. And, as you know, I work here every now and then."

He came closer. "She can't be paying you much…"

"It's not about the pay."

"You're good to your friends," he said.

Ellen blinked in surprise. "Is that…a compliment?" she asked uncertainly.

His eyebrows slid up. "You can't tell?"

"It sounded like a compliment," she said. "But it was coming from you."

He studied her for several moments, long enough to make her even more uncomfortable.

"What?" she said, somewhat defensively.

He grinned—a warm, inviting grin she'd never seen him turn on *her* before. "What if I'm not the ogre you've made me out to be?"

Ellen didn't know how to respond. Even though she didn't want to feel anything, that damn grin warmed her from the pit of her stomach all the way out to her fingers and toes. "There are…there are a lot of people who think you're great."

"Just not you."

She cleared her throat. "We're in an unusual situation."

"I didn't choose my role in what happened any more than you did," he pointed out.

"Yeah, well, sucks to be Stuart's favorite, right?" she said with a humorless laugh. Did he expect her to feel sorry for him? He had everything she'd ever wanted—what she would've had if his aunt hadn't stolen her father.

Hendrix glanced at Leo, who was still preoccupied looking through the large front windows for people who might come in, and lowered his voice. "You know what your mother is like, Ellen."

Ellen. He didn't usually say her name. She told herself she didn't like the sound of it on his lips, but deep down she knew if there was no history between them she would've liked it a lot. He reminded her of Brant in some ways, and Brant was special enough that it'd been hard for her when he'd moved on—not that she'd ever begrudged him and Talulah the happiness they'd found. She wasn't like Averil. She understood she just wasn't the right fit for him. They hadn't even slept together, so they hadn't gotten especially close. It wasn't as if he'd broken her heart or anything. Besides, she'd always believed that if someone didn't or couldn't return her feelings, she was better off letting that person go.

"What's that supposed to mean?" She tried to remain focused on his words and not the deep rumble of his voice, or the dimples that had appeared in his cheeks when he grinned at her.

"It means that your dad wouldn't have stayed with her for long even if he hadn't run into my aunt. There would've been *someone* else. He wasn't fulfilled in the relationship."

"You're saying I should be mad at my mother instead of my father?" she demanded.

"Not exactly. Just reminding you of the whole situation. Your father should've stood up to my aunt and delivered for you. There's no doubt about that. But he'd just been through a divorce, and I think he didn't want to risk another one."

"Forgive me if I'm not feeling too sorry for him, either."

"I'm not done. Then there's Lynn. She probably deserves the most blame. After not meaning nearly enough to her first husband, she demanded her next one sacrifice too much to prove his devotion and loyalty. She was determined to have her life just the way *she* wanted it at last and wouldn't compromise by including a child who wasn't her own. Or," he added, "wasn't connected to her by blood."

She stared at him, stunned. She'd never expected Hendrix to share his thoughts on the matter, let alone have him lay it all out so neatly for her. But in her view, he deserved some of the blame, too. He could've made things easier, could've reached out and tried to help bridge the gap—and yet he never did. Not even when he grew older and probably understood how unfair the situation had been to her. And he certainly hadn't been happy when she moved to town. "I don't remember *you* offering me any kindness," she said.

Her comeback caused him to sober and straighten.

"Or is that *my* fault?" she continued. "I'm just *that* unlikable?"

The compassion that filled his blue eyes embarrassed her. She'd used a snarky tone, but she knew he'd felt the pain underlying her words. "You're not unlikable at all, Ellen," he said gently. "I should have done more. I'm sorry I didn't."

Before she could recover from the shock of his response, Leo spoke as if he was so disappointed he could hardly bear it. "No one's coming in! How am I supposed to work if we don't have any customers?"

Ellen could tell Hendrix had said his piece and wanted to leave—get away so they could both escape the awkward strain of being near each other. But he didn't go; he stepped up to the counter. "You don't need any other customers, bud," he said. "You haven't served me."

Immediately brightening, Leo hurried around the counter, and Ellen had to respect Hendrix for always going out of his way to make his cousin happy. Whether she liked it or not, that said something very flattering about him.

"What do you want?" Leo asked. "I'll get you whatever you ask me for."

Ellen would've smiled. Leo was so easy to please. But she was too torn. Did she owe Hendrix her forgiveness? Would she become the jerk in this situation if she couldn't or wouldn't offer it?

She almost wished he *hadn't* taken responsibility for his part in the situation and apologized, because now she had to decide how to react. Forgiving him would mean letting go of the resentment she'd held for so long. But how could she ever get beyond the jealousy that'd caused the resentment? Forget that her father had preferred him to her?

And still did…

Hendrix pointed at one of the cakes under the glass. "I'll have the carrot," he told his cousin.

Leo wrinkled his nose. "That has raisins in it."

Hendrix laughed. "Well, I wasn't planning on sharing it with you. You can't eat while you're working, Leo."

"Can't you just give me a bite?"

"No, because it's not professional."

Leo gazed longingly at all the other cakes and pies. "What if I'm not working? Can I have my own cake then?"

"We didn't come here to eat," Hendrix reminded him. "And you know you'd just beg to go back to work as soon as you finished your cake."

Leo gave him an impish smile. "Yeah," he agreed as if Hendrix had caught him. "I want to work for Ellen."

"I'm happy to hear that," Ellen said and handed Leo a plate and the cake server. "Do you think you can get your cousin's cake while I ring him up?"

"Of course I can," he said, but Ellen watched him out of the corner of her eye while she accepted Hendrix's debit card. She was afraid Leo might accidentally dump the entire cake on the floor when he removed it from the display case. But he moved very slowly, trying to be extra careful, and managed to get it onto the counter without mishap. Since all their cakes and pies were scored, he had a guide for where to cut, which he followed fairly well. The only thing he did wrong was use his hand to slide Hendrix's cake off the server and onto the plate—and then he licked his fingers.

"Yum. The frosting is *so* good," he said, completely unaware that he shouldn't have touched the food. "Isn't it good, Hendrix?"

"I'm about to find out," he replied.

Ellen let the finger-lick go. She figured she'd just warn Leo when the next customer came in. He'd be more likely to remember if she told him at the moment he needed to know.

Hendrix took the plate and accepted a fork from Leo, as well. "Thanks, bud. Great job."

Leo's smile stretched from ear to ear. "Let me know when you want another piece."

"I won't want another piece," Hendrix assured him. "One will be enough."

Leo hovered over and around his cousin until Hendrix let him scrape the excess frosting off the plate and eat it. Fortunately, no one else was in the restaurant to see that, so it didn't matter.

"I'm just going to hang out in town for an hour or two so I can take him home with me," he said when he handed Leo the plate and Ellen told Leo to take it to the sink in back.

Ellen lowered her voice so Leo wouldn't be able to hear. "It's fine if you want to leave him here with me. I can give him a ride after we close." If it would save her from having to be around Hendrix again, why not? She could pull down his drive, let Leo out and take off.

"To my place?" he clarified.

"I can promise you I'm not going to my father's house," she responded.

"Right," he said. "That works. Just…call me if something comes up or you change your mind."

A trio of older women Ellen recognized from when she'd worked at the diner before came in, saving her from having to say anything else to Hendrix. As she greeted them, she heard him admonish Leo to behave and to listen to her as his boss or he'd have to come back for him. Then he left.

While the women chatted about what was especially good at the diner and who was going to order what, and Leo was busy telling them he was there to help and he'd get them any cake they wanted but really thought they should get the chocolate because it was his favorite— Ellen allowed her eyes to follow Hendrix out the door. She even watched through the window as he climbed into his truck. She didn't trust him, but she couldn't deny that he had more than his fair share of sex appeal.

He could have any friend he wanted. With that face and that body he could have any woman, too. So why was he suddenly being so sweet to *her*?

Eleven

Leo wasn't home yet. Hendrix frowned as he checked his watch. Five thirty. He was fairly certain the diner was closed. So where was his cousin?

Surely, Ellen hadn't gotten frustrated or mad at Leo and left him to his own devices. She'd been so kind to him whenever they'd come into contact with her recently that he hated to think she might do something like that. Or it could be that Leo got upset over something he did wrong—or felt he did wrong—and took off on his own. He couldn't tolerate conflict. If someone so much as raised his or her voice at him, he'd try to escape. Maybe he'd dropped a cake or a piece of pie on a customer who got angry and ran out the door, and she was looking for him. It could even be that she was having to keep an eye on him while handling an entirely different problem.

Hey, everything okay? Need me to come get Leo?

He sent Ellen that text, then flipped through a few more channels on TV while waiting for a response. But fifteen minutes later, he hadn't heard back.

He figured he should drive by the restaurant just in case there was a problem. Stuart and Lynn were expecting them for Sunday dinner at six thirty, and he didn't want to have to explain that he'd left it up to Ellen to get Leo home. Lynn was going to be mad enough when Leo announced that he'd been helping Ellen at the diner again, because even if Hendrix told him not to say anything, Leo would probably talk about it all through dinner. Then Lynn would stare daggers at him for going against her wishes, and Stuart would keep his gaze fastened to his plate and shovel down his food to get the meal over with as quickly as possible so he could escape. When it came to conflict, Ellen's father wasn't unlike Leo.

Hendrix knew Lynn would find out, so he expected that much to happen. He just hadn't expected to run into any additional complications…

He was halfway to town when his phone signaled a text. He'd finally heard from Ellen.

Sorry. Leo wanted to see my house, so we swung by after leaving the diner, and Talulah and Brant happened to walk over with a bottle of wine. We're just sitting out front for a bit. Is it okay if I bring him back after they go home?

She probably couldn't imagine that Leo would have anywhere else to go tonight. She didn't know Sunday dinners were a regular event in the Fetterman household because she'd never been invited.

Hendrix was beginning to feel guilty about everything she'd missed. Through the years, it'd been easiest to keep his mouth shut and just do his thing—go along with the status quo his aunt had established almost from the beginning of her second marriage. That was the pattern Stuart had followed, too.

But the more he considered the situation from Ellen's perspective, the worse he felt. Which was why he'd apologized today.

There wasn't anything else he could do about the past, he told himself. He could only try to get Leo home so that Lynn wouldn't freak out any more than he'd anticipated from the start. If he drove over to Ellen's to get Leo right now, they could still make dinner on time.

The drive didn't take long. Ellen lived on the other side of town, but he was there in twelve minutes and could see her, Talulah and Brant sitting around a small table on the porch when he pulled into the drive. Leo was drawing with chalk on the concrete nearby but came galloping toward him soon as he heard Hendrix pull in and recognized his truck.

"Look," he cried, holding up a thick piece of blue chalk as Hendrix climbed out. "I'm drawing pictures."

"Where'd you get that?" Hendrix asked.

"I bought it! Ellen took me to the store to spend the money I earned today."

"You earned money?"

"Yep! And I bought this," he repeated proudly.

If Ellen wasn't careful, she was going to have Leo begging to see her every day. Or maybe she wasn't too worried about that. She was usually working, like he was, so she couldn't take him very often. Working at trying to put him and Stuart out of business, Hendrix reminded himself. But somehow there wasn't any fire in his anger over that. Where had it gone?

He had no idea, but he still had a problem with Ben, who'd probably be coming to him for a job next week, and he wasn't sure how he was going to handle it. "You must've been a big help," he told Leo.

"I was."

Hendrix turned his attention to the three people who'd gotten up and were now walking toward him. "Hey."

"Didn't you get my text?" Ellen asked, visibly perplexed.

"I did, but I was already in my truck, coming to see if something was wrong, so I decided to drop by so you wouldn't have to bring him home later."

"I'm sorry you had to come all the way out here," she said. "I should've texted sooner. I guess I assumed you wouldn't be paying such close attention to the clock."

For the first time, they were acting like friends, as if they'd gotten along for years. It felt much better than the animosity that'd defined their relationship so far. "Just didn't want to put you out," he said. He didn't plan to mention the dinner Lynn was making. That would only highlight why they'd had so many problems in the past. "Thanks for being so good to him." He gestured at the stick figures and various shapes Leo had drawn and colored on Ellen's driveway. "He's obviously had a blast."

"He was a lot of help," she said. "Weren't you, Leo?"

Leo was too busy finishing his latest masterpiece to respond, and the conversation quickly moved on as Brant, whom he'd known most of his life because of his friendship with the younger Elway boys, and Talulah, who'd been a few years ahead of him in school, both said hello.

"Come have a glass of wine with us," Brant said, motioning him toward the table and chairs they'd been using.

Hendrix was feeling pressure to get to Lynn and Stuart's house. But he hesitated to say he had to take Leo and go, because he didn't want to seem unreceptive now that Ellen was becoming less combative with him. She'd been very kind to his cousin, and since Lynn was going to be mad anyway, he figured he might as well stay for a few minutes. "Sure thing," he said. "Thanks."

Ellen went inside, and while she was gone, Talulah patted the chair between hers and the one Ellen would apparently be taking when she returned. "Have a seat. It's such a beautiful evening."

Intending to text his aunt once he settled into the group and they were no longer giving him their full attention, he set his phone on the table rather than slipping it into his pocket. "The diner seems to be doing well."

"We've been lucky—haven't we?" She turned to her husband. "I thought it would take a lot longer to establish the sales volume we've been doing recently. The breakfast buns have been such a big hit. That really helps."

Brant nodded. "I admit I was more than a little worried when Talulah decided to sell her interest in the restaurant in Seattle to open one here," he told Hendrix. "Going from the big city to such a small town—it could easily have been the wrong call."

"Good food sells anywhere," Hendrix said.

"She's put a lot of blood, sweat and tears into that diner." Brant clicked his tongue. "I'm just glad she doesn't regret giving up what she had before to marry me."

"I could never regret marrying you," she said, reaching over to take his hand.

"Now that the restaurant's up and running, the hardest part should be behind you," Hendrix said.

Brant kissed his wife's knuckles. "Here's hoping. But you know what it's like to run a business."

Before Hendrix could respond, Talulah leaned forward and lowered her voice. "I'm glad you and Ellen are starting to get to know each other. She's a much better person than you probably realize."

"I've never thought she was a bad one."

"She's special," Talulah pronounced.

Hendrix couldn't disagree. "I know."

His response caused her to rock back in surprise. "You do?"

The door opened and Ellen stepped out with another wineglass, and he was glad. It saved him from having to clarify his feelings.

Ellen didn't say anything when she handed Brant the glass and he poured Hendrix some red wine. "Here you go," he said.

As Hendrix accepted the wine, he hoped Ellen didn't mind that he was joining their small group. Judging by her expression and body language, she was tentatively okay with it. But when she sat down their legs accidentally brushed. Since they were both wearing shorts, it was skin-to-skin contact, and she immediately slid her chair farther away so it couldn't happen again.

"Did the diner get busy after I left?" he asked.

"It was slow for a bit but picked up around three thirty," Ellen replied. "I was grateful to have Leo there to get customers water and silverware and carry dishes into the back. He did a great job."

"I did a great job, Hendrix," Leo echoed, suddenly tuning in.

Leo's response drew an affectionate smile from Ellen, and the fact that she seemed to have such a big soft spot for him made Hendrix feel a certain amount of affection for *her*. Which was crazy. Considering how unreceptive and antagonistic she'd been to him in the past, unless he wanted to have it thrown back in his face, it was dangerous to feel *any* positive emotion where she was concerned. "I don't think he was expecting to get paid."

"But you should've seen how excited he was to have his own money to spend at the store," she said.

Brant set his empty glass on the table. "That's all he's talked about."

Hendrix took a sip of his wine. "I bet."

"I'm drawing a picture for you, Ellen," Leo announced. "Because you're my favorite."

Ellen was suddenly Leo's favorite? "Whoa, what about me, bud?" Hendrix said, pretending he was wounded. "Some pretty girl catches your eye, and you drop me?"

"You're my favorite, too," Leo quickly assured him and cast an uncertain glance at Talulah and Brant, making it obvious he was hoping they wouldn't say anything because he hadn't included them on his list.

Everyone laughed at how obvious that look was. "I love you, Leo," Talulah said. "You always tell the truth."

"Am I being funny?" Leo asked uncertainly.

"Only in a good way," Hendrix reassured him, and Leo was so used to trusting him to navigate anything he found too confusing that he was immediately mollified and went back to drawing more pictures.

Brant talked about some acreage he was hoping to buy adjacent to his family's ranch, Talulah talked about a new oven that would make it possible for her to bake more breakfast rolls at one time, since they were so popular, and he and Ellen simply commented on what they said. He wasn't about to bring up his own business, and he guessed Ellen steered clear of introducing the subject of drilling for the same reason—that could cause some contention between them.

After ten minutes, during which he hadn't had the chance to text his aunt, Hendrix picked up his phone and stood. He needed to take Leo and go before Lynn started blowing up his phone with calls and texts asking where they were.

But he would rather have stayed, which surprised him. He'd been enjoying himself. He liked seeing Ellen out in front of her own house, relaxed and happy in a yellow sleeveless shirt with tiered ruffles at the bottom and a pair of cutoffs with no shoes. She had her bare feet tucked underneath her and was smiling as she slowly sipped her wine, and he couldn't help thinking, When did she get so pretty? So sexy?

He let his gaze lower over her muscular, gymnast-type of body but quickly pulled it up to her face when he realized she'd noticed he was looking at her. "Thanks for the wine. But I'd better take Leo and go."

"So soon?" Talulah said. "Just before you got here, we were talking about grilling some burgers. You and Leo should stay for dinner."

Ellen seemed slightly startled that her best friend had extended such an invitation, but she didn't say anything, and Hendrix actually wished he could accept the offer. "It's nice of you to include us. We can't stay tonight, but I hope there'll be another opportunity."

"We have to go home now?" Leo said, a whine in his voice. "I don't want to go yet. I'm having fun. Can't we stay here and eat?"

Hendrix didn't want to remind him that they were supposed to have dinner with Lynn and Stuart. "Not tonight."

"If you have to be somewhere, he can stay and I can bring him home later," Ellen offered.

He shifted his gaze to her with her unusual eyes and pixie-like face. "I'd love to let him, but I can't."

"Okay." She got up and started gathering the chalk.

"Leo, you have to go now, but you can come back soon. Do you want to take your chalk with you or leave it here for next time?"

"I can come back?" Leo said, clearly pleased by the idea.

"Of course. Whenever I'm home and not too busy."

"Okay," he said and chose to leave the chalk.

At first that surprised Hendrix. He couldn't imagine Leo wouldn't want to take it home, if only to show his mother and stepfather what he'd earned. But then he realized Leo probably understood that leaving something that belonged to him at Ellen's place would help ensure he'd really get to return.

Hendrix helped pick up the chalk and handed all the pieces to Ellen, who put them back into the big plastic bucket they'd come in.

"I'll store this in the garage for next time," she promised Leo and set it down before walking out to the truck with them, where she gave Leo a hug.

"I can come back?" he confirmed once again when she let go of him.

"Of course," she said.

"When?"

"Hendrix has my number. We can arrange something for this coming week."

Seemingly placated, Leo climbed into the truck, leaving Hendrix and Ellen standing there, looking at each other. After the affection she'd shown Leo, it would've been natural for her to hug him, too—if he were anyone else.

But he wasn't.

"Thanks for everything you've done for him," Hendrix said, gesturing vaguely to the passenger seat, where Leo was putting on his seat belt.

Ellen shoved her hands in the pockets of her cutoffs as if she felt the same awkward tension between them. "No problem."

He started to open his door but turned back at the last second. "Maybe I can come back sometime, too," he said and was gratified when she didn't react as negatively as he'd expected. As a matter of fact, she didn't react negatively at all. She seemed surprised but ultimately gave him a somewhat confused response.

"If you want to."

He grinned at her. "I want to," he said. Then he waved at Brant and Talulah who were still sitting on the porch. "Night," he called out and couldn't resist whistling to Neil Diamond's "Cherry, Cherry" which was playing on Leo's favorite radio station as he drove with his cousin to the Fetterman house. There was something exciting about Ellen's reaction when he'd shown interest in returning. It hadn't been an unequivocal, excited *yes*. But it'd been a yes that suggested he wasn't the only one who was feeling differently about their relationship.

"I love Ellen," Leo said.

Hendrix chuckled. "I can see why."

"That went well," Talulah said, smiling coyly as Ellen returned to the porch.

Ellen chose to play dumb. "What went well?"

"Having Leo and Hendrix here," Brant replied, also smiling like the Cheshire Cat.

"I much prefer Leo to Hendrix," Ellen said, reclaiming her glass.

"Of course," Talulah said. "Leo's harmless. He could never hurt you."

"Hendrix couldn't hurt me, either," she argued, pretending he didn't matter enough to make that possible.

But she was leery of him for a reason. She tried telling herself it had everything to do with how he'd made her feel on the occasions she'd seen him while she was growing up—unaccepted, unattractive, unwanted and inferior—but that wasn't the entire truth, and she knew it. The way he was talking to her and looking at her lately was…discomfiting. But in a much more positive sense. It was almost as if he found her attractive—not that she could believe that was truly the case. She didn't think she'd be Hendrix's type even if they didn't have good reason to dislike each other. "He's just grateful that I'm being so good to Leo," she said. "Leo means a lot to him."

"I'm sure he is grateful for that," Brant said. "He's been protecting Leo ever since he moved in with Lynn and Stuart. It's probably a breath of fresh air to have someone else care about him, too."

"Everyone who knows Leo cares about him," Ellen said, shrugging off Brant's words.

"Not necessarily," Talulah said. "They know him and might give him a kind word or a wave when they see him, but they don't take a personal interest and help entertain him the way you have."

Ellen finished what was in her glass. "Maybe that's true. But I'm not doing it for Hendrix."

"He's still grateful," Brant pointed out.

"Why *are* you doing it?" Talulah asked.

"I don't know. I guess it's because…because Leo's so easy to love."

"And you need someone to love. I've been telling you that for a long time."

She needed someone to love *her*. But she'd needed that for years, which was why she'd finally allowed Talulah to convince her to try online dating. The person she was looking for wasn't Leo. "I just enjoy being around him." His innocence and sweetness made her feel good. So did his lack of criticism and judgment.

"Could befriending Leo have anything to do with your father?" Talulah asked.

"In what way?"

"Just to bug him? Get back at him a little bit?"

If she wanted to get back at anyone, it'd be Lynn more than her father. Well, maybe not. She held her father accountable for allowing Lynn to do what she'd done. So maybe she was subconsciously taking some sort of joy in becoming one of Leo's favorite people. But it wasn't anything she was doing specifically for that reason. "Making Leo love me wouldn't be enough to give me any sort of revenge. He loves everyone."

Talulah eyed her closely. "What about making *Hendrix* love you?"

"That would be impossible," she said with a laugh, pretending to dismiss it out of hand. But she wasn't entirely convinced of that anymore. He'd just asked if he could come back to her house sometime. Why? What did he want?

The way he'd looked at her when she was wearing her robe and how he'd behaved ever since made her think he wasn't just seeking peace. And yet she couldn't fully believe he wanted more than that, either.

Twelve

As expected, Lynn wasn't happy they were late.

"Where've you been?" she demanded as soon as he and Leo walked through the front door.

Hendrix would've preferred to be the one who answered that question. He would've remained vague—said they got caught up, apologized and left it at that. But Leo piped up with the full truth before he could respond, which was also predictable. "We were at Ellen's, Mom. She took me to the store, and I bought sidewalk chalk, and I drew all over the driveway."

Lynn almost dropped the casserole she'd been taking from the oven. Hendrix reached out to grab the hot dish but fortunately didn't have to because it landed on the stove with a thump, sloshing a little over one side. And Stuart, who was already sitting at the table waiting to eat, jerked his head up.

"Did you say *Ellen*?" Lynn's eyes narrowed accusatorily as she glared at Hendrix. "What's going on?"

Hendrix did his best to downplay the fact that he knew he'd been doing something she wouldn't like. "Nothing, really. Leo saw Ellen while we were driving through town yesterday and asked if he could help at the diner again. She said yes. So I took him over there earlier today."

"She doesn't own the diner," Lynn said. "Talulah does. Why's she there every weekend?"

"It's not *every* weekend," he explained. "She helps out now and then, which is kind of her. Otherwise, Talulah would hardly ever get a break."

Lynn's mouth parted as though his response had taken her off guard. "Kind of her…" she repeated, stunned.

"You can't hate *everything* about her," he said drily.

Probably because there was no rational way to argue with that statement, she didn't follow up on it. "Why would she let Leo come to her place?"

"Why wouldn't she?" he countered.

"You know why. She hates all of us."

"No, she just hates you, Stuart and me. She doesn't hate him."

"She's taking advantage of the fact that he doesn't know to stay away from her. She's been trying to hurt us any way she can ever since she came to town. She's just switched weapons, that's all."

"Not really," he said as he took a piece of watermelon from the bowl that was waiting to be placed on the table, then popped it in his mouth. "She's still going after our business."

"And you can be friendly to her, considering that?" she cried.

"We wronged her first."

"In what way?" she demanded.

"In just about every way," he replied.

She threw her oven mitts into the sink. "What the hell are you talking about?"

He swallowed the watermelon. "I'm not trying to upset you. Just…calm down, okay?"

"I'm not going to calm down!" she snapped. "I want to know what we've ever done to hurt her!"

Hendrix should've backed off. His aunt had a temper, and it took her a long time to forgive and forget—if she ever did. But the truth was the truth, and it was high time someone said it. "If you'll just take a moment to think about it, you'll know," he said, speaking as gently as possible.

"Are you mad, Mom?" Leo asked, growing distressed. "Did we do something wrong?"

She was angry enough to ignore him. "So now you're finding fault with *me*?" she said, keeping her focus on Hendrix. "You're blaming me for the past, taking her side over mine?"

Hendrix shoved a hand through his hair. Everything to do with Ellen was somewhat irrational. There was probably no way to convince his aunt that she should've done more for her new husband's daughter. She'd had her own problems to deal with. "I guess I'm wondering why there are two sides to begin with," he said.

"You have no idea what that girl was like as a child. She was a little demon! I wasn't about to have her teach you and Leo how to be so naughty—and ruin the peace and happiness we were trying to establish."

But would Ellen have been that difficult if they'd been able to give her the love and security she needed?

Hendrix wasn't in a position to make that call; his aunt was right about that. But he felt terrible for Ellen. Stuart was her father, after all. He could've done a lot more to support and include her. "Calm down," Hendrix said again. "I'm not judging you. Just…asking you to relax and let me deal with Ellen however I see fit."

"What does that mean?" she demanded.

"It means I might want a better relationship with

her than you have. Leo wants to be a friend to her, too. And would that be so terrible, if we were no longer enemies?"

"You don't get to speak for Leo," she said. "That's up to me."

"When it comes to Ellen, he can speak for himself. Tell Mom, bud, what you said in the truck. You told me you love Ellen, right?"

"I love Ellen," Leo said, but he was starting to choke up, as he always did when emotions ran this high.

"She's not a nice person," Lynn insisted. "You need to stay away from her!"

Leo's face contorted. "She has my chalk!"

Hendrix touched his arm to reassure him. "We'll get it back. Don't worry."

"She said I could come over next week," Leo said. "She said I could help her mow the yard."

Lynn threw up her hands. "See? She's trying to use him!"

"She's not trying to use him," Hendrix said. "You know her grandparents left their riding lawn mower in the barn. I'm guessing he saw it, and she told him he could ride on it."

Lynn looked horrified. "What's gotten into you?"

Before he had a chance to answer, she turned to Stuart. "You tell him!" she said. "You tell him what Ellen was like back in the day."

Stuart hadn't said a thing so far and probably wouldn't have, except Lynn was suddenly demanding he get involved.

"Well?" she prodded when he still hesitated. "Are you just going to sit there and let this fall on me?"

Stuart sighed. "I don't see any harm in letting Leo see Ellen now and then," he said.

"That means I can go?" Leo looked from one to the other to determine if he had anything to worry about.

"Yes, you can go," Hendrix said, but Stuart's lack of support and his own opposition made Lynn walk out of the room.

A few seconds later, they heard her slam the bedroom door.

"Why's Mom mad?" Leo asked, bewildered.

Hendrix pinched the bridge of his nose. "When something has to change, it can be hard to get used to," he told his cousin.

Stuart was watching him contemplatively. "Why now?" he asked.

Hendrix frowned at the delicious-looking meal he'd ruined by getting into an argument with his aunt. "Why now...what?"

"Wasn't it just last week that you told me I have to do something about Ellen? That she was going to ruin our business if I didn't step in? Why are you suddenly defending her?"

"Because it's about time someone did!" he said and walked out of the house. He wasn't going to stick around here, where he'd feel pressure to apologize for speaking his mind. He was going back to Ellen's to have a burger with her, Brant and Talulah. That was where he'd wanted to be in the first place.

Ellen felt her jaw drop when Hendrix walked onto the patio carrying a big bag of chips and a six-pack of beer. He'd let himself into her backyard and lifted the chips in lieu of a wave as he approached.

"Is...is something wrong?" she asked him, confused that he'd reappear after leaving.

His lips curved into the charming smile with the

dimples. "Nope. My plans changed, that's all. Turns out Leo was the only one who had to be somewhere else, so I decided to come back and join you—if that's okay."

Brant was grilling burgers a few feet away; she and Talulah were putting out plates, silverware and the salads—one pasta, one fruit—they'd just made in the kitchen.

"Of course it's okay," Brant said, speaking up right away and using the tongs in his hand to motion toward the cooler. "Grab yourself a cold beer. Burgers will be coming off any second."

Ellen was glad Brant had answered so quickly. Otherwise, there might've been an awkward silence. She was too shocked to manage a welcome.

"Smells good." Hendrix put the chips on the table before taking the beer he'd brought to the cooler. "Is there anything I can do to help?"

While he had his back to them, Talulah shot Ellen a look that was part "what the heck" and part "this is so exciting." Ellen's response was more heavily weighted toward "what the heck." Having Hendrix show up and want to join them for dinner was nothing she'd ever expected. Leo wasn't even around. She could see it if Leo was still there and Hendrix stayed to have a burger while picking him up. But coming back all on his own?

"Brant just has to toast the buns," Talulah told him. "Then we'll be ready to eat."

Ellen knew she should say something, too. That would be the polite thing. But what? She'd never been particularly good at small talk. Instead of reaching for an uncomfortable "glad you came back" or something similar, she simply handed him a plate. "Here you go. I'm just… I'm going inside to slice the lettuce, tomato and onions."

Once she was in the safety of her own kitchen, she drew a deep breath. She was grateful to be alone and took as much time as possible to prepare the burger toppings. Talulah and Brant were certainly capable of entertaining Hendrix. It was Talulah who'd invited him, after all.

She heard the door as she finished arranging sliced jalapenos on one of two plates.

"Hey, you," Talulah said, entering the kitchen. "What's taking so long?" She lowered her voice suspiciously. "You're not hiding out in here, are you?"

"Of course not," Ellen said.

Talulah gave her a disbelieving look. "You *have* been hiding out in here. But your time is up. The burgers are done."

Ellen leaned over to take a quick peek out the window. Brant was carrying everything over from the grill and Hendrix was standing behind one of the chairs across the table, talking to him. "Why do you think he came back?" she whispered as she grabbed the tomatoes and onions.

Talulah picked up the plate of lettuce and jalapenos and started out ahead of her. "Because he's starting to like you."

"There's no way that could be true."

"You'll see."

"I don't want to see!" she snapped.

Talulah turned back before opening the door. "Come on. He's on his best behavior. I say we just…roll with it."

"He and I can't be friends," Ellen insisted. "I don't trust him."

"Maybe it's time to let the past go, Ellen. Maybe that's what he's trying to do."

Ellen got the same impression. But Talulah didn't

understand that this wasn't really about being friends. It was about the sudden crazy attraction that'd welled up, making her want more.

Talulah and Brant had a lot more to say than Ellen did. As Hendrix visited with them, she ate quietly, listening. But he could feel her watching him when she didn't think he was paying attention. She was wary of most people, guarded in general, which was why she tended to be such a loner. Given who he was, and how things had gone through the years, particularly since she'd moved to town and they'd basically become open enemies, he could see why she wouldn't give him a chance.

Why did he suddenly want to be one of the few people she liked and fully accepted? He had no answer to that question. By getting close to her he'd only be asking for problems, and he knew it.

But every time he tried to mentally dismiss her, to get himself back in line and focused on life as he knew it, he failed miserably. Probably because she'd been on his mind for a long time. It'd become a habit to think of her on an almost daily basis. And now that his perspective had shifted, and his emotions were drifting toward the positive, he felt unsettled and hungry for a better resolution.

"We have to get going," Talulah said as they finished cleaning up after the meal. "Brant promised his parents we'd stop by tonight."

Ellen's eyes flew wide. "You're leaving? Right *now*?"

Talulah shot her an apologetic look. "I'm sorry. We haven't seen his mother since she got COVID two weeks ago. We really need to drop by for a few minutes before it gets too late."

Hendrix smiled. It was obvious that Ellen didn't want to be left alone with him. Talulah was the one who'd invited him; Ellen had merely tolerated his presence. But he had a few things he wanted to say, and he was eager to have some time alone with her. He'd actually been waiting for Talulah and Brant to leave.

"Okay," Ellen said, grudgingly enough that it came across as, "I can't believe you're leaving me with him."

He chuckled.

"What?" she said, hearing him.

He wiped the smile from his face. "Nothing."

She studied him for a moment. "It's okay if you have to go, too."

"I'm good for now," he said, allowing his smile to widen.

Catching the exchange, Talulah glanced between them. "I admit—this is a day I never saw coming."

Neither he nor Ellen asked what she meant by that. They both knew—and didn't want to hear her state it expressly.

Brant and Talulah each gave Ellen a hug; Talulah hugged Hendrix, too, and Brant stuck out his hand to shake. "See you soon, bro."

Talulah and Brant didn't bother to go back around front. They cut across the field to their own house.

Once they were out of earshot, Ellen looked over at him. "What's going on?" she asked.

He could tell she wasn't trying to offend him. She was honestly confused and looking for an answer. "You're finally going to speak to me?" he said.

Taking umbrage, she lifted her chin. "I've been talking to you all evening."

"No, you've been talking around me. You wouldn't even catch my eye."

"Because I don't understand what you want."

"I want to be your friend," he said simply.

She stiffened. "What for?"

"Why continue to be enemies? What good does it do either one of us?"

"I could argue with that. But…we'll let it go if you answer this. Why now?"

"I don't know," he replied. "It's just…time, don't you think?"

"No. That won't work."

"Because…"

"You know why."

"What are you afraid of?" he asked.

Leaning back in her chair, she folded her arms. "I'm not afraid of anything."

"Then prove it. If you and Leo can be friends, why can't you and I?"

"Leo has never done anything to hurt me."

"I haven't gone out of my way to hurt you, either. I've done my best to ignore you. That's about it."

"You tried to steal my driller."

"And I'm sorry for that."

"I appreciate the apology. But I still have to find a new driller."

"No, you don't. Don't let him go. We'll both sit down with him and explain that the situation—and the opportunities as he understands them—have changed."

"He told me you need a driller. That one of yours is leaving."

"He is, but I'll hire someone else."

"And leave Ben without a job?"

"I'm trying to save his job *with you*."

"I'm not sure that's going to work. He's gotten so full

of himself. You have him believing he's in high demand and worth more than he is."

"Which is why I'm willing to set him straight."

She said nothing. He could tell she was still looking for a good reason for shoving him away in an emotional sense.

"You got anything else?" he asked.

She bit her lip. "I don't know what you mean."

"Some other reason to hate me?"

"I don't need a reason," she said, but she sounded like a petulant child, and that only made him laugh.

"You're not as tough or as mean as you want me to believe," he said and surprised himself as much as her by standing up, lifting her chin with one finger and kissing her gently on the mouth. "Good night, Ellen."

She didn't move or even answer. She stayed exactly where she was as he walked away.

Thirteen

Ellen touched her lips. She couldn't believe it. Had that really happened? Had Hendrix *kissed* her? He'd said he wanted to be friends. So then...why'd he kiss her?

Trying to figure out his motives was confusing enough. What made it even worse was that she'd liked it. A lot. Her heart was nearly beating out of her chest as she listened for the sound of his truck around front.

She could barely hear it when his engine started, and the noise quickly receded as he pulled out of the drive. Still, she remained where she was long after he was gone, reliving the moment his mouth had touched hers.

His lips had been so pliable and warm...

Had he been testing her? Taunting her? Trying to neutralize the threat she posed to Fetterman Well Services?

Maybe he'd decided that winning her over was the best way to gain the upper hand. If that kiss had been some sort of chess move, merely a way to win the power struggle between them, he'd use any leverage he gained against her...

She was tempted to call Talulah. She needed to talk to someone, and she knew her friend would be as shocked as she was by this latest development.

But she didn't dare tell her what'd happened. That would make it too real. She wasn't sure she'd enjoy hearing Talulah's take on it, anyway. Talulah seemed to like Hendrix. She was probably just trying to be objective; Talulah was fair that way. But having her best friend be so open-minded where Hendrix was concerned made Ellen feel as if she was switching sides. And that frightened her, made her feel vulnerable, because it once again left her all on her own against the people who'd hurt her deeply.

Ignore what happened, she told herself. *Pretend he never touched you.* She'd been completely on her own before. For most of her life, as a matter of fact. She could manage.

It wasn't easy to get up, go inside and finish out the day. She'd start something, then find herself staring off into space, thinking about how Hendrix had shown up out of the blue, talked and laughed with her friends as casually as though they hung out together all the time and teased her affectionately, as if he knew her better than he did and they hadn't been enemies as far back as she could remember. She hated to admit it—would never admit it to anyone else—but she'd enjoyed being around him even before he kissed her.

You're not as tough or as mean as you want me to believe.

This was an entirely new tack—and it was an incredibly effective offense. She had no idea how to combat a happy, joking, friendly Hendrix.

Her phone signaled a text. She hoped it would be someone with whom she could share her thoughts. She was suddenly lost. He'd managed to take her back to when she was much younger, when she felt isolated and hungry for a connection with him, Leo and her father—

if not Lynn. But the thing that completely shocked her
was that she wanted a different kind of connection now
than she'd ever wanted back then, at least with Hendrix.

Only with Hendrix.

Her own heart seemed to be turning on her...

"Damn you," she muttered as she tracked down her
phone.

She found it in the kitchen where she'd left it while
using her computer to lodge a complaint against Jordan
Forbes on the dating site. She'd been eager to put an
end to Friday night, hadn't wanted to put that off any
longer. Then she'd handled the billing for her business.

As she picked up her phone, she assumed Talulah
was back from her mother-in-law's and was eager to see
how the rest of the evening had gone with Hendrix. She
had no idea what she was going to say about it. But she
didn't have to decide. It wasn't Talulah; it was Jordan.

Really? You reported me? You're the one to blame for
Friday night. Your fucking boyfriend broke my nose!
I was going to let it go—just file the whole incident
under "crazy dating stories"—but now I'm going to
report YOU.

Ellen stared at his words. This was how he was going
to react? He was the one in the wrong!

She knew better than to respond. He obviously didn't
see reality the way she did. But she couldn't help herself.

Report me for what? You got what you deserved.

I think you invited me to Coyote Canyon just to make
your bf jealous. You probably had him come by hop-

ing he'd see you with me, and when I kissed you good-
night, he went ape shit.

That isn't what happened, and you know it!

That's exactly what happened.

In other words, he was going to twist everything to
make *her* look bad.

You attempted to assault me! I could go to the police!

And tell them what? That I kissed you goodnight after
taking you out to dinner? That's what you're calling
assault? I have several texts showing that you invited
me to town. Lots of people saw us having a great time
at the bar. And you have no injuries to prove any kind
of force. You'll only be making yourself look worse if
you attempt to lie.

"I can't believe this!" Dumbfounded, Ellen shook
her head. What an asshole! But how could she refute
his version of events?

She was tempted to tell Hendrix what Jordan was
doing. He'd been there. He could corroborate her story.
But would the company behind the dating site really
care to investigate? Would the police? She didn't file
a report the night it happened, and Jordan was right in
that she had no injuries. The dating site would probably
kick them both off the platform and tell them to take the
incident to the authorities, and the authorities would say
there was nothing they could do because there wasn't
enough evidence to even warrant their involvement.

Jordan might be able to convince them to file assault

charges against Hendrix, however. He was the only one who'd sustained any injuries, and if it was true that he had a broken nose, there'd most likely be medical records to prove it.

The evidence was on his side. What was she going to do?

Jordan could follow through with his threat to report her as she'd reported him, she decided, but she wouldn't retract her complaint. Although she wasn't particularly thrilled to have a new enemy, especially when she'd spoken the truth, other women needed to be warned that Jordan wasn't quite right. She had to stand by the information she'd provided.

If you feel the need to report me—even though I did nothing wrong—go for it.

She'd been planning to leave the dating site, anyway. She'd just pull her profile down right now. She hated that it might make his version of events seem like the truth, but she didn't want to be contacted and questioned. She didn't have the time or the mental fortitude when she knew it wouldn't ultimately go anywhere. She had a business to run, and what was going on with Hendrix—and Ben, of course—was causing enough of a distraction. She was finished with Jordan and, for the time being, dating in general.

You won't retract it? he wrote back. You're going to damage my reputation for nothing?

It's not for nothing. Your reputation should be damaged. You were way out of line.

She was tempted to say a lot more. But what good

would trying to convince him do? She was afraid he might be totally disconnected, with no awareness of cause and effect, devoid of empathy and unwilling to take responsibility for his own actions. That certainly seemed to be the real Jordan. And she wanted him out of her life as soon as possible.

That's a no? he wrote.

Although it was taking a risk, she felt empowered calling his bluff. That's a no.

Then you're going to regret it.

How? She was afraid to ask. Let's just agree to go our separate ways, she wrote back. Then she blocked him, deleted her profile from the dating site and went back to working on her billing.

But his threat haunted her for the rest of the night. Was it all talk? Or...exactly how vengeful would he be?

Ellen had a difficult time getting out of bed the following morning. She'd tossed and turned most of the night, remembering Hendrix's kiss in her backyard and worrying about the ugly text exchange she'd had with Jordan Forbes. But she had to forget about that stuff and get to work. It didn't matter how tired and sluggish she felt. Mondays were important. There was always so much to do at the start of the week.

Today, she was supposed to put in Jay Haslem's well, and she was hoping to get that done while she still had Ben's help. Knowing she had to bring her only employee's expectations in line with reality sooner rather than later cast a dark cloud over the future of their relationship.

But she needed to put up with him a little longer,

because she had to keep Jay happy. He was a friend of Hendrix's. He'd mentioned that when she bid on the job—said he felt a bit guilty going with her instead of Hendrix, who was his neighbor—so she'd hate to give him anything to complain about. If she screwed up and something went wrong, she had no doubt Hendrix and her father would hear about it, and that was the *last* thing she wanted.

As she drove to the Haslem property, she planned what she'd say to Ben when the time was right. She'd do it by making it clear that Hendrix was no longer interested in hiring him. Maybe then she'd be able to talk some sense into him, and they'd all be better off for it.

Jay was waiting for her when she arrived, standing in the knee-high weeds that covered most of his property, wearing a pair of coveralls and clutching a cup of coffee. Ben was supposed to be there, too. When she'd spoken to him before going to bed last night, she'd told him she wanted to get an early start and asked him to arrive at seven, and he'd indicated he was back in town, as promised, and would be on time.

But she didn't see his truck.

"Looks like you're as good as your word," Jay said, approaching her as she climbed out of her rig.

"Of course." She wished Ben was there, too. She needed him to take her back to her place to get the water truck. Only then could they truly get started. But she didn't mention that to Jay. "I emailed you the estimate with the details—how deep I'll be drilling, how much casing I'll be using, the size of the hole, the type and size of pump I'll be installing. That sort of thing." She opened the clipboard she'd taken out of the rig with her and handed him two sheets of paper. "This is the contract, which says pretty much the same thing but requires your signature."

After he looked over the paperwork, he signed it and pulled a check from his pocket to cover the deposit. "How long will it take?"

"To drill the well? Provided all goes well, a day or two."

"Then let's hope all goes well. My dad's coming to help me build my new house, so he and Mom will be staying here in an RV for the summer. He'll need power and water."

Ellen knew the power was already in. The pump required electricity to work, so that was an important element. "When will he be here?"

"On Friday."

"Shouldn't be a problem." Of all the wells she'd drilled, she hoped this one went the smoothest.

She fastened the check and the signed contract onto her clipboard and returned it to the rig. Then she walked the property with him to make sure she knew exactly where he wanted her to put the well.

"You need me to stay out here for anything?" he asked after she'd positioned the rig in the proper location.

Relieved that he wouldn't be standing around watching the whole process, she said, "No. I've got it. I'll call you if we run into any trouble."

"Sounds good." He checked his watch. "I'd better get over to the auto shop."

After he left, she climbed into the cab of the rig, leaving the door open to let in some fresh air. She was hoping Ben would show up any second, but another fifteen minutes passed and there was still no sign of him.

With a sigh, she plucked her phone from the seat beside her and texted him. Where are you? I'm at the

Haslem property, waiting. Can't start without you. Did we get our wires crossed?

Sorry, but I don't think I'm going to make it today.

She blinked several times as she read his response. What???

I just woke up, or I would've texted you sooner. We had engine trouble on the drive back.

Ellen could understand that a breakdown would be outside his control, but this didn't make sense. When she'd talked to him, he'd indicated he was home. And he obviously wasn't too worried about letting her down if he could casually say, "Whoops! I fell asleep, or I would've notified you."

You said you were back in town.

Because I thought I would be back in town. We were supposed to get in early this morning.

You were going to come to work after driving all night?

They worked around heavy machinery. A sleepy driller could lose a limb or get even more badly hurt.

I planned to catch a few hours in the car while my girlfriend drove. But we only got halfway home before we ran into engine trouble.

And it was something he couldn't fix? He was a decent mechanic—not an expert when it came to specialized systems like transmissions or starters, but he could make general repairs. She knew because they had to repair equipment here and there all the time, and he'd been a quick study for anything his father hadn't already taught him. What's wrong with your truck?

Radiator leak. Have to wait for someone to fix it. So we might not be able to get back until tomorrow or even the next day.

That meant she'd lose Monday, Tuesday and possibly Wednesday, as well as the days he'd cost her last week?

Where are you?

In the middle of nowhere, somewhere along the road.

That was vague. Ellen was getting a bad feeling about this. You don't have any idea where?

Does it matter? I'm nowhere near home. I know that.

Can you take a picture of the closest road sign?

While she waited for his response, she did what she could in the rig by way of returning calls and following up on various supply orders. She also scheduled a pump replacement job she'd bid on over a year ago that was finally coming through. That was a bright spot.

By the time she was done, an hour had passed, and she still hadn't heard from Ben. She tried calling, but he didn't pick up. Was he lying again? Had he let his girlfriend talk him into staying in Salt Lake for another day or two?

Her intuition insisted what he'd told her wasn't the real story. But did it matter? He'd already lied to her once, causing her to arrive at a jobsite with no way to get started. She could've used the additional sleep, if only he'd shown her the courtesy of letting her know he was stranded.

If that was true...

She'd have to go to Jay and reschedule, she decided. If she was lucky, he wouldn't cancel the contract and take his business to Hendrix and her father. But if he could get the well drilled sooner, he might actually do that. He'd said his parents were coming on Friday.

That would be a financial blow. But it would be better than trying to drill the well herself and being unable to complete it, thanks to Ben. Letting go of it would save her that embarrassment, at least. And if she couldn't rely on her driller, she might as well fire him now and start looking for someone else. She couldn't continue to offer him the kind of flexibility he was demanding. Doing that would ruin her business.

Don't worry about hurrying back. I'm going to hire someone else. I'll mail you your final check.

She stared at those words for a full minute before squeezing her eyes closed and hitting the Send button. *There*, she thought when she opened them again. *It's done*. She'd most likely lose the Haslem well, but she was too afraid to drill it now, anyway. She'd rather have Hendrix drill it than screw it up somehow and have him hear about it, especially after he kissed her last night. Somehow that seemed to give her even more to lose.

Ben responded immediately, which convinced her he'd been getting her calls and texts all along but was ignoring them because she was pressing him for proof of his story.

Are you firing me???

She drew a deep breath. She was this far in; she had to see it through. I'm letting you go, yes.

Why? It'll take you a lot longer to train someone else than to wait for me. I'm only talking two days.

How do you know the truck will be fixed by then?

It will be.

Because there's nothing wrong with it? She knew she shouldn't send that but couldn't stop herself. She was too disappointed, frustrated and embarrassed that she was going to have to give up the Haslem well.

Are you calling me a liar?

Yes, she was. And because she realized she'd be doing that before sending her last message, she felt she had to answer this honestly.

I don't think you're being truthful, Ben. That's why I'm letting you go. That and I can't afford your new salary.

Tossing her phone on the seat, she started the rig and drove off the property. It wouldn't look good to Jay to see that the drill was gone when he got off work. But thanks to Ben, she couldn't leave it. She had no other ride. She wouldn't have any way to drill this week, regardless, so it didn't matter. She'd just have to tell Jay the truth and recommend he go with Hendrix.

When she got home, she parked to one side of the barn, still trying to figure out how to salvage her day. Other than spreading the word that she was looking for someone she could train as a driller, she supposed she could finish up what little paperwork she hadn't done yesterday. Then, if she had time, she'd start tearing out the old carpet in the other rooms of her house.

None of that would earn her any money, which would be a problem if she couldn't make up for the missed time, but there was nothing she could do about it. Ben had left her in the lurch.

She picked up her phone before getting out and saw that she'd missed a flurry of texts from her former employee.

Are you serious right now? Give me a break! We had engine trouble.

Hello? Are you not going to answer me?

"How does it feel?" she mumbled.

Don't be a bitch!

The last one got to her. Even though she'd told herself she'd said all she was going to say, she responded, anyway.

Am I being a bitch? If so, feel free to prove me wrong. Send me a picture of anything that shows you're no longer in Salt Lake. If you can do that in the next five minutes, you can keep your job—if you still want it.

I can't, he wrote back. We broke down before we left Salt Lake.

She chuckled humorlessly. He'd already said he was "in the middle of nowhere."

Sorry, Ben. I think it's best that we go our separate ways.

I can't believe this. I've been a good employee! I could've left you for your competition. Instead, I remained loyal. Now you don't have any loyalty to me?

"You would've left if I hadn't paid you to stay. That's not loyalty," she said but another text came in before she could clarify that he didn't deserve credit for something he used to his benefit.

I'll just go to Fettermans. I don't need you. I'll help them take back wells since you won't be able to drill until you hire someone else.

Now he was after revenge? She could have informed him that Hendrix was no longer interested in hiring him. But she figured it would be smarter to stay out of it. If Fetterman Well Services wanted to hire Ben, they were more than welcome, especially now that she'd seen what he was like when he held a little power.

Good luck with that.

You'd better send me my check right away, or you'll be sorry.

She rubbed her forehead before heading into the house. She seemed to be making enemies everywhere...

Fourteen

Ben's call came in while Hendrix was trying to repair a generator he needed to test a pump. He paused to look down at his screen, almost ignored the interruption, then thought better of it. If Ellen's driller understood that there was no other opportunity except the job he had with her, maybe he'd settle down.

He pressed the Talk button. "Hey, Ben. How are you?"

"Not so good," he said, clearly upset.

Hendrix cringed. "What's going on?"

"I'm done with Ellen. I can't deal with her anymore. I'm ready to move on."

Hendrix nearly groaned. What did he say now? "Um... listen, Ben... Whatever it is, I suggest you try to work it out with her."

"I don't want to work it out. I'd rather drill for you. I should've made the jump when you offered me a job that night when we saw each other at Hank's."

"Except...when you didn't come over right away, I made other plans," he said. "I'm sorry." That wasn't strictly true. He still hadn't filled the position that would be empty when Randy Bettencourt left, but there was no way he could replace Randy with Ben. He'd promised Ellen he wouldn't. He was just trying to let Ben down as easily as possible.

"That fast?" Ben sounded even more upset. "Who'd you hire?"

"No one. But Stuart and I are... Well, we're thinking about holding off—in case it's possible to get by without another employee." That wasn't strictly true, either, but it could take a while to find someone else so it could easily look that way. Even if Ben heard he was searching for someone or had hired another driller, it would mean Ben would probably have kept his job with Ellen or found another one by then.

"How are you going to do that?" he asked. "Summer's the busiest time of year."

He had a point, but Hendrix knew better than to try to defend his excuse. He'd only talk himself into a corner. He simply reiterated what he'd already said. "Why not stick with Ellen for the time being, and I'll let you know if any opportunities develop on this end?"

"I *can't* stay with her! She's being completely unreasonable," he snapped and disconnected.

"Shit." Hendrix started to slide his phone back into his pocket but pulled it back out at the last second to text Ellen.

Ben just called me. What's going on?

I fired him.

Why? I told you I wouldn't hire him. Was it the money?

That and more. It couldn't be avoided.

But why not keep him on until you find someone else?

Because he's no longer reliable.

How will you get by?

I don't know. But you should be glad. Your buddy Jay Haslem will probably be calling to have you drill his well. I was supposed to start it today but had to pull out. Ben never came back from his trip to Utah like he said he would.

Firing her only employee—especially at this time of year—would cause a huge disruption to her business, and for how long? It might not be easy to replace Ben, especially if they were both looking to hire someone at the same time. "Damn it," Hendrix cursed. Why'd he ever approach Ben at the bar?

The fact that he was now disappointed that he might get the Haslem well was too ironic. It wasn't very long ago that he'd been furious about losing it. But he was suddenly rooting for Ellen's success even if it came at his own expense.

What should he do about the problem he'd caused?

He was just pondering that question when he got a text from Lynn.

I can't believe how you behaved last night.

Hendrix was too mad at himself to play the penitent, as she obviously expected.

I only behaved the way I did because of how you've behaved toward Ellen for so many years. He typed that and sent it off quickly—probably too quickly. He understood what was required of him to be able to get along with his aunt, and he had to get along with her for the sake of the business, if not for the sake of peace in general. He also owed her a great deal for taking him in. He would've gone into the foster care system otherwise. That gratitude had held him hostage from the beginning.

He felt a moment's regret after it was gone, knew it would cause an even bigger problem. But he was suddenly tired of turning a blind eye to the injustice he'd witnessed where Ellen was concerned.

Why are you standing up for her all of a sudden? What's gotten into you?

He liked Ellen, he realized. Way more than he should. But that wasn't what he wrote. Fair is fair.

He sent that message. Then he texted Ellen again. Meet me at the Haslem property as soon as you can get there.

What for???

I'm going to help you drill Jay's well.

Ellen wasn't convinced she should allow Hendrix to help her. Why would he come to her rescue when he could take the job for himself? What would they do when it came to getting paid—split the money? If so, how would they figure out who would get how much?

If they used her license, insurance, equipment and supplies, she should retain more than half, but she had no idea how much Hendrix would expect. She'd have to pay him more than she'd pay Ben—that was for sure. He was worth more, and his assistance would help her out of a jam, so it made sense.

But how much would be enough? And how would he explain what he'd done and why he'd done it to Lynn and Stuart?

Why would he put himself in the position of having to explain when he could simply let her languish and step in to claim the entire job for himself? If she couldn't find a new driller quickly enough, he might be able to take some of her other jobs, too. Surely, he could see she was vulnerable...

Although Ellen was as dubious as she could be, her curiosity and need to keep working instead of just filling time until she could hire someone to replace Ben brought her back to the Haslem property. If she started the well today as originally planned, she could finish close to when she'd promised, and it would also buy her a few days to try to replace Ben so that her future schedule wouldn't be disrupted.

And she wouldn't be the only beneficiary. Jay's parents could come as scheduled, and if something did happen to go wrong in the process of finding water—always a possibility when dealing with an imperfect science—Jay couldn't make her look bad to Hendrix because he'd see Hendrix as equally responsible. There'd be some consolation in that even if she didn't walk away with much of the money.

A call came in from Talulah as she sat behind the wheel, waiting for Hendrix, but Ellen didn't want to answer. She wasn't quite ready to tell her best friend that Hendrix had offered to help her drill the Haslem well. Because she couldn't understand *why* he would step in on her behalf, she couldn't completely trust that it would work out the way she hoped. Part of her still believed this had to be some sort of prank...

She'd send Talulah a message after Hendrix arrived

and she knew more about what was going to happen today, she decided, ignoring the call.

Shading her eyes against the sun, she gazed back toward the road but didn't see anyone coming.

She checked the time on her phone. It'd been forty minutes since she'd received his message telling her to meet him here. Maybe he'd had to finish something else and would appear at any moment. Or maybe he was at another jobsite—one of his own—laughing his butt off that she'd believe he'd help her drill a well on a job he felt should've gone to him in the first place. It wasn't hard to recall how angry he'd been when he'd confronted her about her sales tactics at the Slemboskis'.

Don't make me put you out of business...

Saving this job for her was hardly putting her out of business. So...he couldn't really intend to help her, could he?

She was just about to start the engine of her rig and drive off when she saw a white truck turn down the long drive. She couldn't quite read the logo emblazoned on the door. It was still too far away. But she knew what it said: *Fetterman Well Services*.

Ellen had climbed down from her truck and was waiting for him as he'd hoped she would be. Hendrix could see the doubt in her body language as soon as he parked and got out, but he'd been expecting that reaction. He'd certainly never offered to help before. Although—except for the incident with Ben—he hadn't purposely gone out of his way to hurt her, he hadn't made things any easier, either.

As she'd pointed out.

"What's going on?" she demanded.

"Sorry. Had to take care of a few things before I could get away," he replied.

She stepped closer. "No, I mean...why are we here?"

He yanked on the leather gloves he'd taken from the door of his truck. "I told you. We're going to drill this well."

She studied him closely. *"Why?"*

"Because it's my fault you lost Ben," he said. "I feel responsible. So I'm going to make it possible for you to get this done."

She narrowed her eyes, didn't seem to be buying it. "What about all the things you're supposed to be doing for your own business?"

He'd visited his drilling crew, who were fulfilling a maintenance contract with the county, to make sure they had everything they needed. He'd have to be available by phone in case they ran into trouble. But Stuart wouldn't know he wasn't out visiting jobsites, trying to garner new business or picking up supplies. Hendrix was more of a manager these days than an active driller, which gave him plenty of autonomy. And Stuart would be busy managing the other drill crew.

Still, his uncle would probably hear he'd helped Ellen at some point. How would he react? Would he tell Lynn?

Chances were better that he'd quietly pull Hendrix aside to see what was going on or completely ignore the gossip. Neither one of them liked to upset Lynn. "I may have to stop here and there to handle various details, but with any luck I'll be able to squeeze this in around my own stuff."

She made no move to get started. She just stood there watching him as though he might surprise her by yanking off the sheep's mask she must've felt he was wearing to reveal the wolf inside.

"Come on. Let's go get your water truck." He gestured at her attire. Although she was wearing a hard hat, work boots and jeans—all acceptable clothing for their line of work—she was in a tank top, which might help with the heat but would do nothing to protect her arms. "And you need to put on a shirt with long sleeves."

"You realize you could've stolen this whole job," she said, ignoring everything he'd said.

He gave her a pointed look. "You mean... I could've stolen it *back*?"

Her eyebrows slid up. "I bid on it fair and square."

"You undercut me," he said. "But I forgive you."

She stepped back when he approached the rig—probably so he could get around her without brushing against her. "Why?"

"I'm not entirely sure of that myself," he admitted and stopped to survey the ground with a critical eye. "This is where we're putting the well?"

Finally distracted enough to turn her attention elsewhere, she kicked a dirt clod, sending it rolling before it fell apart. "It's where Jay said he wants it."

Hendrix clicked his tongue. "He set on that?"

Her forehead wrinkled in consternation. "Why wouldn't he be?"

"I drilled the well on the next property over. Ran into a lot of sand, and this looks to be in the same culvert."

"How much sand?" she asked.

He rested his hands on his hips. "Enough to require a sleeve."

"That sucks."

"An expensive pain in the ass. We don't want that to happen here. So...given the geology of the area, we might be better off putting the well along that slight rise on the opposite side of the parcel. Could give us a better chance of avoiding the sand."

She looked in the direction he indicated, her expression finally a bit less skeptical and more contemplative. "Want to call Jay to see if that'd be okay?"

"This is your job," he said. "Why don't you call him?"

He preferred Jay not know he was involved. With any luck, he could handle this quickly and quietly and be done without causing any more problems between him and his family.

She cleaned the dirt off her boots by knocking them together. "What am I going to owe you when this is over?" she asked.

He settled his hard hat more squarely on his head. "We can talk about that later."

"I'd like to handle it up front," she said. "I appreciate your help—if that's what it really is. But I have to know what I'm leaping into."

There was something about her ongoing struggle to hide or refute all vulnerability—to pretend to be so tough she couldn't be hurt—that made him feel strange things. Empathy for her struggles. Admiration for her strength and stubborn pride. Protectiveness. Attraction. *Affection.*

It was the affection that scared him most. Coupled with the attraction, it could get him into a lot of trouble, which was why he attempted to ignore his own reaction. "What do you think I'm after, Ellen? What do you have that I want?"

Her gaze lowered to his mouth, tempting him to pull her up against him and kiss her again. He got the impression she was either remembering yesterday or imagining what it would feel like to kiss him again.

At least…that was what he was thinking about.

"I know you'd like to hurt me or my business in some way."

Surprised, he blinked at her. "That's not true."

"You've stated as much," she said simply. "I'm only taking you at your word."

"When?" he started to say but remembered the day he'd approached her, not too long ago, at the Slemboskis' and threatened to ruin her business. "Oh…that." He gestured as if it was nothing. "I was mad," he explained. "Didn't mean it."

"So…why are you here?" she asked again. "What do you want from me?"

"Everyone who does you a favor must be after something?" he challenged.

She didn't look away. She was staring into his eyes so intently he suspected she was trying to peel back the layers to determine if he was being kind and sincere or something else. Something unkind and insincere… "In my experience, yes."

What was he going to do with this strong, determined, defiant woman? He couldn't go after the friendship and interaction he was starting to want. He knew that wouldn't be good for either one of them.

Allowing himself to lean in close enough, he ran his lips up the side of her neck. "If I'm the devil you think I am, I must be after your soul, right?" He grinned as he pulled back to let her know he was teasing. But she didn't look all that reassured.

Hendrix insisted she didn't have to pay him, that he was helping her to make up for his mistake with Ben and fitting his time with her in around his other work. But Ellen couldn't believe he'd allow the arrangement to be that favorable to her.

She'd give him as much as she could afford to out of Jay's final check, she decided. Worse than trying to get by without that money would be feeling she owed Hendrix. That—and the gratitude his kindness would engender—would make it much harder to keep him neatly categorized as no one she'd like to associate with. Thinking of him as anything other than that would include infinitely more risk. She'd been hurt badly enough by Stuart, and Hendrix had been a large part of the reason. As she'd promised herself before, she wasn't going to give either one of them the power to hurt her ever again.

By dinnertime, they were both dusty, dirty and tired. She'd been up since before six. The same was no doubt true for Hendrix. But he insisted he could push through until sundown. He said he wanted to finish the well as soon as possible. He was probably afraid someone would realize he was helping her.

He also needed to get back to his own jobs. So, tired though she was, she continued to watch the rig for any signs of trouble and shovel the pilings away from the hole while he took a turn welding the casing.

The confidence with which he handled the equipment showed his level of experience. He knew what he was doing; she had to give him that. Today certainly hadn't been anything like working with Ben. She just hoped Hendrix was right about moving the well to the other side of the property. Jay had agreed. He didn't want to pay for a sleeve to keep the sand out of his water. So they'd made the adjustments before getting started and were about two hundred feet down in their new location, hoping they would hit plenty of water but no sand.

"Aren't you getting hungry?" she asked as her own

stomach rumbled. She'd been in such a hurry this morning that she hadn't eaten much breakfast. Then, wondering if Hendrix was really going to help her out of the jam she was in, she'd dashed out of the house at noon without grabbing lunch for fear any type of delay would blow the opportunity.

"I was hungry hours ago," he admitted.

"Then why don't we stop for a few minutes, and I'll run into town to grab us a bite to eat?" She knew better than to suggest they go together. That would start too many tongues wagging around Coyote Canyon. The fewer people who saw them, the better. She hadn't even mentioned Hendrix to Jay. She'd just explained the odds of hitting sand in that particular culvert, and he'd gone with her suggestion to move the drilling site, which was really Hendrix's idea, of course.

Hendrix hesitated as though he might insist on working through dinner. But then he shut down the rig. "Okay," he said with a tired sigh. "Let's take a break. It'll help us get through the next few hours a little more comfortably."

After deciding what they were interested in eating, she called in an order to the local pizza joint. But instead of starting the drill back up until she needed to leave to get the food, he walked over to a copse of trees and sank down onto the ground in the dappled shade, leaving her with nothing to do except follow him.

They'd been talking most of the day—banal chitchat mostly. Conversation was all they had to help pass the long, tedious hours. They had to speak over the motor of the drill, which didn't always make it easy to be heard, but she'd told him about Ben and how he'd lied about returning from Salt Lake City. Talulah must've mentioned that she'd helped decorate her and Brant's Victorian, because Hendrix had asked her about that, and she'd told him she loved bargain-hunting and often drove to one of the bigger cities to pick up a couch, chair or other secondhand furniture she'd seen advertised online. She thought she might even start up a resale business one day—when drilling became too rigorous for her. He'd seemed interested in that, for some reason. And then he'd told her about various drilling jobs where he'd experienced something out of the normal routine—one where his rig had been struck by lightning—which in turn spurred some of her own drilling stories.

So far, they'd managed to steer clear of any emotionally charged topics—like her mother, her father and his aunt. And Ellen was glad of that. She didn't enjoy talking about those people. Talulah was the only one who truly understood what she'd been through and how she felt about it, and that was only because they'd spent so many evenings sitting out on one porch or the other, discussing almost everything.

As she and Hendrix sat beneath the trees, waiting for their pizza to be cooked, they'd used up their small talk. So it felt natural to delve a bit deeper when she asked, "Do you ever wonder about your father?"

He leaned back, propping himself up with his hands. "You mean my sperm donor?"

She bit her lip. He didn't sound surprised she would know—or particularly resistant to talking about it. Maybe he assumed everyone knew how he came to be. After all, Lynn hadn't made a secret of it. She'd had to have something to say when asked where his father was, and she'd gone with the truth. He'd told his friends and classmates, too, so most people in Coyote Canyon knew. "Yeah."

"Not very often. It's just too bad my mother didn't know she had cancer when she decided to become a single parent, huh?"

Ellen knew his mother had died when he was only eleven and Lynn had taken him in immediately—just months after she'd married Stuart—but she hadn't heard many of the details. What information she did get came from Grandma and Grandpa Fetterman, and she'd been so determined not to let them know how left out and hurt she felt that she rarely spoke of Stuart, Lynn or Hendrix.

It was a sore subject for her grandparents, too—the way Stuart had treated his daughter—so they rarely mentioned Stuart or the others themselves, which didn't exactly give her easy access to what was going on in her father's life or the lives of his new family.

"She had it since before you were born?"

"No one can say for sure. But they didn't find it until it'd progressed to stage four. That suggests she'd had it for a while. Then she went through various treatments for six years."

Ellen dipped her head. She'd been so busy blaming him for replacing her in her father's affections that she hadn't spent much time looking at the situation from his perspective, which was probably why she couldn't hold his gaze when she said, "Must've been hard to lose her."

He'd been teasing her on and off today, making the hours pass quickly, and work that was generally long and grueling had felt like fun. She'd tried not to respond with her own teasing and banter but had failed many times. It was just too hard not to like Hendrix when he was being so charming.

Anyway, the playful version of her nemesis was gone now; she could tell he was dead serious. "At that age?" He nodded.

"I'm sorry."

He met her gaze. "It's okay. As you know, I had it pretty good, considering."

Ellen plucked a blade of grass, which she twirled between two fingers. "Can I ask you another question?"

"Is it personal?" he asked with a chuckle.

"I guess it is."

His smile returned. "Okay. But then I get to ask you one."

She tossed away the grass. "Never mind."

"You're *that* closed off?" he said with a scowl.

From him? Yes. She needed to be. Getting to know him was tearing down the walls she'd built up, and she needed the protection those walls provided. "I just don't like talking about myself."

"I've noticed." He extended his legs, crossing them at the ankles. "But now I'm curious enough to let you ask your question, anyway. What is it you want to know?"

"Do you have any DNA information on your father?"

"I do. No identification or anything but some info that would be helpful for medical purposes—just in case."

"Are you ever tempted to try to identify him?"

"No."

He seemed resolute. "Because…"

He shrugged. "When you come from a sperm bank, you understand the donor doesn't want to be identified or contacted, and you leave him alone. I won't be that guy who goes chasing after someone who'd rather not be found, you know?"

She understood. In a way, that wasn't too different from how she felt about her own father. She wasn't going to chase after Stuart and beg him to love her. She'd made up her mind on that years ago.

There was something else she wanted to ask Hendrix, but it was a bit trickier, because it involved the people she'd been so grateful they'd avoided talking about thus far. Only the fact that she'd wondered since she was a child compelled her to ignore that it would reveal too much about herself and her own needs. "Why do you think Lynn was able to accept you and not me?"

He didn't answer right away. He sat still for several seconds, his eyes resting on her as though he was carefully forming his response. Then he said, "I can't point to one reason, Ellen. That's a complicated thing, right? No doubt it had something to do with the fact that I was already a blood relation. I was big for my age, so I'd be able to help Stuart with the business. I gave her son a protector, and I helped their bottom line. It made sense from a practical standpoint, I guess."

"So that's it? It was strictly practical?" she said. "She saw me as a weakling who couldn't do what you could do and saw you as someone who could drill?"

"I'm not finished. From a not-so-practical standpoint, she may have felt too obligated to refuse. She and my mother were close. When I was little, they traveled to see each other whenever they could and talked on the phone all the time. And since I don't have a father, there was no one else to step in, which placed the responsibility squarely on her shoulders. My mother might even have gone to her before deciding to have a child and asked if she'd be there as a safety net, if necessary."

"And she probably said yes, assuming she'd never be needed."

"Exactly."

That made sense. Ellen had explored those ideas herself. But it was still difficult to figure out what was so terrible about her that she couldn't have been accepted, too.

"Some of it might even have been about timing," he continued when she didn't speak. "My mother died only a few months after Stuart divorced your mother and married Lynn. Everything was new and most likely overwhelming. Stuart was still having trouble with your mother, trying to kick loose of her long after the paperwork was final. I've heard stories about her driving from Anaconda and showing up drunk out of nowhere, throwing things through the window, screaming at him or my aunt in public and refusing to let him see you. It simply might've been too much for him—easier to put some distance between the two families and take away the leverage having you gave Jan. On top of that, since Lynn was taking me in, she probably felt she couldn't deal with another child. You had your mother—at least in her mind—and I had no one. Also, *I* wasn't any threat to her, you know? With you… My guess is she was insecure enough that she didn't want any competition when it came to her new husband's affections."

"Competition…" Ellen muttered, scarcely able to believe a woman could be that threatened by a child.

"I know. It's immature and unkind and says a lot of things about her I'd rather not face. Because, for all her faults, she's been good to me. But…those kinds of rivalries crop up—"

"With certain small-minded people." She hated the bitterness that crept into her voice. She was afraid he could hear it, too. But it was too late to think better of speaking; the words were already out.

"It must've been rough for you," he said gently.

That she was tempted to lean into the kindness in his voice and let his empathy soothe some of her deepest wounds brought her to her feet. He couldn't care. Not sincerely. He was one of *them.* "The pizza's probably ready. I'd better go grab it."

Fifteen

Hendrix was exhausted by the time they struck water, but he was relieved to see that it wasn't too sandy. "Once we develop this well, it's going to be just fine," he said as they watched water spout from the top of the rig and cascade onto the ground.

Ellen looked as though she was tired, too. She stood back, wearily shading her eyes against the setting sun as she admired the success of the new well. "Thank goodness."

Hendrix glanced toward the road. "I'm surprised Jay hasn't been out here."

"So am I." She checked her phone. "It's getting late. But I haven't heard from him."

If she hadn't heard from him, maybe there was still time to get off the property before his neighbor dropped by to check on the well's progress and caught him helping Ellen. It would be harder to spare the time to finish up tomorrow when he'd be more pressed to take care of the demands of his own business. But he'd have less chance of bumping into Jay while he was with Ellen if he came back during regular working hours. "I'd better get going," he said. "Thanks for dinner."

"It was the least I could do," she said. "Thanks for jumping in to rescue me. Again."

"Could you have said that any more grudgingly?" he said with a laugh. "God, you hate needing anyone."

"I do," she admitted, laughing, too. "I'd much rather be self-sufficient." She sobered. "But I am grateful."

He nodded. "It doesn't hurt to accept a little help every once in a while."

"If you say so. But I definitely plan to pay you for your time, so…don't worry about that."

"I'm not worried about it, because I'm not taking anything. It's your job. You keep the money."

She looked stunned. "No way! This cost you a whole day, and unless we can make quick work of the rest of it tomorrow, it could cost you another. Your time is valuable. I can't accept your help for free."

"It's not up to you," he said with a shrug. "It's up to me."

"I'm going to pay you," she insisted.

"Don't bother because I won't take it."

"Of course you will."

He gave her a look that said to drop it. Then he helped her shut everything down and started toward his truck, only to turn back at the last second. "Hey, you haven't heard anything from that dentist guy you had trouble with last Friday, have you?"

She hesitated as though she wasn't sure how to respond.

"Have you?" he pressed.

She cleared her throat. "Everything's…fine."

He could tell everything wasn't fine—or, at a minimum, she wasn't sure if it was fine. "It was a simple question. You wouldn't give me a yes or a no. What happened? Did you report him to the police?"

"No. I didn't want to risk getting you in trouble."

"So…"

"I just… I reported him to the dating site. I felt I had to alert other women, at least on the site where he's actively trying to date, that there's something wrong with him."

"And? How'd that go?"

"They must've contacted him about it, because he texted me to say I'd better retract my complaint."

"Did you retract it?" he asked, slightly apprehensive that she might've just picked another fight with Jordan.

"No."

Of course not. Ellen wasn't someone who was easy to intimidate. "And did he let it go?"

"So far," she said.

He walked back to her. He was getting to know her well enough to be able to pick up on various nonverbal clues. "Why do I get the impression there's something you're not sharing with me?"

She waved a dismissive hand. "Because it's probably nothing. I mean…he said I'd be sorry, but… I think he was just talking. What can he do?"

Depending on how far he was willing to go, he could do a lot. Hendrix didn't like that he'd even made the threat. "You don't think he'll come back here…"

"No," she said. "But I do wish he didn't know where I live."

"You need to listen to your intuition and keep an eye out. If he shows up, call the police immediately."

She shoved her hands into the pockets of her jeans. "It's a long drive from Libby. I can't believe he'd come all the way down here just to harass me."

Unless getting back at her would give him some kind of pleasure. Maybe he'd connected with other women on the site and was furious they'd be given negative information about him.

Hendrix opened his mouth to say she needed to be cautious regardless of the illusion of safety a five-hour drive might create, but before he could get the words out, the sound of a motor drew their attention. A red truck had turned onto the property. Jay. Hendrix had waited too long to leave. "Damn it," he cursed.

"Do you want to go?" Ellen asked. "I can handle this."

Maybe he should. There was no reason he needed to stay and field Jay's questions. Jay hadn't hired *him*. "I think I will," he said. "What're you going to tell him?"

She blinked several times. "Are you saying…you don't want him to know you helped?"

"I don't see why that would be necessary. As far as I'm concerned, no one needs to know. Just say I stopped by to tell you off for undercutting my bid. He'll believe that."

"You're not going to take any of the credit *or* any money?" she asked.

"Nope. But I *will* let you make me dinner this weekend," he said with a wink and hurried back to his truck so he could take off before he had to face Jay.

Make him dinner? What was Hendrix thinking?

Ellen shook her head as she watched Jay get out of his truck and walk toward her. She'd rather pay Hendrix, she told herself. But the truth was she'd enjoyed being with him today. They'd spent hours and hours together, and she'd loved every second of it.

"That's dangerous," she mumbled to herself. But she didn't have long to stew about it.

"That was Hendrix Durrant I just passed, wasn't it?"

Jay asked, gazing after Hendrix's truck. "What was he doing here?"

Hoping to divert Jay's attention as soon as possible, Ellen located the video of the water spouting from the well. "Nothing. He's just pissed off that I'm drilling this well instead of him."

"Was he giving you any trouble?"

She didn't know how far Hendrix wanted her to go to keep what he'd done a secret, so she hedged as best she could. "Nothing I can't handle."

Jay winced. "I'm sorry if he said something he shouldn't have. I can see why he might be upset. He's my neighbor and was expecting the job."

"He's a big boy. He'll get over it." She stuck her phone under his nose before she had to elaborate any further. "Look at this," she said. "We, er, I... I mean Ben and I... Well, not Ben exactly, because... Well..."

Fortunately, he wasn't listening to her, so she just let her words fade away. The water gushing in the video had completely distracted him.

"You didn't run into any sand like we were worried about?" he asked.

"Doesn't look that way." She could smile now that she'd gotten away with her gaffe of a moment before. "But we'll know more when we finish up. We've still got another fifty feet to go."

"What time will you start up again in the morning?"

Ellen covered a yawn. She'd forgotten to ask Hendrix when he could make it. "I'll come when I can. I've got some other things to do first," she said in case Hendrix couldn't start right away. "But don't worry. The well will be finished before your folks arrive."

He rubbed his beard growth as he nodded. "Perfect."

They spent a few more minutes talking about the size

of the pump and if she'd drilled a big enough hole, and she assured him both would be sufficient for his needs. Then she stumbled wearily to her water truck. Tomorrow morning would come far too soon, but she'd get up whenever Hendrix said he could make it. She was so relieved to be able to do this job, after all, that she was willing to push through any inconvenience.

As she drove off the property, she felt a great deal of gratitude to Hendrix for stepping in and saving her from the consequences she would've faced otherwise.

Smiling dreamily, she headed toward town, allowing herself to revel in what she was feeling for a moment. Then she sat up taller and gripped the steering wheel more tightly. Was his help really as good for her as it seemed? Spending time with him, feeling so grateful, it was changing the dynamic between them.

It was difficult to hold a grudge when she was no longer angry…

She was so caught up in trying to figure out if she was still on safe and stable ground that she almost missed it when a white Audi that looked exactly like the one Jordan had been driving raced past her. White Audis were common enough, but not so much in the country.

Still, it didn't have to belong to Jordan. But she adjusted her rearview mirror to get a better look just in case—and could've sworn it had a green tree and blue sky license plate.

Montana had never issued a license plate like that.

But Oregon had.

"Do you really think it was Jordan?"

Talulah had brought over a plate of pastries. Because the diner was closed on Mondays and Tuesdays, she cleaned out the display cases and brought home whatever she had left, since it wouldn't be fresh enough to sell on Wednesday. What Ellen didn't eat or freeze—which usually wasn't much since she wasn't all that big on sweets—Talulah gave to Brant to take over to the ranch. His brothers could seemingly devour any number of calories without gaining an ounce.

Ellen had inspected the barn and the rest of her property as soon as she got home to make sure everything was as it should be. From what she could see, nothing had been disturbed. But she couldn't get the vision of that Oregon plate out of her mind. "I'm not positive." She scooted her chair closer to the kitchen table as she took a bite of the toasted almond coconut cake that was her favorite Talulah creation. "It was odd to see that license plate when I looked in the rearview mirror. That's all." She didn't add that it probably struck her as more ominous than it should have because Hendrix had seemed so concerned about how Jordan might react to her refusing to remove the complaint she'd lodged. So far, she'd left Hendrix out of the conversation.

Talulah watched Ellen take another bite. "How long ago did Jordan move from Oregon?"

The sweet creamy frosting—her favorite part of the cake—melted in her mouth. "Last year. At least, that's what he told me."

"Shouldn't he have changed his plates over by now?"

"Depends on when his registration expires, right? Not everyone does it immediately."

Leaning back, Talulah folded her arms. "What kind of license plate did he have on his Audi when he came here?"

Ellen sipped the tea she'd made to go with the cake. She'd poured Talulah a cup, too, but Talulah had refused to have anything with it. She said she did enough taste-testing for quality control and didn't need more calories. "I didn't notice," Ellen said. "I wish I had."

Talulah left her tea on the table and went into the living room.

"What are you doing?" Ellen called after her.

"Just taking a look outside."

"It's nearly ten o'clock," Ellen said. "You're not going to be able to see anything."

Talulah's voice drifted back to her. "The porch light's on."

Ellen took another bite of cake while waiting for her friend to return. "I don't think he'd come and stand in the porch light."

"Talking about him coming here at all makes me nervous," her friend said.

Ellen swallowed another bite of cake. "I shouldn't have mentioned it. It's nothing."

Talulah reappeared in the doorway. "It might not be nothing. Maybe you should come stay with us for a while."

The man Talulah had dated before marrying Brant had once thrown a rock through her window, so it was little wonder she was taking Jordan's threats seriously. "That won't stop him from doing something to my house or one of my vehicles," Ellen said. "And if he hurts my rig, I won't be able to work."

"You're worried about your rig?"

"Of course. That's the most valuable thing I own."

"You're not going to stay up all night in the barn to defend your equipment…"

"No. I have to get some sleep. I just feel… I should stay close in case I hear something."

"What would you do if Jordan showed up here?"

"Call the police."

"*Things* can be replaced," Talulah argued. "*You* can't."

"You don't believe Jordan's *that* dangerous, do you? I did an internet search on him before I agreed to date him. It's not like he has a record or anything."

"First offenders start somewhere. Who can say what might cause him to do something he ordinarily wouldn't? You've wounded his pride, and he's angry. Just stay with us for a few days—until he has a chance to calm down and start thinking straight."

"I bet Brant would love that," Ellen muttered.

"Brant wouldn't mind one bit. He loves you, and you know it."

"I'll be fine," she insisted. She was actually more worried about the threat Hendrix posed to her peace of mind. "There's something I haven't told you," she said, putting down her fork.

Talulah looked alarmed. "About Jordan? What'd he do? Does it get worse?"

"No. This is about Hendrix."

Obviously intrigued, Talulah returned to her seat. "Go on..."

"You know I fired Ben this morning..."

"Yes. You were supposed to drill the Haslem well today and couldn't because of him."

"Right. I was going to rip out the carpet in the guest bedrooms instead. But I didn't do that. I was able to proceed with the well, after all."

"*How?*" she asked, holding her cup in midair.

"Hendrix helped me."

Immediately slamming her cup down, Talulah jumped back to her feet. "He didn't!"

"He did. He was there with me for hours today."

"Helping *you*, his competition."

"Yes. He said it was his fault—what happened with Ben—and he was going to make sure I could get the well done."

"What a great guy!"

Ellen gave her a rueful look. "He's the one who caused the problem in the first place," she pointed out.

"But he could've left it at that. He didn't have to try to make it right."

Good thing she hadn't told Talulah about his apology for trying to steal Ben. That would've softened her heart even further. "I hate him," she grumbled.

Talulah started laughing. "No, you don't."

"How do *you* know?"

"Because if there wasn't something more going on, you would've called me the second he made the offer to help. But you weren't planning to tell me, were you..."

Ellen scowled. "I'm telling you now."

"Because you're confused and don't know what to make of it and you need my opinion!"

"I shouldn't have said anything, after all," she muttered, shoving another bite into her mouth, even though she couldn't even taste it. She was so preoccupied with her misery.

Talulah didn't seem remotely penitent for teasing her. "Does Jay know Hendrix helped you?"

"No one does. Except you—now."

"This is exciting!"

"No, it's not! I don't know whether he's my worst enemy or..."

"Or..." she prompted.

Ellen lowered her voice meaningfully. "The only man I'd like to sleep with in Coyote Canyon."

A slow smile stretched across Talulah's face.

"What?" Ellen snapped, too tortured to see the humor in what was happening.

"You're going to be fine. I've seen the way he looks at you. I'm pretty sure he feels the same. But oh, boy, is Lynn going to be mad."

"No doubt. And I have no idea how much that will affect him."

"You think she still has a strong hold on him?"

"I know she does! She took him in when he had nowhere else to go. And they're in business together. His future is entwined with her and my father's."

"I say you give him a chance to work that stuff out, leave it up to him."

"Just trust that he can do it? That would be risky," Ellen said, immediately rejecting her advice. She had no doubt allowing herself to fall for Hendrix would backfire, and she'd be the one to get hurt in the end.

Sixteen

Hendrix was surprised when he didn't hear from Lynn that night. He tried calling her, planning to check in without mentioning Ellen or their disagreement. He was hoping they could move on as if nothing had happened, because he didn't feel he'd done anything wrong.

But she didn't answer. And she didn't call back.

He guessed she was trying to punish him for taking Ellen's side and not apologizing for it afterward. But he couldn't see why the respect, love and loyalty he owed his aunt had anything to do with Ellen. He didn't have to feel the same way she did, did he?

Honestly, Hendrix wished he'd befriended Ellen sooner. But when he was younger, he'd been doing his best to cope with his own issues. Having to be taken in and raised by an aunt left him feeling indebted in a way a son or a daughter would not. He'd seen Ellen rejected and didn't want the same thing to happen to him. He'd been too desperate to prove he was worth rescuing.

But that was before, when he was younger. He could easily have been kinder to Ellen in the past ten or twelve years. Now that he was getting to know her, he couldn't really say why he hadn't. The general feeling in the Fetterman household, he supposed.

He tried watching TV. But there wasn't anything on that could hold his attention. He was too caught up in what it had been like to spend the day with Ellen—what she'd said, how she'd looked, her incredible smile (when she deigned to offer him one) and the skepticism he saw so often in her beautiful eyes when she looked at him.

After turning down the TV, he retrieved his laptop, propped his feet on the coffee table and navigated to the dating website Ellen had mentioned. He was curious to see if she'd removed her profile and if Jordan Forbes was still on there, trying to meet women.

Unfortunately, he had to sign up and create a profile of his own before he could check. Online dating was something he'd never done. But he was offered a free trial he could cancel whenever, and it only took a few minutes to answer some basic questions and slap up a single picture.

After that, he was able to find Jordan immediately. The son of a bitch hadn't left the site. And there was no warning about him that Hendrix could find. Maybe Dr. Forbes had convinced whoever researched complaints at the company that Ellen was lying. A dentist held considerable credibility. And as Ellen had said, he didn't have a criminal record. Perhaps they did enough research to feel they wouldn't be held liable if something terrible happened and that was as far as they went.

Since Jordan was still allowed on the platform, would he be satisfied and leave Ellen alone? Was there no longer anything to worry about?

Hendrix hoped that was the case. He was tempted to let Jordan know he was keeping an eye on Ellen, but he was afraid that would only backfire by antagoniz-ing the dude further.

He'd just decided to wait another week to see what, if anything, happened, when his phone signaled a call from Stuart.

Before he answered, Hendrix glanced at his watch. Eleven fifteen? It wasn't like Stuart to be up so late.

He pressed the Talk button. "What's going on?"

"About to go to bed," Stuart told him. "What's going on with you?"

"In what regard?" There had to be a reason behind this call. Otherwise, they could talk in the morning. He, Lynn and Stuart showed up at the office at 6:00 a.m. sharp every Tuesday, Wednesday and Thursday to co-ordinate and plan for the business. Then they got to-gether more loosely, or by telephone or text, the other days as needed.

"Lynn's been pretty upset since you walked out of here," Stuart told him.

Hendrix had suspected as much. Had she put Stuart up to contacting him so she wouldn't have to lose face? "Is she there with you?"

"No. She's in the bedroom, asleep. I wanted the chance to talk to you in private."

This was completely unexpected. Hendrix couldn't remember another time Stuart had sought him out for a conversation he didn't want Lynn to hear. "You were there when we had the argument. Did you agree with Aunt Lynn or with me?"

"It's not that simple."

Of course he'd equivocate. Stuart would never say a bad word about his wife, even if she was clearly in the wrong. And he rarely made a concrete statement about Ellen. He dodged the subject of his daughter whenever he could—seemed more interested in pretending she didn't exist. "Then why don't you break it down for me?"

Silence.

"Stuart?"

A long sigh came through the phone. "I feel bad about Ellen, Hendrix. I should've done more for her while she was growing up. I think you realize that. But just between you and me—and this is something I've never breathed a word of to Lynn or anyone else, so I'd appreciate you keeping it strictly confidential…"

When he paused, waiting for confirmation, Hendrix said, "Of course."

"I'm not sure she's mine."

Hendrix almost dropped his phone. "As in…*not your daughter*?"

"That's exactly what I mean."

"What makes you think she might not be yours?" Hendrix had always thought he saw a strong resemblance between the two, but that could be the power of suggestion.

His question was met with another long silence. Stuart was obviously reluctant to be having this conversation. But now that something had happened to threaten Lynn's happiness, he was jumping in.

"The way Jan was acting back then," he said at last. "I had no idea what she was doing when I went to work. I was up and out of the house early, had to put in long hours, and she just…seemed to crumble into nothing after Ellen was born. She had no determination to be a functioning member of the family, no willpower, no direction. Nothing I did made her happy. I couldn't get her to help me in any way. She wouldn't even make dinner. I'd get home at night, completely exhausted, only to find Ellen sitting on our neighbor's lap, both he and Jan high as kites."

"A *male* neighbor…"

"Yes."

"You believe he and Lynn were sleeping together?"

He made a clicking sound with his mouth. "She claims they weren't. But…who knows? I couldn't trust her."

"Why didn't you get a paternity test, for God's sake?" Hendrix asked. "If Ellen isn't yours—"

"I wouldn't have owed any child support," he broke in.

"Exactly."

"She would've been worse off with that neighbor as a father than me, Hendrix, and I knew it. He was the biggest loser I'd ever met. So I *wanted* to send her money, and I didn't want Lynn to get upset about what it was costing us or try to stop me."

"You wanted to pay child support for a daughter you didn't even know was yours?"

"She could be. And I raised her as my own for ten years. If I was going to walk away, I wanted her to at least have some financial support."

"But I remember a friend of yours—or a business associate—coming to the house when I was thirteen or fourteen who said Jan was telling everyone in Anaconda that you weren't paying what you owed her."

"She'd say whatever she could to shift the blame for her situation. She may have claimed that, but it was a lie to make herself look like the martyr. I sent my child support every month."

"If Jan was doing drugs, was Ellen even the beneficiary of that money?" he asked.

"I don't know. I had no control over what happened

on that end. All I could do was fulfill my obligation and hope for the best. Jan was *so* difficult. I figured my money had to buy them some food, at least."

Hendrix wondered how Ellen would feel to learn this. Would it make the situation better—or worse? "I get what you were trying to do," he said. "Sort of. But… don't you want to know now whether Ellen is yours? For peace of mind if for no other reason?"

"No."

His tone was unequivocal. "Why not?"

"If she *is* mine, I'll only feel worse for not staying more involved in her life. And if she's not mine, it'll just make Lynn mad at me for not speaking up sooner. Fetterman Well Services had some lean years immediately after we married. There were months when we could barely make ends meet, and yet I sent that money to Jan. Considering how difficult that period was, I think it's best to let sleeping dogs lie, don't you?"

Hendrix wasn't sure. The truth mattered, didn't it?

He got up and began to pace in his living room. "I'm guessing she has no idea you have doubts."

"I've never breathed a word of this to anyone else. But if her mother did cheat on me, maybe she's mentioned the possibility that I'm not Ellen's biological father either to her or someone who's told her."

"I doubt it. That'd be letting you off the hook. As bitter as I've heard Jan is, I don't see her doing that. Besides, if Ellen didn't believe you were her father, she wouldn't be so determined to damage our business."

"True. I guess that makes it unlikely. But Jan used to fill her head with all kinds of terrible things where I was concerned. I heard what she was saying from friends and clients who lived in Anaconda at the time. I couldn't have a relationship with Ellen under those circumstances. It would keep Jan front and center in our lives, and she relished having that hold on me, really tried to take advantage of it. We just couldn't live like that. Lynn was upset all the time. Dealing with Jan and Ellen almost ruined our marriage. I had to choose. I could keep Lynn, you and Leo from experiencing that toxicity, which meant letting go of Ellen. Or I could try to hang on to Ellen and possibly lose the rest of you. And even if I'd chosen Ellen, given Jan's antics, she probably would've wound up hating me as much as she does now."

There could be some truth to that. Lynn had always made Hendrix feel being loyal to her meant not associating with Ellen. Although it had never been expressly stated, not that he could remember, he'd always known better than to cross that line himself. It'd been a messy, emotionally charged situation on every side.

"I can tell you Lynn was right about one thing," Stuart continued. "Ellen didn't do herself any favors. She was *very* difficult at that age. We couldn't deal with her. A weekend with us here and there wasn't going to be enough to counteract the influence of her mother. She was always mouthing off, acting up, running away. We just had to…to put a stop to all the drama."

Hendrix shook his head. His uncle seemed to believe his situation had been like the lifeboats on the *Titanic*. If he'd pulled Ellen aboard their boat, she would've brought Jan with her, and Jan would've caused them all to go under.

Those kinds of decisions weren't easy. Hendrix was glad he'd never had to make one. He hoped, had he been in the same situation, he would've figured out a way to fulfill all his roles. But with Jan as part of the equation, was that even possible? "I see."

"I thought if you understood what things were like back then, you might not judge us so harshly. You know how much Lynn adores you. I don't want Ellen to come between the two of you."

"It's not my place to judge anyone. Lynn's mad at me. I'm not mad at her. But…just to be clear, I don't think I'm willing to take her side over Ellen's any longer."

"What does that mean?"

Hendrix could immediately tell he'd said the wrong thing and tried to explain. "It means I like Ellen, Stu. I want to feel I'm free to be her friend."

He waited but there was no response.

"Hello?"

"Is this one of those situations where you want something simply because you feel we disapprove?" Stuart asked.

"No. Of course not. I'm not a teenager."

"So…what's the sudden attraction?"

He'd been watching Ellen for a while, growing to appreciate her unique beauty, and now he was learning more about her personality. He'd seen how kind she was to Leo. He knew how much Brant, his brothers and Talulah liked her—all people whose opinions he could trust. And everyone knew how hard she worked. From what he could tell, she was sensitive, determined, hardworking and honest, or he would've heard otherwise by now—all of which eroded what he'd believed before. That she'd been a terrible child who'd grown into a terrible adult. That she was "just like her mother" as Lynn claimed. And that she was unfairly targeting their business.

If he were in her shoes, he probably would've done as much or more. "I think she's a good person," he replied and left it there. No way was he going to admit that he was quickly coming to see her as one of the sexiest women he'd ever met...

"Are we still talking about the woman who's been stealing work from us?" Stuart said wryly.

"She's angry, Stu. We just spent fifteen minutes discussing why she might have reason to be."

"I'm not saying you have to mistreat her. I hope you never got the impression I wanted that from you. I'm just saying there are plenty of women in Coyote Canyon, Hendrix. You don't have to be especially close to Ellen, do you? There's just no reason to go in that direction."

He supposed Stuart had a point. As long as he was nice to Ellen and did his best to defuse the rivalry that'd developed between them—to give them all some peace—he didn't have to make any public statements. As strongly as his aunt felt about Ellen, his becoming too friendly with her would not only endanger his relationship with Lynn, it would ruin the work environment at Fetterman Well Services, and if things got bad enough, it could even endanger his job.

And for what? He doubted any kind of relationship with Ellen would work out too well in the end. She was obviously jealous of him, and jealousy was a difficult and inexplicable emotion. One of the hardest to overcome. "No, I don't have to be especially close to her," he said.

"Fine. Let whatever kindness you show her fly under the radar," Stu said, "and all will be good."

Hendrix thought of the moment he'd kissed Ellen at the barbecue. That certainly couldn't be considered "flying under the radar." He shouldn't have done it, especially since he wouldn't be able to follow up on it. "Okay. No problem."

"Great. All's well that ends well," Stuart said. "I'll see you in the morning."

After their early meeting, Hendrix would be going to help Ellen finish the Haslem well. He'd have to dodge any calls he received from the Fettermans and pull away to handle a few things to make it look as though he was working. But he couldn't leave Ellen in the lurch, not when they were so close to finishing. And there was no way he was going to tell Stuart what he was doing, not after this conversation. He knew his aunt would've loved nothing more than to be able to reclaim the Haslem well. That he'd stood in the way and actually made sure Ellen got the job had cost them a significant sum of money. Stuart might let that slide, but he knew Lynn never could.

He'd just help Ellen finish up the well and hope no one ever mentioned that he'd been out at the Haslem property to his family. He'd gotten through one day without anyone noticing; he could get through two. Then he'd try to keep his distance. "Yeah. I'll see you in the morning," he said.

Talulah generally used her second day off to run errands, do some grocery shopping, clean her house and take care of other things she didn't have time to do when she was working. She'd just put some supplies in the back room of the diner and was locking up when she turned and saw a white Audi with Oregon plates parked on the street a few cars down from where she was planning to pick up some dinner.

Taking a few steps toward it, she tried to peer through the front windshield. As far as she could tell, no one was in the car, and she didn't see where the driver had gone, but she was thinking this might be the vehicle that'd made Ellen believe her terrible online date had come back to exact revenge.

If this car was parked in plain sight, right in the center of town, Talulah couldn't imagine it belonged to Jordan Forbes. He wouldn't just hang out indefinitely five hours from where he lived and worked.

Or would he? Maybe he'd taken a few vacation days and was making his presence known as a way to frighten Ellen.

Hoping Ellen could confirm it wasn't Jordan's vehicle, so they'd all be able to rest easier, she pulled out her phone to snap a picture. But just as she was texting that picture to Ellen, she was interrupted by a voice she never liked to hear.

"Well, look who it is…"

The *whoosh* that signaled her text had been sent sounded as she forced her eyes up. It was Charlie, all right—the man she'd left standing at the altar when she was only eighteen. In her opinion, not getting married at that young age had turned out to be the best thing for both of them, but it didn't matter. He and his family would never forgive her.

She often lamented that falling in love with Brant meant moving back to Coyote Canyon. Now she had to face Averil, Charlie or someone else in the Gerhart family on almost a daily basis.

"Hey," she said, faking a smile.

He gestured at her restaurant. "Diner's not open today, huh?"

"No. I'm closed every Monday and Tuesday." As far as she knew, he'd never been inside the diner. He was probably the only person in town who hadn't crossed the threshold at least once. Even his sister, Averil, and his parents had come in, although his parents only deigned to visit when they were with other people on a night out. And they wouldn't acknowledge her when they came in. They treated her no differently than they would an employee who was a total stranger.

"Seems to be going over nicely," he said. "Congratulations on your success."

Seems to be? Hadn't he seen the long lines that formed outside her door every Saturday? Because there wasn't a lot of breaking news in Coyote Canyon, there'd been several write-ups about the diner in the paper, too. "Fortunately," she said. "But owning this kind of business is a lot of work."

"I bet."

He didn't sound as though he cared.

"How's Brant?" he asked.

Like her and Averil, Charlie and Brant used to be best friends. Brant had been the best man at the wedding where she'd almost married Charlie, and Charlie had been the best man at the wedding where she did marry Brant. But relations had been and still were strained. She believed Charlie had only been part of the wedding to save face by pretending he didn't care that his best friend was marrying his ex-fiancée. If she had her guess, he'd also been hoping—maybe he still was—that they wouldn't be happy together. She was betting the whole family would gloat over a divorce.

Whether that was true or not, he and Brant hardly spoke to each other these days, and Talulah was sort of relieved about that. Otherwise, she'd have to face Charlie a lot more often. "Brant is good," she replied. "Busy with the ranch."

"As always."

"As always." She could've asked how he was doing with his real estate business. He sold homes and buildings, even raw land—it was difficult to specialize in such a small town. But he wasn't very successful, probably because, according to Brant, he didn't put much effort into his career. Brant said he did everything *but* work.

That wasn't the reason she didn't ask, however. She didn't care to prolong the conversation. Feeling as though she'd been cordial long enough and could now move on, she was about to say, "It was nice seeing you," except he spoke before she could.

"Averil told me that you're hanging out with Ellen these days."

Had that incident in the grocery store not occurred, she would've been surprised by the change in topic. Given that it had, Charlie would want to rub salt in the wound by reminding her that her former friend had said some very unkind things about her. "Ellen and I are friends," she said.

"So are you and Jane Tanner, but I never see you with her anymore."

Talulah did see Jane occasionally. She loved Jane and always would. "Since she met her boyfriend, she's been gone a lot. You probably know this, but he lives in Bozeman."

"She still works here," he pointed out.

Jane owned a secondhand shop only a few blocks away. They could see each other more. But she had to be diplomatic about their relationship. Growing up, it'd always been the three of them—Averil, Jane and her—so Jane was trying to be neutral and remain friends with Averil, too, which wasn't easy. Averil demanded more from her, and since she'd married, Talulah had stepped back to ease the tension.

Besides, it was more comfortable for her to be with

Ellen, who had no prior loyalties to anyone in town and lived so close.

Charlie was just needling her, she decided. He did that whenever he could—tried to shame her or make her feel uncomfortable. It was his way of getting back at her for the hurt she'd caused him.

"I see her whenever I can," she said and started to turn away.

"The only reason I mentioned Ellen is because I saw something really weird yesterday," he said, stopping her.

The curiosity his question evoked was obviously what he was going for. "What's that?" she asked as she turned back.

"A Fetterman Well Services truck and a Truesdale Well and Pump Services truck on the same property *for hours.*"

He'd seen Hendrix helping Ellen drill the Haslem well? That was bad luck. He and his family knew everyone in town and loved having something to say that others might find shocking or interesting. They considered themselves well-connected and always in the know. "How odd," she said, adding a dismissive tone to her voice so she wouldn't simply confirm that he'd hit on a juicy bit of gossip. "Are you sure that's what you saw?"

"Couldn't miss it. I listed the property next to Jay Haslem's last week and was out there putting up my For Sale signs. I had a bit of trouble getting them into the ground and had to leave to get some more tools. Then I got busy doing other things, so it was several hours later by the time I got back. And yet those two trucks hadn't moved."

She blinked at him. "So? What are you saying?"

Lines creased his forehead as he frowned at her. "I'm saying it's weird that Hendrix and Ellen would spend so much time together. Don't you think? The last I heard they weren't even on speaking terms."

"Maybe Jay stipulated they work together," she said.

"Why would he do that?"

"Who knows? It's none of my business," she said. *Or yours*, she wanted to add but didn't. "Anyway, things can always change."

He shoved his hands into the pockets of his wrinkled chinos. "I never expected *that* to be one of them."

"Maybe it isn't. I don't know anything about it." She hiked her purse up higher on her shoulder. "Well, I've got a lot to do. I'd better go."

"Of course," he said. "You're a busy person."

She managed another smile despite the sarcasm in his response. These days, he could barely conceal how much he hated her. But at least she hadn't married him. That would've been worse.

Lifting her chin in an attempt to make it appear he didn't bother her, she started to walk away but had taken only a few steps when her phone dinged. She'd received a text.

Because she was still conscious of that white Audi, which might or might not belong to Jordan Forbes, she paused to see if it was from Ellen.

Sure enough, it was. But her friend's response wasn't what she was expecting.

That looks like his Audi to me.

"Shit." Talulah would've gone back and tried to look through the stores and businesses nearby to see if Jordan was really there and to find out what he was doing. But she'd just gotten rid of Charlie, and she didn't want to run into him again.

Seventeen

"What is it?" Hendrix could tell that Ellen had just received a text message that bothered her.

"Nothing." She had to yell above the sound of the machinery to be heard as she slid her phone into her pocket.

"It's something," he insisted, also raising his voice.

She gestured to signify the noise was too difficult to talk over, no doubt assuming that would put an end to the conversation. But they'd just hit their depth target, so he shut the drill down. After that phone call from Stuart last night, he'd been trying not to interact with Ellen too much today. But trying not to speak to someone he actually enjoyed speaking to seemed so contrived it required too much effort. It came much more naturally to tease and joke around with her, especially since she had such a quirky personality and could be so sarcastic, which he found amusing. They'd even shared some of the food they'd brought for lunch. "What aren't you telling me?" he asked.

She scowled. "I can handle it."

That could be true, but she was worried about something. He'd seen the alarm that'd crossed her face when she looked at her phone. "You won't tell me what's going on?" He gestured at the rig. "We still have to set and wire the pump. We've got nothing but time."

When he came to help this morning, he'd assumed they'd finish in half a day. But thanks to a worn-out bit and a trip to the hardware store, it was nearly three and they still had several hours of work to go. He'd left a few times to pick up parts for the Fetterman drilling crew he was in charge of and to drop some paperwork by the office—to put in an appearance and keep things moving forward somewhat while he was away—but then he'd returned.

With a sigh, she pulled her phone out and showed him what Talulah had sent her.

"That looks like Jordan's Audi," he said as he studied the picture.

"I think it is," she responded.

"Can you be sure? There are more trucks and SUVs than anything else in this part of the state, of course, but Audis are popular enough, especially white ones."

She moved closer to be able to point at the license plate in the picture. "This Audi has Oregon plates."

He grimaced. "What reason could that asshole have for coming back?"

"I have no clue, but I saw this car last night, so if it's him, he's been here for a while."

"On a Tuesday. Doesn't he work?"

"Maybe he's so weird that he's already ruined the practice he purchased and doesn't have enough patients to keep him busy."

Hendrix laughed at her response. "That would certainly make him available. But what's his purpose in coming?"

"To make me regret lodging a complaint against him, I guess."

"Do you still have his number?"

"I do, but...why do you want it?" she asked. "I've blocked him."

How could they get rid of this guy without any more problems? "Maybe you should unblock him and send him a message. See how he responds."

She cast him a dubious look. "What kind of message?"

"Tell him you saw him in town and are wondering what he's doing here. I'd like to get a read on how hostile he's feeling. It might give us an indication of just how nasty he might get."

He expected her to argue. She definitely had a mind of her own. But she surprised him by saying, "I suppose more information is better than less."

"Not knowing will only make us both imagine the worst," he said.

After she unblocked Jordan's number, he watched her type out a message: Hey, I thought I saw your Audi. Are you by any chance in Coyote Canyon?

A ding sounded a few minutes later. "He says it's none of my business," she told him.

"Of course it's your business," Hendrix said. "You live here and want to feel safe. Tell him to go back to Libby."

She hesitated. "If I want this problem to disappear, it wouldn't be smart to antagonize him. Why make him any angrier?"

"If he drove five hours, and he paid for a motel so he could stay the night, he's angry already." *Something* had motivated Jordan to return to Coyote Canyon, and since Ellen was the only person he knew here, it wasn't difficult to guess that his presence had something to do with her. "See if we can draw him out, learn what he intends to do," Hendrix added.

Her chest lifted as she drew a deep breath, but she started another message. I can't imagine why this small town would hold any interest for you, she wrote and then showed it to him.

He nodded, she sent it, and he stood next to her while they waited for the reply.

There's a lot here to like, Jordan wrote back with a winking emoji.

"So he *is* here," Hendrix said.

"Apparently." Ellen began to nibble at her bottom lip. "Maybe this is about pride. Maybe he's just trying to prove that he won't let us push him around."

Hendrix shook his head. "I don't think it's safe to make the assumption that he's only putting on a show."

Not if you came back to cause trouble, she wrote to Jordan.

You're the one who's asking for trouble, came his response.

"They're allowing him to remain on the dating site," Hendrix told her. "I don't think they did a damn thing about your complaint, so reporting him hasn't hurt him. He has no justifiable reason to be mad. He's the one who acted out, which is why I hit him—and you reporting him didn't make any difference."

"How do you know they're letting him stay on the site?" she asked. "I wanted to check but decided not to. I knew if he was still there it would only make me mad."

"I created an account so I could take a look."

"You were that concerned?"

He probably shouldn't have revealed that. It told her he'd been thinking about her way too much. In an attempt to downplay it, he answered without directly addressing her question. "I get the impression he doesn't like anyone finding fault with him. I mean…no one enjoys criticism, but he seems to take greater exception to it than most. There's something wrong with him."

"There's definitely something wrong with him," she agreed and texted Jordan again: The complaint I lodged hasn't gone anywhere. Why don't you just move on with your life?

You're the one who started this.

What are you talking about? We had dinner together. It didn't work out. Time to see who's behind Door #2.

Except it didn't go quite like that. You didn't even give me a chance. And then that friend of yours jumped me.

That's not true!

He didn't argue. In his next text, he wrote, I met someone who knows you last night.

"Why would he change the subject and bring that up?" Ellen asked.

Hendrix shook his head. "See if you can find out."

Where?

Hank's.

"I think he's getting off on trying to intimidate you," Hendrix said. "Or he came back hoping for another chance at me. He could be spoiling for a fight, looking to get even."

"You broke his nose. I doubt he wants to tangle with you again."

"Well, that's what's going to happen if he doesn't back off." He was supposed to be distancing himself from Ellen—had planned to do so as soon as they finished Jay's well. But he wouldn't allow Jordan to harm her.

"I don't want to drag you into this," she said. "Who knows how dangerous he is, how far he'll go."

"That's exactly what I'm concerned about," he said.

That's a long drive to get something to eat, she wrote.

Maybe it is, he responded. But I'm glad I went to the trouble. The woman I met there is a hell of a lot more fun than you. Prettier, too.

Since Hendrix was reading Jordan's texts as they came in, he saw that message the same moment she did. "He's full of shit," he said. "There's no one prettier than you, especially around here."

When she blinked at him, he could tell she was slightly stunned by what he'd said. He was a little surprised he'd blurted that out, too.

"You don't mean it…"

She probably assumed, as one of her chief detractors, that he didn't like anything about her, even her appearance. Maybe especially her appearance. He'd witnessed the polarizing effect it had on the people of Coyote Canyon in general. Some were drawn to it, but he'd heard others say things like, "She'd be attractive if she didn't have all those tattoos…" or "Why doesn't she grow her hair out like a woman should?" She'd probably heard the same things, but she refused to conform, and he admired that she remained true to herself and lived so authentically. "Why would you say that?" he asked.

"Because you've always hated me."

"I have never *hated* you." Although she gave him a skeptical look, he forged ahead. "But even if that were true, hate has nothing to do with looks."

"It definitely factors into whether or not you find someone attractive."

Another text came in from Jordan, interrupting their conversation.

Aren't you going to ask me who I'm talking about?

Ellen rolled her eyes. "He's obviously baiting me," she said and wrote, I'm not sure I care.

Fine. Then I won't tell you.

"Who could it be?" she asked Hendrix.

He shrugged. "I have no idea."

"Whatever. As long as he leaves me alone it doesn't matter."

He got the impression she planned to let it go at that, but Jordan texted her yet again.

I will give you a hint—she hates you as much as I do.

"Now *I'm* curious, too," Hendrix said.

"Hmm. A woman from around here who hates me…" She gave him a sly grin. "Don't tell me he's hooking up with your aunt."

He laughed. "Good one."

"The only person I know who's single, our age, hangs out at Hank's fairly often and has any reason to dislike me is…" She sobered instantly. "No… It couldn't be."

"Who?" he asked.

"I'm thinking… Averil Gerhart?"

"Talulah's friend? Why would she hate you?"

"Because she hates Talulah, too. She's been talking all kinds of crap about her, so much that I had to confront her when I overheard her in the grocery store a few weeks ago."

Hendrix jerked his head toward her phone. "See if you're right."

If it's Averil Gerhart, she can go to hell.

When Jordan didn't write back, she looked up. "It's Averil, all right."

Ellen had just gotten out of the shower and pulled on her robe when a knock at the front door caused her to tense. That would be Talulah, she told herself, coming by to talk about the Audi she'd taken a picture of.

Although…it could also be Jordan and Averil, teaming up to confront her. He had to have come to town for a reason. And Ellen could only imagine how having Averil chirping in his ear would make him feel that much more justified in his hatred of her.

Jordan and what he might have planned had been all she could think about since she'd gotten home. She knew it was just a matter of time before she found out what he was up to. But in a perverse way, she was sort of grateful for the distraction. While she was worrying about Jordan—or Jordan and Averil, depending on how involved Averil decided to get—she couldn't obsess over Hendrix and how effective he'd become at quashing any negative feelings she had toward him.

After quickly running her fingers through her damp

hair to get it to lie right, she padded, barefoot, into the living room and peered tentatively through the peephole.

It wasn't Jordan or Averil. But that didn't mean she could relax. Hendrix was standing on her stoop, looking freshly showered, and he was holding a bottle of wine in one hand and a bouquet of flowers in the other.

What was he doing here? And why would he bring *flowers*?

Although she'd received an arrangement here and there on special occasions, she'd never had a man show up with a bouquet. It seemed sort of old-fashioned—and yet it was the flowers, much more than the wine, that struck her as special.

Hendrix knocked again. "Ellen? It's me."

Since she normally wasn't the giddy type, feeling that excited over flowers made her strangely uncomfortable. She had to wipe the smile from her face before she cracked open the door and leaned into the opening. "Hey. What's going on?"

His gaze moved down over her. "Oh, God. Not the robe again."

"What?" she said, completely taken aback.

"Nothing. Never mind." He lifted the wine and the flowers. "I come bearing gifts."

"Because…"

"Because I thought you'd be more likely to let me in," he said with a laugh.

She eyed the flowers again. They weren't the more conventional roses or carnations. They were an assortment of Montana wildflowers—exactly the ones she would pick for herself. "But…why are you here?" she asked. Surely it wasn't because he wanted to hang out with her…

"If Jordan's going to do something while he's here,

it'll probably be soon. I can't imagine he'll stick around indefinitely. So instead of waiting for you to invite me to dinner next week, I thought I'd spend the evening with you, make sure everything's okay."

"Jordan's not your problem," she pointed out. "You don't have to protect me."

His grin slanted to one side. "But since I'm already here, you might as well let me in." He lifted the flowers again. "I feel sort of stupid holding these. I don't think I've ever brought flowers to a woman before. But they reminded me so much of you I had to get them."

They reminded him of her? Why? She wanted to ask but didn't.

Opening the door wider, she took the bouquet and stepped back to make room for him to come inside. "They're spectacular," she admitted.

"You like them?"

"I do."

"I wasn't sure you'd be a flower type of girl, but they just… I don't know. Screamed your name."

She admired the delicate blue petals of the mountain bluebells, the proud stalks of the purple lupine, the exotic-looking pink prairie smoke and the common yarrow. The flowers were probably less expensive than the wine, but it was the fact that they served no practical purpose—and they'd been such an impulsive purchase—that made them meaningful to her. "Thank you," she said. "I'll just…put them in some water."

"No word from Jordan?" he asked while she was in the kitchen.

"Nothing so far."

"Have you eaten?"

She returned to the living room to find him examining the geode she'd found on her doorstep. "Isn't that pretty?"

"It's gorgeous. Where'd you get it?"

"Someone gave it to me—I don't know who. They left it on my stoop a couple of weeks ago."

"Without taking credit for it?"

"Without taking credit for it."

"Weird."

"I know. The mystery has been driving me crazy. I have no idea who would think of such a thing, but I love it." She placed the flowers, now in a canning jar, on her coffee table, and he put the geode beside them.

"You need to get a critter cam."

"For my doorstep?"

"Then you'd be able to see if Jordan comes back here."

"I might just do that."

"Have you had dinner?" he asked since she'd never answered his question about eating.

"Not yet. I had to clean up the equipment and put it away. I also swung by Jay's repair shop to collect the final check for drilling his well. I was going to call you to see how much I owe you, but since you're here, we can take care of that."

"I told you, I won't accept anything," he said.

She gaped at him. "I won't let you work two whole days for free!" She would feel *way* too indebted to him…

"Keep the money," he said. "I'm hoping it'll hold you over until you can find someone to replace Ben."

She looked from the flowers to him and back again. "Why are you doing this?" she asked softly.

"It's part of that truce I was talking about. See?" His dimples flashed. "A truce wouldn't be an entirely bad thing."

"The kind of truce you're offering includes wine and flowers?"

"If you like…"

She tilted her head to study him. Was he sincere? "What else does it entail?"

"No more animosity, for one. A meal together now and then, maybe with Leo, since he likes you so much. A game of pool if we happen to be at Hank's at the same time. Basically, peace, good feelings and friendship."

Had he forgotten who she was? She was an outcast. And she was convinced that without him her father would never have cut her off. Stuart would've needed someone to help him build the business he'd started, especially during the rough years after the divorce when he couldn't afford to hire a full-time employee, and maybe he would've fought for custody. But Hendrix took her place. He was Child 2.0, an upgraded version of whatever she could've offered—and that was difficult to accept.

Still, shouldn't she blame Stuart instead of Hendrix? She'd had that thought before, of course, but Hendrix had always been so aloof and uncaring she'd been able to lump him in with the Fettermans without feeling too much guilt. Whenever she'd told herself it wasn't fair, that she should focus her anger away from him, she'd just remind herself what a jerk he was.

But now that he was separating himself from Stuart and Lynn and proving to be a much better person than she'd ever dreamed, she wasn't quite sure what to do.

"And your aunt and uncle?" she asked. "They won't like you associating with me."

"Why would they even have to know about it?"

She sank onto the couch. "Have you forgotten that we live in the same small town?"

"We just act normal, casual. No big deal."

"So…it's a *secret* friendship you're after."

"Not secret, no. Just low-key, like I said, in that it's not disruptive to your life or mine."

She didn't believe they could have it both ways, but he seemed convinced of it. Maybe she should let him worry about the Fettermans. "Is this how you're trying to neutralize the threat I pose to your business?" she asked.

He sat across from her. "What you're doing to Fetterman Well Services is a pain in the ass, but so far you're only working in the immediate vicinity. We cover a much wider area, go all over the state, so we'll get by. I admit it's annoying to lose jobs that would fall so easily to us otherwise, especially since I'm in charge of sales. But I'm not calling for a truce to get you to stop underbidding us. You should understand that already. I just helped you drill a well for my *neighbor.* If I wasn't trying to be a good friend to you, I wouldn't have bothered, right? Also, I came over tonight to make sure you don't get hurt by that loser you met online. I'm not out to take advantage of you in any way."

"It's the sudden change in your behavior that's confusing to me," she said.

"I'm sorry. I was angry over your business tactics. But I've apologized about Ben and tried to make it right."

She cleared her throat. "Okay. Supposing I accept all that. How do you see our separate businesses going forward? How do I know you won't just…get angry again?"

"I guess you won't know that. But I'm hoping there'll be no reason for there to be any more trouble between us. With luck, there should be enough work for both companies. The Fettermans might just have to travel a bit more."

Which would bite into their bottom line. That wouldn't make them mad? She couldn't travel. She wasn't well established enough to find those jobs, let alone bid on them. She was in a much more precarious situation, living month to month—not that she was willing to admit that to him. "Are you sure? Because if a truce means I can't compete with you—"

"It has nothing to do with business," he assured her. "But…could you at least go out to each jobsite and create your own bids instead of simply using mine to undercut my price? That seems predatory to me."

If she agreed, this friendship was going to cost her time and money—both of which were in short supply. But all she could think about was how he'd come to her rescue with Jordan, how he'd made himself show up and apologize after trying to steal Ben and then helped her drill the well she would've lost as a result.

Besides, she could understand why her business practices would upset him. She wouldn't want anyone using her bids to undercut her, either.

Or maybe those were just excuses to give up the fight. She was tired, she realized, tired of carrying a grudge. She'd been enemies with Hendrix, Lynn and her father since she was eleven years old. Maybe she'd be happier setting all of that aside—at least when it came to him. Just doing that would lighten the emotional load.

"You're considering it…" he said.

"I'm considering it," she admitted.

He came to her and crouched at her feet so he could take her hands. "Let's give it a shot."

She stared down at his long, tanned fingers. He had a few nicks and cuts—proof of the physical kind of work he did—but his hands were large and warm, and even though he wasn't trying to be evocative in any way, she found his touch oddly stirring. "Okay," she said. Then she shocked herself by leaning forward and pressing her mouth to his.

Eighteen

This was the last thing Hendrix had ever expected to happen. Ellen had been so wary and tentative with him. He hadn't even been sure she'd allow him to stay and look after her tonight. And yet she'd just pressed her lips to his as if…as if she'd been so compelled she couldn't stop herself?

He certainly didn't mind. He could smell the shampoo or conditioner she'd used in her hair, which was damp, and feel the warmth emanating from her body only inches away while her hands still gripped his tightly in her lap—and felt slightly intoxicated by it all.

Instead of breaking off the kiss right away, as he feared she might, she opened her mouth for him. That was when he let go of her hands to cup her face and hold it steady as he deepened the kiss. She wasn't being aggressive. She'd started this, but he'd been eager enough to take the lead the second he felt he could do so without scaring her off, and she seemed just fine with letting him. At least she was willing to explore the spark they both must've felt when he kissed her after the barbecue. Despite their history, she seemed as curious and intrigued by what was happening here as he was.

The second their tongues met, he heard himself groan. He couldn't remember ever having such a strong reaction to a simple kiss, but as he allowed himself to melt into her, he felt her melt into him, as well, and the next thing he knew, her hands were clenched in his hair, holding him right where he was. Then *she* groaned, and he knew they weren't going to break apart. Not tonight. This kiss was merely the beginning…

He was dying to slip his hands inside her robe. He'd started to crave the feel of her body when she'd answered the door in the same robe a couple of weeks ago. The thought of being able to explore the shape of her breasts and the contours of her stomach and thighs made him hard as a rock. But he didn't dare move too fast. He wasn't sure how far she'd be willing to go.

He was hoping she'd take off his shirt or do something else to signal that this was more than just a make-out session. But then she drew back.

The disappointment that welled up proved so acute he almost said, "No!" and pulled her close again. But he wouldn't pressure her. He knew, as much as he wanted to continue what she'd started—or maybe he'd started it when he kissed her at the barbecue—they'd probably regret it tomorrow. Given the past and who they were to each other, he still couldn't quite explain how they'd come to be perched on this dangerous precipice in the first place. She was the last person he should be getting so intimate with. He'd just promised Stuart he'd keep everything to do with her low-key and casual. Making love to her hardly fulfilled that promise.

Closing his eyes, he rested his forehead against hers as he caught his breath. "That was incredible," he whispered. "I don't think I've ever experienced a kiss in quite the same way."

Her hand lifted his chin so that he had to look into her eyes. "This is crazy."

"It's crazy," he agreed. "But it's good, right? You feel it, too, don't you?"

"I feel it," she admitted.

"What are we going to do?" he asked.

"I don't know. There's so much going on inside my head—a cacophony of voices. On top of all that, it's been a long time for me since..."

"Since..." he repeated.

"I've been with a man."

The fact that she'd even bring that up made his heart race. It showed he wasn't the only one thinking about taking this a lot further. "How long?"

"Nearly three years—since before I left Anaconda."

She hadn't slept with anyone since moving to Coyote Canyon?

Actually, he wasn't all that surprised. He saw her as a warrior—someone who tended to push others away, mostly out of a lack of trust. Someone who insisted on charging ahead, sword drawn, to take life on alone. "It's been a little over six months for me," he said, thinking of Jennifer Pullman, his ex-girlfriend. "But...you've heard it's like riding a bike, haven't you?" he said jokingly. "No matter how long it's been, it's easy to slip right back into it."

"I don't know about that—not with you."

"Especially with me," he said and reached for the belt on her robe. "Can I see you?"

When she hesitated, he moved his hand away. But then she untied the robe herself, and he could scarcely breathe as she opened it enough that he could see two or three inches of her all the way down to her belly button.

He wanted to pull it open even further. But he was

being careful not to spook her. He allowed his fingers to graze her waist instead, before sliding his hands around to her bare back.

"Are you sure you're okay with this?" he asked but didn't give her a chance to answer before adding, "God, I hope you're going to say yes."

She didn't laugh as he'd expected. She was too busy staring into his eyes. What she was looking for, he couldn't say. His level of sincerity? His level of desire? Some kind of reassurance?

Or was she feeling slightly victorious for making him want her?

He couldn't tell but decided to assume the best when she let him kiss her again. Then he moved his hand to cup her right breast, which was small like the rest of her but just as perfectly formed, and the way she let her head fall back and closed her eyes let him know that, for good or bad, she was giving herself over to the experience.

"You're beautiful, Ellen," he murmured as he parted her robe a little wider and lowered his head to take her nipple in his mouth.

The sound she made sent so much testosterone through him he wasn't sure he'd last long enough to get inside her. He had to lift his head and take several deep breaths to calm down.

He got the impression she didn't fully buy the compliment he'd given her, but she was caught up in what they were doing, too. He knew that when she held his head, encouraging him toward her other breast, and he suckled her while sliding one hand up her thigh.

She stiffened slightly as he drew closer to the sensitive area he was seeking.

"It's okay," he whispered and gently pulled her forward as he nudged her legs open wider.

She put up a hand as if to stop him—obviously unsure. But as he continued to caress her, waiting and hoping she'd quit fighting what she was feeling, her eyes slid closed and she relaxed, allowing him the access he wanted.

"Oh, wow," she gasped as he pressed a finger inside her. She really seemed to enjoy that, enough to lean back to give him even more unobstructed access, but when he began to kiss his way down her stomach, she sat up.

"Hendrix…"

He was so intent on what he was doing—and what he wanted to do—that he couldn't even answer. He was excited to touch and taste as much of her as possible.

"Don't worry," he told her, and that seemed to reassure her, because she let him lift her legs over his shoulders. "Everything will be okay," he said and remained on his knees in front of her as he pulled his finger from her warm wetness and replaced it with his mouth.

This was far more than Ellen had expected, but the desire she felt had overcome her usual caution. She couldn't even bring herself to think about the reasons she shouldn't allow Hendrix to touch her so intimately. What she was experiencing in this moment crowded out everything else.

As the pleasure increased, her breathing grew ragged. She was edging closer and closer to climax and was beginning to worry about the opposite of what she'd been worried about a few minutes earlier—not that he'd touch her but that he'd stop touching her.

Fortunately, he didn't. As the tension built, she felt

her body go taut—then the pleasure broke over her like a tidal wave crashing through a barrier. She jerked and gasped and he lifted his head, wearing a self-satisfied smile as he watched her recover. "Was it good?" he asked.

"One of the best," she admitted, and his dimples deepened as he tugged her to her feet and led her down the hallway to her bedroom.

This is my chance, she thought. She should say something to stop the madness before it went any further.

But he wouldn't appreciate her bailing on him at this point, and she wouldn't blame him. Besides, she'd been careful for so long. Right now, it felt like she'd been *too* careful. Was she any happier not having a love life and doing nothing but work?

No. The years were passing, and she wasn't taking full advantage of them. If she wasn't careful, she'd wind up like Talulah's aunt Phoebe, who passed away a year ago in her eighties never having had a long-term relationship. She'd grown so cautious she shut out all possibility of romantic love for fear of the pain it could cause. Ellen didn't want to end up dying without feeling as though she'd truly lived.

So she was going to be brave enough to remain open to certain possibilities, even if they felt dangerous and could result in getting hurt.

Right now, with Hendrix lifting her and playfully tossing her onto the bed, the risk certainly seemed to be worth the reward. But it probably wasn't the best time to make such a judgment call. Her ability to reason was gone—had been lost when she'd opened her robe and other, more pressing needs filled her head.

They could talk later, she told herself, and regain the emotional and physical distance they should've kept—then move ahead as friendly acquaintances, just as they'd already agreed.

"Do you have any birth control?" he asked.

She'd gone off the pill before she'd ever moved to Coyote Canyon. "Sorry. I told you it's been years for me."

He checked his wallet and seemed relieved to find a lone condom. "It's been so long for me, too, that I wasn't sure it'd be there," he said. "Thank God it is."

He didn't seem to be having second thoughts, which surprised her. What he'd done in the living room was one thing. But making love in the traditional sense? They'd been enemies since she moved to town! And not a lot had happened to change that. This was sudden and reckless, but it was also the most exciting thing she'd ever experienced.

She opened her mouth to warn him that they were probably making a terrible mistake. Or, at a minimum, to offer him something more like what he'd done for her in the living room. Surely, he, too, had to be worried about the ramifications of going so far.

But then he pulled off his shirt.

"Oh, wow…" she said.

He gave her a quizzical look. "What?"

He didn't know? She could've said, "You look incredible, that's what." But she bit her tongue. As far as she was concerned, she was revealing enough for one night.

"Nothing," she said and welcomed him into her arms—probably too readily—as soon as he climbed into bed. She might pay a high price for her actions later but…whatever this was, she wasn't going to miss it.

Ellen woke to the sound of Talulah banging on her door. "Ellen! Ellen, open up! I'm worried about you. Are you okay?"

Too groggy to immediately gather her faculties, she rubbed her face. It was early enough that it was still dark. Talulah must be on her way to the diner. So why had she stopped by? What was going on? They typically didn't see each other until the workday was over.

She was about to roll out of bed when she felt movement beside her—and the brush of a warm, well-muscled leg. It wasn't until then that everything that'd happened last night came tumbling back to her in full detail. She and Hendrix, of all people, had made love. When she drifted off to sleep, she'd assumed he'd get up and leave before morning. They couldn't have his truck discovered at her house. But he was still there.

"What's going on?" he mumbled, obviously still half asleep himself.

She climbed out of bed as fast as possible and scrambled to find clothing. She'd left her robe in the living room, but, thankfully, there weren't any underclothes out there. She hadn't been wearing any when he came over...

"Talulah's here," she said. "Because Jordan's in town, she tried to get me to stay with her and Brant, but I wouldn't do it, so she's probably coming to check on me."

"I'm glad she's looking out for you, but...why'd you refuse?"

"Because I'm not going to let Jordan scare me out of my own house. And I felt like I needed to stay and protect my equipment and my belongings, keep an eye out so I could call the police if I heard or saw anything unusual."

"But then I came over..."

She grabbed a sweatshirt and yanked it on, not bothering with a bra. "Yes."

"Well, I, for one, am happy you were here," he said with a lazy smile as she pulled on a pair of sweatpants.

She couldn't believe he didn't seem to be more concerned. "You understand we could be discovered, don't you?"

"You said it was Talulah. You don't trust her not to say anything to anyone?"

She didn't answer that question. She didn't want anyone to know, *including* her best friend. "Don't make any noise. I'll be right back."

Talulah knocked again as Ellen hurried down the hallway. "Ellen? You in there? I'm going to call the police if you don't answer—"

"I'm here," Ellen yelled back before she could finish that sentence and opened the door—only to realize a second later that she'd forgotten to toss the robe puddled near the couch into the kitchen or somewhere out of sight.

That wasn't a big deal, though. She could talk her way out of it easily enough—as long as Talulah hadn't also seen Hendrix's truck.

"What's going on?" She was breathless and her heart was pounding, but she could see that Hendrix's vehicle wasn't in her driveway, as she'd feared it might be. He must've parked somewhere else, farther away, like he had the night he'd busted Jordan's nose.

"I've been texting you, but you haven't answered. Normally, you're up by now."

She shoved a hand through her hair. "What time is it?"

"It's only six thirty, but when I didn't see your lights on as usual, it spooked me—what with Jordan being in town. Otherwise, I wouldn't have thought anything about it. I mean…it's still early."

Ellen covered a yawn. She hadn't gotten much sleep. She and Hendrix had enjoyed each other on and off for hours before they'd both grown so exhausted they'd fallen asleep for the rest of the night. "Sorry to scare you. Everything's fine. I just...didn't rest well."

Talulah grew concerned. "You look a little flushed. Are you feeling okay?"

She was embarrassed, not feverish. "I'm fine. Just... warm from being under the covers."

"Oh. Okay. Well..." She turned to look out over the yard.

Ellen caught her breath for fear she'd spot Hendrix's truck, after all—wherever he'd left it—but it was still dark enough to offer some protection and nothing seemed to register as unusual.

"I'll head over to the diner, then," Talulah said. "Just wanted to make sure Jordan hadn't been an asshole last night."

"I have no doubt Jordan's always an asshole, but maybe he can't help it," she quipped. "At least he didn't show up here."

"I hope he goes home and leaves you in peace."

"Me, too. Thanks for checking on me."

"Call me if you hear from him."

"Will do." Ellen watched Talulah walk to her SUV, get in and drive off before closing the door.

"Are we in the clear?"

She turned to see Hendrix at the entrance to the hallway, wearing only his jeans, which weren't buttoned all the way. "We are," she said, sighing in relief. "She seemed to have no clue. Where'd you park your truck?"

"On the far side of the barn, where it can't be seen from the road or their place."

"Good thinking."

He yawned as he scratched his bare chest, which had been such an irresistible sight to her last night. It looked just as good this morning but the shock of having Talulah show up at her door had pulled her out of whatever craziness had gripped her before.

"Any chance you'll be making coffee this morning?" he asked.

"Yes. Eggs and toast, too. But we don't have long. You'll have to eat and hurry out of here before it starts to get light."

"It can't be *that* late already. Seems so early."

"Only because we had a short night."

"What time is it?"

"Nearly six thirty."

His eyes flew wide. "Are you kidding me?"

"No."

He turned and jogged back to the bedroom without another word.

She went into the kitchen to put on a pot of coffee, but he came out fully dressed—boots and all—before she could even get the beans ground.

"Gotta go," he said. "I'm late for a meeting."

"Where?"

"At the office."

"With Stuart?"

"And Lynn, who's already mad at me."

"Why's she mad?"

He hesitated, then seemed to think better of explaining. "It's a long story. I'll tell you later."

Would they even be talking later? She'd resolved that she'd allow herself only one night with him.

She gestured to the counter where she'd been using the grinder she'd purchased from Jane Tanner's vintage furniture and gift shop a few months ago. "So…no cof-fee?"

"Not today. But thanks. I'll… I'll call you later."

She said okay, even though she wasn't sure he'd ac-tually do it. She wasn't sure she wanted him to. It'd be smarter to move on as if last night had never happened. After all, what could they say? There was nowhere to go. Sex with her hadn't changed his relationship with Stuart, Lynn and Leo.

And yet… Part of her hated the idea of him walk-ing away and never thinking of her again. A *big* part.

She expected him to turn and go. He was obviously feeling some pressure. But he surprised her by taking the time to cross the floor and kiss her on the forehead. "Don't worry about anything. It'll be fine," he said. Then he hurried out of the house, and she went to the window to watch him stride to the barn. Although he soon disappeared from view, memories of their time together paraded through her mind.

She'd never felt quite the same with any other man, which worried her.

All the more reason to keep your distance in future.

His truck passed in the gathering dawn, and she sighed. Sleeping with Hendrix had probably been the stupidest thing she'd ever done. She was supposed to be looking for a man who could love her and make her happy, not creating more problems than she already had.

But she'd just experienced one of the best nights of her life. So much about the way he'd behaved—generous, tender, funny and sweet—made it hard to simply forget and move on.

She could do it, though, couldn't she? If she got back on track immediately, maybe they'd get away with what they'd done. As far as she was concerned, life owed her a freebie. Until now, anything that could go wrong typically had.

She allowed herself a smile as she remembered Hendrix pressing himself inside her. *That* had been a moment.

She was still thinking about it an hour and a half later while standing outside the bank, waiting for it to open. But her good mood quickly dissolved when Jay Haslem called to say someone had vandalized his new well.

Nineteen

Jay had found the well cap removed and "Ellen's a bitch" spray-painted on the only building on the property—a rickety old chicken coop. There were tire tracks in the mud by the well itself, and after trying to run the pump and getting no water, Ellen knew what had most likely happened.

"What do you mean someone's put trash or rocks or something down the hole?" he asked after she explained. "Who would do such a thing?"

"I have no idea," she said. The graffiti on the coop told them the reason was her. Whoever it was probably hadn't realized she'd already finished the well—finished it and been paid. That shifted the liability to Jay, which was lucky for her, but she felt terrible for him. He didn't have the money to withstand this kind of loss any more than she did.

He shoved his hands into the pockets of his freshly laundered coveralls and scowled at the hole. "Hendrix couldn't be responsible for this, could he?" he asked. "He was pretty mad that he didn't get the job—"

"No," she assured him. "Hendrix would *never* do something like this."

When Jay looked up, obviously surprised by her response, she knew she'd been too quick to defend her rival. To everyone else, Hendrix was her mortal enemy, and it would be better if they didn't realize that had changed. "I mean, *you* don't really think he'd sabotage your well, do you?" she said, backing off so she wouldn't sound quite as positive.

The way he shook his head showed a measure of uncertainty. "I don't want to think that. But you should've seen him when he met me out here not too long ago... He was pissed that I had him bid on the job, then gave it to you."

No wonder Hendrix had gone after her driller. She hadn't realized he'd been quite that mad. "He might've been upset, but I can't imagine he'd risk his career and his reputation over losing one well. That would be stupid. And Hendrix is anything but stupid."

"True," he allowed, somewhat grudgingly. "But... who else could it be? Who else would even know I'm having a well drilled out here?" He gestured at the graffiti. "And that you're doing it?"

She winced as, once again, she read her name written in sloppy red paint. If Ben was finally back in town, *he* could be responsible. She would've suspected Jordan, too. He'd also had both motive and opportunity. But she couldn't see how he'd know she was working in this particular location. He wasn't familiar with the area, had no idea what jobs were on her schedule. "I wish I could tell you," she said.

She could've informed Jay she'd fired Ben—that, at the moment, he was far angrier than Hendrix. But she didn't want to make a big deal of it. Jay might ask who'd helped her with the well if she didn't have Ben, and then she'd have to admit it was Hendrix, which would seem weird since she hadn't told him before.

Nothing good could come of heading in that direction. Besides, she didn't want to cast any aspersions on Ben in case she was wrong. He'd certainly be able to tell that the well was finished. All her equipment, including her rig, had been moved off the site. But maybe he was so angry he simply didn't care and was out to cause any trouble he could.

"Can you fix it?" Jay asked.

That depended on whether she could get whatever had been put down the well out. "I can try." She had to reschedule her other jobs, anyway, until she could replace Ben. She'd been planning to take care of that this morning, then post notices online and in town. She just hadn't had the chance to get started on that yet. She'd already given herself today as a cushion, in case she ran into problems drilling Jay's well. At least a day in between jobs was customary for her. But it was already Wednesday, and she was supposed to repair a pump this week. She could also get an "out of water call" at any point and have to head over to another well. Fortunately, those types of calls could keep her in business until she could drill again.

"How much will it cost?" he asked.

She lifted her hands, palms up. "Depends on what I find. If I can get whatever it is out relatively easily, it won't cost that much."

He scratched the back of his neck. "And if you can't?"

"Let's hope I can." She knew he didn't want to hear that he might be looking at drilling a whole new well, not when this one had turned out so beautifully. That would cost him what he'd already paid, and there was no guarantee a second well would produce the water this one had, even if it was on the same property. "I'll do what I can for you today without charge," she told him. "And we can reassess the situation after I've diagnosed the problem and determine how we want to proceed."

"You're going to work for free?"

When she nodded, he visibly relaxed. After all, it wasn't as if he could go to any insurance company. Most people didn't carry insurance on raw land. That was rare, so rare she knew better than to even ask.

"Thanks. I appreciate your help."

"No problem." After all, she felt partially responsible. Whoever had done this obviously hated *her*, not Jay.

She glanced once more at the writing on the coop. Was this Ben's doing? Jordan's? *Averil's?* Jordan had connected with the woman she'd confronted for being a terrible friend to Talulah. Maybe the two of them had a few drinks, riled each other up and did this together.

That was somewhat plausible, but how would Averil know where she was working?

"Let's just keep our fingers crossed it's something I can handle in one day," she said. "Then we'll both get out of it relatively unscathed."

"I've got my fingers *and* toes crossed," he said. "My wife is going to freak out about this."

"You might want to install a critter cam after work in case whoever it is comes back. We don't want any further problems."

"Good idea. I'll do that." He pulled his key fob from his pocket. "I've gotta get over to the auto shop. I'm behind enough as it is. Will you call me as soon you know more?"

"Of course."

She watched his truck bounce and sway over the

ruts in the drive as he took off, probably a little too fast
since he was two hours late for work, then squatted to
take a closer look at the tire tracks in the mud around
the well. She'd seen enough forensic shows to wish the
police would at least attempt to match the tread to a
specific tire, but she couldn't believe the department
in Coyote Canyon would go after a mere vandal using
forensics, even if they were sophisticated enough to
have the capability.

Still, the tracks were so clear she decided to take
a picture before she tried to repair the damage that'd
been done.

While she had her phone out, she received a text
from Hendrix.

Jay just called me. He said someone threw something
down his new well.

She frowned as she read the message. Looks that
way. Did he ask if it was you?

He did.

What'd you tell him?

That I couldn't have done it because I was in bed with
you. :)

Her heart skipped a beat. What?

Kidding. Told him it wasn't me, of course. But I'm not
sure he believed me. He's pretty upset.

I can see why. This is such a bummer.

Her phone rang. Apparently, Hendrix was tired of texting because he was calling her instead. "Hello?"

"Jay told me what was written on the coop," he said. "You don't think it could be Jordan, do you?"

"Jordan came to mind right away, of course. But how would he know where I've been working?"

"Averil. She and her family seem to know everything about everyone."

"True. But where I've been working the past two days? That's a pretty minute detail. I don't really speak to any of the Gerharts. Although... Do you know if she's friends with Jay or his wife?"

"It's possible."

Ellen hated how much she liked the sound of Hendrix's voice. After last night, she'd formed too many positive associations with it. They hadn't wanted anything to do with each other for most of their lives and yet they'd certainly been compatible in the bedroom. He'd been an excellent lover, confident without being pushy, intuitive, naturally good in the way he moved and handled her body...

She cleared her throat. "Then she could've heard about it, I suppose."

"Averil has lots of family in the area. Maybe word got around to her."

"What about your aunt?" Ellen asked, finally voicing the question she'd been suppressing all along.

"You think *she* told Averil?"

"I think she may have sabotaged the well."

"No," he said. "No way."

"I can't imagine she's very happy that I ended up with the Haslem job."

"She's not. But she knows better than to do something illegal."

Lynn had never seemed like a paragon of virtue to Ellen. Ellen believed she'd do what she could to get even. The question wasn't whether it was illegal; it was whether she believed she could get away with it. And maybe she'd somehow been presented with the perfect opportunity last night.

But Hendrix loved Lynn; she didn't share what she was thinking because she didn't want to cause an argument. "If you say so."

"Do you think you'll be able to drill whatever's in the well out?"

"Hard to say at this point. I don't even know what it is."

"Let's hope it's not cement. Or dynamite, like Stuart used back in the day to remove obstructions."

"Trust me. I'm hoping."

"Jay said you're trying to fix everything for free."

"If I can. Depends on the extent of the damage."

He lowered his voice. "That's nice of you, Ellen. You're such a good person, you know that?"

That wasn't something she was used to hearing. She'd had to prove herself to everyone here in Coyote Canyon. It hadn't been much different in Anaconda, actually. "Yeah, well, don't let the word get out. You'll ruin my reputation."

He chuckled. "The people who matter already know."

Like him? Did *he* matter?

Sadly, after last night he seemed to matter more to her than he should. As much as she'd enjoyed herself, she lamented getting caught up with him like she had.

Shading her eyes, she gazed across the lot at the chicken coop. *Ellen's a bitch.* "Your aunt and my father don't think much of me. Are you saying they don't matter?"

"Lynn's just plain wrong."

"And Stuart?"

"He's trying not to upset the woman he lives with. He prizes peace more than anything, and he can't have peace if he doesn't agree with his wife."

"Forgive me if I don't feel any sympathy for his 'difficult' position."

"Deep down, he loves you, Ellen. I firmly believe that."

She wished *she* could believe it. But he'd proved otherwise. "What he feels doesn't matter to me anymore. If he can't treat me any better than he's treated me over the years, what good is love?"

"I can't blame you for feeling the way you do. My aunt's done a lot for me, so I feel guilty saying anything negative about her, but the raw truth is she deserves a large part of the blame. Stuart tries to keep her happy, but she's high-strung and temperamental—"

"Not to mention petty and selfish."

There was a slight hesitation before Hendrix spoke again. "I won't go that far, but I will acknowledge it can be hard to get along with her. For some reason— a reason I don't fully understand—she's got her mind set against you and won't give you or anyone else the chance to change it."

Had *he* tried to change it? Was he alluding to some effort of his? She couldn't imagine he'd done much. He'd only recently started interacting with her in a friendly way. "I don't expect any major improvement after so long." She climbed back into her truck. "I'd better get busy. I've got to go home and get my drill so I can fix this mess."

"Wish I could help you, but after being away from my own job for two days, I'm backed up over here. I'm afraid if I disappear again, it'll send a red flag to Lynn and Stuart."

He'd already done far more than she expected. "I appreciate the help you've already given me. Have a good day." She was about to disconnect when he stopped her.

"Ellen?"

"What?"

"Can I see you again?" he asked.

Her chest grew so tight it felt like she was caught in a vise. "I'm sorry, but... I don't think continuing what we started last night would be a good idea," she said and forced herself to press the End button right after. Otherwise, given a few more seconds, she was afraid she'd change her mind.

To get her phone out of her hands as soon as possible, she tossed it on the passenger seat as she got behind the wheel, waiting to feel some sort of elation—or even relief—for having done what she should've done last night.

But it didn't come. She felt terrible instead, as if she'd lost or broken something meaningful and important.

Trying to ignore the dark cloud that hung over her, she spent the next five hours removing what was clogging the well, which turned out to be a chunk of cement. Someone had poured a bag down the hole, but it hadn't encountered enough water to set up correctly and came out much more easily than she'd expected.

When she called Jay before heading home, she was relieved and excited to be able to give him the good news. But the sick feeling in her gut that'd started when she hung up with Hendrix never went away.

Since Stuart had taken Leo with him, Hendrix was alone in the office with Zeus when he had lunch. He had a lot of work-related things he should've been thinking about, but he couldn't get his mind off Ellen and the negative answer she'd given him when he asked to see her again.

"Damn it." He'd been afraid she'd turn him down. He probably shouldn't even have posed the question, but he hadn't been able to resist. He'd enjoyed her so much last night. And he knew she'd enjoyed him, too. He could tell by the way her body had risen to meet his, how readily she'd welcomed his kisses and how she'd curled into him as they slept.

Those were all classic signs he couldn't have missed, right? And yet...that was it? What they'd had last night was over, and there'd be nothing more?

He frowned as he gazed down at his phone. He was tempted to call her back, or text her, or order chocolates or something else to be delivered to her house. She seemed to like the flowers he'd given her last night. As awkward as it had been to carry them to the door, he was convinced he'd made the right call. That she'd kept looking at them—as if no one had ever done anything quite so nice for her—made him want to do it again. That he was so eager to change her mind where he was concerned was hugely ironic, though. She was the only woman in the world he knew he should stay away from—for his own good.

He thought of Jennifer Pullman. His ex-girlfriend's chief complaint was that he didn't seem to be fully invested in their relationship. She'd said he was too quick to shrug her off or see her only when it was comfortable and convenient. He felt bad that he hadn't behaved the way she wanted, but he hadn't felt very strongly about her or any of the other women he'd dated. He'd thought he was flawed in some way, destined to be somewhat indifferent in his romantic relationships.

So why did he feel so compelled to follow up with Ellen? Was it just because he'd been without a woman for six months and was looking for more great sex? Or was he simply acting as the contrarian because he couldn't really pursue Ellen?

He had no idea, but all he wanted was to be with her again. He kept picturing the sight of her naked body with all the tattoos he now found so beautiful, and remembering the way she'd locked her legs around his hips as he moved inside her. His enjoyment had fed off hers...

But he'd gone too far with her, damn it. Now she was in his blood. "What am I going to do?" he asked himself.

"Who are you talking to?"

Startled, he looked up to see Lynn. He hadn't expected her back so soon. "Just myself, I guess," he said, stuffing his sandwich back into his lunch container.

She frowned. Since their argument, they'd both attended their usual morning meetings, where she'd treated him coolly—proof that she hadn't yet forgiven him—but they were on speaking terms. Mostly. It could depend. She had moments where she seemed to soften a bit, and others when she was clearly holding a grudge. It depended on her mood and what she was thinking about at the time, he supposed. "What was it you were saying to yourself?"

"Nothing." He glanced at his watch. "I thought you went to town to get your nails done." It'd been only an hour since she left, not the usual two hours. No wonder she'd managed to surprise him.

"I did, but Sally's mother cut her hand while slicing

an onion and needed to be taken to the doctor. We had to reschedule."

"I hope her mother's going to be okay."

"Didn't sound serious. The wound just needs to be cleaned and stitched."

"That's a bummer all the way around, since you had to waste a trip to town."

She put her purse on her desk, which faced his and sat down. "I don't mind. I actually learned something interesting while I was there."

"What was that?"

"Have you heard what happened to the well Ellen just drilled?"

Hendrix sat up taller. He *had* heard, but he thought it was odd that she already knew. "I have. Jay called me an hour or so ago, wondering if I was the one who'd thrown something down it."

She gaped at him. "He thought it might be *you*?"

"He knew I was upset that Ellen got the job and couldn't imagine anyone else who'd do such a thing."

"What's he talking about? A lot of people don't like Ellen."

"I wouldn't say that." A lot of people didn't *trust* Ellen, but that was because she dared to be different— and because of Lynn. All the things his aunt had said over the years had certainly fanned those flames. Hendrix could see attitudes changing as time went by and more people got to know Ellen, however. In his opinion, Lynn didn't allow for that change. She saw only what she wanted to see, or she'd be aware of the shift in public sentiment, too. "Besides, it would have to be someone who also knew she was drilling that well."

Disgruntled, probably because he'd stuck up for Ellen again, Lynn made a face. "I think it serves Jay right, if you want the truth. That was a dirty trick, giving Ellen our estimate and allowing her to undercut us. You don't treat a neighbor like that."

Hendrix stood. He needed to take a load of pipe over to a jobsite and was already running an hour behind schedule. Ellen was disrupting more than his sleep. He couldn't seem to concentrate or get anything done. And now Lynn was causing further delay.

He hated to think his aunt might be responsible for sabotaging the Haslem well. But Lynn was in the well business, too, and had been for years. She would know how easy it would be to cause a problem. "Who told *you* about what happened?" he asked.

She pulled her chair closer to the desk. "Sally."

Her nail tech couldn't have been too worried about her injured mother if she was wasting time passing along town gossip, Hendrix thought. But maybe he was hypersensitive at the moment. He was certainly more defensive of Ellen than he'd ever been before. "And who told Sally?"

"There wasn't time to ask. Jay's wife, probably. Sally does her nails, too. Why?"

"Just wondering."

She powered up her computer. "Where's Leo? With Stuart somewhere?"

"Yeah. Stuart took him to Monicello."

She looked up in surprise. "Utah? What're they doing going clear down there?"

"An old friend from Anaconda told Stuart about a pump puller that's for sale. Since we need another one, he went down to grab it—was afraid he'd lose it if he delayed by even a day—and Leo wanted to go with him."

"Why didn't he call me to say he was leaving?"

Zeus came up beside him and nudged Hendrix's leg,

looking for a scratch. Hendrix complied as he answered. "He tried. You didn't pick up."

She pulled her phone out of her purse and must've seen the missed calls because she seemed satisfied. "How long will they be gone?"

"If all goes well, they'll head home tomorrow." Hendrix dug his key fob from his pocket and approached the door.

"Where are you going?" she asked.

He didn't want to get specific. So many of the errands he needed to run should've been done Monday or Tuesday, when he'd been helping Ellen, and she might recognize that and call him out on all he hadn't accomplished this week. "I've got a laundry list of things to do."

"I wonder if Ellen knows about Jay's well," she said. "Sally told me someone wrote 'Ellen's a bitch,' on the chicken coop."

Her satisfied smirk irritated Hendrix, but he tried not to show it. "Jay didn't mention that," he lied. "So…was it meant to be an attack on her or on Jay?"

"Probably both of them," she said.

And Lynn just happened to be mad at both. He wanted more information, but he knew that was all the clarity he was going to get—from her. She was already calling Stuart back. As he filled his water bottle at the cooler by the door, he heard her say, almost gleefully, "You'll never believe what happened to the Haslem well…"

Twenty

Did you sabotage the well?

Ellen had typed that text, intending to send it to Jordan, but hadn't done it yet. If it wasn't him, she was afraid it'd be a mistake to engage him.

On the other hand, he might say something that would convince her one way or the other, and she was so eager to learn who'd poured that bag of concrete down the Haslem well she almost couldn't stop herself from hitting Send.

"Did you do it?" she asked out loud. She was home alone, exhausted after staying up so late with Hendrix, then working in such a stressful situation all day—not sure whether she'd be able to save the well or not. She was relieved it had worked out but still angry at whoever had caused the problem in the first place. And she was tired enough that she wasn't getting anything else done.

"I bet you did," she said and finally hit Send.

She didn't get an answer. She hoped that meant he'd blocked her and gone home, that the brief Jordan era of her life was over once and for all. It would suck not to be able to figure out who'd vandalized the Haslem well and written on the coop, but if it meant the dentist from Libby was out of her life for good, she figured she could live with the mystery.

She was just about to make herself climb off the bed, where she'd been relaxing since showering after work. She had to replace the pipes under the sink in her guest bath. Now that she had the parts, she'd been meaning to do that for the past several days. And it wasn't yet seven o'clock. She hoped to accomplish a few more things before going to bed. But she decided to make a few calls in search of a new driller first.

She posted a couple of online ads but knew she could probably make something happen faster if she asked around to find out who the seniors were at Coyote Canyon High. Someone graduating this spring who didn't plan on attending college might make a good candidate for a driller. That was how she'd found Ben. Brant knew Ben's mother and had mentioned that Ellen was looking for help. Then Ben had contacted her to see if he could come and meet with her.

Maybe something like that would happen again, except…she was hoping to get an employee with a little more life experience this time. It would be better if she could hire someone who was a few years older, maybe twenty-two to twenty-four.

Propping several pillows behind her back, so that she could lean against the headboard, she sat up taller and dialed Ross Moore, who'd given her the opportunity to get into the business.

"There you are, girl. I thought maybe you'd forgotten about me," he said when he answered.

She smiled at the rich baritone of his voice. He was a gruff old guy—had been drilling for years. But he had a soft spot for her, and she knew it. He wouldn't have done all the things he'd done otherwise. She hadn't been a likely candidate for a driller, especially at that age. But he'd taught her and encouraged her and had always rooted for her success. "I could never forget about you," she said.

"Good. You back in town? If so, let's grab some dinner."

"Unfortunately, I'm not in Anaconda at the moment. I'm still in Coyote Canyon, but I would love to do dinner with you. I'll call you next time I'm back that way."

"Sounds good. I ran into your mother on Monday."

"What was she doing? Should I be embarrassed?" He, of all people, knew what she'd been up against with Jan. He'd witnessed a lot of her mother's dysfunction when Ellen worked for him. But he blamed Stuart for not taking care of his ex more than he blamed Jan for her own actions. Ross was generous with women; not so much with other men.

"No. You should be proud. She hit me up for a job."

"She did?"

"Asked if I needed someone in the front office."

"Really! She didn't tell me." Probably because she knew Ellen would ask her to stay away from Ross. She liked him too much to burden him with Jan, didn't want him to feel he had to do her yet another favor. "And… do you? Need someone, I mean?"

"Figure…couldn't hurt."

"So you *don't* need anyone, but you're trying to create a job for her," she said with a laugh. That was *so* like him…

"I could use her," he argued. "She was just here for the interview. Actually kept the appointment we made, which I saw as a good sign. So I gave her the job. But I told her she'd better show up on time, and if she calls in sick without a doctor's confirmation even once, she's gone."

"You think that makes you sound tough?" Ellen rolled her eyes but felt no real irritation, just a surge of affection. "You're all heart!"

"Yeah, well, I figure you don't need her dragging *you* down," he said. "And if she's looking for work… We both know what that means."

Ellen had often felt as though she was completely alone in the world, but she was pretty sure this old driller loved her. "You've always tried to help me where you could."

"I haven't done anythin', darlin'. You worked your butt off when you were here. And if I did do a little somethin' to help you out, I don't know a little girl who deserves it more."

She blinked back the tears that were welling up. "I'm not a little girl anymore, Ross," she said, chuckling as she sniffed.

"Well, I'm not getting any younger. You'll always be a little girl to me," he said. "But you musta gone soft since you left, because if I'd ever said somethin' like that to you while you were here, you'd have had my hide."

She'd called him on his sexist bullshit more than once, wouldn't tolerate him treating her as though she were any less capable than his male workers. But that'd only made him say or do misogynistic things just to get her mad.

She freely forgave him for that and all the fun he'd had at her expense, though. He didn't like talking about anything deeply emotional. He may have teased her mercilessly, but he'd done more than most employers would to take care of her. "Thanks for giving my mom a shot. I really, really hope she doesn't let you down. But—and this is me keeping it real—I can't promise you won't be sorry."

"I know. It's nothing for you to worry about. She and I will either make a go of it or we won't."

She dropped her head into her hand. It was so good to talk to him she was beginning to wonder why she hadn't kept on working for him and let him worry about how to stay in business, find new jobs, pay for equipment, insurance, employees and all the rest of it. It would've been a lot easier, and she probably would've made almost as much. It was the possibility of future earnings that would have been lost—owning a very productive business like his one day. But still… As beleaguered as she was feeling right now, it was tempting to crawl back into the safety of what she'd known before. "Maybe I need to return to Anaconda and go back to work for you myself…"

"I would love to have you here, and you know it. But you wouldn't be satisfied working for me. Not after getting a taste of being your own boss. Now that you've flown the coop, you need to soar, little girl. Tell me you're still giving Fetterman Well Services hell."

She winced as she thought of welcoming Hendrix into her bed. She'd given him a lot last night, but she certainly hadn't given him hell. When she got home, she'd moved the flowers into her bedroom, since that was where she planned on spending most of her evening. But, of course, she didn't say that. "I am. I'm stealing all the jobs from them I can get."

"Good for you."

She smiled at his response, but because she was still emotional, she had to sniff again. "I'm in a bit of a jam right now, Ross."

He sobered. "What's going on? What do you need?"

"Fortunately, just the benefit of your knowledge."

"In what regard?"

"I had to fire Ben."

"Wasn't he your only employee?"

"He was."

"Wait—you're not trying to drill alone, are you? You know it's not safe."

It wasn't easy to accomplish, either. She could handle a few small jobs on her own—some out-of-water calls and pump repairs—but others would be impossible. "I'm hoping I won't have to resort to that. I've been rearranging my schedule to allow for some downtime, but I can't go very long without working. It'll hurt my cash flow too badly."

"I know what that's like. Need me to loan you a worker?"

She hadn't thought of borrowing someone, but the idea sounded like it could save her—as long as it didn't hurt him. "Only if you have one to spare. But I'd rather hire someone of my own right away. You don't know anyone who's looking for a job, do you?"

"There's nobody around there who wants to work?"

"Not that I've found," she said with a sigh. "But I admit I've just started putting out a few feelers."

"I'll check with my crews. Coyote Canyon's not that far away. I'll see if anyone's interested in moving."

"I didn't mean you had to give up one of your own employees!"

"I wouldn't mind. I'm overstaffed at the moment, anyway. And I have guys walk through my door all the time, looking for work. If necessary, I can find someone else easily enough."

"But then you'd have to train them. There's a cost involved."

"There's a constant ebb and flow around here, anyway."

"I wish it was that easy for me to find and train help!" But she wasn't there yet, didn't have his reputation, his longevity in the business or his army of employees, since, like Hendrix and Stuart, he covered several states.

"You will one day," he predicted. "Let me ask around, and I'll get back to you."

Sliding under the covers of her bed, she closed her eyes in relief. Thank God for Ross. Leave it to her former employer to do what he could—again.

Talulah couldn't believe it when she got Ellen's text. She was so stunned that Jane, who was visiting with her after hours at the diner, took notice.

"What's wrong?"

Talulah wasn't sure whether to tell her since Jane and Averil were still close. There'd been nothing to try *their* friendship, other than the strain Jane no doubt felt trying to remain friends with Talulah instead of siding completely with Averil.

Even that problem had been largely mitigated when Talulah married Brant. Since he and her business— and Ellen, who Talulah felt needed her more—took up the majority of her time, she didn't put Jane in the position of having to choose between her and Averil very often. Maybe once a week, they caught up with each other on nights like this, when Jane walked down the street after closing her vintage furniture and gift shop and hung out with Talulah while she finished cleaning the diner. Sometimes Talulah went to her shop, if Jane was the one working later. But these days they rarely got together otherwise.

Jane set down the iced mocha Talulah had made for her and leaned across the table. The restaurant was now clean, so Talulah could go home, but they were having a drink and relaxing and chatting a bit longer. "Lu? You're not going to tell me?"

"It's about Averil." She set her phone back on the table next to her bowl, which was filled with sliced berries and a dollop of whipped cream instead of one of the more calorie-dense desserts she could've chosen. "I don't... I don't like talking about her with you, for obvious reasons. I know it puts you in an awkward position—"

"That's okay. You two haven't had an easy go of it. I believe she would've been able to get past the whole wedding thing. When you came back to town, it seemed you two were moving in that direction—"

"But then I 'stole' Brant," Talulah broke in.

"You and I both know he wasn't interested in her, anyway. Still, she's so jealous she can't get over it."

"I'm sad about that. I never meant to hurt her. But I'm happy I allowed myself to love Brant, so it's tough to regret what happened."

"She'll find the right guy eventually," Jane said. "Then maybe things can change. I admit, I'd like to see that wound finally heal."

"It can't be fun feeling as though you're always in the middle."

"It's better than being either one of you," Jane said with a chuckle. "But, yes, it'd be easier if we could all be friends again." She gestured at Talulah's phone. "So... was it Averil who just texted you?"

"No, it was Ellen. She told me that Averil's hooked up with a guy she met online."

Jane scowled. "Averil's doing some online dating?"

"No, I talked Ellen into doing some online dating," Talulah said and told her what'd happened.

"Wait… You're saying Averil likes this guy?" Jane asked when she was done, clearly alarmed.

"Apparently so. I mean… I don't know how much, but he looks good on paper. I could see her getting excited about an attractive dentist, especially one who hates Ellen."

Jane winced. "After what Ellen said to her in the grocery store, I can see that, too."

"Averil told you about that?" Talulah had purposely not mentioned it. It was just another thing that would put Jane in a position to have to choose between them.

"She said Ellen accosted her."

Talulah lifted her eyebrows to indicate she didn't agree with that interpretation. "Did she tell you why?"

Jane looked slightly confused. "She said Ellen doesn't think Averil's treating you right, that she should forgive you for Brant. Is that what you mean?"

"It wasn't about Brant, Jane. What Averil apparently didn't tell you was that Ellen overheard her say she hopes the diner fails—that I would deserve that. Then maybe Brant would divorce me, and I'd move back to Seattle and get the hell out of town so she wouldn't have to see my ugly face."

"Oh, wow. Now I get it." Jane tucked her long blond hair behind her ears. "Then I'm glad Ellen didn't just let it go." She took another sip of her drink. "No wonder Averil didn't get too specific. Just said that Ellen's a bitch."

The text Talulah had received from Ellen indicated

someone had spray-painted those exact words on a broken-down chicken coop on the Haslem property. Calling someone a bitch was a common enough occurrence. And yet the echo was a bit jarring. "You don't think Averil would try to get even with Ellen by sabotaging a well she's drilling, do you?"

Jane set her drink down again. "Sabotaging? You mean…damaging it in some way?"

"Yeah. Like putting cement down the hole so the water can't come out. Last night someone did that to a well Ellen just finished drilling, and she had to spend all day getting it out."

"No…" Jane shook her head, but her voice revealed a desire to remain loyal more than rock-solid belief.

"Even if she was influenced by some hot guy she'd met and was excited to have the chance to finally strike back at someone who's embarrassed her in public and outed her where I'm concerned?"

Jane's expression grew more and more doubtful as her conviction began to crumble. "I don't *think* she'd ever do that," she said. "But…"

"What?" Talulah prompted.

"She wasn't home last night."

"How do you know?"

"I stopped by her place. Her mother had Mitch."

"Did you text her to find out where she was?"

"I did." She seemed somewhat reluctant to admit it when she added, "She didn't answer."

As far as Hendrix could tell, Jordan had left town. He'd been driving for over an hour, cruising past the motels and the eateries, looking for the white Audi with Oregon plates. But he hadn't seen any sign of it. He was considering stopping by Averil's parents' house. He

didn't know her well; she was a few years older than
he was. But he remembered her from school, and he
saw her at Hank's quite often, where they nodded and
said hello. In the past six months, since Jennifer had
moved away, she'd even asked him to dance on occasion. He'd always agreed but had kept their interaction
light and friendly, since he'd never been especially attracted to her.

Given their lack of a deeper relationship, it would
seem strange to randomly show up at her house. But
they'd never exchanged numbers, so it wasn't as if he
could call or text her instead. And he felt he should warn
her about the kind of man she was getting involved with.
Ordinarily, that would seem like overstepping, but Jordan's presence in town could have a significant impact
on Ellen's life.

Not only did he need to tell Averil what Jordan had
done to Ellen and let her know the dentist might not
be everything he seemed to be, he was hoping to learn
where Jordan was last night. It was possible he had
nothing to do with the Haslem well. Maybe he'd left
Coyote Canyon before the damage occurred, and he
was no longer a threat to Ellen or anyone else—at the
moment. If that was the case, there'd be one less thing
to worry about.

Hendrix hated to think of who else might have been
responsible, however. He definitely didn't want it to be
Lynn. But he decided to go ahead and visit Averil, just
in case he managed to learn something. Even if she got
mad at him for it, or she wasn't home, he was fighting
the desire to drive over to Ellen's place again, and this
would provide an immediate distraction to keep from
doing that.

According to Brant, who provided the address, the

older Gerharts lived on twenty acres along the highway and had been there for years and years.

Hendrix slowed as he drew close to the house in question and waited for oncoming traffic before making the turn. It'd grown dark since he'd left his place, so the porch light was on, and a number of cars were clogging the drive. The Gerharts had several grown children with spouses and kids of their own, so he assumed there was some kind of family party going on.

Pulling to one side to make it possible for others to get out, he cut the engine and climbed from his truck.

He could see a woman, then two men, pass in front of the kitchen window as he approached and, although it took a minute, Charlie, Averil's brother, whom Hendrix also knew from Hank's and various mutual friends, answered the door when he knocked.

"Is Averil around?" Hendrix asked.

"Yeah, she's inside," he said. "Let me get her for you."

Hendrix stepped back so he wouldn't be crowding the doorway when Averil arrived. Charlie had left the door standing open; she only had to come through a wooden screen door, which was hanging slightly askew.

"Hendrix…" she said, obviously surprised to see him.

"Hey, Averil. How are you?" he asked.

"Good. What…what's going on?"

Shoving his hands in the pockets of his jeans, he took another step back so he wouldn't come across as too strong or overpowering. "Something's come up. I hope you don't mind me stopping by to talk about it."

"Of course not. What is it?"

"Do you know a dentist from Libby by the name of Jordan Forbes?"

Her expression grew less open and more suspicious. "Yes…"

"Did he tell you his version of what happened at Ellen's the other night?"

She blinked several times as, he guessed, she was trying to determine how he might be connected to Jordan, Ellen and this line of questioning. "He said she talked him into coming all the way from Libby to make some dude jealous. Whoever it was blindsided him with a punch that almost broke his nose."

"*Almost* broke his nose…" That was news. Jordan had obviously portrayed his injury as worse than it was.

"Yeah. It's swollen and has a cut on it right here." She pointed to the bridge of her own nose. "I saw it. And considering what I know about Ellen, I believe she'd set a guy up like that, don't you?"

Averil didn't know *he* was the guy who'd punched Jordan? Why not? Jordan knew his name. They'd played pool together. He must've chosen not to include it in his story for some reason. Maybe he'd kept the tale as vague as possible so he couldn't accidentally relate something she might not believe or could easily verify—and that meant leaving as many details out of it as possible, including Hendrix's name.

Hendrix had to hand it to Jordan. He was smart. He'd focused his revenge on Ellen alone—and in Averil he'd found the perfect person to believe everything he said about her. That had to have taken a little bit of luck, too. "He didn't tell you who hit him?"

"He didn't know. Said some guy sprang out of the bushes when he dropped her off."

"He didn't drop her off, Averil. He followed her home after she tried to end the date, forced her to kiss him and looked as though he was ready to do a lot more."

"How do *you* know?" she asked, almost belligerently.

"Because *I* was the guy who hit him."

Her jaw dropped. "What were *you* doing at Ellen's?"

Since he and Ellen weren't known to be great friends—or friends at all—he could see why she might ask that. "I wanted to talk to her. She'd just taken a job I thought we'd be getting, and I'd reacted by doing something I regretted."

Understanding dawned on her face. "Is that why you were helping her drill that well? Charlie told me the two of you were right next to the land he just listed, working together all day, but I didn't think anything of it. I assumed the owner must have stipulated you do it that way or something."

She knew he'd helped Ellen drill the Haslem well? He hadn't realized anyone who would bother to take note had seen them. "The owner didn't stipulate it. I was trying to make up for what I'd done, yes."

"Are you two friends now?"

He'd just slept with Ellen. They certainly weren't enemies. But he felt it was in their best interests—especially for the purposes of this conversation—to seem as neutral as possible. "She and I are still competitors, right? We both own a well business and will go head-to-head on more jobs in the future. That might make it hard for us to be friends. But I wish her the best. And we're cordial when we see each other."

She swatted away a moth drawn by the porch light. "So…why are you here?"

"Two reasons, actually." He cleared his throat. "I wanted to warn you about Jordan. He's not a good guy, and I'm afraid for you or any other woman I know to get involved with him."

"He seems pretty nice to me," she said, growing defensive.

"He comes off that way. I was at Hank's when Ellen and Jordan came in. Kurt knows Ellen through Talulah and asked them to play pool with us. Like you, I thought Jordan seemed normal—until I saw him start to get rough with her later on. I'm telling you, she was doing everything she could to fight him off, and he wouldn't let her go."

"That's not how he tells the story," she said. "Besides, it's hard to feel too sorry for Ellen."

Hendrix had to swat away the same moth that'd been bothering her. "I'm telling you the truth. And the problem is…if he'd do something like that to her, he might do it to someone else. I think he has anger issues. Or he can't bear to hear the word 'no,' or feel criticized in any way. *Something*."

She still seemed reluctant to accept what he was saying. Maybe she was planning to see him again. He'd obviously won at least some of her loyalty. "What's your other reason for coming?" she asked.

"Last night, someone sabotaged the well Ellen just finished drilling. The one I helped her with. It's on Jay Haslem's property on Stockman Road. And I was wondering… You don't think it could've been Jordan, do you?"

He realized she'd most likely say no. Saying yes would suggest she might've had something to do with it, too. After all, Jordan would've needed help to locate the well. It wouldn't be easy to find a piece of empty land after dark, especially since he was unfamiliar with Coyote Canyon in general and the more rural parts surrounding the town in particular. Hendrix was looking for the little telltale signs in Averil's face and body language that might indicate she knew more than she was saying, but she seemed perfectly composed when she said, "There's no way he'd do that. How would he even know where she was drilling?"

"*You* knew where she was drilling. You didn't tell him?"

"No!" she cried. "I don't like Ellen. I've made no secret of that. But I would never vandalize someone's property."

He hadn't asked that. He'd only asked if she'd told Jordan where Ellen had been working. "Then…would you mind letting me know where you were last night?"

Her body went rigid and anger flashed in her eyes. "I don't have to answer to you. You're not a police officer," she snapped and went in, letting the screen slam behind her before also slamming the heavier main door with a loud bang.

Twenty-One

Ellen's phone lit up where it was charging on her nightstand, waking her from a deep sleep. She'd meant to get up and fix the sink in her guest bath, but she'd never actually done it. After talking to Ross, she'd been so exhausted she'd immediately fallen asleep, was still in her robe.

So…who was trying to reach her at—she saw the numerals on her alarm clock as she grabbed her phone—nine thirty?

It was Rocko Schneider from Burgers and Shakes. Ellen couldn't believe it when she saw his name on her screen. How dare he call her after how he'd behaved the last time they talked? She'd had Talulah return his ten bucks. Other than accepting that tip, which she hadn't known how to refuse because she was so preoccupied with Hendrix and Leo and their lady friend at the time, she'd done nothing wrong.

With a sigh, she let the call transfer to voice mail. No way was she going to wake up enough to talk to him right now. She probably wouldn't be able to go back to sleep if she did, and she was eager to snuggle down and drift off again. Whatever she'd been planning to do before bed could wait.

But then a thought occurred to her. It couldn't have been Rocko who'd sabotaged the well, could it? Would he do something like that?

He'd definitely been unhappy when she'd turned him down for dinner. Or had he mentioned his attraction to her to his ex-wife, and Debbie was the one who'd taken revenge? She'd nearly run over her last romantic rival. Ellen wouldn't put anything past her.

Sliding up so that she had her back to the headboard, Ellen took a moment to gather her wits. Then she returned his call.

"Hello?"

He sounded wide-awake, which shouldn't have come as a surprise. Most other people probably hadn't gone to bed yet. "It's Ellen," she said. "You just called me?"

"I did. I was leaving a message, telling you to call me back, which you can now ignore. What are you doing?"

"I was asleep." She didn't bother to hide the irritation she felt. She'd tried hard enough to be nice to Rocko—without much positive reinforcement. "Did you get the ten dollars I sent back to you through Talulah?"

"Yeah. I feel...kinda like a dick for what I said. I'm sorry."

Was that what he was calling about? Because she didn't want his apology any more than she wanted anything else from him. She wished he'd just go on with his life and let her go on with hers. "No problem."

"You're not mad at me, are you?"

"No." She thought of the mysterious geode which had arrived the night he'd called to ask her out. "You didn't give me a geode you now want back, too, did you?"

"A *what*?"

"Never mind." She was already regretting waking up for this. "What is it you need, Rocko?"

"I don't need anything. I just… I wanted to let you know about something that happened last night that struck me as kind of odd, considering what Jay Haslem told me about his well when he was at my burger joint a few hours ago."

The drowsiness weighing on her limbs and eyelids fell away as his statement registered. Did he know who'd sabotaged the well? Was it a white Audi with Oregon plates? "What'd you see?" she asked.

"I was out joyriding with my new girl—"

"You're seeing someone?" she said. *Joyriding? New girl?* His diction alone highlighted the age difference between them.

"You know Maribeth Woodson, don't you?"

She worked at the front desk of the veterinary clinic. Ellen knew that much, but not because she had reason to visit the vet. She wasn't home enough to have a pet. It was just general knowledge from seeing her around town and knowing people who knew her. "I'm familiar with who she is. It's not like we've had much occasion to interact."

"Well, I was taking her for a ride on my motorcycle around midnight. We were the only ones on the road, so we were just flying along, enjoying the freedom, when a white truck pulled out onto the highway *right* in front of us."

"You didn't smash into it…"

"No, but it was a close call."

She was sorry to hear that. Still, she couldn't figure out why he'd bother to tell her about it. "I'm glad you're okay."

"Guess where it came from?" he asked.

Where was he going with this? "Not over by the Haslem property…"

"Not *by* the Haslem property. It came *from* the Haslem property. Drove out of there like a bat out of hell."

Throwing back the covers, she jumped up and began to pace. "Did you tell Jay that?"

"Not yet. I'm kind of afraid to point any fingers. It all happened so fast, you know?"

"Are you saying you didn't get a good look at it? What kind of truck was it?"

"A Ford, I think."

She was immediately disappointed. She needed that information, and he'd had a chance to get it. "You couldn't tell?"

"No," he said, "but it had a Fetterman Well Services sign on the door."

She froze. "Are you kidding? Did you see who was driving?"

"I didn't. Happened too fast. I only saw that much because we nearly ran into it. Then I swerved, and by the time I managed to stop, all we could see were the taillights."

Ellen sank down onto the bed. Hendrix had been with her at the time. That meant either Lynn or her father had sabotaged the well—and her father didn't seem nearly vindictive enough.

After leaving the Gerharts', Hendrix had stopped off to have a beer. He wanted to tell Ellen about his encounter with Averil, but he knew if he went over there, he probably wouldn't leave—not if she let him stay. He was already afraid word would get back to Lynn that he'd helped Ellen drill the Haslem well and she'd freak out and demand Stuart fire him or something.

He believed that, especially when it came to him and Leo, she meant well, but she had a temper and could be rash and impetuous—not to mention touchy where Ellen was concerned.

He was walking to his truck, which he'd parked at the curb near the Stardust, a dive bar he frequented on the rare occasion he wasn't in the mood for Hank's, when he received a text from Ellen.

Rocko Schneider just called me.

He'd been thinking of her all day and couldn't believe how relieved and excited he was to get a message from her. It was ridiculous.

He paused to respond before climbing behind the wheel. That dude wants you bad, he wrote but, apparently, so did he. He couldn't remember ever being so caught up with a woman.

This time it wasn't to ask me out.

Rocko had tried asking her out? When Hendrix had arrived at the diner with Veronica Salvo, he could tell Rocko wanted to, but he was surprised the burger joint owner had finally worked up the nerve. What'd he want?

To tell me about something that happened last night. I think you should hear it. Can you come over?

Hendrix rubbed his forehead. If word got back to Lynn that he'd helped Ellen with the Haslem well, he'd already be in trouble. He was curious to learn what Rocko had said, though. And, more than anything, he was dying to see Ellen—and this gave him the perfect excuse.

"Fuck it," he muttered and texted her back: Be there in ten.

Ellen could've told Hendrix what Rocko had told her over the phone. But she'd wanted to see his face when he heard the news. She knew he'd have a hard time believing what she'd learned. In some ways, *she* had a hard time believing it. She'd always known Lynn didn't like her and wasn't happy she'd moved to town. But for a grown woman, well-known with a solid reputation in the community, to go out in the middle of the night and cause what could've been a lot of damage to someone else's property...

It was hard to imagine Lynn would go that far.

Ellen was pacing in the living room when Hendrix knocked. Taking a deep breath, she smoothed the peace-sign tank top she was wearing with a pair of faded cut-offs and answered the door.

His gaze lowered over her, but he didn't reach for her. He had to be slightly confused. She'd told him she wouldn't see him again, and yet here she was, asking him to come over. Her head and her heart demanded opposite things, and each had their own small victories in the tug-of-war between them.

Chalk one up for my heart, she thought.

"Come on in." She stepped aside so that they wouldn't touch as he passed by, even though touching him was exactly what she wanted—when she wasn't able to think better of it.

"What's going on?" he asked. "What'd Rocko Schneider have to say?"

"He called to tell me what happened when he was

riding his motorcycle past the Haslem property late last night."

"How late was it?"

"Close to midnight."

"The roads must've been deserted at that time."

Most people in Coyote Canyon went to bed early—on weeknights, anyway. They were farmers or ranchers who started at dawn. But Rocko's burger joint didn't open until eleven. Even then, he had employees who could probably open the restaurant for him. "That's true. Which is why you'll be even more shocked by what he said."

Hendrix definitely seemed interested. "Which was…"

She'd thought it would be easier to tell him it was his aunt who'd most likely harmed the well. But she didn't want him to think she was taking any pleasure in being right about the woman who'd been so good to *him*. He had to feel a great deal of gratitude toward Lynn and probably plenty of love, too. "He said he nearly wrecked into a white truck that came barreling out onto the highway right in front of him."

"From the Haslem property."

She nodded.

"What kind of truck?"

"He didn't know."

"Did he get a look at the driver?"

"No. He said the truck had a Fetterman Well Services logo on the door, though."

Shock replaced his scowl. "You can't be serious…"

"I'm afraid I am."

He hung his head for several seconds. When he lifted it, he said, "You know it wouldn't be Stuart."

"I *don't* know that," she said. "It's possible Lynn put him up to it." After all, she'd been behind almost all the pain Ellen had suffered since her parents' divorce, and Stuart hadn't shown a heck of a lot of resistance. Lynn had a great deal of power over him.

"I can't imagine he'd go that far. Even for her. He pretty much tries to remain neutral. Never says anything when she's complaining about you."

"Does she complain about me a lot?" Ellen asked drily.

"Come on," he said with a gently remonstrative look. "You know she talks. I'm not revealing anything."

Still, it stung to hear the truth. Although she had no idea why she cared what Lynn thought, especially after so many years. It was about finally winning the approval of the one person who could've made such a difference but had never even given her a chance, she supposed. It was a very different situation, but it reminded her of how she'd felt in high school when the boy of her dreams seemed to like her—and then suddenly backed away without any sort of warning or explanation. She'd spent the whole of her senior year trying to understand what she'd done wrong so she could finally achieve closure and feel okay about it. But he would hardly speak to her afterward. That it hadn't worked out and she'd never know the reason was just something she had to live with—like her rejection by her father and his second wife. "I *did* know," she acknowledged. "But…never mind."

Sympathy filled his eyes. "I'm sorry, Ellen. The more I get to know you, the worse I feel about what's happened. If my aunt sabotaged the well…" He stretched his neck as if trying to ease the stress he was under.

"If she did, then what?" Ellen asked, prompting him to finish. "I can't imagine you'll want me to go to the police."

"No. If she put cement down that well it was a stupid move—one she must've made in the heat of the moment. She gets impulsive when she's mad. I won't lie about that."

"Saying it was a rash decision makes it okay?"

"Not at all. But…" He combed his fingers through his hair, causing it to stand up in front. "Shit. I don't know. If she did it, you have every right to make her pay the price. A little justice would have to feel good after all the hurt she's caused you."

Ellen could hear the regret in his voice. "And yet…"

"I don't want to see her humiliated in front of everyone she knows. She's a proud person, cares a lot about her image and how she's perceived. Even if she claims she didn't do it, if Rocko saw a Fetterman truck drive off the property at that hour, it won't look good. She can deny it all she wants, but there are probably very few people who'd believe her, given the animosity between you two."

Most people still thought there was animosity between her and Hendrix, too. The pendulum of public favor might finally—*finally*—swing in her direction. She'd been waiting a long time for that. Deserved it. Didn't she?

"So what are you suggesting I do?" she asked. "Just… let it go?"

He stretched his neck again. "Let me talk to her, see if I can get her to tell me the truth. If she admits it, apologizes and pays you reparation, will that be enough? I hate to ask this of you, but if I can get her to that point, is there any chance we could handle it quietly—just the three of us? And your father, of course."

Ellen knew she'd be justified in saying no. She didn't owe him or the Fettermans any favors. Or…maybe she did. Hendrix had helped her drill the Haslem well. But he was the reason she'd had no other help. And it was his aunt—or her father—who'd tried to sabotage it, costing Ellen an entire day of work. If she hadn't been able to save the well, it would've cost Jay thirty thousand to drill another one.

"Do you think she'll tell you the truth?" she asked.

"I don't know. She'll probably get mad at me for even asking. She's already mad at me."

"Because of me?"

"She's not happy we're…friends."

"Why?" Ellen demanded as more anger and frustration rushed through her. "How can that possibly hurt *her*?"

"I don't know. I don't get it, either. My best guess is that it's her way of continuing to believe she did the right thing back then. She can't ever be wrong, can't accept any blame. She wants to believe it was you."

"I was ten!"

"I know," he said with a wince. "Anyway, it's possible she won't even talk to me about what she did last night. But I'd like the opportunity to try. If it was her and not Stuart—"

"If it was Stuart, she probably still had a hand in it."

"That's true. And I want to understand what she was thinking and feeling, if she's remorseful and all that. It would…it would make it easier to decide what should happen as a result."

Ellen had Lynn at *her* mercy, could *finally* hurt her back just as she'd dreamed of doing since she was a child and so crushed by Lynn and her father's rejection. Those fantasies were the only things that'd kept her going in high school when she was drowning in the responsibility of trying to help her mother keep a roof over their heads and food on the table. Back then, it'd seemed like she was fighting on all fronts, battling the whole world just to eke by.

But did she really want to be the kind of person who delighted in revenge?

She stared at the carpet as she thought back over all the times she'd been snubbed by her father's second wife. How Lynn had refused to let her come and stay. How Lynn had refused to let Stuart come over when she was staying with her grandparents. How Lynn hadn't wanted Leo or Hendrix to play with her. How lonely and lean her Christmases and other holidays were by comparison to theirs. And how Lynn had tried to turn everyone in Coyote Canyon against her when she first arrived in town.

So much of the pain and anger she'd suffered had been caused by this one selfish, jealous woman. There was a part of Ellen that wanted to shout what Lynn had done to the Haslem well from the rooftops. Print it in the paper! Then everyone would know *she* wasn't the terrible person in this situation—*Lynn* was.

But then she *would* be the same kind of terrible person as her stepmother, wouldn't she? If she abused power when she held it, too, how would she be any different?

"It's so ironic…" she muttered.

Hendrix bent his head to try to catch her eye. "What'd you say?"

She looked up at him. "I'll hold off to give you the chance to talk to her." She couldn't speak for Jay Haslem once he found out, though. Even if she didn't tell him, Rocko could. But that didn't matter. At least *she* wouldn't be out for vengeance. That was somehow a win despite how tempted she was to let the full consequences of Lynn's actions hit her right in the face.

"Thank you."

His expression made her glad she'd chosen mercy over justice, which only demonstrated how desperate for love and positive attention she really was, she thought.

She couldn't speak because of the emotion that was welling up, so she nodded. It was getting late, and she didn't know if he planned to talk to his aunt tonight or wait until tomorrow. If Rocko was spreading what he'd seen around town, Hendrix needed to act quickly...

But he didn't turn toward the door. He pulled her into his arms and held her against him. Then he kissed the top of her head. "You do something to me I can't explain," he said and brushed his lips against hers before seeing himself out.

Twenty-Two

Ellen stood in the middle of her living room for the next fifteen minutes. She couldn't bring herself to move. She was afraid it would break the spell of what'd just happened, and what she was feeling seemed even more magical than the time she'd spent with Hendrix last night. Sex she could attribute to hormones and the drive for pleasure. This was something different, something deeper. It terrified her at the same time it excited her. She'd never felt anything like it, wanted to take the time to imprint the last few seconds of Hendrix's visit on her long-term memory.

She wished she could talk to someone, share her excitement but also her doubts and fears. But she couldn't tell her mother. Jan would freak out when she heard that Lynn had tried to sabotage the well and would probably show up in town tomorrow and raise havoc, trying to get Lynn thrown in jail. Jan had reason to dislike Stuart's second wife, too.

And Ellen couldn't tell Talulah. The issue wasn't a matter of trust; it was that she knew Talulah would only saw off the branch she was trying so hard to cling to so she wouldn't get swept away and be hurt. Talulah thought Hendrix was "a good man." She couldn't see how fraught with danger this situation truly was—or she assumed the danger was being overstated or everything would turn out right in the end.

Ellen wasn't so sure.

Knowing she wouldn't be able to go back to sleep—not after Rocko's call and Hendrix's visit—she headed to the guest bath, hoping to finally repair her sink.

She'd just torn the whole thing apart and was replacing some of the pipes when she heard the ding that signaled a text.

Dropping her wrench, she nearly banged her head on the cabinetry in her hurry to reach her phone. She thought maybe Hendrix had spoken to his aunt and was letting her know what'd been said. It was getting late enough that she couldn't imagine it being anyone else.

But it wasn't Hendrix. It was Jordan.

Averil told me you sent your boyfriend over to accuse her of doing something to a well? Breaking it or something? You sent me a text about it, too. I don't know what the hell either of you are talking about. But you'd better not be trying to ruin things between Averil and me or we're going to have a major problem.

By now, he had to know Hendrix wasn't her boyfriend. But he had to hang on to that idea. It was jealousy that made his version of events credible. There was no reason a mere friend or acquaintance would strike him unless he was acting out, as *she* claimed, and he refused to admit the truth.

She hadn't even known Hendrix had gone to Averil's. He hadn't mentioned it when he came over, probably because they knew who'd most likely damaged the well

by then, and what she'd learned impacted him far more
personally.

She wondered how Averil felt about Hendrix showing up at her door. Jordan didn't like it for obvious reasons. But if Averil became convinced of the truth, she
might refuse to see him again.

Ellen wondered if he'd come to town intending to intimidate her—or prove that she and Hendrix didn't intimidate him—and wound up meeting Averil at Hank's
instead, which switched his attention to her and meant
he no longer felt compelled to act on his earlier threat.

That was the impression she was getting—that he
was satisfied to leave her alone as long as she didn't
interfere with what he had going on in Coyote Canyon now.

She hated that dating Averil might mean he'd continue to return to town, but she supposed it was better than what could've happened—at least to her. She
didn't need another problem. And maybe he wouldn't
treat Averil as badly as he'd treated her.

She texted Hendrix:

Jordan just sent me a message. He said you went to
Averil's house?

She thought he might be asleep, but she got an immediate response.

I did. I felt someone should warn her that she's getting involved with a man who isn't quite right when it
comes to women.

How'd she take the news?

She wouldn't believe me.

"Love is blind" is a cliché for a reason.

Apparently so.

At least you tried to protect her. Have you talked to your aunt about what Rocko saw?

No. Didn't even try. She goes to bed early. I'll drive over first thing in the morning.

I hope it goes well.

Don't hold your breath. Averil's brother Charlie recently listed the property next to the Haslem place, so he was over there when you and I were working together and found it unusual enough to notice.

Averil told you that?

She did. And I have no doubt word will get around to Lynn eventually. I'm just hoping it hasn't already. I'd rather get through this first.

I can see why. Will you call me and let me know how it goes?

When I get away from the office.

Ellen almost set her phone aside. But it was difficult to let him go. Drawing it back at the last second, she typed another message: Is there anything I can do for you tomorrow to help you catch up on the time you lost working with me?

Assuming he'd say no, or that he wouldn't be able to accept her offer for fear Lynn would find out, she was shocked when she read his response.

Seriously? Are you free? Because if you could drive over to Missoula and pick up some flat hose I need for an irrigation job, I'd really appreciate it—and I'd pay you for your time and the cost of gas, of course. Stuart's out of town, and I've got one guy on my drill crew who has a pregnant wife and will be moving away soon. I can't get him to work much now that he knows he'll be leaving. He left me a message a few hours ago saying he won't be coming to work tomorrow. So I'd be able to take his place and drill if you picked up the hose.

She used her phone to calculate how long the drive would be. Nearly three hours. She could do it in one day. Sure, she wrote back. Just text me the address and a list of what I'm supposed to pick up. I'll bring it all here, and you can come for it after I get home. That way, no one will even know I helped.

And I won't have to explain why I haven't made it over to Missoula myself. Thanks a lot.

No problem.

Ellen began to sing along with the music she had playing in the background as she went back to fixing her sink. As worried and stressed as she'd been lately, and as frustrating as this repair was continuing to be, she was somehow happy. She told herself it was because she was glad Jordan seemed ready to leave her alone, she'd been able to save the Haslem well and she had some valuable information on who'd most likely sabotaged it. Those were all good things that'd happened today.

But she knew the way she felt had nothing to do with her problems and everything to do with Hendrix.

Lynn was already in the office when Hendrix arrived. He knew it would be more awkward between them than it had been lately, because Stuart and Leo wouldn't be there, giving them other people to interact with as they avoided speaking to each other—or, at least, filling the silence and keeping Lynn from getting too worked up.

But he supposed it was for the best. He needed to talk to her in private, and this gave him the perfect opportunity.

She looked up when she heard him come in but didn't say anything. Going back to her computer, she continued to work as if she hadn't been interrupted in the first place.

"Morning," he said.

She glanced at him, slightly startled—and maybe even a little smug that he'd been the first to break the silence. She always made those around her be the first to apologize, even if she was the one at fault—or at least equally to blame.

When she didn't reply, just went back to work for the second time, he knew she planned to punish him a bit longer. She was trying to teach him a lesson, he supposed. To show him what it was like when he fell out of her good graces.

Normally, he focused on her better traits, which allowed him to tolerate these episodes. Stuart had trained him to turn a blind eye until the situation finally worked itself out. Today, however, it was harder to shrug off her behavior.

"You're not going to say anything?" he asked.

"You want to hear me say good morning? Good morning," she replied sarcastically.

He put his lunch box and water bottle on his desk but kept the coffee he'd purchased on his way over in one hand as he stepped closer to her. "We have a problem," he announced.

She finally gave him her full attention. "What problem are you talking about?"

"Rocko Schneider."

She seemed unfazed. "The guy who owns Burgers and Shakes?"

He took a sip of his coffee. "That's him."

"How could he be a problem?"

If she'd almost crashed into Rocko, she didn't seem to be aware of it. Or she was a better actress than he'd realized. "He saw you the night before last." That wasn't strictly true, but Hendrix didn't believe it could be Stuart.

Again, she didn't bat an eye. "Where?"

"Driving off the Haslem property."

Lines of irritation appeared, forming deep grooves on either side of her mouth. "What are you saying? I haven't been over at the Haslem property."

"He claims otherwise," he said, pushing harder.

She remained resolute. "Then Rocko doesn't know what he's talking about. Why would he tell anyone I was at the Haslem property?" she asked. Then it dawned on her. "He's not claiming *I* sabotaged Jay's well!"

"He's not saying that, no. What he's saying is that you

almost crashed into him when you came from the property on Tuesday—the night the well was vandalized—at nearly midnight, going way too fast."

She jumped to her feet, from all appearances genuinely stunned. "That's almost the same as saying *I* sabotaged it. Why else would I be there?"

"It certainly invites suspicion, especially considering how you feel about Ellen."

"Who's he telling this to?" she demanded.

"Who knows? Maybe everyone."

"How'd *you* hear about it?"

"He called Ellen, and she called me."

"He's lying!" she cried. "Or Ellen's trying to gain your sympathy by pinning something on me I didn't do."

Hendrix studied his aunt's face. The shock, the offense an innocent person would feel—it was all there. "You're saying you think she's making it up?"

"I don't know," she said, still seeming flabbergasted. "She hates me, so she has to be behind it somehow. Maybe she sabotaged the well herself and enlisted Rocko's help to place the blame on me."

Rocko had shown obvious interest in Ellen, but there was no way Ellen would use that to her advantage. She wouldn't harm a well she'd just drilled, either. She wasn't duplicitous like that. Besides, if she was behind the accusation, she would've gone to the police instead of granting him time to talk to Lynn.

Unless… She couldn't be playing him, could she?

"What?" Lynn said when he didn't speak. "You don't believe me?"

"I *do* believe you," he admitted. That was the problem. If Lynn had done it, there'd be some telltale sign. She had a hot temper, but he'd always known her to be up-front and honest. "Something isn't making sense."

"It's *her*," she insisted. "It's Ellen. She's trying to get me in trouble, make me look bad."

"It's *not* her," he said, even though part of him was terrified it was and this was some grand scheme to get back at them all. Ellen certainly had reason to be bitter.

"How do you know?"

Because she wasn't like that and if Lynn had remained open-minded about Stuart's daughter, she'd know it, too. "I just...do," he insisted. But what was going on? Could they both be telling the truth? "Could Rocko be mistaken?" he asked.

"He's mistaken if he claims he saw *me*, because he didn't!" she yelled.

"He didn't say it was you specifically," Hendrix admitted, speaking softer so the emotion wouldn't continue to escalate. "He told Ellen that what he saw was a Fetterman Well Services truck. So if it wasn't me and it wasn't you, it would have to be Stuart."

"No way would he vandalize anything," she said.

He scratched his head. He believed that, too. "Then *someone* has to be lying."

Ellen found herself smiling almost the entire way to Missoula. She should've been worried about what she was going to do with her own business. She'd received no calls regarding the ad she'd placed online for a new driller, and there'd been no response to the flyer she'd created on her computer late last night and dropped by the high school as she was driving out of town. That would take more time. But she'd managed to push off a couple of jobs to give herself some breathing room. With any luck, she'd find someone soon—or Ross would—and she'd be able to complete them before they got canceled and her situation grew dire.

Meanwhile, she was going to allow herself to enjoy the day helping Hendrix, she decided. She'd woken up to a text from him telling her exactly where to go and what to get and was nearly there. She figured she'd load up and then have lunch before heading back. She'd been hoping he'd call her and tell her how his conversation with Lynn went, but she hadn't heard from him. She guessed he hadn't yet had a chance to talk to his aunt. Or he was slammed. She knew how hard it was for bigger outfits to gather all the materials needed for each job and get the drilling crews off; she'd witnessed it firsthand while working for Ross.

A call came in from her mother while she was loading up, but she silenced her phone and waited until she was sitting at a burrito place before calling Jan.

"There you are," her mother said. "Why didn't you pick up?"

"Mom, I'm working," she said. "I can't pick up every call that comes in."

"Oh. Well, I was just excited to give you some good news."

"I can always use good news. What's up?"

"I got a another job!"

Ellen swallowed the first bite of her *carne asada* burrito. "With Ross's outfit?"

"How'd you know?"

"I talked to him." She took a drink of her soda. "He said you'd been in."

"And you didn't call to congratulate me?"

"Sorry. There's been a lot going on around here." That was the understatement of the year, but the real reason she hadn't called was because she wasn't comfortable with her mother once again cashing in on *her* hard work and reputation—the credibility *she'd* established—because of how Jan's actions might reflect on her. Ross had told her not to feel responsible if her mother flaked out, but she knew she would. She'd been embarrassed by Jan's behavior for a long time and cared about his opinion, wanted to make him proud. That included not having Jan let him down after he'd tried so hard to help her.

"A lot going on? Like what?" her mother asked.

"I lost my driller, for one," she replied. "Been trying to replace him. Something went wrong with my latest well, for another, and I almost couldn't save it." She decided not to go into any more detail. The last thing she needed was to make her mother any angrier at Lynn and Stuart. Who knew what Jan might do? She'd gone way too far in the past... "There's a whole list of things," she went on, "including trying to repair the sink in my guest bath. I spent hours on it last night and still haven't been able to stop the darn leak."

"You'll get it." Jan didn't sound concerned, but she'd never owned a home—not since the one she'd had with Stuart was sold after the divorce—so she shrugged off maintenance as if it was nothing.

"When do you start your new job?" Ellen asked after taking another bite of her lunch.

"On Monday. I'm thinking of quitting the diner."

Ellen winced. This was meant to be a leading statement—her mother's attempt to get Ellen to approve of that plan. Then she'd be partially responsible if the new job didn't work out and her mother ended up in dire straits again. Ellen recognized the pattern because she'd seen it many times. "Why not stay on two or three nights a week until you settle in with Ross and make sure it's going to last? Office work is a big change. It means forty hours a week instead of twenty or twenty-five. It's not flexible, either. You can't just give up a shift when you want to go do something else, like you can in the restaurant world. And you don't know how you'll take to pushing paperwork around."

"Yeah, that's probably a good idea," she agreed, but with so little conviction Ellen was willing to bet she'd *already* quit.

"If you need any help with anything after you start, be sure to call me. I was in and out of that office for years, as you know. Plus, I do my own paperwork these days, so I should be able to help."

"Thanks. I'm a little nervous," she admitted. "You know I'm not good at book learning and that sort of thing."

Ellen did know that, which was why she thought Ross was making a mistake hiring her. Jan had no experience and a very short attention span. But Ross had such a huge heart. He tried to give everyone a chance.

"You can do it. It's all about learning the process and then repeating it. So don't be too hard on yourself. It's always the first few weeks that are the most difficult when you're learning a new job." Her phone buzzed to signify she had another call coming through. She pulled it away from her ear to check who it was, saw Hendrix's name and told her mother she was getting an important call she had to take. It still took Jan so long to say goodbye that she almost missed it. She caught Hendrix just before his call was transferred to voice mail.

"Hello?"

"Sorry it's taken me so long to check in. It's been busy here. How's your day?"

She glanced outside at her truck. "Going smoothly. I have the hose you need. I'll be heading back as soon as I finish my lunch."

"Thanks for your help."

"You bet. Have you had a chance to talk to your aunt yet?"

He hesitated as though he wasn't eager to embrace that subject.

"Hendrix?"

"Yeah. I talked to her first thing this morning."

"What'd she say?"

"That she didn't do it."

A knot began to form in Ellen's stomach. She had Lynn dead to rights. They had a credible witness. It was Lynn or Stuart or both of them. Why else would Rocko call her and say what he'd said? "How does she explain what Rocko saw?"

"She swears up and down he must be lying."

"But...*why* would he lie?" she asked.

"I have no idea."

Was he going to let Lynn wriggle out of what she'd done? "Don't tell me you believe her..."

After another brief hesitation, he said, "I don't know what to believe, Ellen. Lynn has some difficult aspects to her personality. I've already acknowledged that. But I've never known her to be a blatant liar. She manipulates in other ways—with emotional blackmail and the sheer weight of her temper and displeasure. So...there must be something else going on here."

Suddenly unable to take another bite, Ellen pushed the rest of her burrito away. "Like what?"

"I don't know. But I'm on my way over to Burgers and Shakes to see if I can talk to Rocko right now."

Ellen stared down at her half-eaten food. "You don't think *I'm* lying, do you? That I'm somehow trying to... to frame your aunt?"

"No, of course not. Just...let me do some poking

around, and we'll talk about it tonight, okay?" he said. "In the meantime, don't worry about anything," he quickly added.

She tried to take those words to heart, to relax and enjoy the drive back to Coyote Canyon as much as she'd enjoyed the trip to Missoula. But her stomach churned the whole way. Somehow, no matter what Lynn did, she got away with it. It was always Ellen who was the troublemaker or not measuring up and somehow deserved to be the outcast Lynn had made her.

Ellen had thought she was finally beyond Lynn's ability to hurt her. As a matter of fact, she'd begun to pride herself on how well she'd recovered from the past. Maybe she'd been a little lonely, but she worked a lot and didn't have enough social interaction. That was to be expected. In other ways she'd been happier than she'd ever been.

And yet…because she'd allowed herself to start caring about Hendrix, she was vulnerable again. Even though his aunt was the one who'd sabotaged the Haslem well, Lynn was going to be able to turn it around and make it look as though Ellen was somehow behind it. Not only would that ruin her fledgling relationship with Hendrix, it would poison everyone against her all over again and damage her business, ensuring that Fetterman Well Services remained on top.

Had Lynn known exactly how she'd play it from the moment she poured cement down that well?

Twenty-Three

Hendrix could tell Rocko was surprised he hadn't come in for a burger, like everyone else who was standing in the fast-food restaurant.

"You want to talk to *me*?" he'd said when Hendrix stepped to the side of the three registers to catch his attention.

They didn't know each other well, had never had any business together. Hendrix stopped in for a meal now and then, and they nodded or waved if they saw each other around town. That was it. "If you can take a minute."

He looked at his staff as though he was hoping they'd appear too busy to allow him to step away. Or that someone would have a question for him that would keep him behind the counter. But the lunch rush was nearly over, and they had what was left of it well in hand. "Okay," he said, sounding baffled by the request. "Where do you want to talk?"

"At an empty table will be fine." He couldn't say why Rocko seemed so put off. It wasn't as if Hendrix expected to be invited into the kitchen.

"What's going on?" Rocko asked as they both slid into the closest unoccupied booth.

"Ellen told me you saw something that has me a bit concerned."

Rocko smoothed his white polo shirt, which had his logo in red, with matching piping. "What was that?"

That he hadn't already guessed seemed strange. What he'd reported definitely pertained to Hendrix and the people he'd grown up with. "It's about the truck you saw on the Haslem property on Tuesday night."

"Oh, that." He made a dismissive gesture. "It was late and dark and…it all happened so fast. I couldn't really see anything."

"Except a white truck with a Fetterman Well Services placard on the door, right?" Hendrix clarified. "Isn't that what you told Ellen?"

"That's what I *thought* I saw. But now that I've had more time to go over those memories… I don't know. I don't want to accuse anyone, because I can't be certain. Like I said before, it happened too fast."

Hendrix studied him. "Did you tell *her* that?"

"Of course."

"You told Ellen you didn't really see anything."

"I told her it all happened so fast I can't be sure."

"So…what *are* you certain of? What did you see?"

"A truck came flying off the property and nearly hit me. That's all."

"While you were riding past on your motorcycle…"

"Yes."

"How'd you manage to avoid an accident?"

"I slammed on my brakes and swerved."

On a motorcycle? How did he avoid skidding and laying the bike down on the concrete? "But you didn't wipe out."

"No, thank goodness." He whistled as he shook his head to emphasize that it'd been a close call. "I got really lucky."

"Do you remember the color of the truck you saw?" Hendrix asked.

"I think it was white."

Now even the color was in question? "You told Ellen it was white and had a Fetterman Well Services placard on the door."

"I didn't say that."

Hendrix blinked in surprise. "You didn't tell her you saw our company name on the door?"

"She must've come up with that on her own. You know how she feels about you, Lynn and Stuart. She probably added that part herself." He glanced back at the registers to see that a few stragglers had wandered in. "I've got to get back to work," he said. "I wish I could tell you more, but that's all I remember."

Hendrix nodded and watched as he got up, hurried back behind the counter and started barking out orders as though they were in the midst of a huge crush. Rocko had always been a little self-important. But…was he also dishonest?

Hendrix couldn't believe Lynn had been out at the well in the middle of the night. He'd seen her reaction— the genuine shock and anger—and considered it authentic. So…what was going on?

Could Ellen have made up the Fetterman branding part of the story?

No way. And yet… Hendrix had to admit that if she *was* out to get even for all the hurt Stuart and Lynn had caused her over the years, enlisting his support and sympathy so she could divide them and cause turmoil in their lives and business would be a clever way to go about it.

Making him want her would be even better.

Talulah frowned. "You've hardly said a word."

Ellen glanced listlessly around the bar. After hearing from Hendrix and learning what Rocko had said when he visited Burgers and Shakes, she didn't really want to be out in public. It was Talulah who'd insisted she stop moping around the house and meet her at Hank's for dinner while Brant was busy with his cattle and a livestock agent. Her best friend mistakenly thought getting out would cheer Ellen up, but they'd paid their bill and Ellen didn't feel any better. "I don't know what to say," she said. "It feels as though I've fallen right into Lynn's trap—that she had this planned from the time I got the Haslem job. The worst of it is that Hendrix has to believe her instead of me, especially now that Rocko's changed his story."

Talulah folded her arms on the table as she leaned forward. "But you don't care what Hendrix thinks, remember?"

Ellen stared down into her peach smash, which she'd been nursing since she arrived. She wished she could go back in time to before she cared what Hendrix thought—before he'd punched Jordan in the face for manhandling her and helped her drill the well and slept with her. If she hadn't allowed the last two things to happen, maybe she wouldn't be thinking of him obsessively, craving the sound of his voice and hoping to see him again, despite telling him she wouldn't.

What had she done?

She'd handed Lynn and Stuart the perfect weapon to use against her—that was what she'd done.

"Rocko's mad you won't go out with him, so he has no loyalty to you," Talulah said. "And, knowing him, he's probably afraid of choosing the wrong party to support in this situation. Most people respect Hendrix and the Fettermans. They're well established, with lots of friends, clients and acquaintances. That's why he backed off his story. He doesn't want to get on their bad side."

She'd tried calling Rocko this afternoon, but he wouldn't pick up. "I don't know why he did it, but now it looks as though I sabotaged my own job so I could frame Lynn."

"Anyone who knows you will never believe you're capable of something like that."

"You're the only one who knows me that well. I'm still considered new in town, remember?" She'd spent all her time working. She hadn't been out making friends. What trust and respect she'd been able to garner had come slowly over time, as people saw for themselves what she was like and began to form their own opinions independent of what they'd heard Lynn Fetterman say about her.

"This thing isn't over yet," Talulah insisted. "We'll get to the bottom of it."

"How?" If no one would tell the truth, what could they do?

"Didn't you say Rocko had someone with him?"

"Maribeth was riding on the back of his bike."

"Why don't we go talk to her? Maybe she saw something he didn't—or could back up what he first told you."

"If she's dating Rocko, I have no doubt she'll support whatever position he takes. Besides, she was riding behind him. If *he* couldn't even get a good look at the truck that came barreling off the property, how would *she* be able to do it?"

"Who knows? But it can't hurt to ask. I say we at least talk to her."

Ellen wasn't optimistic. "I don't think it'll do any good."

Talulah checked her watch. "It *won't* do us any good to go there tonight if we don't hurry. It'd be kind of weird to show up after dark, and it'll be dark in an hour. We need to get going."

Too disheartened to even finish her drink, Ellen left it, like she had her food, only halfway eaten and followed Talulah to the door.

Hendrix had been busy all afternoon. He was still trying to get caught up, and with Stuart being out of town, it wasn't easy. He needed to pick up the supplies Ellen went to Missoula to get, but he wasn't ready to go over there quite yet. Something Rocko had said earlier had bothered him all afternoon, and now that he finally had a break, he was hurrying out to the Haslem property to take a look at the area around the driveway while he still had enough sunlight.

As he approached the turnoff, he pulled to the side of the road and got out. He assumed Rocko would have been coming from town when he saw the truck, but that hadn't been established, so he planned to check both directions, if necessary.

He walked ten, twenty, thirty, forty and then fifty feet from the Haslem drive and saw none of the skid marks he'd expected to find on the pavement. He didn't see any areas on the shoulder that'd been disturbed, either. So...if Rocko had slammed on his brakes and narrowly avoided a collision, where was the telltale rubber that should've been left on the road? And, if there were no skid marks, where was the evidence that he'd been forced over onto the shoulder?

There was no proof of that, either.

Hendrix examined the other side of the drive just as carefully. No skid marks; no evidence of a motorcycle or any other kind of vehicle stopping on the shoulder.

Trying to figure out how this incident had taken place, he turned to look at his truck and immediately noticed the impressions his own tires had left on the soft dirt. There should've been some sign that Rocko had nearly been in an accident, even though it was a few days ago.

"What the hell," he mumbled and drove down the driveway, wondering if he'd see anything on the property itself that might back up Rocko's story—like evidence of a motorcycle turning around to head back after narrowly escaping a life-threatening collision.

He found no sign of that. But that didn't mean anything. He and Ellen—and Jay, too—had been in and out of the property with various vehicles. There were all kinds of tire tracks but nothing particularly suspicious or unusual about any of them.

He was just climbing back into his truck when his phone went off. It was Stuart.

He punched the Talk button. "Hello?"

"What's going on? I just heard from Lynn. She's beside herself. Claims Ellen's trying to say she sabotaged the Haslem well."

"I don't think it's quite the way she's making it sound," he said, hoping against hope he was right. "But something's up, and I'm trying to figure out what it is."

"Hi, Hendrix!" Leo called from the background. "I'm almost home. I can't wait to see you."

"Tell Leo I'm excited he'll be back."

Stuart relayed the message, but Leo must've grabbed the phone, or Stuart let him take it for a minute, because his voice suddenly came through much more stridently. "I miss you, Hendrix."

"I miss you, too, Leo."

"Why's Mom mad at Ellen, Hendrix? I like Ellen. I want to go back to her house. She has my chalk."

There was no way to make Leo understand the complexity of the situation. "There's been a little confusion around here since you left, bud, that's all."

"Confusion?"

"I've got some stuff I need to get done before the sun goes down. Can you put your dad back on the phone?"

"Okay. But…will you take me to get a donut tomorrow morning?"

Hendrix chuckled. "You're going to have to talk to your mom about that. I don't dare cross her right now, not even for you."

He could hear Leo hitting Stuart up to let them go get a donut tomorrow as the phone changed hands.

"Is there anything I can do to help?" Stuart asked when he came back on the line.

Hendrix gazed out toward the highway where he'd found nothing to indicate Rocko had nearly crashed, like he claimed. "I don't think so. Not right now."

"Will I see you at the house later tonight?"

"No. But I'll probably see you tomorrow or sometime this weekend, if only for Sunday dinner." If Lynn was still going to have it…

"Okay."

"You don't think Ellen would sabotage her own well, then claim it was Lynn, do you?" Hendrix asked.

There were several seconds of silence. Then, Stuart said, "You can only judge future behavior by past behavior."

"Meaning...you agree with Lynn? You think Ellen was a difficult child who's turned into a difficult adult, and she'll stop at nothing to get revenge for past slights?"

"Ellen has been in Coyote Canyon for two and a half years, Hendrix. If she was going to do something beyond what she's already done—which is to show me that she's just as capable of building a well-drilling business as I am—she would've done it."

"So...you don't believe it?"

"I might've believed it two and a half years ago, when she first came to town. But after watching her establish a pattern of working hard and smart and building a good reputation, I can't see her suddenly being dishonest enough to sabotage a well just to blame someone else for it, even if that someone is Lynn—or me. What's changed? Why would there be such a marked deviation in her behavior?"

Hendrix had slept with her. That was what had changed. His involvement could easily have caused the whole paradigm to be turned on its head. But there was no way he'd ever admit that to Stuart. Not if he didn't have to. "Right. Okay," he said and disconnected.

Talulah drove because she knew where Maribeth lived. She often delivered breakfast rolls and other treats to Maribeth's grandmother, who was in her eighties and bedridden and living in the same house. "You ready?" she asked Ellen as they pulled to a stop at the curb.

Her friend nodded and opened the passenger door. "Let's go."

Ellen was one of the toughest people Talulah had ever known. That was what she most admired about her—or, at least, one of the things. Not only had she come through some difficult experiences, she continued to blaze a bold trail in a man's world.

But she didn't seem like herself today. She was agitated and worried and seemed to be second-guessing her friendship with Hendrix.

Talulah understood. You couldn't be strong all the time, and Ellen seemed to believe that allowing Hendrix into her small circle of friends had been a catastrophic mistake. "We're going to get to the truth," she told her.

Ellen nodded but didn't speak as they approached the door.

Serena, Maribeth's mother, answered Talulah's knock. Other than taking care of Hazel, she worked at the ice cream parlor on weekends, presumably when Maribeth was home and could take over with her grandmother. Maribeth's father had passed away five years earlier, so there was no longer a man in the house. "Is Maribeth here?" Talulah asked.

"She is," Serena said. "We just finished dinner, so she's been helping me clean up. Let me get her."

"Thank you." Talulah cast another encouraging glance at Ellen.

"I feel stupid interrupting them like this," Ellen muttered.

"It'll only take a few minutes."

When Maribeth stepped outside, she had her long brown hair piled on top of her head and was wearing a pair of sweats. "Hi, Talulah," she said with a friendly smile. "How are you?"

Ellen had indicated on the way over that she didn't really know Maribeth, had just seen her around town and at Hank's on occasion, so it was understandable that Maribeth gave her only a polite nod.

"I'm doing great," Talulah said. "Listen, we hate to bother you, especially out of the blue like this, but something happened on Tuesday night, and we really need to talk to you about it."

Maribeth's eyes went wide. "What's that?"

"You know when you went riding with Rocko Schneider on his motorcycle?"

She looked even more confused. "The last time I went riding with Rocko was a month or more ago."

Talulah didn't look at Ellen, but she could feel the surprise that hit her on hearing this response. Talulah was equally surprised. "You weren't with him when he was out by the Haslem property around midnight?"

"Jay fixes my car, but I've only ever been to his repair shop. I don't even know where his property is."

"Rocko told Ellen that you were with him when he nearly had an accident Tuesday night. He said a white truck came tearing out of the Haslems' vacant land just as you were passing by, and he had to swerve. According to him, the two of you only narrowly avoided a terrible accident."

"There's no way," Maribeth said, shaking her head. "He must've been with someone else. I could never stay out that late on a weeknight. I have to be at the vet clinic by seven in the morning."

"I see." Talulah didn't know where to go from there. "Maybe Ellen misunderstood. I'm sorry to have interrupted your evening."

"No problem. I feel sorry for whoever was on that bike, though. It sounds like a harrowing ordeal. And Rocko's weird to begin with. Once he sets his sights on someone, he won't back off. I'm just glad I finally got him to stop calling me."

"He wouldn't leave you alone?"

"No. After I told him I didn't want to see him anymore, my mother caught him sitting out front, watching our house late at night. It was creepy."

"That *is* strange."

"I was excited about him at first," she admitted. "But after we started dating, it just...didn't work. He was far too obsessive about certain things. That was what put me off."

"And you wouldn't want any trouble with his ex," Talulah joked. She was trying to lighten the conversation, but Maribeth didn't laugh.

"Debbie's nothing to worry about compared to him," she said as she went back inside.

"What does *that* mean?" Talulah whispered to Ellen as they walked back to her car.

"It means Rocko's up to something," Ellen replied, her voice velvet over steel. "The question is...what?"

"And why? Why would he claim Maribeth was with him if she wasn't?" It was comforting to see Ellen's usual strength and determination return. She never backed away from a fight—not if someone brought the fight to her. But lately, Hendrix seemed to be acting as her kryptonite.

"I have no idea," Ellen said. "But I plan to find out."

Twenty-Four

It was nearly ten that night when Hendrix called to say he was coming over to get the hose Ellen had picked up for him in Missoula. She was anxious to see him and worried about how he might behave at the same time. Would they end up in an argument that would make them enemies again? Was their brief attempt at friendship over already?

Ellen wouldn't be surprised if that was the case. Things had gotten so strange and unusual lately, what with letting him in her bed. Then there was the damage to the well and the question of who was responsible. Because she'd wandered off the safe path of her usual routine, it felt like she'd inadvertently kicked a beehive—and now she could hear the buzz of the swarm coming after her.

The note she'd found on her door when she got home had a lot to do with the sense of impending doom that hung over her. It was from Lynn, who'd never come to her house before. Lynn had been careful not to open herself up to a direct confrontation—until tonight, apparently, and then Ellen had been out with Talulah. Ellen knew the fact that her feelings had never really been addressed was probably why they sat deep in her gut, rotting like an old piece of meat.

In an attempt to ease her agitation, she took a deep breath, smoothed open the note she'd crumpled in one hand and read it again.

Ellen—

I can't believe anyone, even you, would stoop low enough to try to frame me for a criminal act. But you won't get away with it. Unless you retract the accusations you've made and tell the truth about what really happened to that well, I'm going to make sure everyone finally understands what a terrible person you are—including Leo and your father.

Remember, I know you best—Lynn

"I know you best," she repeated as she paced to the fireplace, then marched back across the living room. Her stepmother didn't know her at all! She'd never taken the time, never opened her heart, never had any interest.

Or...was Lynn right? Was she really as unworthy of love as Lynn made her feel—and had made her feel since she was just a child?

A lump swelled in her throat as she turned back toward the fireplace—one she fought hard to swallow when the shine of headlights coming through the picture window suddenly lit the room. That had to be Hendrix. She didn't want him to know how much this whole thing upset her. She could only protect herself from him and the Fettermans if she didn't let them know they held any power over her.

Blinking rapidly to rid her eyes of tears, she opened the door as soon as she felt capable of speaking without her voice cracking. "Hello."

"Hey," he said back. "I hope it's okay that I parked in the driveway this time. I thought it would be easier to transfer the hose and other stuff you got for me today."

"That's...fine." She'd never been opposed to it. He was the one who had to worry that Lynn might find out they were associating with each other. "If...if it's okay with you."

"It's silly for me to have to park so far away."

Was it? What had changed? She didn't dare ask, and she didn't know whether to step aside and let him in or walk out to help him transfer the hoses. As far as she knew, he believed Rocko, felt she'd been lying to get Lynn in trouble and no longer wanted anything to do with her.

"Can I come in?" he asked when she hesitated.

She had to swallow again—that damn lump had come back—as she moved out of the way. "Sure."

He waited until she'd shut the door, then he took her by the shoulders as he gazed into her face. "You okay?"

The concern in his voice almost proved her undoing. She'd expected him to shun her again, to fall back in line with his aunt and her father. "I'm...fine," she insisted stiffly, but when he looked at her more closely, she sighed. "I don't know," she admitted. "I'm...confused."

"So am I, especially after what I found at the Haslem lot this evening—or, more accurately, *didn't* find."

"What do you mean?" she asked, instantly alarmed. "The well hasn't been damaged again, has it?"

"No. The well's fine—at least as far as I know. I was looking for skid marks or any other evidence that there'd almost been an accident near the driveway, but

I couldn't find anything. There were no black marks on the pavement and neither shoulder looked as though it'd been disturbed, not recently and not within the area Rocko would've been for his version of events to be true."

She folded her arms. "To be honest, that doesn't really surprise me."

He scowled. "What?"

"Talulah and I spoke with Maribeth Woodson tonight. Rocko told me he had her on the back of his bike when he almost collided with the white truck with the Fetterman Well Services logo on it. But she claims she hasn't been anywhere with Rocko for well over a month."

Releasing her, he stepped back. "Why would Rocko claim she'd been with him?"

"I really don't know." Lifting her hand, she showed him the crumpled note. "And when I got home, I found this."

His scowl increased as he took the paper from her and read it. "Where was it?"

"It was peeking out from under my doormat tonight."

"You can't pay attention to this garbage," he said. "My aunt doesn't know what the hell she's talking about."

"I didn't sabotage the well," she said. "And I only repeated to you what Rocko told me about seeing a Fetterman truck. I didn't make that up, Hendrix."

"I believe you." He tossed the note on a side table before pulling her into his arms. "I'm sorry, Ellen. I know what my aunt has done has cut you deeply—both over the years and now. It's all been so…unfair."

Her pride demanded she claim Lynn and Stuart no longer had the power to hurt her. To do less would show weakness, and in her experience, weakness was always exploited.

She started to push him away, but he used the few inches she created between them to lift her chin and kiss her so gently and sweetly she couldn't bring herself to do more. *Nothing* had ever felt so good. The sense of security that filled her when she was in his arms was something she'd never been able to find, not since her parents' divorce.

Then there was the intoxicating scent of his cologne and the sight of his eyes, filled with emotion, as he gazed at her again…

She wanted nothing more than to give herself up to the desire to be loved. But she couldn't allow it. She was frozen with fear. If she kept things as they were, at least she knew she'd be able to continue to limp along as before.

If she allowed herself to love Hendrix and he turned on her…

"It's okay," she told him. "I don't need you or your sympathy. I don't need *anything* from you. I can take care of myself."

He winced as though her words stung. But that had to be an illusion. This was Hendrix. He'd lost his mother early on, which couldn't have been easy, but he'd always had plenty of people to love and support him. Stuart. Lynn. Leo. The whole community. He certainly didn't need *her*.

"Ellen…"

"It's getting late," she said. "You'd better transfer the stuff out of my truck and go."

"Are you sure that's what you want?" he asked. "I feel… I feel different with you than I've ever felt with anyone else. I think we could have something, if only…"

He didn't finish that statement, but she knew where he was going—or what needed to happen, at any rate. They could have something if only she could trust him.

Problem was, she couldn't. It was far too big a risk for someone whose heart was already so battered and bruised. She had to keep her fists up so she could protect herself in case he ever decided to side with Lynn and Stuart again, which would come as a blow. "Really?" she said. "Because I don't feel *anything*."

His mouth opened, closed and opened again. "What about the other night—in your bed?" he finally asked.

"When we had sex?" She shrugged. "That wasn't about anything except getting off, right?"

He rocked back as though she'd slapped him. "It seemed... I mean... You didn't feel anything...deeper?"

"I enjoyed it," she said. "But no more than with the guy before you. And I'm sure I'll enjoy sex just as much with the next guy."

He pressed a hand to his chest. "Ellen, stop. You don't have to act like this—"

"Act like what?" she broke in. "It was fun while it lasted. At least I know you won't tell anyone, because then you'd have to admit to consorting with the enemy." She forced herself to laugh and prayed it sounded believable, because she certainly wasn't feeling any mirth. The opposite was true, in fact. Something inside her seemed to be shriveling up and dying—and stealing all the power from her soul at the same time.

"Right," he said. "Okay. I guess..." His throat worked as he swallowed. "I must be wrong. I apologize. Apparently, some things just can't be fixed."

With that, he walked out and didn't even bother to close the door. She could hear his feet on the porch steps, broadening the distance between them as he hurried to the driveway, where her truck was parked beside his.

She'd done the right thing, she told herself in the silence that ensued—what had to be done. She wouldn't allow him or her father or his aunt to hurt her ever again. That was a promise she'd made to herself when she was just a girl, and she'd keep it. She didn't need anyone.

Besides, she could never truly expect him to choose her over Lynn. Lynn was his aunt. Actually, she was more like his *mother*.

Too charged up to stand still, she was breathing hard and turning in a circle, wishing there was some way to release the terrible pain inside her. It felt as though someone had stabbed her, weakening the defenses she'd built so carefully over the years—the defenses that held back the pain of her childhood, including her parents' divorce, her father's abandonment, her mother's far-too-heavy reliance and all the things she'd missed as a child because of it.

I'll be fine. I've always been fine. I have my business. I have Talulah. I have Ross. I have… I have my mother even though she's part of the problem.

That kind of thinking had always worked before. But as she heard Hendrix unloading the hoses out front, she realized it wasn't working now. She'd never felt so forlorn or bereft.

Then her eyes landed on the geode on her coffee table, and a memory she'd suppressed because she couldn't bear thinking about it—sealed off like a coffin she'd buried deep in the earth—suddenly rose to the surface. She was eleven and staying with her father and Lynn during one of her early visits before she was cut off from the family. She'd wandered into Hendrix's room right after he'd come to live with Lynn and Stuart—she'd been so curious about this interloper who was loved far more than she was—and picked up a geode he had on the dresser that, if memory served, looked a lot like the one that'd been left on her doorstep.

She'd never seen such a thing before, didn't even know they existed, and had been entranced by the beauty of all the purple crystals—so entranced that she hadn't heard Hendrix come into the room, hadn't realized she'd been caught in his private space looking at his personal possessions, and he'd absolutely exploded in anger. He'd shouted for her to put it down and never touch it again, that she wasn't even to *look* at it, and when Lynn came to see what all the fuss was about, Ellen had been punished with a crisp slap on the hands. Then Lynn had grabbed Hendrix, pulled him in for a hug and started to cry with him, and it was only later that Stuart had explained that she'd been in the wrong for invading Hendrix's space and touching something that was special to him because it had belonged to his mother.

She eyed her geode more carefully. Surely Hendrix hadn't been the one to leave this on her doorstep. He would never give her such a priceless possession, one that meant so much to him.

As she stared at the rock, she realized that if it wasn't the exact same one she'd been punished for touching, it was almost identical.

He remembered she'd liked it; that was why he'd given it to her. Who else would think of such an unusual gift? And why would whoever it was give it to her anonymously?

The sound of his engine rose as he started his truck. She wanted so badly to go to him, to stop him and tell him he *did* mean something to her, and everything could be fixed, as he wished.

But she couldn't. That would only bring more pain.

She began to tremble as she stood there, and as he started to back down the drive, more and more tears rolled down her cheeks. Then something snapped inside her, and the next thing she knew, she was running out the door.

Hendrix almost didn't see Ellen. He was too upset, too eager to get the hell away from her house. That he'd even tried to reach her on an intimate level seemed foolish now.

But as he shifted into Drive, he caught sight of her white billowing shirt as she came charging down the driveway, saw the streaks of tears on her cheeks in the moonlight and had to stop. No matter what it was, she needed him, and he cared too much about her to drive away.

After he put the truck in Park, he opened his door and got out, half expecting to hear her scream every vile thing she'd ever thought about him.

But she didn't say anything. She ran right up to him and threw her arms around his neck, and all his own pain and anger evaporated as he held her small body against his. "Don't go," she said. "I don't want you to go."

He smiled as he kissed the top of her head. "Okay, I won't."

"I don't know why I'm crying," she said. "This is stupid."

Feeling he might finally be allowed entrance into the fortress she'd built around herself, he buried his face in her neck. "It's not stupid. You need to let it out. Let it all go, Ellen. We all have a heart." He cupped her face and looked down into her eyes. "Even me—and I hope you won't break it."

He held her for several minutes while she cried, but as her tears began to subside, he started to kiss her neck, and then her mouth and the next thing he knew, she wanted him to come back inside.

"Just let me pull my truck into the drive for the night," he said.

"Don't you think you should move it down the road, out of sight, like usual?" she asked as she wiped her eyes.

He kissed her forehead and then the tip of her nose. "No."

"Why not?"

"Because as often as I'm going to want to see you, I won't be able to keep it a secret, anyway," he said.

Twenty-Five

Ellen began to stir, waking Hendrix before his alarm went off, but he didn't mind. He needed to be up early. It was Friday. He had one more workday ahead of him before the weekend and had to get a lot done. He still had to make up for all the hours he'd lost earlier in the week helping Ellen.

Besides, despite the passion and bravado he'd been feeling last night, he wasn't eager for someone to spot his truck in Ellen's drive, notice it'd been there all night and report it to Lynn and Stuart. If he left before the sun came up, maybe he could get away with having spent the night here. Relations with his aunt and uncle were strained enough as it was. The fact that Lynn had made the trek to Ellen's house to deliver such a nasty note was proof she wasn't going to let the Haslem thing go. Now that he wasn't feeling the rush of euphoria and relief he'd experienced when Ellen came running out to stop him from leaving, he understood it would be best to work through a few things first. There was a lot on the line—they needed to be as smart as possible so they could successfully navigate whatever was coming.

"You're awake?" Ellen yawned as he reached over to pull her tighter against him.

"I am. But I don't want to get up. I wish I could stay in bed with you all day."

"Last night was…" Her voice drifted off as if she couldn't—or wouldn't—finish that sentence.

"Good?" he suggested. Fortunately, he'd remembered to buy more condoms yesterday, because he'd definitely needed them.

"Unlike anything I've ever experienced before," she admitted.

"Does that scare you?"

"Doesn't it scare *you*?" she asked.

"If you weren't smashed up against me, totally naked, it would."

They both chuckled as she began to use her finger to draw an imaginary design on his chest. "What are we going to do? I don't want to get you in trouble with Lynn and Stuart, and yet… I don't want to give you up, either."

Ellen was showing more trust than he'd expected her to have—and that gave him hope they might be able to hang on to each other and somehow make a relationship out of what they felt. At least she wasn't telling him sex with him was only about pleasure, she didn't really care about him and all the other stuff she'd tried to say before.

"It doesn't make any sense to me that they'd try to keep us apart," he said.

"And yet you know they will. Lynn, for sure."

"For now, let's just…keep things on the down-low as much as possible. I don't mean we have to sneak around—" he felt she deserved more than that after what she'd been through "—but let's not make any grand announcements until we can work through the Haslem well problem. It'll be easier for me to approach my aunt about you if she doesn't have anything else she can blame you for." And waiting until then might give him and Ellen a chance to become more confident in what they felt and what they wanted from each other before the relationship could be targeted by those who'd like to see it destroyed.

As she slid her leg over his, he moved his hand up her bare thigh to curve around her firm ass. "Okay," she said. "But…what if we can't get anywhere with that? What do we do then?"

"It's got to be Rocko," he said, thoroughly convinced. "He's the one who made up all that bullshit about the motorcycle accident, and I bet he did it to get you into a fight with Lynn and Stuart—and probably with me, as well."

"I've been thinking it has to be him, too. Maribeth made him sound a little obsessive. Said her mother caught him stalking her. Maybe, since he's turned his attention on me, he's been watching *my* house and has seen you come over—"

"Or heard from Charlie, or someone Charlie told, that I helped you drill the Haslem well."

"And thought he'd put a stop to anything that might be developing between us."

Hendrix breathed deeply, taking in the appealing scent of her warm skin. "That sounds plausible. Except… Rocko doesn't seem smart enough to come up with such a diabolical plan."

"He's not very self-aware," she agreed, "but he's been quite successful with his business. He must be smarter than he seems."

While he was still skeptical, Hendrix couldn't think

of any other explanation. "Maybe. But how do we prove it was him so that everyone who's involved can relax, and Lynn will put her guard back down?"

Ellen leaned on her elbows. "Has her guard *ever* been down when it comes to me?"

"You know what I mean," he said, tucking a strand of her short hair behind her ear. "If she'd go so far as to come to your house to confront you, this situation with the well has brought all her animosity to the forefront."

Ellen lowered her head and began pressing her lips against his neck. "I don't know." She kissed his jaw. "Without a witness or something—" another kiss—this one on the lips "—how can we prove it was him?"

Catching her face, he brought her mouth back to his for a longer, lingering kiss. "I'm hoping we'll get lucky. Otherwise, my aunt will keep going after you until everyone believes you sabotaged the well and blamed her."

"She can't really believe *I'd* sabotage the well…"

"She believes you'd do anything to make her look bad. Probably because she deserves it," he added as an afterthought.

Ellen seemed slightly surprised by his last statement. He was surprised himself. He owed Lynn his appreciation and respect. But the more he got to know and care about Ellen, the more torn he began to feel.

"She's never really known me." Ellen paused. "Wait…"

"What?" he asked.

Rolling away from him, she grabbed her phone off the nightstand. "When I arrived at the Haslem property the morning after the well had been sabotaged, I found a tire imprint in the mud. I didn't think I'd really be able to use it for anything, but I snapped a picture, just in case."

"Wow!" he said as he took her phone from her. "You got a good shot."

"Thanks. Just before you came over tonight, I stopped by the police station and spoke to Sherman Wilkes. I've known him since I fixed the pump on his well right after I moved to town and he was new on the force. He said Jay would have to file a police report, since it happened to his property, but then he'd look into it."

"Are you going to talk to Jay about it?"

"I plan to."

He continued to study the photograph. "Even if Jay files a report, who knows how long it'll take the police to make any kind of determination—or if they ever will."

"There's also a chance Jay won't bother, now that the well's been repaired."

"We could use this to check the tires of the people we suspect," he said. "There's a lot of detail here. We should be able to tell if Rocko's tires are similar or vastly different, at least."

"Vastly different could work as a means of elimination."

"And if we find that any of Rocko's tires *are* similar, we could press him harder—maybe even accuse him outright to see what he might give away under pressure—because there'd be no reason for his vehicle to be anywhere near that well." He sent the picture to himself before giving her phone back to her. "Why do you think he claimed Maribeth was on the back of his bike if she wasn't? That was such a risky lie. All you had to do was check with her."

"Honestly? I think he was embellishing to make the lie more believable—providing a good reason for being on his motorcycle so late at night that far from his house—and never thought I'd check. He used to date Maribeth. He might be aware that we don't know each other. Without Talulah, I never would've approached her."

"And he has to be familiar with how you felt about me and Lynn and Stuart. He owns and works at one of the most popular businesses in town, so he hears most everything. I bet he thought it would be easy to cause a fight between us—that he'd set it up, and we'd just go after each other and never investigate further."

"Then he'd have his revenge on me for turning him down, and you'd no longer be a romantic rival—meaning there'd be a chance I'd change my mind about him."

"Would you ever date him?" Hendrix asked.

"Absolutely not," she replied. "But he doesn't know that."

Hendrix sighed. "The last thing we needed was for him or anyone else to cause more trouble between you and my aunt. Things have been bad enough for the past twenty years."

"Well, if things get so bad between you and your aunt and my father that you get fired, at least I can offer you a job." She lifted her head to grin down at him. "In case you haven't seen the notices posted around town, I'm looking for a good driller."

He laughed. "Working with you every day doesn't sound half-bad. But if I'm not going to be able to buy Stuart out of the business I've been helping with for years, you'd have to make me more than just an employee. Would you be willing to do that?"

She tilted her head to the side, wearing a skeptical expression while making it obvious she was teasing him. "We'll see. At least we both know the demands of the job."

He'd hate to lose all he'd put into Fetterman Well Services. The equipment alone was worth millions. But all the power was in Stuart's hands, who was heavily influenced by Lynn. There was a very real risk Hendrix could be cut off.

Was he going to allow Stuart and Lynn to use the business to control his personal life? That they might even try made him angry. But taking up that fight came with huge risk. What he felt for Ellen was exciting and hopeful, but it was also brand-new. He had no idea where it would go. And if it didn't go anywhere, he'd be risking his financial future, as well as his relationship with the only family he had, for what? Would Lynn block him from seeing Leo? Refuse to forgive him if he chose Ellen over her?

They all lived in the same small town. It would be miserable if a serious rift occurred.

The ramifications were daunting. But he wasn't going to think about all of that right now. He'd solve the mystery of who'd sabotaged the Haslem well and mitigate some of Lynn's anger that way—show her that Ellen wasn't out to get her. Then, hopefully, she'd feel bad for assuming it was Ellen and be more tractable in the future.

"For the first time since you moved here, I'm glad you're in the same business," he said as he rolled her beneath him. "There could certainly be some advantages."

Her arms tightened around his neck as she pulled him in for a kiss. When he lifted his head, he couldn't help thinking how beautiful she'd become to him, which was so weird, given how he'd reacted to her at first sight. She was probably the only woman in town who wore her hair so short, but it made her eyes look that much bigger. "On the other hand, maybe we'd never accomplish anything if we worked together. It's getting harder to leave you by the second..."

"That could prove to be a challenge."

"Even if we got to a jobsite, I probably wouldn't be able to let you out of the truck." His alarm sounded, making him groan in disappointment. "Damn."

Reluctantly, he got out of bed to silence it. "I still need to go home, shower and change into my work clothes, so I'd better take off."

She covered another yawn. "You don't want breakfast first?"

The longer he stayed, the greater the chances someone would see his truck in the drive—especially if Rocko was watching Ellen's house, as they'd guessed. "I'd better not. But I'll be back tonight, since you owe me dinner," he said and shot her a grin when she didn't argue.

Leo called just as Hendrix was ready to walk out the door of his house.

"It's me, Leo," he said as soon as Hendrix answered.

"I'm glad to hear from you, bud. How are you this morning?"

He didn't answer the question, just moved right on to the reason he'd called. "Are you coming over to see me? I was gone for a long time, Hendrix. I bet you missed me."

Hendrix had been hoping to avoid Lynn and Stuart until their next regularly scheduled meeting on Tuesday. He felt it would be smarter to keep his distance until he could, hopefully, learn who'd sabotaged the well and use that information to take the fire out of his aunt's anger. Otherwise, the friction between them would just continue.

But he hadn't accounted for Leo and the fact that his cousin could never wait that long to see him. "Do you want to go to work with me today? If so, I can swing by and pick you up." He always enjoyed Leo, but thinking his aunt and uncle might cut him off made him eager to spend time with his cousin while he could.

"Yeah! You'll come get me? I'll be ready, Hendrix. I'll change out of my pajamas and brush my teeth right now."

"Good. Go ahead and do that because I'm on my way."

Leo didn't even bother to answer. He must've gotten so excited he forgot to finish the call, because Hendrix heard him yell to his mother that he needed to hurry up and get dressed. Then the phone went dead.

He smiled as he strode to his truck. He wasn't sure where his life was heading. Just a week or two earlier, his future had been predictable. Now it seemed much less so. But he'd never seen Ellen as a major or intimate part of his life before. Now he did, and that changed everything.

Another call came in as he was climbing into his truck; he answered on Bluetooth so he could still drive.

"Dude, is it true?"

It was Kurt. When Hendrix saw his name on caller ID, he'd assumed this call would be about going out tonight or maybe target shooting or riding ATVs tomorrow. "Is *what* true?"

"Are you and Ellen friends, after all this time?"

"Who told you that?"

"When I was at Hank's last night, everyone was talking about how you helped her drill a well for Jay Haslem. I said that was impossible, that Ellen owns a business that competes with yours, and you were pissed off when Jay hired her instead of you. But Charlie Gerhart was there, and he said he saw you with his own eyes."

News of him helping Ellen was already starting to circulate around town. He needed to figure a way out of the mess he was in before the gossip reached Lynn. "It was nothing," he said, hoping he wouldn't have to clarify further.

"You're saying you *didn't* help her?"

Hendrix couldn't go that far. Charlie had seen him there. And the more he dodged the question, the more Kurt would press him. He figured a semblance of the truth might serve him best. "I screwed things up for her with her driller, so I took his place for a couple of days, that's all. It was a unique, onetime situation."

"But you hate her. You two are like oil and water. So, why would you step in to help?"

Judging from how things had gone in bed last night, as well as the first time they'd slept together, they weren't nearly as incompatible as people thought. They weren't nearly as incompatible as *he'd* thought. "I just told you—I felt bad that I caused her to lose her driller, so I stepped in for a day or two."

"I see. And…what'd your aunt have to say about that? She didn't care about you helping her greatest enemy? Did Ellen split the money with you or something? Was it just a way to get a piece of the job?"

Hendrix hadn't charged her. If Lynn found *that* out, she'd be even more pissed. Damn it! Why couldn't Charlie mind his own business? "I was just making up for something I'd done wrong."

Silence. Then Kurt said, "I'm still a little confused. Was that all there was to it? You two haven't become friends or anything, right? Because Charlie said it looked like you were having a pretty good time together."

Hendrix cursed under his breath. Jealousy was causing his friend to push so hard it left him very little wiggle room. "We were working, Kurt. That's it. It was just a...a business deal."

"Right. Okay. Well, I was thinking of going over there tonight to fix the sink in her guest bath. You wouldn't mind if I did that, would you?"

Yes. Yes, he would mind. There was no way he wanted Kurt trying to move in on Ellen right now. He was too excited about her himself, and he didn't want to lose her to a relationship that would be tempting if only because it was far less complicated. "Actually..."

"Actually?" Kurt repeated.

Hendrix wished he could keep their relationship quiet for the time being, but the world was pressing in on him from all sides. He didn't have that luxury. He had to push forward with the truth, because he wasn't willing to risk what he'd found with Ellen. His head was still filled with the memories they'd created last night—the taste and feel of her—and he was already eager for more. "I'll be there myself. I can take care of it."

"You've got to be kidding me..." Kurt said.

"I'm afraid not. I know you like her, too, and I want you to know I didn't have any designs on her when you told me that. But... Well, things have just sort of progressed in that direction since we were at Hank's that night. I have no idea where it'll go from here. But I'd like to give it a chance."

"Wow," Kurt said.

"I'm sorry if that makes you mad."

"Do you really think you two can make it work?"

"We have a lot of obstacles to overcome, but..."

"You like her that much."

"I do."

"Shit, Hendrix. You were the last dude I was worried about," he said and disconnected.

Befriending Ellen seemed to be causing a problem with everyone he cared about. But, fortunately, Kurt hadn't sounded truly pissed—just a little irked and disappointed. He'd come around eventually, once he stopped kicking himself for not making a move on Ellen before something like this could happen.

The radio had come on the second his call disconnected. He lowered the volume as he turned down his aunt and uncle's road. With everything that was stacked against him and Ellen, maybe Kurt would have another opportunity. He didn't like picturing her with his friend. It would suck to see them together around town. But what were the chances he and Ellen would be able to come out of this mess with each other?

Not great.

He pulled into the circular drive of his aunt's house. But it was seeing Lynn—and not Leo—standing outside waiting for him that put the exclamation point on that thought.

Twenty-Six

Hendrix's heart sank. Judging by the steely set of his aunt's jaw, she was furious.

Leo had to be aware of his mother's emotions, too, because he was hanging back in the entryway of the house. Although the shadow of the porch made it difficult to see much detail, Hendrix saw his cousin open the door, poke his head out and then close it again as though he couldn't bear to watch what was about to happen.

Leo had just opened the door and closed it for the second time when Hendrix came to a full stop and lowered his window. "What's going on?" he asked Lynn.

She drew herself up straighter. "Why don't you tell me?" she asked, her words clipped.

To buy a few seconds to decide how to handle this ambush, Hendrix reached over and turned off his radio. But she was so upset she couldn't wait even a second for him to answer.

"Have we not been good to you?" she demanded. "Have Stuart and I not treated you like our own child? We took you in, raised you, gave you everything you could ever want. And you repay us by taking money out of our pockets and putting it in Ellen's—of all people!"

So this *was* about helping Ellen drill the well and not about something else he'd done—like spending the night with her. He hadn't been sure what, exactly, Lynn had heard. In Lynn's mind, developing a relationship with Ellen would be just as bad. But he felt his actions there were easier to defend, since he should have the ultimate say over his personal life.

She had him on the issue of money and the success of their business, though—not that he believed he'd harmed Fetterman Well Services.

"You can take what we would've made on that well out of my next several paychecks," he said, hoping to mitigate the problem before his aunt could take things too far.

There. He'd offered her a very expensive *mea culpa*, but he couldn't see how Lynn could continue to be mad—not on *this* scale—if he acknowledged his fault and tried to make it up to her.

"You wouldn't have done that if I hadn't caught you?"

"*Caught* me?" he echoed. "Can't I help whoever I see fit?"

"Not if it's our biggest competitor!"

Apparently, he'd underestimated his aunt. It wasn't enough that he was willing to make reparations. "I'm sorry. I thought it was the right thing to do."

"You did," she said bitterly. "What about what's right where *we're* concerned?"

Leo poked his head out of the house again, and this time he didn't go right back inside. He was watching and listening, unable to leave them to themselves but also afraid of the high level of emotion.

Hendrix wondered if Lynn was aware of how the confrontation between them was affecting her tenderhearted son. She was usually more attuned to Leo's wants and needs, but at the moment, she was too angry to rein herself in. Hendrix wasn't sure he'd ever seen her quite *this* upset. And Stuart wasn't going to help. His truck wasn't in the drive, anyway. If Hendrix knew his uncle, he'd taken off at the first sign of trouble. "I didn't see it as a personal betrayal," he explained, trying to keep his own voice calm so he wouldn't escalate the situation. "And since we didn't get the job in the first place, there was no loss to the business."

"It probably would've come to us if you hadn't helped her!"

"But it was only because I interfered that she lost her driller!"

"Stuart said you offered Ben a job. Big deal. We need a driller, too, and we have every right to hire anyone we wish, even someone from another outfit. That's called competition. How's that any different than what she's doing to us by underbidding our jobs?"

She was the underdog! Couldn't Lynn see that? Didn't she care? Would she stop at *nothing* to destroy Ellen? "I just thought it was the right thing to do," he said again. "Obviously, you don't agree with me. But I already said I'll pay the business whatever we would've earned."

He thought this should disarm her. They didn't pay him a huge amount. Most of the value of what he'd done remained in the business he was supposed to buy out at a significant discount the day Stuart retired—or inherit along with Lynn and Leo if something happened to Stuart before that point. It'd been Stuart's business long before Hendrix had come along, and Stuart had trained him, then paid him for his help. Hendrix felt their arrangement was fair if not overly generous. It didn't leave him with a lot of extra cash right now, though, and Lynn had to realize that. She could take however much she felt he'd cost the business over time.

Giving him a dirty look, she folded her arms. "What about the hours you spent doing it? It must've taken several days—days when we thought you were on *our* jobs."

"It took two days, and I did *some* stuff for us during that time. I'll get everything done that needs to be done, so there'll be no damage to Fetterman Well Services."

"Hi, Hendrix," Leo called, but his voice was high-pitched and worried. "I'm right here. It's Leo."

Hendrix waved, but Lynn didn't even turn around. She acted as though she hadn't heard her son.

"I'm afraid that's not good enough," she said. "If you don't care about us and you're not grateful for all we've done for you, you can just find work elsewhere."

Hendrix reared back. "What are you saying?"

Tears welled up in her eyes, but she remained stoic. "You know what I'm saying."

"You're firing me? What about Stuart?"

"He won't stand for this, either."

"You've asked him?"

"I don't have to, because I *know* him."

So did Hendrix, and he was afraid she was right.

"I don't want to see you ever again," she snapped and turned to go back in the house.

Hendrix had expected his aunt to be angry, and he knew she lost her filter when she was angry. But in typical Lynn fashion, she'd gone too far. And he was tired of putting up with her behavior. He'd worked hard, done what he could for them, too—because he *was* grateful they'd given him a home. For one thing, raising Leo would've been much harder without him. Growing the business in the early years, when they didn't actually pay him, would've been much more difficult, too.

"You know what?" he yelled after her. "I'm surprised you took me in. I'm surprised you cared enough about my mother to do it, since you don't really care about anyone other than yourself." He started to go but slammed on his brakes before she could finish escaping into the house. "And, while we're being so honest, what you've done to Ellen is *unconscionable*. How could you reject a ten-year-old child who needed you so badly? Cut her off from her own father and leave her to flounder with a mother like Jan?"

Lynn never backed down from a fight. Whipping around, she started screaming at him. "She was a little monster! A nightmare child! You have no idea—"

He wasn't going to listen. He continued to speak right over her. "She was a child, for God's sake! You could've stepped in and helped her. But you chose not to. You were too threatened by her—too worried about having to share the smallest sliver of your husband's heart."

She came rushing toward him again. She was pointing and screaming about what an ungrateful bastard he was, but he refused to hear any more. Stomping on the gas pedal, he peeled out of the drive, but his window was still down, so he could hear Leo calling after him before he could even reach the road.

"No! Mom, why did you do that? Don't go, Hendrix! I love you!"

He made the turn, anyway. He couldn't stay any longer. But a glance in the rearview mirror showed Leo barreling out of the house, running past his mother, who wasn't strong enough to stop him, and charging after Hendrix's truck.

"Hendrix!" Leo called again, sobbing uncontrollably. "Don't leave me. I'm sorry! Do you hear me? I'm sorry! Please, come back."

Hendrix slammed on his brakes. He couldn't leave Leo like that. He'd never seen him so upset. But Lynn was rushing up to her son and pulling on his arm, insisting he go back to the house, and Hendrix knew he had no choice. Going back would only make matters worse for Leo, because Lynn would just keep the fight going.

He kept one eye on the rearview mirror as he pressed the gas pedal again and traveled more slowly while watching Leo have a complete meltdown in the middle of the road.

Ellen should've been stressed out of her mind. She'd only received one call on her driller opening, and it was from some headhunter who wanted to charge her for filling the position. He said he had a website that matched job openings with job candidates, that he specialized in rural areas and he'd "only" take half her driller's wages for the next three months plus a hefty fee from her for his services.

She couldn't afford that and was pretty sure whoever she hired wouldn't be able to, either, so she'd told him she wasn't interested. But she wasn't as frustrated or upset as she would've been if she hadn't already been happier than she could ever remember. She was looking forward to seeing Hendrix after he got off work, she'd finally been able to fix the leak under her sink this morning before she left the house and the weekend felt as though it was full of promise.

She'd worry about her business later, she told herself. She'd done all she could for now. After all the hard work it had required to get to where she was, she deserved three days of simply enjoying the latest developments in her life.

That meant Hendrix, of course. It was shocking how finding someone she enjoyed as much as she enjoyed him could make everything else seem inconsequential. She still had all the same challenges she'd faced yesterday, and yet she couldn't quit smiling.

She stopped to see if Talulah needed any help opening the diner—Fridays were her busiest night of the week—and Talulah remarked on Ellen's mood the moment she walked through the back door.

"Wow! Look at you grinning from ear to ear," she teased. "You must be having a good day."

In lieu of a wave, Ellen lifted the soda she was still nursing after having a burger at Rocko's next door. She hated to patronize his establishment after what he'd done to her, but she'd been hoping to talk to him and had been unable to reach him by phone.

He hadn't been there, though. That meant she couldn't inspect his tires while his truck was parked in the alley, either.

She hoped he'd show up while she was helping Talulah, and she'd have the opportunity to do both of those things before heading home to make dinner for Hendrix. She hadn't heard from him since he left early this morning, but she knew he was busy and figured he would've let her know if he wasn't coming.

"It's Friday," she told Talulah. "The weekend's almost here."

Talulah was frosting a lemon cake that also had lemon filling. "It's the arrival of the weekend that has you so excited? What do you have planned?"

Ellen averted her gaze. "Nothing special. What do *you* have planned?"

"Work. You know Mondays and Tuesdays are my weekend," she said with a laugh.

"Right." Ellen felt slightly embarrassed over the gaffe. Her head was definitely in the clouds. "Well, weekends are good for your business..."

"That's true." Ellen looked up at her again. "Any potential candidates for your new driller?"

Ellen set her purse and her drink on the stainless-steel counter farthest from where Talulah was working. "Not yet."

"With a smile like that, I would've thought you'd filled the position."

"Do we have to talk about work?" Ellen asked while running hot water into the sink so she could wash the dirty pans scattered about the kitchen.

"No. I was just trying not to talk about your personal life." She sent Ellen a knowing smile. "I wanted to wait until you were ready to tell me about Hendrix."

Ellen poured in some dish soap, creating massive suds. "You know about Hendrix?"

Talulah winked. "I own the property next to yours, remember?"

"That doesn't mean you notice every little thing I do," Ellen grumbled.

"You live alone. I check your place to make sure you're okay, and so does Brant. He called me after he left this morning to tell me Hendrix's truck was parked in your drive, and he was pretty sure it'd been there overnight." She turned the cake around to be able to reach the other side. "Was it?"

Ellen winced as her friend looked up again. "Do I have to answer that question?"

"No," Talulah replied with a chuckle. "But not answering tells me the same thing."

Ellen put several pans in the hot, soapy water. "Do you think anyone else noticed he was over at my place?"

"Who can say? Brant and I have reason to look, since we care about you and want to make sure you're okay, and no one else lives quite as close to you."

"So...there's a chance."

"I guess, but it's not that big a chance considering everyone's been talking about Hendrix helping you drill that well. Brant called me again over his lunch hour to tell me one of his brothers said something to him about it after he got to work, so I know the Elway boys have heard."

"Word must be traveling all over town."

"Yes. It's only a matter of time before everyone hears the latest."

"Damn."

Talulah used her forearm to adjust her hairnet. "Would it really be so bad to have your name linked to his?"

Ellen started to scrub a pan. "Not for me."

"You're worried about him?"

"Of course I'm worried about him. Dating me could destroy his relationship with his aunt and...uncle."

"Dating you? You're saying it's not just about sex?"

"I don't know what it's about," she admitted. "It's too new. But... I know I like him."

"I'm so glad, Ellen," Talulah said, grinning widely. "I hope he knows what he's getting in you. Instead of feeling smug for being able to get Hendrix to defect and risk what he's risking, you're concerned for him."

"I don't want to see him hurt," Ellen said. Nothing else mattered quite so much.

Talulah set the finished cake aside. "Boy, have things changed."

"I was never out to hurt him."

"No, but you certainly didn't like him."

Ellen couldn't argue with that statement. "I guess I can just...finally understand what my father sees in him."

"He's no better than you are, Ellen," Talulah said. "Your father had no reason not to love you. That's on him and his nasty, hard-hearted wife."

A knock at the back door interrupted, causing Ellen to look at Talulah expectantly. "Is that a delivery?"

"I don't think so."

"Maybe it's Rocko." Ellen had asked for him when she was at the burger place. It was possible they'd sent him over. "I'll get it," she said, drying her hands. Talulah was busy emptying the pastry bags, so it would be harder for her.

But after Ellen walked over and opened the door, she took a step back.

The man at the door wasn't Rocko, it was her father.

Twenty-Seven

Hendrix hadn't called Ellen all day. He was afraid of what she'd ask him and didn't want her to know about the argument he'd had with his aunt this morning. Losing his job was something he'd never truly anticipated. He'd known it was a possibility, of course. Although they'd mostly been joking, he and Ellen had discussed it just that morning. He'd also been aware of his aunt's temper and her animosity toward Ellen—how possessive she was of all the men in her life when it came to Stuart's daughter. But he'd never truly believed she'd cut him out of their lives the way she had Ellen.

What she'd done had come as a blow to Leo, too. Leo had been calling continually, and despite the fact that Hendrix answered each and every time and tried to calm him down, he'd call back twenty or thirty minutes later, and they'd have what was essentially the same conversation. Yes, Hendrix was still his cousin. Yes, they'd still see each other. Yes, Hendrix would take him out for donuts when he could.

Hendrix had never seen the poor guy so upset. Leo also kept asking Hendrix to come get him. "You said I could go with you today... I was supposed to go to work with you," he kept saying. "I'm all ready."

Hendrix would've been happy to have him around, but he knew Lynn would never allow him to take Leo. Not now. She'd try to use her son as a weapon against him—like she had his job—and he didn't see the point of subjecting his cousin to another big scene.

He didn't see the point of subjecting himself to a repeat of this morning, either. And it wasn't as though he could simply reach out to Stuart and Stuart would step in and solve everything. His uncle would never oppose Lynn, or he'd have hell to pay for it. And since Hendrix was Lynn's nephew and technically no relation to Stuart, Stuart would be even less inclined to get involved. If he wouldn't stand up to Lynn for the sake of his own daughter, Hendrix knew better than to expect any help to come from that direction. He hadn't even tried to call him, had no idea what he was thinking about what was going on.

After taking care of several details for the business in spite of being fired, he'd been on a mission to find out who'd sabotaged the Haslem well. If he could prove it wasn't Ellen, he felt Lynn would have to acknowledge she'd been wrong about *that*, at least.

Or...maybe she'd never admit it.

Slowing as he reached the clearing where Ben lived with his girlfriend—a woman named Delia from what Seth, one of Kurt's brothers, told him, and he should know since they used to date—Hendrix studied the surrounding area. It wasn't cool to sneak onto someone's property and start snooping around. But he had to get a look at the tires on Ben's truck. His girlfriend's SUV, too. Since both vehicles were sitting out front, it wouldn't be hard. The only problem was that Ben and

Delia were most likely home, and they might not appreciate what he was doing.

Turning his own truck around so that he could get out of there quickly if Ben came charging from the trailer with a gun or a baseball bat, Hendrix cut his engine. He hoped no one had heard him pull in, but the trailer door opened as soon as he started toward Ben's truck.

"Hey," Ben said, standing in the doorway and looking down on him from a small wooden landing that was four stairs up.

Hendrix felt even more uncomfortable when Ben smiled. He could easily see how Ellen's former driller might assume he'd come to offer him a job. And since Fetterman and Truesdale were the only two water well outfits in the region, he knew it probably wasn't going to be easy for Ben to find work—not in the same field. "Hey," Hendrix replied.

Delia appeared behind her boyfriend, and Hendrix recognized her. She worked at the drive-through coffee stand on Grove Street, he realized. Like Ben, she was quite a bit younger than he was, so he'd just never known her name.

"What's going on?" Hendrix asked.

"Nothing much. We're just hanging out," Ben replied as Delia peered around him. "What's going on with you?"

Hendrix sighed. He'd been planning to do this quickly and quietly. He'd already checked Jay's tires and Jay's wife's tires. He didn't believe they'd sabotaged their own well, but he didn't want to be searching for the owner of a particular tire if the picture in his possession corresponded with a vehicle that had good reason to be out there. "I'm not sure if you've heard," he said, "but someone poured concrete down the well Ellen drilled on Monday and Tuesday—out at the Haslem property. Whoever it was also spray-painted something rather... unflattering about her on the old chicken coop. You wouldn't happen to know anything about that, would you?"

The open and eager expression on Ben's face quickly shifted to dark and closed. "No. Why would I?"

"You weren't happy when she let you go. I feel bad about that, by the way, because I'm sort of to blame."

"Is that why you helped her drill it?"

So Ben had heard, too. It stood to reason. He would know she couldn't drill something like that alone. No doubt he'd been interested enough to ask around, and the answer was out there. "That's exactly why I helped her drill it. And I'm not happy that someone damaged it."

"You think it was me..." Ben said.

"I want to be sure it wasn't," Hendrix clarified.

Ben used the bottom of his T-shirt to wipe his forehead. "It *wasn't*," he insisted. "I'm pissed off at Ellen. I admit that. She didn't have to leave me high and dry. But I didn't vandalize anything."

"I don't even think we were in town," Delia piped up.

Ellen had mentioned that Ben had gone to a wedding in Utah. "When'd you get back from the wedding?"

"Not until Tuesday, late." She spoke as if that should cover it, but that wasn't the case at all.

"Unfortunately, that's exactly when the incident occurred," he told her.

"Doesn't matter," she insisted. "I'd know if Ben did something like that. I was with him all night. I've been with him every minute since we left for Salt Lake."

Hendrix lifted his phone to show them the picture

of the tire imprint. "Then you won't mind if I compare the tires on your truck to this photograph?"

"There's no need," Ben said. "Like Delia just told you, I didn't do it."

"Then why not allow me to eliminate you using this?" Hendrix asked.

"Maybe you should," Delia muttered to Ben. "I mean…why not? There's no way it could match because it wasn't you."

"I don't care," he told her. "I don't have to let him. He's not the fucking police."

"Why are you the one who's checking?" Delia asked.

"And why are you suddenly so keen to help Ellen?" Ben chimed in. "I thought the two of you were sworn enemies."

Hendrix wasn't going to go into that. He decided to stick to the reason he'd come and ignore the rest. "Rocko told Ellen it was someone with a Fetterman Well Services logo on the door."

"So… Rocko's blaming you?" Ben said.

"Or my aunt or uncle. One of us."

"He's just trying to make sure he doesn't get blamed," Delia told Ben, pointing to Hendrix.

Ben scowled at her. "I'm glad you're concerned for him, but I don't want to get blamed, either!"

Hendrix gestured toward Ben's Dodge Ram. "If you didn't do it, there's nothing to worry about. I'll tell the police this picture doesn't match the tires on your truck, and they'll have to look elsewhere." He wasn't sure the police would ever really get involved. As far as he knew, Jay hadn't even bothered to file a report. But he was using whatever leverage he could to make this happen. He needed something solid to present to his aunt.

Uncertainty replaced Ben's earlier conviction. "I didn't do it!" he said, more emphatically this time.

"Then the tread won't match, and you'll be eliminated," Hendrix repeated.

"Oh, go ahead and let him," Delia said.

Ben still seemed torn, but he didn't argue with her, so Hendrix walked to Ben's truck and knelt down to compare tread patterns.

Ben, who'd followed him, stood over him while he did it, hands jammed in the pockets of his worn jeans. Delia came out, too.

"See?" Ben said, clearly relieved when it became evident that the patterns weren't anything alike.

Hendrix said nothing, just walked the few steps required to reach Delia's old Tacoma.

"Now you want to check *my* tires?" Delia cried as they watched him.

Hendrix said nothing as he worked his way around the vehicle. Since they weren't actively trying to stop him, he didn't see any reason to leave without getting what he'd come for. But none of her tires were a match, either.

He stood to face them. "You're good. I'm sorry to have bothered you and appreciate your cooperation."

"Of course we're good," Ben snapped, ignoring his apology. "What, did you think I might've taken Delia's Tacoma to ruin that well? Or she might've done it with me?"

Hendrix raised his hands, making it clear he wasn't looking for a fight. "Like I told you, I'm just trying to eliminate anyone who has any motivation to see something terrible happen to Ellen."

"You and your aunt and uncle have disliked her the longest—and the most," Ben pointed out.

Hendrix slid his phone in his pocket. "Exactly why I'm worried about where the blame will fall."

"Maybe it *was* your aunt who sabotaged the well," Delia said. "We have the same stylist, so I've been at the salon when she's been there, too. I've heard some of the things she has to say about Ellen."

"She had no business saying those things," Hendrix said as he started toward his own vehicle. "She doesn't know what the hell she's talking about."

"Wait… You're on Ellen's side now?" Ben called after him, but Hendrix didn't bother to answer.

Stuart had asked Ellen if she could take a few minutes to talk to him in private, and Talulah had said she had to go out front and open the diner, anyway, so they could use the kitchen.

It took her a few minutes to get what she needed, however. The two of them had been standing and waiting, feeling uncomfortable knowing they had what would, at the very least, amount to an awkward conversation ahead of them.

Ellen was more nervous than she would've been had she not been involved with Hendrix. Before the past couple of weeks, she had only herself and her own feelings to worry about. Now she had his, too—and didn't want to mishandle this, since she might not be the only one to pay a price if she did.

"I'm just about there," Talulah said as she finished squaring things away and carried the lemon cake she'd frosted into the front, along with an almond coconut cake from the fridge, then returned for a chocolate cream pie and a pan of thick brownies with chocolate chips inside and mint frosting on top.

"I can help you carry everything out," Ellen offered when her friend came back a second time.

"No. I've got it," she insisted and grabbed a cherry cobbler from a cart where she could stack what she baked. "I just forgot this. You're good now."

When the door swung shut behind Talulah, Ellen looked at her father. She had such mixed emotions where he was concerned. Sometimes, she couldn't believe he was as bad as she imagined. Other times she felt his actions spoke for themselves. "What is it you want?" she asked quietly. She'd learned from when he'd visited her at the Slemboskis' that it didn't take much for him to leave without speaking his mind, and she didn't want him to go before telling her why he'd sought her out to begin with. She'd kicked herself for doing that the last time.

"I have a few questions for you," he said. "I'm hoping you'll be willing to answer them."

"If you're going to ask me if I sabotaged the Haslem well so I could make it look like it was your wife, I didn't," she said.

He was holding two manila envelopes, but he slipped his free hand into the pocket of his work pants and stared at the floor for a few seconds before lifting his gaze. "I wasn't going to ask that. I know you'd never vandalize someone else's property."

"Really?" she said, truly surprised. "How would *you* know?"

"You've never been dishonest."

"I don't think you have enough experience with me to make that call. But it's interesting to hear your opinion, especially because your wife seems to think that's exactly what happened."

"Lynn would like to believe it. Then she'd be justified in disliking you."

Ellen blinked at him. "So...*you're* finally going to be honest?"

"I love Lynn," he said. "I can only say so much, but I'll give you that."

"Of course," she said bitterly. "We wouldn't want you to lose Lynn, no matter how unfair she's been to me."

"She's brought a lot to my life, a lot that was missing. Maybe I'm an asshole for grabbing hold of that, Ellen, but I've been much happier with her than I ever was with your mother."

"We all have choices to make in life, and you've made yours," she said. "That includes abandoning me for a woman who's never shown me any kindness."

"You have every right to be angry," he said. "I've let you down in the worst possible way."

She said nothing. She wasn't going to correct him because he was right.

"And now you finally have the chance to take your revenge—on Lynn, if not on me," he added.

Ellen swallowed hard. She could already feel the burn of tears. Although she was determined not to let them fall, it was so hard to control her emotions where her father was concerned. The second she encountered him, she seemed to turn into the ten-year-old girl who was so devastated when he didn't love her enough to demand his new wife accept her and treat her right. "If you're here to ask me not to, you have some nerve," she said.

"I would never presume that much."

"So what do you want, exactly?"

"Are you seeing Hendrix?" he asked.

She didn't know how to answer that question. He'd

just called her honest, but the honest answer to that might be more than Hendrix wanted his aunt and uncle to know. "We've become…friends," she hedged.

"He admires you a great deal. I can tell."

Determined not to give too much away, she didn't respond to that specifically. "Would it be a problem if we *did* start seeing other?" she asked.

"Not for me."

"But it would for Lynn, even though we're both adults and should be able to choose who we want to share our lives with."

"After all she's done for him, she'd take it as a personal betrayal. As a matter of fact, she already has. She and Hendrix had a huge argument this morning, and she fired him."

Her astonishment must've shown on her face because he said, "He hasn't told you?"

"I haven't heard from him," she admitted, and now wondered if there was more to that than just being busy. Would Lynn be able to ruin the happiness Ellen had found? She and Hendrix hadn't been seeing each other long enough to have established strong ties. For all she knew, Lynn had already ruined any chance they had to find out where their relationship might go.

Just the thought of that made her feel sick. But Lynn always won. Why wouldn't she win now?

Except… Her father wouldn't be here if *she* didn't hold at least some power in this situation. Maybe Lynn hadn't gotten the best of her quite yet.

"I haven't heard from him, either," Stuart said. "And he won't pick up when I call."

"I haven't even tried to reach him, but I hope he won't let your wife manipulate him any longer."

"Manipulate him…"

"Isn't holding a job over someone's head manipulation? Isn't emotional blackmail manipulation?"

"Maybe it is," he said, sounding too tired to fight over it. "And that will be Hendrix's decision."

"You won't override Lynn and give Hendrix his job back?"

When he hesitated, she said, "You might want to do that before you lose him, because if you don't, he'll just come to work with me. And then where will you be?"

He chuckled. "She's pushing him right into your arms, eh?"

"I won't allow her to hurt him because of me."

"I believe that," he said. "You're nothing if not loyal."

"Maybe you could take a page out of my book." She'd told herself she wouldn't say anything too bitter, but she'd been unable to hold that back.

"Ellen, I'm here because... Well, let me ask you this— what's your relationship like with John Williams?"

"The guy who lived next door while you and Mom were married?"

"Yeah. He's not part of your life, is he?"

"No, why would he be? Why would you even ask me that?"

"Because I've always wondered if...while I was away at work, and he was hanging out with your mother..."

Ellen pressed a hand to her chest as she began to comprehend what he was getting at. "You think they might've had an affair?"

"I've always suspected that. I hate to even bring it up at this late date, but I can't help thinking I should've brought it up before—established, once and for all, what my responsibilities regarding you really are."

Her heart jumped into her throat. "You're saying... You're saying you're not even sure if you're my father?"

When he didn't respond, just looked at her, she knew that was exactly what he was saying. "Is that why you left us to fend for ourselves and didn't even feel the need to pay your child support?"

"I paid child support," he said, handing her one of the envelopes he'd brought with him. "Inside, you'll find copies of all the canceled checks to prove it."

She didn't want to accept it, didn't want to see the proof. Jan had bitched about the money he owed her almost since Ellen could remember. Ellen had believed her on that if almost nothing else. His lack of love and attention had given it too much credibility. If he'd walk away from her physically and emotionally, why not financially?

But her mother had never been the most reliable person. Was it just that Jan thought they'd deserved more? That she was jealous she didn't get to enjoy everything Lynn was able to enjoy after the divorce? Or was it Jan's way of blaming Stuart for her own shortcomings— making it look like *he* was to blame for the many hardships they'd suffered?

You'll find copies of all the canceled checks to prove it. Of course they'd be in the envelope, just as he said. She should've known better than to take anything at face value when it came to her mother. Jan wasn't trustworthy and never had been. Stuart couldn't even be sure she was his daughter.

As the ramifications of what he said sank in, Ellen's knees went so weak she could barely remain standing. Fumbling to grab hold of the nearest chair, she sank into it to avoid collapsing on the floor. "Why'd you pay child support if you didn't know for sure that I was your child?" she managed to ask.

"Because I wanted to leave you with that much, regardless."

"And you didn't want to find out the truth, even after I got older?" She couldn't even imagine living with such an unknown. *"Why?"*

"I didn't see how it would improve your situation. John was such a flake. I knew he wouldn't give you anything."

"But you must be telling me for a reason. Now you want to know?"

"Considering the unexpected situation we're facing— one that could literally tear my family apart—I think it might be the best path forward."

She thought of all she'd done to compete with Fetterman Well Services, hoping to prove to Stuart that she was just as capable as Hendrix. Had she been chasing a man who owed her nothing? Who'd already given her much more than he had to?

He thought her father might be the guy who'd lived next door. From what she remembered, John Williams had been kind enough, but he'd shown little interest in her personally, rarely had a job, smoked a lot of pot and had moved away from Anaconda when she was fifteen. As far as she knew, her mother hadn't heard from him since. *She'd* certainly never heard from him.

"So…what are you suggesting?" she asked, and he handed her the second envelope.

Inside, she found a cotton swab and some directions. He wanted her to take a DNA test.

Twenty-Eight

Ellen couldn't remember ever being so angry at her mother, and that was saying something. She'd spent most of her teenage years seething at her mother, her father and the world at large. Making the conscious decision to focus most of her anger on her father instead of her mother was the only thing that'd enabled them to have a relationship—that shift in blame and the enormity of Jan's need. If Ellen hadn't been around to take care of her through those years, who else would've done it?

In some ways, she was still taking care of her mother. She was the person Jan called when something went wrong, or she needed money or any other kind of help.

Talulah poked her head tentatively into the kitchen. "You alone?"

Ellen was still sitting in the chair. Stuart had left nearly fifteen minutes ago, but she'd spent the whole of that time simply watching the second hand on the big clock on the wall go *tick, tick, tick.* "Yeah."

An expression of concern replaced Talulah's open curiosity. "Is everything okay?"

"As okay as I can expect it to be," she said dully.

"What does that mean?"

"It means I've had it wrong all these years, and I should've known better."

Leaving the front unattended, Talulah came into the kitchen and hurried over to her. "What is it? What'd he say?"

"That he owes me nothing in the way of child support and never did." She held up the photocopies of the checks she'd pulled out of the manila envelope after he left. "But he paid it, anyway. He brought me proof."

Talulah accepted the stack and thumbed through the individual pages. "There are a lot of canceled checks here. But... I don't understand. What do they mean? Your mother was lying about his support when you were growing up?"

"Among other far more important things."

The bell went off in the front, signaling a customer. Hearing it, Talulah glanced over her shoulder but didn't move.

Despite feeling as though she had a dagger in her chest, Ellen summoned the strength to get to her feet. "Go. You've got a business to run. I'll be fine. We can talk about this later."

"No! You're upset. I don't want to leave you on your own. Just...let me tell whoever's out there that something has come up and I'm going to have to close. Then you and I can hide out back here, have a cup of coffee and a piece of cake, and talk about what your father had to say."

Tears filled her eyes but, again, she blinked them back. "That's just it. He told me he doesn't think he's my father—and took a swab of my cheek so he can prove that, too."

The empathy on her friend's face made it that much

harder not to break down. "Oh, Ellen. I'm so sorry. Does Lynn know?"

"He said she doesn't, that she has no clue he's ever even wondered, and he thinks it would be best not to tell her until after the results come back."

"Since the results might not change anything, that's probably wise."

"I guess so."

"Wow. You must feel terrible. I can't even imagine how much what he had to say must've hurt."

"I feel like I can't breathe," she admitted.

"I'm going to close the diner for the day—"

"No, you just opened. I won't cost you what you could earn. Like I said, we can talk later. Nothing's going to change between now and then. The only person I need to speak to right away is my mother."

Talulah's forehead creased with worry. "You're going to call her, then?"

Ellen started laying the photocopied support checks out on the desk and taking pictures of them. "You bet I am. But first, I'm going to send her these."

Hendrix had been dreading this visit. He wished he could wait for dark, so he'd have some cover, but the floodlights in the drive would never allow him to see Lynn's tires in enough detail, even if he used a flashlight.

It wasn't as if he could just move on to someone else, though. He'd already checked all the tires of the people on his list—at least the ones he could. The Haslems had allowed the inspection; their tires didn't match the picture. Although far more reluctantly, Ben and Delia had allowed the inspection; their tires didn't match the picture. And, as a bonus, he'd managed to check Charlie's tires without Charlie's knowledge when he spotted Averil's brother's SUV parked in the lot at Hank's.

He hadn't truly believed Charlie could be the saboteur. Charlie was a bit too far removed from Ellen. But he'd been aware of where Ellen was drilling, and he was closely related to Averil, so Hendrix had decided to check on the off chance he'd helped her.

But Charlie's tires hadn't matched the picture, either. Maybe Averil's would, but her old rusted-out Nissan Altima was nowhere to be found. Hendrix had driven back to the Gerharts', hoping to take a peek without her knowledge—as he had with Charlie's—but he hadn't found it in the drive, and he hadn't seen it around town. He'd been looking for it when he stumbled upon Charlie's Explorer.

Maybe Averil was in Libby, visiting her new boyfriend. Hendrix hoped to check Jordan's tires, too. Jordan probably didn't know much about wells—how to find the one Ellen was drilling or how to harm it—but it wasn't that hard to figure out and whoever did it didn't do that great a job. With Averil's help and/or input, Jordan could easily be the one who'd poured cement down that hole. If it wasn't the weekend already, he'd go to Libby. He didn't know where Jordan lived, but he'd seen what he drove and could google the location of his practice. That was why he had to wait until Monday—he'd have a much greater chance of finding Jordan at work.

Although…what he found here, much closer to home, might make the long drive unnecessary.

After parking down the street, he got out to walk the rest of the way to his aunt and uncle's property. At least it wouldn't take long to do what he had to do, and no one was expecting him, so he should be able to get it done and leave without incident.

He eyed the drive before he drew too close. Lynn's truck was there. So was Stuart's.

Great. He could check both.

He looked at his watch. He'd been hoping to come while they were eating dinner, when they'd be together and preoccupied, so no one would startle him by coming out of the office or pulling into the drive at the wrong time. His aunt was pretty methodical and typically adhered to a routine. Unless what was going on between them had somehow caused her to deviate from the norm, he should be able to get what he wanted without their even knowing he was there.

Stuart's truck was closest, so he checked that first. Although he was skeptical, there was a possibility that Lynn had pressured her husband into damaging the well. Or she could've driven *his* truck to the Haslems' property that night and done it herself.

But Hendrix hadn't expected to find a match, and he didn't.

It was Lynn's truck that worried him. He'd believed her when she denied any involvement, but belief was different from proof. He hoped to get something he could show Ellen.

To document what he found, he'd been taking pictures of the tires he checked and labeling them. If he was going to the work of trying to use the tire-imprint impression to find the saboteur, he figured he might as well.

He glanced at the house. Leo's day was less structured and predictable than Lynn's or Stuart's. And if Leo saw him, he'd scream his name and come running from the house…

But all remained quiet.

Hendrix kneeled to check the back tires of his aunt's

ride. The body of the truck would block any view of him from the house. He'd only be exposed once he circled around to the front, so he was saving those tires for last.

No match.

Allowing himself one more glance at the house, he strode to the front. If they caught him, they caught him, he decided. He didn't want to make matters any worse, but he was bent on finishing his inspection, regardless.

The front left tire didn't match the tire impression— and the front right tire had the same tread as the front left, so it wasn't a match, either.

"Thank God," he muttered and breathed a sigh of relief as he took a few pictures.

He'd just finished and was eager to show Ellen what he'd found and who he could eliminate—if the picture she'd taken that day truly meant what they thought it did. But before he could get out of the yard, Zeus started to bark and jump against the front door of the house, trying to get out. Then the door swung open, Zeus came running across the yard to greet him and Leo was right behind him.

Ellen had reached her house, but after pulling into the drive, she just sat in her truck. She was too focused on her telephone call to bother getting out. "I sent you the proof, Mom. He mailed those checks religiously on the first of each month—and you cashed them. Didn't you take a look at what I sent?"

"I couldn't really see it on my phone."

"Then get your glasses on and enlarge the photos, because it's all there. Why'd you lie to me?"

"I didn't lie, *exactly*—"

"You told me he didn't pay. That's a lie!"

"Well, he didn't pay enough. It should've been a lot more."

"That's a dodge!"

"Fatherhood isn't a few hundred bucks a month!"

"Then why didn't you take him back to court? And why did you always discourage me from trying to help you do that once I got older?"

"Because it's negative. We didn't need that in our lives. He let us down no matter how you look at it."

"That depends, doesn't it? It was generous of him to pay anything at all if he's not my father!"

The phone went silent for a moment. "What'd you say?"

Ellen let her head fall back onto the headrest. "You heard me. Did you have an affair with the pothead next door?"

"John Williams? No!" her mother cried, but Ellen wasn't sure she could believe it.

"What would make Stuart think you might've been sleeping with him?"

"I have no idea, but this is exactly why I didn't want you moving to Coyote Canyon in the first place. I thought you weren't talking to Stuart. But you obviously are. Why are you letting him fill your head with all this... stuff? He's just trying to turn you against me!"

Ellen stared up at the ceiling of her truck. "He had me take a DNA test, Mom."

Jan said nothing.

"You still there?"

"You don't have anything to worry about," she said matter-of-factly, but was that confidence or the same stubborn denial she'd seen in her mother about other things she didn't want to face?

"I don't? I've had to worry about everything since

I was just a little girl, because you won't stand up and take charge of your life. I don't know if I'm going to be able to forgive you if you've been lying about this, too. If you've been calling Stuart my father just because he was your husband, when you knew you'd cheated and I could belong to someone else, you'll be on your own from here on out. As far as I'm concerned, that's… crossing a line I thought even you would never cross."

"What are you talking about?" her mother asked. "Does it really matter? You're an adult, on your own, and that's all in the past!"

Ellen could no longer speak. The outrage was simply too much for her. She didn't want to continue this conversation, anyway. If her mother didn't understand the hurt and damage she'd caused by now, she never would.

"We'll see what happens when the results come back," she choked out and disconnected.

Her mother tried calling her back several times, but she ignored every attempt. Talulah tried to reach her, too. But the world had become so inhospitable, all Ellen wanted to do was crawl into bed.

Thankfully, it was Stuart who followed Leo outside and not Lynn. For all Hendrix knew, she was sulking inside the house, hoping Stuart would take a turn at blasting him for his disloyalty.

"What's going on? What are you doing here?" his uncle asked.

Zeus sat at Hendrix's feet, wagging his tail, and Leo stood next to Hendrix, hanging on to one arm as though he was afraid to let go for fear his cousin would disappear for good if he did.

"I had to pick up a few things from the office." Hendrix hadn't even considered going after the belongings he kept in his desk. He'd been too focused on other things, but it was as good a reason as any to show up at the house, so he went with it. He wasn't about to volunteer that he was checking their tires; he knew that much.

"You don't have anything to say to your aunt?"

"After what she said to me this morning?" he said. "Hell, no."

Leo clapped a hand over his mouth but spoke through his thick fingers. "Oh! You swore, Hendrix. Mom's going to be mad again."

"I don't care," Hendrix muttered.

His cousin gasped in shock. "How come you don't like Mom no more?"

"It's your mom who doesn't like me," Hendrix corrected. That was a childish way to state the problem, but it was about the only way he could make Leo understand he hadn't instigated the rift.

"Just say sorry," Leo prodded. "Everything will be okay if you say sorry."

"I won't say sorry." Although Hendrix spoke softly, he knew the steel in his voice revealed his determination. Stuart might not have a limit when it came to how far Lynn could push him, but Hendrix had reached his. Someone had to call her on her behavior, especially when it came to Ellen.

His uncle rubbed the beard growth on his chin. "You like her that much."

He was obviously referring to Ellen. "What I would like is to see a change around here—and I don't think continuing to indulge Aunt Lynn is the way to get it done."

"Even if it costs you your job…"

"You know I don't deserve to lose my job, not over this."

Stuart seemed uncomfortable, but he didn't say anything.

"You're going to stand behind her on that, too?" Hendrix prodded.

His uncle twisted around to look at the house as if he was afraid Lynn was watching or listening. "I don't know," he replied. "I think we all need to take some time to reflect and decide how we should move forward."

"Aunt Lynn comes before me."

"She's my wife. She comes before everyone and everything."

Hendrix shook his head in disgust. "Even what's right?"

Probably alarmed by the tone of the conversation and the pervasive frown on Stuart's face, Leo glanced between them. "What's happening?" he asked. He didn't know exactly what was going on, but he could tell it wasn't what he wanted. "Hendrix is coming back, right? Everything will be the way it was?"

"Everything's going to be okay," Hendrix told him. "But it definitely won't be the way it was."

Twenty-Nine

Hendrix knew who'd sabotaged the well. It had to be Jordan. He'd been able to check everyone else off his list. After leaving his aunt and uncle's place, he'd swung by Burgers and Shakes and found Rocko there. And wherever Averil had gone earlier, she was home now. Since he'd had to go past the Gerharts' to reach Ellen's, anyway, he'd looked for her car one more time and, lo and behold, there it was.

Rocko had been so appalled that Hendrix would ever believe *he* could be the one who'd damaged the well that he'd led him directly to the alley, where his Explorer was parked, and waved Hendrix forward. That he'd had no qualms with such a close inspection had come as a surprise *and* a disappointment. After the inconsistencies in his story, he'd seemed like the best candidate—especially after Hendrix had eliminated his aunt and Ben.

Averil, on the other hand, wasn't even aware Hendrix had checked her tires. The sun had been setting by the time he realized he had the opportunity.

Still, he felt confident, despite not having the best light, that her car wasn't the one they were looking for.

Her tires were too bald to leave such a detailed impression in *any* medium.

Armed with the evidence he'd collected, and the determination to travel to Libby on Monday where he would, hopefully, find the tire that matched the picture, he was eager to tell Ellen what he'd found. He knew she wouldn't be happy to hear about his argument with Lynn, the loss of his job or his conversation with Stuart. It couldn't feel good for her to learn that the man she was starting to care about had people in his life who were *that* opposed to their relationship. But at least he was able to bring her some good news, too, and tell her he was homing in on the person responsible for causing so much extra trouble recently.

When he pulled into her drive, he'd been expecting to go in, have dinner and a long conversation—and maybe more. The "more" was what excited him most.

But after he parked and walked to the house, he couldn't get her to let him in. Although her truck was where she usually left it, he got no response when he knocked—then pounded—on the front door.

Was she angry he was late for dinner? As he was driving away this morning, she'd texted him to say she'd make chicken enchiladas and told him to come at seven thirty.

He checked his watch. He was a little late. But, surely, she wouldn't be that upset over ten minutes. And it was strange that all the lights were off. It didn't look as though she'd been cooking enchiladas or anything else.

What was going on? She hadn't canceled their date...

He circled around to check the back door. It was locked, too, and she didn't answer when he knocked there, either.

"Hendrix!" a male voice called.

He'd just pulled out his phone to call her again but turned to see Brant crossing the field, coming from his and Talulah's place. "What's going on?"

"That's what I'd like to know," Brant replied. "Talulah called me from the diner a few minutes ago. Said she was worried about Ellen and asked me to look in on her."

"Why would she be worried?"

"I guess Ellen hasn't been answering her calls and texts—not since your uncle stopped by the diner."

"Stuart was at the diner?" His uncle hadn't mentioned that when they'd spoken today.

"Apparently."

"Why would he go there?"

Brant grimaced. "Talulah said he wanted Ellen to take a DNA test."

Shit. Stuart had chosen this, of all times, to finally reveal his doubt to Ellen? "You've got to be kidding me."

"That's what Talulah told me."

"How did Ellen take that?"

"As you can imagine, she was upset when she left the diner." He gestured at the house. "But it's completely dark inside, so she must not have come home."

"Her truck's here," Hendrix informed him.

"You think she's inside?"

"I can't imagine she'd go anywhere else—except maybe Anaconda to talk to her mother. But she'd need her truck for that."

"I guess you've already tried knocking…"

"Many times."

"So…what do you think we should do? I could go over to the diner and stand in for Talulah so she could—"

"No," Hendrix interrupted. "Let me check inside the house before you do anything."

"How are you going to do that?"

"Since she won't come to the door, I'll have to break in."

Brant sucked air in between his teeth. "Are you sure that's a good idea?"

If he had to break down walls to reach her, he'd break down walls. After all, that was what he'd been doing so far—they just hadn't been quite as physical as the ones on her house. "We'll soon see," he said, and Brant followed and watched as he got a crowbar from the tool chest in his truck and used it to force open the back door.

Ellen had hoped she could hide out in her room, under the covers, and close out the whole world for a while. According to the internet, an accredited lab should take only one to two business days to return DNA results once all samples had been received, so depending on how Stuart had decided to ship their swabs, she had at least three days to wait for some indication of who she was—or who she wasn't.

That sounded like an eternity, an eternity during which she didn't feel she could move forward with her life. She'd built her entire foundation—as well as her career—on believing she was Stuart Fetterman's daughter. If that wasn't true, would she be relieved? Glad to have that conflict removed?

Or would she suddenly feel rudderless? Would she then have the former neighbor take a paternity test?

No. What would be the point of that? She didn't want a relationship with him. He was nothing to be proud of. At least in some ways she'd been proud of Stuart—

how hard he'd worked and what he'd established. She'd looked up to him for those things in spite of what he'd done to her.

There were other considerations, too. What would be left of her relationship with her mother? Or her career? If she had nothing to prove to Stuart, would she continue drilling water wells? If not, how would she earn a living while she transitioned to something else?

She'd been foolish to be so happy about Hendrix. What chance did a relationship with him really have? He'd been fired because of her and had to resent it. If not now, he soon would. They'd joked about having him come to work for her—or *with* her—but she couldn't offer him what he'd had with the Fettermans. Considering all their equipment and the extensive book of past clients which had taken thirty or more years to build and from which they'd get a lot of their future business, he'd be taking a huge loss.

She needed to stay away from him. He'd be much better off without her. She'd heard him pounding on the door and ringing the doorbell but hadn't been able to make herself get out of bed. She assumed he'd leave eventually—and move on as if the past few weeks had never occurred. It was early in their relationship. He probably wouldn't have to think twice. Even *he* had to know he'd be a fool to continue to pursue so much as a friendship with her.

But just when she thought he'd left, she heard a loud bang—it sounded as though a bulldozer had crashed into the back of the house—and sprang out of bed.

"What are you doing?" she cried as she ran down the hall and found him in her kitchen.

He didn't have to answer. She could see what he'd done. He'd broken her back door. It was flapping open, and Brant stood just outside, in the halo coming from the light Hendrix must've turned on.

"You broke into my house?" she said. "Have you lost your mind?"

"I'll let you handle this," Brant said with a wince. "And I'll tell Talulah that Ellen is fine, but you might not be."

Brant left, but Hendrix remained. He tried to get the door to shut and couldn't manage it because of the damage he'd caused. He turned to give her a sheepish look. "I'm sorry. I'll fix that, I promise. I was just... worried about you."

"I'm fine." Her face had to be red and her eyes swollen, which was part of the reason she hadn't answered the door. She didn't want him to see her like this; it was embarrassing. But she was also angry enough to tell herself she didn't care. "If I'd wanted you to come in, I would've answered the door."

"Ellen..." He moved toward her, but she held up a hand to stop him from getting too close.

"Don't. We can't make it, Hendrix. We were stupid to even try. You lost your job today because of *me*! How long will you be willing to live with that kind of treatment before you...before you..."

"What?" he prompted.

"Realize I'm not worth it?" she blurted out. Why not be honest?

"That's not true," he said. "You *are* worth it. And not everyone walks away when the going gets tough. If breaking down your door doesn't tell you that, I'll have to spend a lot of time proving it in other ways. But I can do that—because I'm not going anywhere."

She shook her head. "I don't have anything to offer you."

He closed the gap between them and took hold of her upper arms as he gazed down into her face. "I liked what you were giving me before."

"Sex—"

"Love," he corrected. "Love *and* sex and fun and all the other things that go into a relationship. That's what I want—that's all I need."

The misery she'd been feeling threatened to swallow her whole. "It won't work. Don't you understand? I can't *believe* it. After…after everything that's happened, I have no trust."

He rested his forehead against hers. "Trust is something that can be built over time, Ellen. Drop by drop. Day by day. I'll help you."

"Why?" she demanded. "Why would you take on someone who's so broken when you could have anyone else?"

"Because I don't want anyone else," he said. "I want *you*."

More tears rolled down her cheeks and dropped off her chin. She hated to cry, but she also couldn't stop. "I don't understand."

He wiped her cheeks with his thumbs. "Because you don't see yourself the way *I've* come to see you."

What could he see what Stuart had missed, whether he was her father or not? "What about everything else?" she asked. "What about your job?"

He gave her a peck on the mouth. "I saw a notice in town. Truesdale Well and Pump Services is hiring. We might not make much money at first, but we're young and strong, and we're damn good drillers." He kissed her more deeply. "Together, I think we could really build a business. What do you say?"

Was this for real? Dared she reach for the kind of happiness he seemed to be offering her?

Her heart thudded in her chest, wanting what it wanted even as her mind insisted she'd only set herself up for a bigger fall if she relented. He couldn't make her any promises. She couldn't make him any promises, either. This was too new. It could be entirely the wrong thing for her, or for him, or for both of them.

And yet…nothing had ever felt so right.

If she didn't take the chance, how would she ever know?

"Did you give me the geode in my living room?" she asked, her voice barely above a whisper.

The change in subject had obviously taken him off guard, but he smiled. "I did. I wish I'd given it to you long ago. I knew how much you liked it."

"I can't accept something that precious. It belonged to your mother!"

"It did," he confirmed. "But I want you to have it, and I want you to know that she would've loved you, too."

After making sandwiches for dinner and going straight to bed with Ellen, Hendrix drove her to Talulah's Dessert Diner early on Saturday morning for coffee and breakfast buns. Several people stared at them or murmured in surprise, especially when he held her hand or put his arm around her, but he didn't care, and she ignored the stir they were making, too. They were quickly becoming so caught up in each other no one else mattered.

She made her chicken enchiladas for him Saturday night. They were delicious, but she told him they were about the only meal she knew how to cook. Hendrix had a feeling he'd be doing a lot of grilling and feeding her in the future, but he didn't mind. He was so content when he was with her. The indecision and restlessness he'd felt with every other woman was somehow—inexplicably—gone.

He spent Sunday morning fixing the door he'd broken at her place while she cleaned, and they talked about going to Libby to find Jordan's car the following morning. Ellen insisted she'd be going with him, and he welcomed her company.

"I can't wait to call my aunt and tell her how wrong she's been," he said as they got in his truck to go to his house after lunch.

The dark cloud of worry that'd hung over Ellen on Friday night seemed to roll over her again. He supposed they'd encounter moments like that. As idyllic as their weekend had been, they still had the same problems. He had to expect reality to set in at some point.

"I'm surprised she hasn't tried to call you," Ellen said. "I know how much you mean to her, and I don't want to come between you."

He reached over the console to slide his fingers through hers. "Don't worry about that. I'm happier than I've ever been."

He couldn't explain why they went together so well, but he was beginning to feel a little stupid that it'd taken him two and a half years to realize she was exactly what he wanted and needed in his life. At least he'd gotten it right in the end. "It's impressive you're even worried about that. *She* certainly doesn't care about coming between us. As a matter of fact, she's been trying to do exactly that."

He turned down the dirt road that went past Jay's mobile home before dead-ending at his cabin. He'd told Ellen he had to get organized so they could go to

Libby tomorrow. Then he'd be available to work with her on whichever jobs she could line up for the rest of the week. That he'd be helping her again would infuriate Lynn, but his aunt was the one who'd fired him. What did she expect him to do? Ellen had promised they'd split whatever she earned so they could muddle through what was likely to be an economically trying time for both of them.

Fortunately, he didn't have a lot of debt and, for the time being, could almost get by on what she'd been paying Ben. So even if she could only give him that much, he figured he should be okay. With that, and what little savings he had, he believed he could survive until Lynn and Stuart softened.

And if they didn't? Maybe he'd become Ellen's full-time business partner and see what they could build together. If not for all the equity he'd lose, which he felt he'd helped build, that sounded like more fun than continuing with Fetterman Well Services, anyway.

As he pulled to a stop in his own drive, Ellen pointed to several papers taped to his front door, fluttering slightly in the afternoon breeze. "What are those?"

He knew the second he saw them. "Presents from Leo. He draws me pictures all the time."

She released her seat belt with a click. "Poor guy. He must be so upset. How do you think they got here?"

"Stuart probably delivered them for him," he said as he cut the engine. "I can't imagine my aunt would come over."

She reached for the door handle. "Do you think Stuart's using Leo to make you feel guilty so you'll apologize and things can go back to normal?"

"Who knows?" Hendrix shook his head as he climbed out, waited for Ellen to come around the truck and started toward the landing. "Leo shouldn't have to go through this. None of us should have to go through this. It's so unnecessary."

"Do you want me to try to talk to them?" Ellen asked, slipping her hand inside his. "I could take the blame for what's happened so far. They already don't like me."

"No." He kissed her knuckles. "Nothing's been your fault. They either forgive and accept, or we figure out a way to go on without them."

"You really feel that way?" she asked uncertainly. "I hate what having me in your life is costing you."

"They're the problem, not you." He let go of her so he could get his key ready, but as soon as they reached the landing, a dog barked and jumped against the door. Instinctively, Hendrix put his arm out to protect Ellen from whatever was coming. Then the door flew wide, Zeus ran out and began to run in circles around them, wagging his tail and barking, and his cousin stood in the opening.

"Hendrix!" Leo threw his arms around Hendrix so exuberantly it nearly knocked him down. "There you are. I thought you were gone. I thought you were never coming back."

"I live here, bud," Hendrix told him. "I'm not going anywhere. How'd you get inside the house?"

"I used the key in the little box under the rock," he responded as if it should've been obvious.

Leo had seen Hendrix use his spare key once or twice, but Hendrix was shocked he'd been able to find it and use it himself. "And how did you get over here in the first place?"

Catching sight of Ellen, Leo let him go so he could grab her. "I was afraid I'd never see you again, Ellen. I want to come over to your house, okay? I want to play with my chalk."

"Leo, listen to me," Hendrix said. "How'd you get over here? Do your mom and dad know where you're at?"

Before Leo could answer, Hendrix spotted a rolling suitcase on the floor behind him. It wasn't fastened correctly and some of Leo's clothes were coming out of it. "What's that?" he asked, gesturing toward it.

Leo glanced behind him. "My suitcase."

"Why do you have a suitcase?"

"I ran away," he replied matter-of-factly. "I'm not going home."

Hendrix felt his jaw drop. "What? Why?" he asked, but he already knew the answer to that question. The fighting had upset Leo and made him sympathetic to Hendrix. "Never mind. When did you leave home?"

Leo screwed up his face as he tried to puzzle out the answer to that question. "I don't know. Yesterday?"

"You've been here overnight?"

"No…" he said, immediately shaking his head.

He had to have left this morning, not yesterday. That was the only thing that made sense. Otherwise, Stuart and Lynn would've turned the town upside down looking for him. "You still haven't told me how you got here," Hendrix said.

Leo scratched his head. "I walked."

Hendrix was impressed that he knew the way—and that he could make it six miles. "Then you've definitely been holding out on me when we go to the track," he said jokingly.

Leo seemed confused. "What, Hendrix? What'd you say?"

"Nothing."

Someone else called Hendrix's name, and he turned to see Jay Haslem walking toward them. "Hey, Jay."

When his neighbor got close enough, he gestured toward Leo. "I see you've found your cousin."

"Yeah."

"I hope you don't mind that I gave him and his dog a ride. I just couldn't leave them on the side of the road, you know? When I passed them, they seemed to be okay, but they didn't have any water or anything. And I was afraid he'd wander into the street and get hit—or his dog would."

Hendrix turned back to Leo. "I thought you said you walked…"

"I *did* walk—until Jay picked me up," he replied. "Can I live with you, Hendrix? We could get donuts every day. And I could help you work. And we could watch *Aladdin* at night. And I could visit Ellen whenever I wanted to. I have all my stuff right here, even my toothbrush."

He had it all figured out—except the part where his parents would never allow it. "Leo, you can't live with me," Hendrix said. "You know your mother would be too sad if you moved out."

"Don't tell her where I am, Hendrix."

"I have to tell her, or she'll worry. So will your dad." He pulled out his phone to do exactly that. It sounded as if Leo had left a few hours ago, so Lynn and Stuart had to know he was gone by now. But before Hendrix could even call, a white Fetterman truck came rumbling down the long dirt road leading to his place and turned into the drive.

There was only one person inside it—Lynn.

Thirty

Steeling herself for what could only be a negative encounter, Ellen caught her breath as Lynn got out of the truck and came stomping up to Hendrix's house. "Leo, what are you doing here?" she asked, drilling her son with a remonstrative look. "Do you know how badly you scared me? I've been looking all over for you! I thought I could trust you not to wander off. Am I going to have to fence the backyard and make you play there?"

Obviously feeling out of place in the middle of this family squabble, Jay excused himself and beat a quick retreat, and Leo began to cry. "I don't like it when you're mad," he said. "Stop yelling. Stop yelling!"

She wasn't yelling. She was talking sternly, but he clearly knew she was upset, and all that emotion seemed to be hitting him hard.

"He didn't wander off." Hendrix went in the house and brought out Leo's luggage. "He ran away."

Lynn's mouth dropped open. "You packed a bag, Leo? You left on purpose? You've never done anything like that before! What's going on with you?"

"He's only reacting to what's going on with *you*," Hendrix said.

He figured she'd been trying to avoid interacting with *him*—and she obviously wasn't happy to see Ellen there—but this must've caused her to reconsider speaking to him. "And I'm only reacting to *you*," she snapped.

"What have *I* done?" he asked, spreading out his hands. "I've become friends with Ellen. That's it. Is that so unforgivable?"

"Ellen's nice, Mom," Leo said. "Ellen didn't do anything wrong."

Ignoring her son, Lynn stabbed a finger in Ellen's direction. "She poured cement down Jay Haslem's well and tried to blame it on me. Then she drilled it out for free, so Jay and everyone else would think she was some kind of hero. And this was after she used you to help her drill that well in the first place—which you did, secretly, when you were supposed to be on the clock for Fetterman Well Services."

It was hard for Ellen not to defend Hendrix, if not herself. But she bit her tongue. She didn't want to make things any worse for him—or Leo.

"I only did it secretly because I knew it would cause a fight," Hendrix said. "You've proved me right on that. And Ellen *didn't* sabotage the well, Lynn." He pulled out his phone and showed her the tire impression. "Whoever was driving the vehicle that left this track on the property did. I've checked the tires of everyone in town who'd have the opportunity and the motivation to harm that well—everyone Ellen and I could think of, anyway—and through a process of elimination, we think we know who did it. Ellen and I plan to drive to Libby tomorrow to see if we're right. If we have evidence to prove it wasn't Ellen, will you finally believe us?"

"Libby…" she said, confused, so he explained why

Jordan might've wanted to damage the Haslem well to cause problems for Ellen.

"You're wrong about her," Lynn said with apparent disgust when he was done. "She's got you in the palm of her hand, and now she's calling all the shots."

Ellen expected him to deny it and continue to try to convince his aunt that she was making a big deal out of nothing. But he stepped back and shook his head in disgust just like she had. "The way you've been calling the shots since you married Stuart?" he said. "You used the power you held to shut out his little girl. At least she's been asking me what she can do to heal the rift between you and me, instead of trying to use her power to hurt you back. I think that says it all, don't you?"

Lynn looked stunned. "I can't believe how you've turned on me…"

"I *haven't* turned on you," he said. "You've turned on me simply because I like someone you don't."

"Are you okay?" Ellen asked as soon as Lynn made Leo get in her truck with Zeus and his suitcase.

Hendrix leaned on the banister of the landing as he watched his aunt back out of the drive. "I'm fine."

"Are you sure?" She frowned as she peered closer at him. "I'm so sorry."

"So am I," he said. "But it'll be okay. We'll go to Libby tomorrow, get a picture of whatever tire on Jordan's Audi matches the impression that was near the well and take it to the police. Jay will go to the trouble of filing a report if he feels it won't be a waste of time. Then Jordan can be charged with trespassing and vandalism—or whatever the charges will be—and my aunt will have to believe you had nothing to do with sabotaging that well."

"She's never liked me. Do you think that'll really change anything?"

"Who knows? At least the well issue will be put to rest."

She sighed. "I still don't understand why Rocko came forward to make up that story about being near the Haslem property the night it happened and seeing a Fetterman truck," she said.

"I think he was just looking for your attention. He thought of something he could say that you'd want to hear—then backed away from it once I got involved and everything threatened to blow up in his face."

"I guess," she murmured.

Once Lynn pulled onto the highway, and he could no longer see her, he took Ellen in his arms and kissed the top of her head. "We'll get through this."

"I just feel so bad about what's happening between you and your aunt and what it means for Leo and your job..."

He lifted her chin so that he could look into her eyes. "Don't worry. If I have to, I'll just move in with you," he said.

They both started to laugh, but he had a feeling he'd be living with her soon, regardless. He already wanted to be with her almost every minute. "Now come inside and let me show you my house—while I have it."

The drive to Libby went quickly. Ellen wasn't eager to see Jordan again. She hoped they wouldn't have to run into him. But any time she spent with Hendrix absolutely flew by, in spite of being nervous about the DNA test. The results could come back as early as tomorrow or Wednesday, which weighed on her mind, so this was a good distraction. She was also eager to establish, once and for all, who'd poured cement down Jay's well. It had to have been Jordan. He'd been so angry with her for reporting him to the dating site. And even if she didn't actually participate, Averil had to have told him where to find the property. That could be difficult to prove, of course, but Ellen figured they might learn more about how it happened once they matched one of Jordan's tires to that impression from the site. In Ellen's opinion, he was the kind of person who would implicate his friends and associates if he saw some benefit in doing it, and spreading the blame meant he wouldn't look quite as bad himself.

"After this, Averil might get a taste of what Jordan's *really* like," she told Hendrix as GPS led them to a strip mall on the west side of town.

Hendrix had called, under a fake name, to make an appointment to have his teeth cleaned and examined, so they knew Jordan was working. But they didn't plan on going in. They just had to figure out where he'd parked.

As Hendrix circled the lot, looking for the white Audi, Ellen hoped this would finally be the end of the business about the well. It had to be, she told herself. They'd looked at everyone else.

But once they found Jordan's car parked around back, along with a Toyota Prius that probably belonged to his dental assistant, they were shocked to find the tread on his tires vastly different from what was in the picture.

"This can't be," she said as Hendrix looked up, his expression revealing that he was equally surprised.

"It was no one on our list?" he said. "What...was it just a bunch of teenagers out doing random bullshit?"

"Why would a bunch of teenagers write 'Ellen's a bitch' on the chicken coop?" she asked.

Still crouched next to the last tire he'd checked, Hendrix shook his head. "I have no idea. Should we go in and confront Jordan? Ask him if he was involved?"

"No. He'll just deny it."

Hendrix got up. "What a waste. We drove all the way here for nothing."

"Even if we'd gotten a match, I doubt it would've changed anything with Lynn," Ellen said, trying to make herself feel better. "She's going to believe what she wants to believe about me."

"Yeah. Let's just forget about the well," he said. "We know you didn't do anything to harm it. That's all that matters."

She forced a smile to cover her disappointment. She'd been looking for some kind of vindication—at last. Then, even if it turned out that she didn't belong to Stuart—that she had an even worse father than she'd thought—she'd have this small victory to help console her. She hated that Lynn would still be able to make the baseless claim that Ellen had damaged the well herself.

"I'm going to call Rocko," she said on the drive back, "and ask him why he made up what he did."

"Don't waste your time," Hendrix said. "He has no incentive to tell you the truth."

"I still want to try," she insisted, but Talulah called her before she could act on that thought.

She hit the Talk button. "Hello?"

"Where are you? Your truck's in the drive, but you're not answering the door."

"I'm not there. Hendrix and I are driving back from Libby. Why?"

"I have something to tell you."

This sounded important. Ellen changed her phone to the other ear. "What is it?"

There was a slight pause while Talulah spoke to someone else—Ellen couldn't quite make out what she said. "How long until you're back?" she asked when she came back on the line.

Ellen checked the GPS. "Two hours and fifteen minutes. Why?"

"Can you come straight to my house? Jane Tanner has something to say I think you'll want to hear."

Talulah sat on the porch with Jane. They'd drank half a bottle of wine but barely spoken since she'd called Ellen. She hated to be put in such a terrible position, and she knew Jane felt the same. But right was right. She didn't see how they could do anything except share what they knew, despite the consequence.

As soon as she saw Hendrix's truck coming down the drive, Talulah stood and Jane did the same. Brant was still at work, but she'd already spoken to him and he agreed with what she was about to do.

Jane sighed. "This sucks."

"I think so, too."

They waited expectantly while Hendrix and Ellen got out of the vehicle and approached them. "How'd it go in Libby?" Talulah asked, choosing to start the conversation with something banal and comfortable to help ease them into where they had to go.

Ellen shook her head. "We thought for sure we'd be able to match Jordan's tire to the impression left at the well, but it was a bust. We've now checked everyone on our list and haven't found the culprit. Maybe we never will." She glanced uncertainly at Jane. "What's going on here?"

Talulah looped her arm through her childhood friend's. She and Jane had gone through plenty to test their relationship. Groups of three were notoriously difficult, and navigating this new segment of their friendship with Averil wasn't promising to be any easier. She hoped Jane wouldn't resent her for encouraging her to do what they were about to do. "As much as I wish it wasn't the case, I think Jane might be able to help with that."

Ellen's eyes went wide. "What are you talking about?"

Talulah motioned to Ellen and Hendrix to join them on the porch. Jane took one chair next to the small garden table Ellen had found for her at a garage sale, Ellen took the other, and Hendrix folded his arms and leaned against the railing, facing them.

"What is it?" Ellen asked.

Jane tucked a piece of hair that'd fallen from her ponytail behind her ear. "I feel like such a disloyal friend doing this," she said with a grimace. "I've known Averil since before we went to kindergarten. I'm sure she'll take it as a betrayal, and we'll never be friends again. But—" her lips turned down "—I can't sit back and say nothing."

Ellen's eyebrows came together. "This isn't about the night the well was vandalized, is it?"

"I'm afraid so." Jane rubbed her palms on her jeans before launching into what she had to say. "Averil called me that evening. Said her mother had taken her car because she had Mitch, and it had his car seat in it. She asked if there was any way she could use mine."

"To go where?" Ellen asked.

"Back to Hank's."

Hendrix rubbed his chin. "Wasn't Jordan in town that night? Why couldn't they have used his car?"

"He'd just left," Jane said. "He had to be at work on Wednesday, but because Averil's mother had Mitch and she didn't have to be home for him, she wanted to go back and play some more pool."

Hendrix straightened. "She didn't ask you to go with her?"

Jane shook her head. "She knows I don't typically go out on weeknights—not that late, anyway. I'm usually getting ready for work the next day."

Ellen slid forward in her seat. "So you let her take your car…"

"Yes. And she brought it back the following morning."

"Meaning she had it all Tuesday night," Hendrix clarified. "You think she might've had something to do with the damage to the Haslem well."

Jane grimaced. "I'd hate to accuse her, but…"

"But…" Ellen repeated.

"Yesterday she called to tell me not to mention that she'd had my car to anyone," Jane said. "I was already worried that I possessed information I should probably share, but once she did that… I knew."

Galvanized by this news, Hendrix gestured to the 1967 Mustang Jane's grandfather had painstakingly restored and given to her for Christmas. "That's the car she borrowed?"

When Jane nodded, he called up a picture on his phone—Talulah could easily guess which one—before hurrying out to the drive, and Ellen got up and followed him.

Jane picked nervously at her cuticles while they waited. "Averil's going to hate us forever," she murmured.

"I'm sorry, because I know what that's like," Talulah said. "She already hates me." But she knew Averil was going to hate her even more when Hendrix turned to face them looking triumphant.

"We have a match."

* * *

That evening, Hendrix dropped Ellen off before driving over to his aunt and uncle's place. He doubted what he had to show them would make much of a difference. Lynn's problem with Ellen wasn't exclusively about the well, or they would've been able to get along up until that happened. Still, he was eager to convince Lynn she'd been wrong about Ellen in at least one regard, and hopefully, it would make Stuart think twice about letting Lynn get overly emotional and try to goad him into destroying the personal and professional relationship that'd existed between them all for so long.

Although he typically walked in—he'd been raised in this house—tonight Hendrix showed his aunt and uncle the courtesy of knocking, even though Zeus had already alerted everyone inside to the fact that they had a visitor.

He expected Leo to answer. His cousin was always eager for company. But it was Stuart who opened the door.

"Hello, Hendrix," his uncle said.

Hendrix dipped his head in greeting before bending down to scratch Zeus, who was far more excited to see him. "Is Aunt Lynn here?"

Stuart glanced over his shoulder as if she wasn't far away, but she must've signaled that she wouldn't come to the door, because he said, "Maybe it'd be best if you just talked to me for now."

"No problem." Hendrix straightened and held out his phone to show Stuart the picture Ellen had taken at the Haslem well. "See this?"

"It looks like dirt…"

"If you look closely, you'll see there's something in

the dirt—a tire impression from the vehicle driven by whoever sabotaged the Haslem well."

Stuart looked up. "How do you know that?"

"Because Ellen found it there and took that picture Wednesday morning, just after Jay called her to tell her the well was no longer working. He saw it, too." Hendrix took his phone and swiped left before handing it back. "And this is the picture of the tire that matches that imprint."

Stuart examined the two pictures closely. "Who owns the car?"

"Jane Tanner. But that isn't who sabotaged the well. She loaned her car to Averil Gerhart that night. It was Averil who poured cement down the hole."

Hendrix heard a sound that made him believe his aunt was just in the living room, listening, but she didn't make herself visible to him.

"Why would Averil Gerhart want to ruin Jay Haslem's new well?" Stuart asked skeptically.

"If you'll remember, she also spray-painted 'Ellen's a bitch' on the chicken coop. She and Ellen had a disagreement a few weeks ago in the grocery store. The well was her revenge. She thought if she used a borrowed car, she wouldn't get caught. But she thought wrong. I just came from the police station."

"Are they going to do anything about it?"

"That depends on Ellen."

Stuart whistled for Zeus to get out of the road. "Why would it depend on her?"

"In the state of Montana, vandalism with damage under $1500 is a misdemeanor. If Ellen charges Jay for fixing the well, and the bill is more than $1500, it would be a felony."

Stuart pursed his lips. "Considering the time required and the use of heavy equipment, we would've charged at least that much," he confirmed. "What's Ellen going to do?"

"She hasn't decided yet." He used his phone to forward the pictures to Stuart and Lynn. "I just sent you and Lynn copies of what I have here."

"We don't need copies," he said.

"Too late." Hendrix wanted them to have them—as a reminder not to jump to conclusions and judge someone before they had all the details, if nothing else. "Where's Leo?" he asked, finding it strange that he hadn't heard a peep from his cousin.

"I guess he's taking a nap."

Hendrix gave him a funny look. "He never takes a nap. It can even be difficult to get him to go to sleep at night."

Stuart sighed as he kicked a rock off the walkway. "He refused to come out of his room for dinner—must've cried himself to sleep. He's taking the...uh...rift between us pretty hard."

Hendrix shook his head. "That's too bad because there doesn't have to be a rift," he said, and he walked away.

When Ellen heard Hendrix come in the front door, she closed her laptop and shoved it away. "How'd it go?" she asked, getting up from the table as he walked into the kitchen.

"About as well as could be expected." He dropped his keys on the counter. "My aunt's being her typical stubborn self. I'm getting to where I don't care if she forgives me or not. I haven't done anything wrong."

Ellen crossed the floor so she could step into his

arms. "I don't want to be the cause of any pain, especially when it comes to you."

Holding her close, he rested his chin on her head. "She's causing all the pain, not you. *You*, for all your toughness, can't even bear to kill a spider. You made me take one outside." He smiled down at her. "But I love you for your inherent kindness."

Not wanting to appear weak, she scowled at him. "Insect populations all over the world are at risk."

"Well, you're certainly doing your part to save them." He let go of her, poured himself a glass of water and gestured at her laptop. "Any word?"

She knew he was referring to the DNA results. She couldn't get them off her mind. Even when she was distracted by who'd sabotaged the well, it was there, haunting her—always. "I wasn't checking," she said.

He raised an eyebrow.

"Okay, I was just logging in to look around."

He laughed. "I can see why you'd be nervous and impatient, but it's far too early to start checking."

"Not necessarily," she argued. "If Stuart shipped our samples overnight, a technician could've opened the envelope and run the test first thing this morning. Maybe he wanted to post the results to have it over and done with before going home."

"Was that the case?" he asked.

She frowned at his skepticism. "No."

"Exactly. You're assuming those technicians are far more diligent and efficient than they probably are. To them, one test is like another. It's just what they do all day."

"But to me…" She went to the freezer and took out a carton of Ben & Jerry's ice cream. "What do you think

Averil's going to say when she finds out that we know she's the one who damaged the well?"

"What can she say?" he asked, getting two bowls and two spoons for the ice cream. "We have proof."

"But will there really be any type of punishment? Plenty of people do worse things and face no consequences."

He took the lid off the ice cream. "That depends on you, remember?"

Ellen pictured her name spray-painted in red on the chicken coop along with the word *bitch*. She wasn't likely to forget that image anytime soon and couldn't believe Averil would go so far. She knew Talulah was shocked, too. "What do *you* think I should do?"

"I'd probably make her pay you $1499 for the day you spent fixing the damage she caused. Then the police can decide what to do from there. If they go ahead and charge her, it'll only be a misdemeanor and won't destroy the next few years of her life."

"All she has to do to ruin the next few years of her life is continue to date Jordan," Ellen said.

Hendrix grinned at her joke. "Then that will be on her. If you keep her from getting into too much trouble, maybe her opinion of you will improve—or she'll be grateful enough to calm down and behave. She has a lot of family and friends in the area who would probably be grateful to you, too."

"Are you saying it might be good for business?" she said with a gasp.

"I'm just saying it doesn't hurt to have so many people in the area think highly of you."

Ellen wasn't holding a huge grudge against Averil. She just didn't admire her very much. But that wasn't new; she never had. Still, what would happen to her son if she went to jail even for a few months? "Yeah. I think that's what I'll do—for her son's sake if not for all the rest of it. Then maybe she'll forgive Jane and Talulah for coming forward and the incident can be forgotten."

He scooped ice cream into both bowls before returning the carton to the freezer. "It's probably a mistake to lead you back to this subject, but I can't quit thinking about it myself. What do you think the DNA results will reveal?"

Ellen carried her bowl to the table and sat down. "I keep asking myself the same thing. Every time I pass a mirror, I stop and look to see if I resemble Stuart in any way—or if I look more like what I remember of John Williams."

He took a bite of his ice cream as he sat across from her. "And? What do you think?"

"I can't see that I look like either one of them," she said.

Thirty-One

The next week, Ellen took down her job-opening fly-ers and posts, told Ross not to bother trying to get her a driller and worked with Hendrix on two out-of-water calls and a new well for a wealthy conservationist who was building a mansion in the mountains overlooking Coyote Canyon. She couldn't believe how much more fun it was to be with him than anyone else, and he seemed to enjoy it, too. They were together almost all the time and typically stayed at her place—even though he did most of the cooking.

She checked the lab website every day but nothing had been posted. The DNA results and what they might signify continued to linger in the back of her mind no matter what she was doing. It didn't help that her mother kept trying to call. It was hard not to answer—she'd al-ways been there for Jan—but she'd decided she wouldn't talk to her until she was ready. She had enough going on, shouldn't have to deal with that relationship in the midst of everything else. As far as she was concerned, her mother needed to handle her own life for a while.

At least the well issue had been resolved. Probably to avoid having to actually speak to her, Averil had mailed her a $1499 check along with a written apology and painted over the chicken coop so it no longer read "Ellen's a bitch." But because her father golfed with the chief of police, who knew their whole family, she wasn't charged.

That wasn't the official explanation, of course. Sherman Wilkes told Ellen that Averil had "learned her lesson," and her actions hadn't resulted in damage beyond the reparations she'd made. But Ellen knew how things worked in such a small town. Had she been willing to make a big stink, she could probably have forced the issue, but she didn't believe there was anything to be gained by doing that, and Hendrix agreed. Why rile up the whole Gerhart family and all of their friends and relatives—make so many enemies—when the problem had been solved? It wasn't as if Averil had a criminal history. According to what Ellen had heard from Sherman Wilkes and others who were talking about the incident, Averil had been angry over their encounter at the grocery store, which had embarrassed her in public. That, taken with the opportunity presented to her when her mother had Mitch and she had Jane's Mustang, she just... went too far. What Jordan had to say about her must've also contributed, since he made it look as though Ellen had wronged him in some way, too.

But she'd been compensated for her time. That was good enough. She also didn't want Talulah and Jane to have to see their friend charged with a crime. They were the ones who'd solved the mystery and been honest enough to let her know who'd done it; they'd feel responsible.

"Earth to Ellen," Talulah said.

Ellen blinked and focused on her best friend, who was sitting across from her at one of the small tables outside the diner on Saturday afternoon. "I'm sorry. What'd you say?"

"I said I also got a letter from Averil, apologizing to me for her behavior in saying what she did at the grocery store."

Ellen grimaced. "Do you think she meant it? Her apology, I mean."

"No. I'm guessing she doesn't want more trouble, so she's playing nice, hoping I'll convince you to be satisfied with what's happened so far."

The wind was beginning to pick up, ruffling Ellen's hair, but spring was in the air. It was the warmest day they'd had so far this year. "You don't have to advocate for her," Ellen said. "I'm satisfied. To be honest, I just want her to go her way and let me go mine."

"That's generous of you." Talulah told someone who approached her that she was out of breakfast buns before continuing. "If your roles were reversed, I doubt she'd be as kind."

"Who knows what she would've done." Ellen twisted around to look down the sidewalk toward the vintage furniture and gift shop. "Where's Jane?"

"She must be dealing with a customer. She'll be here when she can get away." Talulah took a sip of her latte. "How are things with Hendrix?"

"Good," she replied. "We're really happy, despite what's going on with Lynn and Stuart."

"I'm surprised they've held out this long."

"I'm sure they're struggling to keep up with the business. Hendrix did a lot for them. But they haven't admitted that they made a mistake firing him. They did text him to say that Leo was begging to see him, though, so we let Leo stay with us last night."

"I bet he was excited about that."

"He was. It was good for Hendrix to spend some time

with him. But you know they allowed that for Leo's sake, not Hendrix's."

"Lynn would do anything for her son. I bet Leo will bring her around eventually."

"Maybe." In Ellen's mind, a lot depended on the DNA results. Would Lynn treat her differently if she wasn't Stuart's daughter? Why wouldn't she? What threat would she be then?

Although... Lynn would probably still blame Ellen for taking Hendrix away from her.

Crossing her legs, Talulah sat back in her chair. "Where's Hendrix right now? I sort of thought you might bring him along."

"No. He's taking Leo home. Then he has some stuff he'd like to get done at his place. I'll just meet him there."

"Are you hoping he'll be able to make up with his aunt and uncle while he's at their place?"

Ellen wanted Hendrix to be happy, but if they made up and still refused to accept her... She wasn't sure what that would mean. She'd need a driller again, for one. She probably wouldn't see as much of Hendrix. And she supposed he might feel even more torn than he did now.

She was just sipping her coffee, mulling over all the complications while they continued to wait for Jane and Talulah explained to yet another passerby that the diner was out of breakfast buns, when she received a text from Hendrix.

Have you checked the website?

Ellen's heart began to thud against her chest.

Not since last night. It's the weekend. I figured I'd have to wait until Monday to try again. Why?

Whoever Talulah had been talking to moved on, and she leaned forward. "What is it?"

"I don't know," Ellen muttered while waiting for Hendrix's response.

"Hendrix isn't fighting with Lynn and Stuart, is he?" Talulah asked.

"I don't think so."

Another ding signified Hendrix had responded. Stuart wants to know if you'll come over.

Right now?

If you're available.

"Ellen?" Talulah said.

She swallowed hard as she looked up. "I have to go."

Ellen wanted to check the website before she arrived at Lynn and Stuart's, but she couldn't get it to load on her phone. And since Hendrix was waiting for her, it didn't make sense to drive all the way home to get on her computer.

Her chest felt so tight it was hard to breathe as she eyed the vehicles in the Fetterman drive and purposely positioned her truck so that she could get out of there immediately, if she had to. Then she sat behind the wheel, trying to suck enough air into her lungs to speak. The anxiety that had her tied up in knots wasn't going to make whatever was coming any easier.

Zeus ran past her truck, barking. Then Hendrix appeared right outside her window and opened her door.

"You look a little pale," he said. "You okay?"

"Of course," she said, releasing her seat belt. "Why wouldn't I be okay?"

He didn't answer that question. He knew her well enough by now to recognize when she was posturing. "I'm right here," he said. "You don't have to worry about anything."

She could trust him, she reminded herself. He cared about her. Things were different now than they'd been when she was just a vulnerable girl.

She hoped...

"Do you know?" she asked.

He knew she meant whether Stuart was her father without asking her to make that clear. "No."

She jerked her head toward the house. "Does he?"

"He hasn't said. He just asked me if you'd checked the site today, so I asked you."

"I tried to log in on my phone but the website's down."

"Hi, Ellen!" Leo yelled from the doorway. "Are you coming in? You can come in!"

Hendrix glanced in Leo's direction. "You ready?"

She figured she was as ready as she'd ever be. Either way, she didn't want to look scared. Dropping her keys into her purse, she climbed out and felt slightly emboldened when Hendrix slipped his fingers through hers. "Seeing us holding hands might upset them," she said and tried to extricate herself, but he wouldn't allow it.

"I don't care if it does," he insisted.

Leo hugged her as soon as she reached the stoop, even though he'd just seen her that morning. Then he called his dog, bringing Zeus inside, too, as Hendrix led her into the living room.

Lynn and Stuart were waiting for her, both of them sitting on the couch wearing somber expressions.

"Ellen," Stuart said politely.

As she braced herself, Ellen's eyes slid to Lynn. Was

she angry? Upset? About to scream and yell? Her mouth was a straight line—a slash in her face—and her eyes glittered with determination, but Ellen couldn't tell what that meant. Would she let Stuart do the talking, or would this encounter end up in an ugly shouting match?

"You wanted to see me?" she said, looking back at the man she'd always believed to be her father.

Stuart scooted forward and pulled a letter from the back pocket of his crisp, deep-blue Wranglers. "The results of our DNA test came in the mail today. Did you receive a copy?"

Ellen had expected the results to be posted online well in advance of any hard copy notice. She hadn't even checked her box. She paid her bills electronically and rarely received anything besides junk mail so she picked up her mail only once a week. The past several days she hadn't even thought about it. "No."

Taking the letter from the lab out of its envelope, he unfolded it and handed it to her.

Ellen let go of Hendrix. She was shaking and needed both hands to be able to control it. The last thing she wanted was for anyone to notice.

Her eyes skimmed over the numbers and percentages to read the conclusion at the bottom: *The alleged father is excluded as the biological father of the tested child.*

He'd been right. Somehow, he'd known all along.

Trying to tamp down the tidal wave of emotions that hit her until she could get out the door and into her truck, where she could be alone, she nodded and started to hand the sheet back to him, but Hendrix asked if he could see it, so she gave it to him instead.

"You're not a match," he murmured.

"I'm sorry...for everything," Stuart said, looking pained.

"There's nothing for you to be sorry about now," she said and turned to leave. She wasn't sure if she expected Hendrix to go with her or not. He seemed to belong with them. He'd always been with them. But Leo grabbed her and hugged her again, asking if he could come over next week, and Hendrix followed her out.

"Are those not the results you wanted?" he asked.

She didn't know how to answer that question. It wasn't that they weren't what she wanted so much as the drastic change this made to the narrative of her life—the unknown she now faced and her mother's infidelity and deception. "I don't know what I wanted."

"At least this way it'll be a lot easier for us. So there's that. I hope it sort of makes up for what you're feeling."

"Have they offered you your job back?" she asked dully.

He looked down. "Yes."

"Good." She cleared her throat. "I'm happy for you." She opened her door and started to climb in, but he stopped her.

"Ellen..."

Hot and tingly and on the verge of tears, she desperately wanted to get away so she could recover in private. But he caught her arm. "I told them we should buy Truesdale Well and Pump Services and work together."

"You did *what*?" she cried.

"Would you be interested? Or at least consider the possibility? Because I won't go back to work for them without you."

"You want *me* to join forces with Lynn and Stuart? Be part of their company instead of running my own?"

"It'll be *my* company—*our* company—when Stuart

retires. I'm going to get it in writing, the price and everything, before I agree to come back."

"Do you mean that?" she asked in shock.

He pulled her into his arms and held her tight. "I mean it," he whispered into her ear. "I'm here for you. I'll always be here for you."

Epilogue

Six months later...

Six months later...

Ellen was at her desk when Lynn came into the office. It was rare that they were alone together. For the most part, Ellen was careful to avoid Hendrix's aunt. It wasn't so much that she was holding a grudge over the past as it was a lack of emotional trust. She didn't want there to be any problems between them.

But Lynn had been making an effort to improve their relationship as time went by. Ellen had to give her that. She guessed it was partly for the success of the business, since Fetterman had bought her company sixty days ago and they all worked together now. But it was also probably because Hendrix and Leo remained so staunchly loyal to her. Lynn didn't want her son and nephew to move on without her.

Ironically, although Stuart wasn't her father, Ellen was growing to love and respect him more than ever. She thought he should stand up to his wife more often than he did, but if that was the worst thing she could say about him, she figured that wasn't so bad. He was kind, consistent and easygoing. He was also fair when it came to the business. She got along great with him and Hendrix, and she worked with them most often, so she had no regrets about selling out and joining their company. She had more money than ever before, she and Hendrix were living together at her place and selling his, since she didn't have a mortgage, and she no longer had the stress of worrying about whether she was getting enough jobs to cover the payment on her drill. One day in the next two or three years, she'd have enough saved to be able to quit drilling altogether and open her own used furnishings store.

Lynn walked over to her. "Hello."

Ellen's truck was in the drive. Lynn had to have known she was at the office, so...why had she not waited until Ellen was gone to do whatever she needed to do? Although Ellen came to the meetings on Tuesday, Wednesday and Thursday, she went into the field directly after and didn't return until Lynn had left, around four. Then she did her paperwork and put it on Lynn's desk so Lynn could handle the ordering and billing and if Lynn had questions, she'd attach a sticky note to whatever it was and return it to Ellen's desk.

That process had been working well for them; Ellen saw no need to change it. But she smiled, as though she wasn't instantly anxious at the prospect of being alone with the woman who'd been so unkind to her.

"Hi," she said before going back to figuring out the amount and type of supplies she'd need to bid on a job one of their clients had referred to them.

"How's your day going?" Lynn asked.

Surprised Lynn didn't simply sit down and get to work, Ellen looked up again. "Good. Yours?"

"Not so bad. I got Leo into that ceramics class."

"At Shirley's?"

"Yeah."

Ellen had put an advertisement she'd found posted on the bulletin board at Talulah's diner on Lynn's desk. She'd known as soon as she saw it how much Leo would enjoy doing something like that. "I'm glad. He's going to love it."

"I think so, too." She walked over and filled a cup with water from the cooler. "How's your mother?"

Ellen pulled her gaze away from her work once more. "She's…fine."

"Still working for your old boss?"

"Yeah. I actually think they might be dating. Can you believe that?"

Lynn chuckled. "That's lucky, since you think so highly of him."

It meant she didn't have to worry so much about Jan. She was grateful for that. And even though their relationship had been strained since the DNA test which had revealed her affair with their onetime neighbor, they'd been talking fairly regularly again. Her mother was the way she was. There didn't seem to be any point in holding something she'd done thirty years ago against her, especially when Ellen was happier than she'd ever been. "Ross is a *really* good man."

Lynn took a drink of water. "What are you and Hendrix doing tonight?"

"No plans. We don't go out very often midweek."

"Would you like to come over for my polenta and chicken salad?"

Ellen had no idea what to say. Typically, she let Hendrix visit his aunt and uncle and do dinner and other things with his family on his own. He'd tried to invite her occasionally, but she'd always managed to come up with an excuse, and she'd never received an invitation directly from Lynn. "That's the salad you sent home with Hendrix a few weeks ago, isn't it?" she asked, stalling while she tried to think.

"It is. I sent the leftovers, and he said you loved them."

"I did," she said. "That salad's delicious."

"So...you'll come? At six?"

Ellen hesitated. She was trying to think of a polite way out, but she was afraid Lynn would be able to see through any excuse she offered. "Um, yeah, of course— as long as Hendrix doesn't have something planned that I don't know about."

"I already talked to him. He said he was open to it if you were."

"Oh." Ellen blinked several times before curving her lips into yet another smile. "Okay, then. Is there... is there anything you'd like me to bring?"

"No, I've got it," she replied.

Ellen stood and began gathering her stuff. "Let me know if you change your mind."

"You're leaving?" Lynn said.

"There's a few things I have to go do." All she had to do was finish her paperwork, but she was going to do that at home.

"I'll see you tonight, then."

"See you soon."

She crossed the room and was just about to open the door when Lynn said, "Ellen?"

Making sure her smile was still in place, Ellen turned. "Yes?"

"I was wrong about you," she said. "I'm sorry—for everything."

* * * * *

Do you love romance books?

JOIN

on Facebook by scanning the code below:

A group dedicated to book recommendations, author exclusives, SWOONING and all things romance! A community made for romance readers by romance readers.

Facebook.com/groups/readloverepeat

Get 3 FREE REWARDS!

We'll send you 2 FREE Books plus a FREE Mystery Gift.

FREE
Value Over
$20

Both the **Romance** and **Suspense** collections feature compelling novels
written by many of today's bestselling authors.

YES! Please send me 2 FREE novels from the Essential Romance or Essential
Suspense Collection and my FREE gift (gift is worth about $10 retail). After receiving
them, if I don't wish to receive any more books, I can return the shipping statement
marked "cancel." If I don't cancel, I will receive 4 brand-new novels every month and
be billed just $7.49 each in the U.S. or $7.74 each in Canada. That's a savings of at
least 17% off the cover price. It's quite a bargain! Shipping and handling is just 50¢
per book in the U.S. and $1.25 per book in Canada.* I understand that accepting the
2 free books and gift places me under no obligation to buy anything. I can always
return a shipment and cancel at any time by calling the number below. The free
books and gift are mine to keep no matter what I decide.

Choose one: ☐ **Essential**   ☐ **Essential**   ☐ **Or Try Both!**
               Romance   **Suspense**   (194/394 & 191/391
               (194/394 BPA GRNM)   (191/391 BPA GRNM)   BPA GRQZ)

Name (please print)

Address   Apt. #

City   State/Province   Zip/Postal Code

Email: Please check this box ☐ if you would like to receive newsletters and promotional emails from Harlequin Enterprises ULC and
its affiliates. You can unsubscribe anytime.

> **Mail to the Harlequin Reader Service:**
> **IN U.S.A.:** P.O. Box 1341, Buffalo, NY 14240-8531
> **IN CANADA:** P.O. Box 603, Fort Erie, Ontario L2A 5X3
>
> **Want to try 2 free books from another series!** Call 1-800-873-8635 or visit www.ReaderService.com.

---

*Terms and prices subject to change without notice. Prices do not include sales taxes, which will be charged (if applicable) based
on your state or country of residence. Canadian residents will be charged applicable taxes. Offer not valid in Quebec. This offer is
limited to one order per household. Books received may not be as shown. Not valid for current subscribers to the Essential Romance
or Essential Suspense Collection. All orders subject to approval. Credit or debit balances in a customer's account(s) may be offset by
any other outstanding balance owed by or to the customer. Please allow 4 to 6 weeks for delivery. Offer available while quantities last.

Your Privacy—Your information is being collected by Harlequin Enterprises ULC, operating as Harlequin Reader Service. For a
complete summary of the information we collect, how we use this information and to whom it is disclosed, please visit our privacy notice
located at corporate.harlequin.com/privacy-notice. From time to time we may also exchange your personal information with reputable
third parties. If you wish to opt out of this sharing of your personal information, please visit readerservice.com/consumerschoice or
call 1-800-873-8635. **Notice to California Residents**—Under California law, you have specific rights to control and access your data.
For more information on these rights and how to exercise them, visit corporate.harlequin.com/california-privacy.

STRS23